THREE ROADS
TO
VALHALLA

THREE ROADS TO VALHALLA

BY

Catherine Pomeroy Stewart

NEW YORK
CHARLES SCRIBNER'S SONS
1948

Printed in the United States of America

THREE ROADS TO VALHALLA

1

THE *City of Florida* rollicked in the breeze. The paddles of the side-wheel spanked the sea into a ferment and the ship plunged down the waves, wallowed an instant in the depth and then struggled up to sail over the crest again and down. Miss Ferguesson kept her cabin, indisposed as a lady should be. Rows of rag curlers surrounded her head like the halo of a baroque saint, but no sweet saintliness pervaded the gaunt features beneath. She directed the stewardess to bring her an opium plaster. When this had been applied to her tormented abdomen she lay back with a sigh of resignation.

From beyond the panelled walls of her cabin a lively racket occupied the ship.

"I have never known a worse voyage," Miss Ferguesson complained. "Last night I could not sleep for the noise. It sounds as though they were slaughtering cattle."

"It's the elections," the stewardess said. "This is our second boatload since Governor Reed was elected and you should just see the people that are making for Florida. Riff-raff! It's almost as bad as it was in 'Sixty-six."

"Are there any—" Miss Ferguesson hesitated over the word "ladies" and said, "females travelling?"

The stewardess smiled sourly. She had Miss Ferguesson to worry about twice a year. Out of Savannah in July, out of New York in September. This year there were two extra trips. For

Miss Ferguesson had closed her school and gone North in March to attend the death-bed of an uncle, who, it seemed, had then been so ungrateful as to leave his entire estate to his cook. The cook, the stewardess decided, had probably been buxom and deserving. Eying Miss Ferguesson, she could see no reason why any save a mother might be expected to leave her a fortune.

"Well!"

The stewardess started, "A few tourists and one young lady, ma'am," she said, "travelling with her papa. Right out on deck the whole time. A rare sailor for a lady."

Miss Ferguesson moaned and rolled her head. "What do they come South for?" she asked. She believed firmly in conversing during an illness; it took the mind away from bodily discomfort, and if only for an instant it was a welcome instant.

The stewardess sat down on the long padded seat beneath the porthole and folded her hands. There was nothing that she liked better than to sit and talk. While Miss Ferguesson was that contradiction, an austere woman who loved gossip, the stewardess was sharp enough to see the struggle that grew out of this, and to enjoy it.

"The young lady and her papa are with Mr. Tolliver, ma'am," she said, guessing correctly that Miss Ferguesson was not interested in the tourists. She rubbed the side of her long nose and looked at her patient.

"Carpetbaggers!" Miss Ferguesson snorted. "If they're with Tolliver they go on to Jacksonville."

"Most of the passengers do."

"Indeed!" Miss Ferguesson's thin lids closed over her eyes. "My salts," she moaned.

The stewardess administered the salts and went back to her seat. There was a silence in the cabin, interrupted periodically by a low moan from the bunk. After fifteen minutes had passed, the stewardess got up and tiptoed towards the door.

"Where are you going?" her patient demanded sharply. The stewardess sighed and came back to her place.

"There's a man aboard," she volunteered abruptly, "I can't help wondering about. Went North with us last trip and only stayed a week. He's from Jacksonville, maybe you know him, Michael Bourne."

"Michael Bourne!" Miss Fergusson looked over at her sharply, as though to gauge her interest. Women, she thought, [illegible]

[illegible] enemies than any one person could collect in a lifetime."

"Oh, he has enemies, there's no doubt. His house has been burnt twice. But they'll have to drop their matches in his pocket instead of in his house if they want to get rid of him. He's not the kind to be run out."

"Well!" gasped the stewardess with a certain gloomy relish; "whatever would they burn him for?"

The older woman called for her salts again. "Here," she said, "I'll hold them," and she took them with shaking fingers and put them to her nose. In a few minutes she said, "Nobody really knows about Michael Bourne. He was in the Union army and mustered out in Florida. He stayed and watched things and put his finger in this pie and that, and every time he put his finger in a pie some scallawag came off badly. That didn't win him any friends. He talked about going West. He didn't seem to know what he wanted to do. He had a piece of grove-land with a cabin on it and one night it burned down. That just seemed to be what he needed to settle him. He stopped talking about the West and he rebuilt his cabin and put in some young trees." Miss Fergusson put the salts to her nose again and held them there until the tears ran down her cheeks. "Oh my," she moaned, "oh my."

"You know a lot about him," the stewardess said.

The sick woman shook her head. "We board at the same

hotel and I have seen him coming and going for two years. But most of what I know is guesswork. I know that he was burned out and that he stopped talking about going away. The cabin was burned down a second time and he rebuilt and took a partner. So that the place would not be left alone, he said, but a partner is a pretty permanent step, and I think that someone was trying to scare him away and just succeeded in making him want to stay. After that second burning I shouldn't have cared to have him find a box of matches on me! I declare, he looked fierce."

"And why not indeed!"

"As you say."

"He's been elected District Attorney for Jacksonville," the stewardess said. "I heard Mr. Tolliver congratulate him."

Miss Ferguesson cleared her throat loudly and then moaned. "We'll have plenty of trouble in Jacksonville, then," she said at last. "I knew that he was running, but I had not heard that he had won."

"Well, a man like that, you'd just know he'd win."

"It's hard to tell. There are more things going on in Florida today than you can shake a stick at. There's no telling who's going to win what, or why. The darkies do the voting, and there are a hatful of clubs and mysterious bodies telling them whom to vote for. Michael Bourne is a carpetbagger, but he doesn't fit in with that crowd. It's hard to tell how he could win. Maybe Hains Tolliver had a hand in it. Though I would never have thought of those two together. Tolliver is a thoroughgoing scallawag."

The stewardess bridled visibily. "Mr. Tolliver's a fine gentleman," she said.

"What some call a gentleman! Hains Tolliver has everything to make him one, except a heart. He comes from an old family. He is certainly the richest man in the South and the smartest and the crookedest. His own people turn their backs on him."

"I've heard tell," the stewardess said, and she shrugged, "Hains Tolliver was rich and powerful and handsome to boot.

What difference how he came by his wealth. That Valhalla!" she said half wistfully. "I've seen it from the river. It's fit for a king. Why, he must own half the river."

"He owns a large piece of it certainly. And it's an example [illegible]

[illegible]

say you haven't had it easy down there."

"Nonsense! The worst I can complain of is that the ladies turn their backs on me. I fancy they're like the rest of us—good, bad and indifferent. Right now they're full of prejudice."

"Traitors! Trying to break up the country."

Miss Fergusson smiled bleakly. "They had a noble precedent," she said, but the stewardess only stared at her, and for a space both women were silent. The little ship never ceased its lively pace. On the washstand the drinking glass rang against the water carafe. Beyond the walls were running feet, and shouts, and the sounds of loud voices and loud laughter, and through it all the steady chunking of the paddle wheels. Miss Fergusson rolled her head and moaned. The stewardess said, "It's lively weather for May."

Miss Fergusson only moaned, again and again, with each breath. Imperceptibly the sound changed as though the moan had tripped on its way across the vocal cords. Miss Fergusson was snoring gently but firmly.

The stewardess went out of the cabin and closed the door behind her. Miss Kate Rider had asked her to press a dress and it was time for a cup of tea.

The following day the motion of the ship had not subsided, and Miss Fergusson remained in her cabin and applied a second opium plaster.

On the promenade deck Kate Rider leaned against the rail watching the dripping blades of the starboard wheel chop into the water. The pleasant feeling of freedom that she had known ever since she came aboard the fine white ship filled her with a tingling happiness. She was almost ashamed of it, for fear someone would see her excitement and think her very young. But it was impossible not to be excited. For the first time in her life she could do anything she liked, that is, anything that a young lady should do. She could stroll around the deck, pretending to be demure, and showing off her new velvet bonnet with its taffeta ribbon, and her ginger-plaid travelling gown. Or, if she liked, she could go into the salon and write a letter, or order a cup of tea, the way the other ladies did. Or she could go down across the lower deck and up onto the afterdeck where the wind blew more freely and the seagulls sailed down almost within reach. She pictured herself at each pastime in turn, and wondered idly and luxuriously which she would do. But she was tired of pretending to be demure and she hated to write letters, and having tea was a silly business at best. She wanted to pull off her bonnet and feel the wind in her hair and the cry of the gulls in her ears. She wanted to watch the long white wake of the ship rolling away over the green, moving hills of the ocean. "I'll cross the deck," she thought, "in another minute. I've all the time in the world. I've no sewing to do, sitting, when the sun is out and the birds are flying, in a stuffy room with a needle and a thimble and a horrid bit of lawn, so fine that it shows up every mistake! I've no music, I've no aunt. I'm free!"

Kate Rider was fifteen, and had come into her young ladyhood early. Papa and Aunt Enid had thought it advisable and more dignified that she should travel as a young lady. So the hems had gone down and the hair had gone up. And, to Kate's delight, there was lace on her pantalettes where before there had only been ruffles.

Not a little good advice had gone with the new finery. But Kate had borne this affliction nobly, allowing it to be politely received by one ear and swiftly dispatched by the other. Aunt

Enid was bewildered and frightened at the mere idea of her niece's adventure. Kate could not wait to have it start.

For all of the years of her memory Kate Rider had lived within her aunt's orbit; sewing by her side, or practicing her [illegible] day when she left home to marry, starching the curtains the way her aunt liked them starched, with rice-water instead of store starch, rolling the pillows on the beds into stiff bolsters instead of leaving them soft and flat, making bread this way and soup that. And when her father was sick, instead of being permitted to wait on him, she would be sent to sleep in the cold wing with the maid. "I don't want you catching anything," her aunt would say. "One sick person at a time is as much as I want." The cold wing was very cold, but the maid had a featherbed and because of this Kate loved sleeping with her. Though even the featherbed did not make up for the feeling of exile. Now and again her father was not so much sick as he was intoxicated. And still Kate was packed off to the cold wing. She sometimes wondered if her aunt fancied that she did not know! Or if her aunt thought that she might catch something—a little intoxication. Kate would lie in the featherbed and giggle at the thought. And then she would be cross, because she did not like being pushed away from her papa. He was hers. He was not Aunt Enid's.

Aunt Enid was a good woman and very kind to her, as Papa and the maid were both given to telling her. Still it had been a distinct relief when Aunt Enid had elected to remain in Hartford. The past was over and done with. Papa was not likely to get intoxicated any more with her care for him. Besides, he was important now.

Kate smiled, and her plain little face was suddenly bright and very near to being beautiful, so much pride and pleasure shone from it. Papa was very important indeed. Though he had been loved in Hartford, he had not been appreciated as a lawyer. Not until Mr. Tolliver had come and found him out. Aunt Enid had not cared at all for Mr. Tolliver. "He speaks of himself most modestly," she said, "but he is not in the least a modest man. If he says he has some slight influence in his State and can almost promise you a position worthy of you, then he undoubtedly runs the State and will get the position if it suits him to do so. Though whether you will be worthy of it is another thing!" Aunt Enid, Papa said, was apt to be sharp at times.

In the first instance at least she had been right. Papa was going to be head of the Freedman's Bureau in Jacksonville. He was going to take care of all of the poor black men who had been slaves, and who had never been permitted to learn how to take care of themselves. Their owners had treated them like children, or animals, and now, Papa said, they were too innocent to be able to get on in this modern world without help and protection. It was a very important work and Papa was pleased, and Kate thought that from now on everything would be new and fresh and he would always be pleased.

A sudden gust of wind reminded Kate of her decision to visit the afterdeck. She turned quickly and made her way towards the rear of the ship. At the iron stairway leading down to the lower deck she hesitated. She must cross the one below and ascend a similar ladder to reach the lonely place where, even from here, she could see the gulls wheeling and the spray dancing. But unlike the quiet deck on which she stood the one below was teeming with life. Men in pairs or groups or singly paced up and down talking and smoking, staring out at the ocean, or letting their eyes rove with that dazed look of the uncomfortable sea traveller. The bar was immediately beneath her, and the clink of glasses and rattle of dice, the muffled language of card games, floated out through the swinging doors. Kate watched with undisguised fascination as the doors were pushed open, and a large and flamboyant individual stepped out, in the act of tapping his gray beaver to a jaunty angle on his head. He wore on his cherry-colored vest enough gold chain and trinkets to finance a government, she thought. His faun-colored trousers hugged his legs, and he wore a pair of gray- [illegible]

Two men came out of the door behind the gambler and quickly moved up to his side, where they remained much, Kate thought, like carriage dogs trotting beside a coach. They too were outfitted gaudily, though it was obvious that their clothes were of a poorer quality and not so well tailored as their chief's. The men did not speak and Ned King seemed unaware of their presence. As he strolled, he removed a long twisted black cigar from a leather case, and carefully snipped the end with a gadget that hung from the chain on his brilliant vest. Without slowing his pace or turning he allowed one of his followers to hold a sulphur match to the cigar until he had taken several long puffs of the heavy gray smoke.

The men below had passed the foot of the ladder which Kate was about to descend, when something happened that caused her to hesitate again. She wasn't afraid of the gambler, she told herself, though she did not want anything to do with such a person, and she would just wait until he had reached the far side of the deck before she went down. In that moment a man who had been standing by the rail watching the progress of the small group seemed suddenly to come to a decision, and strode over to confront the gambler and block his way. At once the two carriage dogs stepped forward menacingly, and Kate thought, with a sickening surge, that she was about to witness a fight. Ned King had his back to her, but the newcomer faced her and they were still close enough so that she could see him clearly. For a moment he didn't speak, then he grinned slowly, and his deep-set blue eyes narrowed. He was the kind of a man who would have started a fight laughing, she thought, and probably still have been able to laugh when it was done.

He said abruptly, "You don't remember me, King."

"I don't," the man in the cherry-colored vest said coldly.

"It's been a long time, Captain, but I wouldn't expect you to forget a gambling debt!"

The gambler changed as suddenly as though his disdainful manner were no more than one of the fobs he wore on his watchchain, to be picked up and dropped at will. "Thunderation!" he bellowed, "it's Mike. Do I remember? Of course I do. Though it's a devilishly long time, it seems. They said you had stopped a minie ball down in Georgia."

"Just slowed it down a little—not that I couldn't have stopped it if I had wanted to." The two men laughed and then they turned and started to stroll away, and Kate lost the thread of their conversation, only now and then catching a word, or the big sound of the newcomer's laughter.

She went down quickly now, sorry that she had waited. For Ned King was obviously going to stroll up and down, and if she was afraid to cross his path she would never get to the far deck. After all, he was nothing but a prettily dressed fat man. Strangely enough, it was the newcomer who disturbed her most. There was something about him that was both rough-and-easy and knowing, and she particularly did not want to encounter him. Halfway across the deck she passed the group, who had turned back as though suddenly determined to revisit the bar. Ned King was smoking silently, and the newcomer was talking. "Don't stop in Jacksonville, Ned. It's not the town for you."

Kate stared at him at these strange words. The gambler said, "You mean, it's your own personal tenting ground."

"If you want to put it that way," the other shrugged.

"It sounds like a nice little town," she heard King say. "I like nice little towns. I think I will visit it."

Kate caught hold of the railing of the far ladder and looked back. The man, Mike, had stopped squarely in front of Ned King; there was no grin on his face now. On the wind his words came to her clearly:

[illegible]

town," he said patronizingly. "I'm really headed for New Orleans, with a look-see at Savannah. We don't go through Jacksonville. Come along." He took the other's arm. "I'll give you a chance to double——" And they continued on their way to the bar.

The small semicircular deck that Kate climbed to was deserted. A gull whirled down and away again, as light and effortless as a feather on the wind. A path of foam led away from the ship into the distance. Kate sat on the anchor hatch and looked about her. The first thing that she had done was to take off her bonnet, but she no longer felt free and happy and excited. She had unwittingly pictured Jacksonville as almost belonging to her father and Mr. Tolliver. It would be a small town, about like Hartford. She would have her own house and entertain there with her papa, who had the most important position in the town.

But this man Mike talked as though Jacksonville belonged to him, and was nothing but a gambling den. An awareness in Kate, an inner understanding not yet quite born, warned her that her father would like this rough man. Despite all of Aunt Enid's secrecies, Kate knew that her father was fond of both drinking and gambling, and the vision of the rough, laughing gambler who pretended to own Jacksonville filled her with foreboding.

Horrible man! she thought. I hate him. She sat there thinking; half thoughts, half dreams slipping across her consciousness like flecks of foam in the ocean. The gamblers and Jacksonville, and Mr. Hains Tolliver and a house called Valhalla. "It's not a pretty house," he had said. And when she had protested that any house with a name like that must be lovely, he said, "Perhaps you are right—but this house isn't used to the name yet. It was called Hains House before the war. I have borrowed an older name for it—some day I shall have to tell you about it." It filled Kate with a feeling of mystery and beauty.

When the sun had dipped, like a candied apple, into the ocean and all of the colors had faded from the sky, leaving it smoky with dusk, Kate thought that it was time for her to go. She tied on her bonnet and stood up, and she was surprised to see that she was no longer alone. A man and a woman sat on the opposite hatch, their backs to her, and closer to her a large man leaned against the rail. Kate had not heard any of them come, but the wind was loud in this unprotected place and the chunking of the paddlewheels accompanied it like an orchestration. The woman wore a shawl and the man with her had on a flat hat. They were surely deck passengers. Perhaps they even slept up here. Kate shuddered; it was a cold place to sleep. Perhaps the woman had a featherbed. Aunt Enid's maid had brought her featherbed all the way from Germany, and she had slept on deck with it and been very comfortable.

The man by the near rail turned around and Kate saw that it was the man Mike. He smiled at her, and in the dusk his face had a look of kindness that warmed her suddenly.

"Going in?" he asked.

Kate nodded mutely.

"It's late," the man said, "and the deck below is getting lively; perhaps you will allow me to accompany you." He bowed to her, a slight bow, a gesture of a bow.

Kate thought, unhappily, he's not being rude or anything, but he is laughing at me and I don't want him, I don't even want to be seen with a rogue like him. She shook her head and said stiffly, "Thank you, but I'd rather go alone."

The man nodded and turned at once to the rail, and Kate went quickly to the ladder. The deck below was certainly in a turmoil. The entire male population of the boat seemed to have gathered there, and in the fading light their movements [illegible]

[illegible] “I believe it’s a good lesson to you. Out late, and rude to strangers!”

Kate whirled away from him, but not before he had seen the quick look of hurt in her eyes.

“Forgive me,” he cried at once. “I am a great lout, Miss Rider, and I put my feet in my mouth at least twice a day.”

Kate giggled despite herself, and then she stopped. “But, you know my name!”

“Yes, ma’am, and if I may present myself, I am Michael Bourne. I have met your father.”

Kate gave him her hand and said with a simple directness, “How do you do, Mr. Bourne. I am sorry if I seemed rude, I——”

“Never mind, let’s forget it, shall we? We’ve both been naughty.”

Kate laughed, and then she remembered that this man was a gambler and she thought how horrified Aunt Enid would be, and she blushed and was glad of the dark to hide her face.

Michael Bourne was not a tall man, though he towered over Kate. He was not as tall as Hains Tolliver, she thought, but he was broader and stronger-looking, more of a man, while Tolliver looked more of a gentleman. Michael Bourne was not as handsome either, but his wide mouth had more humor, and his blue eyes more warmth.

"I'll be seeing a lot of you this summer," he was saying, impudently.

Indeed you'll not! Kate wanted to say. We are going to lead a different kind of life from that. She let him help her down the ladder and said:

"Why are all these people going South?"

"Carpetbaggers, ma'am, like ourselves," he shrugged. "Scum of the earth, most of us!"

"Oh, but we're not!"

"Enough are so the rest get the name! The South is all disorganized from the war. Every sort of crook and outlaw who has been thrown out of his own State is running South to get some of the plunder. Intelligent Southerners aren't allowed to vote, and a bunch of black hoodlums are!"

Kate looked at him in amazement. "How can you speak that way," she cried indignantly. "After all those Negroes have been through, they might at least vote and not be called names."

Bourne smiled at her with surprising gentleness. He was a man who knew a good deal about women, too much for his own good, he told himself wryly. But this one was different. There was something fresh and alive and strong about her and she was undoubtedly very young—like a gallant little flag. He was reminded of the feeling he had had upon awakening in a field and seeing his company's colors snapping in the breeze over a newly taken position. They had seemed so bright and strong, so high above the heads, and beyond the comprehension, of the men who fought for them. And what else should a woman be but that!

"You'll soon see how it is," he told her seriously. "It's hard to take it all in at once, what with what we've been told at home, and what is going on down South."

"I don't know what you mean," she said.

"Well, you have to admit that the Southerners who governed themselves before the war had some—at least, let's say, education. They knew what government was."

"Slavers?"

"But educated men. Now the blacks, they're not——"

"Don't tell me they're not men!" Kate cried. Her companion laughed.

"They're men, like anyone else, ma'am," he said, "but they've [illegible]

ing to slow 'em down for everybody's good, including their own —and the politicians from the North are trying to use 'em to line their own pockets with gold. It's a considerable mess. So you see, ma'am, the Southerners don't love us!"

"Mr. Tolliver is a Southerner," Kate said slowly, without apparent connection.

"And he loves us! Sure, and why not!"

Kate looked quickly at her companion. He was laughing at her, she thought crossly, and she realized, with a sudden insight, that this was not so surprising a thing as it was that he had been serious with her. Kate tossed her head. Mr. Tolliver was a great man, if a little bit old. For he was thirty-five by Aunt Enid's guess, and Kate would not have been amazed to hear that he was older. And Michael Bourne was nothing but a ruffian and had no business teasing her! She said, "What is Jacksonville like?" quickly, to cover her confusion.

"Not much more than a village, but full of life and spunk," Bourne said, and he wondered, even as Kate had, why he troubled to be serious with her. Seriousness was not his way. He was still ashamed of the quick look of hurt in her eyes that his earlier rudeness had brought, and he thought that she was a girl who had had a cold upbringing, and maybe a lonely one. She would have to learn about laughter the slow way. He found himself thinking that it would be fun to teach her. For something about her drew from him an inexplicable tenderness.

"Jacksonville," he said, "has been burned and plagued again and again, but it's a natural city and will not be stopped. It will be as great a city one day as any in the country! Before the war it had two thousand inhabitants, now it has six thousand. In another ten years——" he looked down at Kate and grinned. "You don't want to know how many inhabitants it's going to have in ten years, do you?"

Kate laughed. Nothing was more annoying than to be talked to in figures, to be told of populations, and that a room was so many feet by so many, a destination so many minutes' walk, a tower so high or a force so strong. She was not unaccustomed to the masculine way of description, for her father was a man of great precision. If she asked him to tell her about some house that he had visited he would look at her blankly and then commence with growing enthusiasm to reckon its dimensions with fractional exactitude, and would be quite unable to tell her whether the curtains in the parlor were red or green.

"You probably don't even know whether it is a pretty place," she said with resignation. "I'm sure Papa would not."

"But I am a very exceptional man!" Michael Bourne announced boldly. Kate looked at him with solemn surprise. It was an extraordinary way for a person to speak of himself, she thought.

"I will tell you how it is," he went on. "Jacksonville is a song of a place. A rip-roaring chorus, like bullfrogs by the river. Everything is big about it, and exciting. Big trees, giant trees, big river, the ocean running inland, big commerce, a navy to carry out the oranges and pine, big thieves, all dressed up like lords and princes. A couple of handfuls of wooden houses inviting another fire, one plank highway and a dozen dirt streets. When it rains you're up to the brim of your beaver, and when it's hot you're like to get consumption for the dust! There's jasmine and night-blooming jasmine, so you're never without a pretty smell, and there are razorbacks in the streets to keep the refuse down!"

Kate laughed helplessly. They had come, in the course of their conversation, to the central deck where a wide companionway opened onto the cabins. She said, eying the door and knowing that she should go and make herself ready for supper, "You say it is pretty, and you make it sound horrible. Do you know Mandarin, too? And is it as bad?"

[illegible]

Bourne smiled. "It was named over a hundred years ago, or so they say, by a lady from a very frosty country. I should think the colder the people the more they'd appreciate oranges in heaven!"

Kate laughed. In the long central cabin of the ship a gong sounded. "Goodness!" she cried, "it's supper time." She made a wry face, wrinkling her nose. "Do you know," she said, "I feel as though I were in a menagerie when I see the funny, heavy dishes and the great, thick glasses they give us to eat from. Why ever do they make them so thick?"

"It's the penny-pinching kind of a thing ship companies do," Bourne said solemnly. "If they're going to have a shipwreck they want to make sure their crockery doesn't get all broken up!"

"Oh!" Kate hoped that it sounded haughty. He was teasing her and it made her feel young and cross. "Papa will be wondering about me," she said quickly. "Thank you for coming with me, Mr. Bourne."

"The pleasure is mine, ma'am." He held her hand and then let her go abruptly and watched her push open the door of the companionway and disappear inside. For a moment he stood there thinking of her. He had noticed her first as she stood watching his meeting with King. She had been so openly curious, like a child who is unconscious of staring, and the fascination and indignation that registered in her eyes were wonderful to see. He thought then that he would like to talk to her. Now that he had talked to her he was delighted. She is a baby, he thought, and as honest as a boy But some day she is going to turn into something very surprising. And he thought that he would like to be the one to see it. She was not going to have an easy time of it in Jacksonville. He thrust his hands into his pockets and swore softly. Her father was a fool to begin with, or he would never have brought her to a place he knew nothing of. And he thought also that she would not have been brought had not Hains Tolliver had some reason to want her there.

"You're suspicious, are you not, Michael Bourne!" he told himself. But he knew Hains Tolliver. And he thought that he was not bringing the lawyer to Jacksonville to benefit the freedmen more than ostensibly. Nor was the daughter coming South to make her father's life an easier one. "Well, you can be wrong," he decided uneasily, and he made his way towards his cabin.

In the dining salon the passengers sat about one long table. It took three of the very largest cloths to cover it, and it was laden, as Kate had remarked, with crockery and glassware of the heaviest sort. Kate finished her supper and sat idly watching her father spoon the bubbles from his coffee. He had a superstitious conviction that every bubble caught meant a fortune would be won, and he never neglected this ritual. Michael Bourne came in for the second serving, and as he passed he bowed to Kate and went down the table to take his place at the far end. Archibold Rider looked up from his cup in time to witness this passage, and frown.

"Making friends, miss?" he asked.

Kate looked at him shyly. "We met on deck, Papa."

"Best keep to yourself, Kate, until we know more." Her father still frowned. "Bourne is a horse of uncertain color. An Irish immigrant gone South at an opportune time."

"I liked him," Kate said simply.

"Still, keep to yourself, girl." Her father's voice was low and not entirely happy. "I cannot be worrying about you now."

Kate studied her plate. He was Irish! That explained his

voice. There were a few of the Irish in Hartford, but Aunt Enid had a strong prejudice against them and would not have one in the house, even to wash the dishes. So Kate had never met one before. She found herself unaccountably sorry that [illegible]

[illegible]

said, clearing his voice sententiously, "but when you have had war you have to resort to superficial standards. Everything and everyone is mixed up. In time, the cream will always rise. But right after the mixing you cannot tell what is what or who is who."

With a loud clattering, three seamen in waiters' coats rolled in a copper soup-tureen on wheels and commenced to dish out platefuls of a transparent liquid. Kate watched them earnestly, embarrassed at her father's words and afraid that in a moment of silence Mr. Tolliver, who sat opposite them, had heard. She should not care, but she did. Mr. Tolliver would think that she was too young to tell a gentleman from an immigrant. From under her lashes she watched Tolliver. He was talking to his neighbor, but indolently as though the man bored him. In the same way he ate his food. What Aunt Enid called "toying" with it, one disdainful hand in his pocket. His neighbor used a gold toothpick, working it daintily, and replacing it after each usage in the pocket of a brilliantly checked vest. Her father ate with grace, too, though he did not hide a hand. While, down the long table, she could see that Michael Bourne's clenched fist was on the table. He wolfed his food as though he were hungry and had no shame of being so. Kate blushed for him and wished that she had not looked.

When she looked up again, it was to find that Hains Tolliver was watching her with the smallest of smiles on his soft lips. She blushed suddenly and unhappily. She was unaccustomed to eating in public and found no pleasure in doing so. Tolliver, as though perceiving her discomfort, turned away at once. Because he is a gentleman, Kate thought gratefully, despite anything Aunt Enid might say. Kate frowned, remembering her aunt's strange words, "I do not trust him, Archibold. The mouth is too soft and the eyes are too cold. It is a dishonest combination."

"A kind and gentle mouth and eyes of strength and reason," her father had protested; "what more would you ask?"

Aunt Enid, with prim New England lips, did ask more "honesty." "There goes a sensual mouth and godless eyes, mark my word, Archibold Rider."

An invisible tremor passed through Kate. She agreed entirely with her father, but she was glad to have Hains Tolliver look elsewhere, for his eyes did seem to see a great deal. Not that there was anything to see, she thought crossly. She did not look towards Michael Bourne again, though she thought once or twice that his eyes were on her, and she found herself listening for his voice above the loud flow of male conversation.

When cigars were brought forth and port served, Archibold Rider took Kate out on deck and walked with her in the quiet evening. They were of a height, the father being a short man, and small-boned. More than father and daughter they looked a happy married couple as they went about together, and indeed they had been taken for such when they first came aboard. No surprising thing that: older men could often better afford to marry than young men whose years had been wasted in war; while the age of the bride was of no consequence so long as she was mature.

Kate hugged her father's arm. "Shall we have a house right away, Papa?" she asked.

"As soon as we can, my dear, though I don't know but what a boarding-house would be more suitable."

"Oh no! A boarding-house would be horrid. You'd never get the food you like and there'd be bound to be someone like that Miss Tillburn last summer, who'd want to manage me."

Her father laughed. "Managing is never going to hurt you, girlie."

"Yes, it will, Papa. I hate managing people."

Archibold Rider sighed. Kate's mother had [illegible]

too could not abide a managing female.

"A house it shall be," he said, "as soon as we can. We shall have to find an older woman to live with us."

"Oh, Papa, how hateful! It will just begin all over again."

"What, my dear?"

"You know, like Aunt Enid. We'll be run."

He patted her hand but his voice reprimanded gently. "Your aunt has done everything for you, Kate, brought you up, and I am afraid that you sound mighty close to ungrateful."

"I'm sorry." Kate pulled him to the railing. The sea was the color of ink, while here and there phosphorus bubbled beneath the surface, like incandescent champagne. "It's just that now I *am* brought up, and I don't want anybody else doing it all over again."

Her father laughed indulgently. "One look at the moon and the stars, girlie," he said, "and then it's time for your bed. Now that you're so grown up you'll have to have a chaperon, you know." He caressed the back of her neck and shook her playfully, as though she were a doll. He laughed at her exclamation of dismay.

When he had seen Kate to her cabin Archibold Rider returned to lean upon the rail. Over the black water and the trailing phosphorus, beyond the little white-caps in the distance where the ocean lay smooth and the eye would have it that sky and sea met lip to lip, there was the hidden future.

Archibold Rider was not a clear-sighted man, in the sense of inner vision. Perhaps because his own needs were simple he tried to read simplicity into a complex world, and so never found a true answer. There was black and white, the ideals of the poet, not of the philosopher. The grays did not exist, nor the luminous blacks, nor the dirty whites. Since the day when he first departed from the ivory tower to practice the things he had learned, in the world he had learned about, he had been looking for that simplicity. The fact that he did not find it did not seem to teach him that it was not there, but served only to impress upon him his own failure. He had failed little Amy, his wife, whom he had introduced to poverty and fear; he had failed the stalwart Enid, whose backbone had not been enough for two and whose ability at hiding the bottle had never been sufficiently ingenious. He did not stop to think that that he had also failed himself, but only looked towards succeeding for Kate where he had fallen so far short of the mark for others.

He caressed a mustache to which many years of favoritism had lent a decided droop. Kate should have her house, and if not the important father she had set her heart upon, at least one of whom she could be proud. It would be simple to be just and strong in dealing with the Negroes. They were children, who needed protection and advice, and Archibold Rider was empowered to give them that protection and advice. Duty and justice could not lie in a more simple path. No right-thinking man could fail so direct a task. He turned from his contemplation of the sea and went towards the saloon. The salt air inspired thirst.

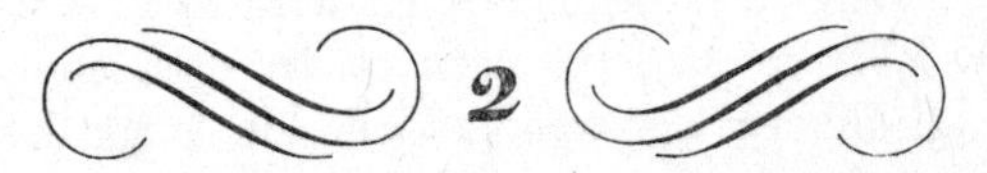

ON Thursday evenings the colored children were put to bed early and the women went into their cabins and pulled the shutters to and barred the doors. Or if they had no cabins they went into their tents, and if they had no tents they hid beneath the pillared porch of some quiet house. Thursday nights the men went to church, swarming through the streets as soon as it was dark, past the watchful sentries, two at the junction where the King's Road crosses Elizabeth Street and on every block from there to the church. [illegible]

the light fell upon them they too were black. They mumbled softly to the sentries and went by them into the church. In the vestibule the inner sentries challenged them and they touched the hands of the sentries and mumbled again and went by into the darkness beyond.

When all had gone through who knew the sign and the word, four men remained in the vestibule. One of these went to the sentry and spoke to him.

"You knows me," he said, "I is Wash'n'ton, that used to be Miss Bellamy's boy."

He turned his head so that the kerosene lamp that hung from the ceiling would throw its pale light upon him.

One of the sentries said, "I knows you."

"I aim to vouch for three brothers," Washington said.

"Does you know 'em?"

"I knows 'em good. They is freedmen and they is good 'publicans."

"They ain't spies?"

"No suh, no suh, they ain't."

In their corner the newcomers fidgeted uncomfortably and their eyes rolled from the sentries and their sponsor to the door that led into night. But now a break would brand them as spies and they would never get past the outer sentries.

The inner sentry rapped twice on the door of the church

and in a moment two raps answered him. Then the door opened and two men came out, they wore black hoods and through narrow slits their eyes glittered like liquid in the light. Washington motioned his three friends to approach. They came reluctantly, their feet shuffling across the dirt floor.

"These is the Tylers of the Altar," Washington said, and he bent as he spoke, as though he would rather have spoken from his knees. To the hooded men he said, "These is good boys, Jim Richards and Jim Oaks and Vinton Oaks. They was all slaves to Colonel Denver in Jackson County."

As their names were called, the three stepped up, bending down, and themselves showing a disposition to kneel. But the hooded men fixed them with menacing eyes.

"Ain't no one asked you to kneel and bend, is they?" one spoke with muffled fury.

"Come and be 'zamined."

The Tylers led the three men into the church. The room was large, though seeming larger because the dim light of candles on the altar did not find out the walls and corners, and in the gloom these stretched indefinitely. Save for an arc of space around the altar, every inch was crowded with colored people. The Tylers clapped their hands and a narrow aisle grew ahead of them like a worm burrowing through the earth.

The altar was festooned with candles and in the shadows of the pulpit a single man was sitting. The Tylers called out the names of the three men and then stood back leaving them alone in the circle of light.

The sound of breathing was heavy on the air and the smell of perspiration and of unwashed clothing was heavy on the air and the feel of fear and the threat of violence were heavy on the air. Suddenly the man in the pulpit spoke and his voice was harsh and alien to the South.

"Brethren, what seek ye?" he asked. And he leaned forward out of the shadow. The candlelight struck his hood and arms and threw a gigantic mass of shadow-creature onto the wall and ceiling.

As he scrutinized the three supplicants before him, the candle flame reflected from his eyes, the men could not see his hard, black eyes, but only the little fires looking down at them.

One of the Tylers stepped up and whispered to the men [illegible]

[illegible] repeated after the president of the meeting, "that I will protect and defend the Constitution and the Government of the United States against all enemies foreign and domestic, and that I will bear true faith, loyalty and allegiance to the same, that I will go to the rescue of a brother whenever I learn he is in trouble, that I will not vote for or assist directly or indirectly any person for any office who is not a brother of this league."

As the last words had died away the Tylers, who were standing by the altar, reached up and extinguished the candles. In the darkness there was a shuffling and from every corner of the room came a low moan of anticipation. When the lights were lit again the three men saw before them, and between them and the altar, a long black coffin. Upon the coffin to the left was a Bible; to the right, set in the triangle made by three naked swords, a human skull.

"No! lordy no, lordy no!" they cried in unison, stumbling to their feet. But the Tylers flanked them and, behind, the wormlike aisle to the door was gone, leaving a wall of unfriendly brothers swaying and moaning.

The president called out to them in his cold, hard voice.

"Kneel!" he cried. "Approach the coffin on your knees. Place your left hand on the Bible, Jim Richards, and your right hand you will place on this skull. It is the skull of a brother,

Jim Richards. If you are honest and true, you have nothing to fear. The man who owned this skull was a traitor. The United States doesn't like a traitor."

Jim Richards did as he was told. His hands were cold and wet and where they rested they left a film so that Jim Oaks, who came after him, screamed when his hand felt the slime on the skull and the Tylers fell upon him and threatened to quell his panic with gag and rope for the remainder of the ceremony. Jim Oaks screamed and jerked in the hands of the hooded men; then suddenly he was still, his terror overwhelming him, and with rolling eyes and palsied tongue he took the oath of secrecy and became a brother.

Back in his pulpit, the president looked down upon his congregation angrily.

"You know why I am here?" he cried.

The room filled with sound.

"Yes, suh."

"Yes, Miste Pres'dent."

"Yes, suh."

"Sho, sho."

"The United States Government has chosen me to save you from being sold back into slavery!"

The brothers cried out and their president held up his hands for silence.

"The Government wants this to be a very special league. You are brothers of Lincoln, who died for you. The Government wants you to keep this secret, so that your enemies will be foiled." He pointed down upon the skull and his voice rose in majesty. "Keep secret everything that happens here, every word that is said, or you will join brother traitor." To the three new brothers he said, "You will each lay two dollars on the altar; after this, you will bring fifty cents every month. If you are asked anything about this society you may say that you have joined a benevolent society. You are now brothers of Lincoln. I greet ye brethren."

A sigh filled the room as though a danger had been safely circumvented, and they were all glad.

"Now then," the president spoke leaning forward on the lectern, "we will call the business of the day." He dug into the cavity of his left ear with the long nail of his little finger, shook it briskly and then, withdrawing it, examined it for an [illegible] about it again before election.

"Now—I hear there are brothers working for Mr. David Snell." The president shook his head. "Don't I tell you, brothers —you don't have to work. The United States Government is going to take care of you. Yes, sir, just as soon as things get settled, every freedman brother of Lincoln is going to have forty acres of his own and a mule too!"

"Glory be," the freedmen cried and moaned with delight.

"If you want to work," the president's soft voice cut across their pleasure like a whip, "work for your friends. David Snell is a Democrat. He's a former slave-owner and he's mad at you because you're free. He would like to put you back into slavery. He would like to whip every one of you. Why!" the president boomed at them, "it wouldn't be a bit surprising if his place got burned some day by a loyal brother. That brother would be a hero!

"Now—Brother Zeke Richards!"

A shuffling and a whispering rose in the church and presently a small black man was thrust into the space that the three new members had but recently vacated.

"I is here," he whispered, and stood with his head bent.

"Brother Zeke, the Lord is pleased with you. The United States Government is pleased with you. You are Lincoln's true brother. You have done well."

Brother Zeke bobbed his head and a grin brightened his face and tears of joy filled his eyes. "I didn't want to do it at first, nohow," he muttered, "but I is glad," his voice rose, "yes, I is proud I has burned out one of de enemy! Dey wants to make us slaves again. Dey is de enemy."

The president smiled at him and the brothers shouted, "Halleluiah!" and Zeke Richards stepped back into their midst.

"One more thing," the president said, "Mr. Michael Bourne is coming back to Florida. You all know he has rebuilt his place. I hear he is going to enlarge his groves—if he can get any labor! He has been made District Attorney and he says he is a good Republican. But we are not sure that he is a Republican at all."

Silence.

"We shall see. I will tell you when I am sure."

Silence.

"All here are good Republicans!"

Cries and shouts.

" 'Publicans, 'publicans!"

"I is."

"We is."

"Sho, sho nuff."

" 'Publicans is good."

" 'Publicans is hones'."

"Jesus Christ," cried the president, bowing his head but lifting his voice like a banner, "Jesus Christ was a Republican."

"Praise de Lord, glory be to God," cried the brothers, raising their arms to heaven and rocking themselves with ecstasy.

"The meeting is adjourned for the week," the president shouted. "Give your dues to the Tylers and go in peace." And he bowed his head on his hands and waited for the church to empty.

When the last brother had gone from the room, the Tylers brought him a flour sack heavy with money. He directed them to lay it on the altar after putting their own donations and those already on the altar into it. Then he came down from his pulpit and, reaching beneath the skirts of the altar, drew out a sturdy red-and-green satchel made of carpet and bound with strips of leather. He took up the sack of money, held it a moment, as though he were speculating upon its contents, before he thrust it into the maw of the bag.

[illegible]

He stepped out of his robe and flung it with a careless gesture across the coffin. It fell like a coif upon the skull, causing it to totter, a grim marionette shaking its head. The two black men cried out and backed away, their eyes rolling so that only the whites showed through the slits in their hoods.

"You fools! Get out of your robes and put all of those things up in the loft." Their leader's tongue lashed them like a whip. "That skull ain't going to hurt you unless you turn traitor. And leaving it out here for everyone to see would be turning traitor plenty. Now, get along." And paying no further attention to their fright, he took up his bag and left them to their unwilling task.

Outside the sentinels saluted. Their torches no longer flared and the night was moonless and dark.

"Goodnight, Mr. President, suh," they whispered as he went, and they watched him go with awe and kindness. He was the black man's friend and protector.

In a room at the St. James Hotel a man of large stature and small head watched the door as a key inserted from the other side turned the lock over.

"Jim?" he said softly. The door swung inwards and James Cutler, the president of the Brothers of Lincoln came in. He nodded to the occupant of the room without speaking, closed and locked the door and then put his satchel on the bed. He was white and small. His face was so thin as to look bruised in places, and his black hair was as smooth as though it were painted on his head.

"Looks like a good take," he said. "When'd you get in?"

"Twenty minutes ago."

Cutler put his beaver carefully on a chair, took off his coat and rolled up his sleeves. "We'll have time to count it before the train," he said, and the two men emptied the bag on the bed and separated the money into denominations.

"Did you get anything done?" Cutler asked as he raked through the nickels, dimes and quarters.

"Hard to tell yet. That black priest has swallowed Jesus. Don't like not knowing what goes on in his church. He don't take much to a benevolent society he's not allowed to preachify at. I told him we're representing the Government, teaching our black brothers how to run their own civic affairs——"

"And——"

"He ain't a real believin' cuss."

"Well, there are ways to fix him if he gets troublesome."

The big man rubbed the side of his nose thoughtfully. "He's mighty popular," he said at last.

Cutler scowled. "We'll leave that particular worry to the boss," he said. After that, the two men were silent, counting.

"Four hundred dollars," Cutler announced at last.

"That's good."

Cutler said nothing. He got ten percent of the take, plus his salary from the Bureau. It wasn't good, not when he did the work and took the risk. He started scooping coins back into the bag.

"It's better than the Freedom League are taking in."

Cutler moved his thin lips contemptuously. When the last penny was put away, he locked the bag and placed it in the bottom of a cupboard which he in turn locked.

"Come on, Sam," he said, "if you ask me it's a fool idea to go all the way to Savannah to meet the new commissioner. But it's the boss's idea so it has the merit of being right, by hell!" And the two men put on their coats and took up their canes and their fine beavers. Cutler carried gloves, but Samuel Hess could not accustom himself to covering his hard square hands. Before the South had beckoned him he had been a professional fighter. If not a very successful one, at least he had led a health[illegible]

[illegible]

pany of richly clothed civilians and dashing officers. For they were as richly clothed as any and they had business to attend to.

AT midday, Jacksonville was as still as though it were instead the middle of the night. An old colored woman shuffled down Caroline Street keeping in the shade of the trees, for the sun was scorching hot. She was a deep African black and her shoulders were thick and stooped. As she passed a small frame house a shutter creaked and a voice called, "Auntie, oh Auntie."

The colored woman stopped, then she shuffled, muttering as she went across the dirt path towards the house, "Yes'm, I is comin', I is comin'."

A white hand held the shutter open and, from the darkened room beyond, a young voice spoke. Her words were gently slurred and as soft as though they had lain for a quarter of a century beneath a covering of wet leaves.

"You want to work?" she asked.

"Cleaning?"

"Yes, the house needs cleaning."

"Is you payin'?"

"Yes."

"Well, ma'am, I doesn't rightly want to. But I is comin' right in." The old woman sighed as she climbed the steps, crossed the piazza and disappeared into the darkened house. In the hall, she was met by a slender girl who led her to the kitchen, walking carefully as though she were not accustomed to the ways of her own house and feared that she might knock into some piece of furniture.

The old woman followed, squinting, for her eyes were focussed to the sun and she was troubled by the dim light. "I's got the misery," she half moaned, half sang, "I's got the misery in my back, but I is goin' to work. Yes'm, I is going to work till I drop. Black is born to suffer by the sweat off his brow. You is Miss Crockett Wilson, isn't you?" she stated, scarcely separating her words with a breath.

The girl looked at her, turning her head slowly, half closing her eyes. In the light of the kitchen it was at once apparent that Miss Crockett was not merely a beautiful girl but, saving the aging look of having been through too harsh a battle, she was even a great beauty. She was over-thin for her height and her eyes were big and round, a dreamy hazel color. But though she was thin and her features were finely cut her face was full and softly rounded and the look of suspicion that she wore now seemed alien to it.

"Yes, Auntie, I am Miss Crockett," she said quietly. "Why do you ask?" And she seemed to listen for the answer with all of her being.

"Nothin', ma'am. I hears you gives food along with pay."

"Food! Yes. I want things clean. You'll get something to eat before you go."

In the corner by the back door a blue enamel sink was cluttered with dishes. A hand pump was attached to the sink and the darkie said, "Water!" with evident satisfaction.

Miss Crockett said, "You'll have to light a fire to heat the water. And do up the floor too." Then she went out of the room with the same quick careful steps she had used before. Once in the hall, she hesitated, listening. A rocker creaked in the front parlor and in the kitchen the darkie had taken up her chant of misery. Miss Crockett bent her head, still listening, and felt along the wall for the knob of a door. She found it at last, pulled it softly and tiptoed into the black depth of a narrow closet. There followed a quiet [illegible]

[illegible]

mending and went to her seat by the window. She felt for the arm of the chair and sat down gingerly. Opposite her, her mother rocked idly, fanning herself rather more energetically with a palmetto fan. Miss Janey Wilson was small-boned but, with the years, the flesh had covered her well so that the bones were only to be guessed at. She wore a white cambric nightgown that clung damply to her body. Now and again she pulled it away from her fat breasts and fanned at her open neck. She watched with a small frown her daughter's progress across the room.

"Is she any good?" she asked at last.

"A cornfield nigger," her daughter shrugged. "She'll have to do. Things have got so dirty. I declare it makes me outright sick." She looked down at her handwork and smoothed it out idly on her knees.

Her mother sighed, "I declare, Miss, there'd be nothing to make you sick if you'd mend your ways."

The girl didn't answer but bent over the piece of embroidery as though studying its pattern.

"Crockett," her mother said sharply, "what were you doing in the hall closet?"

Crockett looked up and her eyes were wide and round. "What closet, Momma?"

"Don't try to fool me, Miss," her mother cried angrily. "I've good enough ears and I heard you go into the hall closet."

"Oh, Momma, I got the girl some soap. Momma dear, what did you think I did?"

Her mother sighed. "Crockett, I declare. Oh, poor little Crockett! I know it's hard for a pretty girl, but you don't make it any easier for yourself. You should straighten out and get married. Cousin George loves you truly, but you must stop, you must stop drinking."

"Momma!" the girl cried. "Momma, what are you saying to me! Have you been telling Cousin George lies about me? Have you!" She stared at her mother, her eyes luminous in the dim light. "Do you know," she whispered, leaning forward, and her voice had a lilt to it, "I think you are crazy. Yes. You are. Poppa and Tom getting killed. I don't think I should stay in the house alone with you."

Her mother paid no attention to her words, as though her ears had long been accustomed to such sounds and they had no power to shock her. She said slowly but decidedly,

"I think that marriage is what you need. It'll straighten you out. Why, I was married, with two children, at your age, Miss. Two in eighteen months." She rocked and sighed. "It near killed me," she said with some satisfaction. "Momma always said it was my own fault for not nursing. Mamie Delahanty didn't have her second for three years. She nursed Ossian till he stood and looked her in the eye. Said it made her uncomfortable. And Bingo! the day he stopped sucking if she didn't conceive again."

Crockett shuddered. "Momma, that story gives me goose pimples."

Her mother laughed. "Guess you're like me. It always made me squeamish to see that young 'un walk up to the tit. Like a pig, or a pup. But I couldn't stand the idea of nursing nohow. You and Tom got black milk. Likely that's why——" she left the sentence unfinished, looking quickly at her daughter.

But Crockett was not listening. Her eyes were closed and she rocked in her chair gently all the time her hands smoothed the work on her knees. The light fell through the shutters in neat slices, ivory as magnolia on Miss Janey's own hands, and white as a rose and as bloodless on Crockett's throat.

"Cousin George hasn't been near us in a week," Miss Janey complained. "Ain't he ever coming again?"

Crockett opened her eyes slowly. "Cousin George?" she asked; "when is he coming?"

[illegible]

ride Hains Tolliver down into the ground where he belongs."

"Oh, hush!" her mother cried.

"He's a red-blooded man." Her daughter pushed herself up from her chair, letting her handwork fall unnoticed to the ground. Her mother held up a hand. "Please, Crockett," she said urgently. The little house was silent, the long complaint of misery from the kitchen had ended. Neither woman spoke, and they listened as though for some expected sound. Presently it came, the soft closing of a door.

"There!" Miss Janey let her hands fall with little slapping sounds to the arms of her chair. "She's gone. You won't get anyone else today either. Crockett, how can you talk that way? You know they listen, and they're so scary these days."

"I don't know what you're talking about, Momma; you're always blaming me about something." Crockett sat down, nursing offense. She had forgotten the piece of embroidery and it lay rumpled under her foot.

Her mother shook her head. "I don't know what to do, I declare I don't," she complained. "Crockett, go fix me a lemon drink, honey, your poor little ol' momma is feeling right puny."

The girl got up readily. As she went across the room the embroidery dragged at her heel.

"Please, baby," her mother called. "Keep away from—keep out of the closet, for your momma."

Crockett went without answering, walking so carefully that

in the dim light it looked as though she were being wafted along on little breezes.

That evening George Morgan came to the house, tying his horse to the ring in the Redberry tree and striding up the path, his left hand in his pocket and his riding crop in the other hand switching nervously at one leg. The shutters of the house were flung wide now and Miss Janey, dressed in black, sat rocking on the porch.

"Why, Cousin George!" she cried, a new vivacity in her voice, "it's that good to see you. We were talking about you only today."

"Were you?" he said eagerly, taking her hand.

"Leave your hat on that chair and come sit near me. Crockett!" she raised her voice. "Crockett, your cousin George is here."

"Good evening, Cousin," Crockett said from the doorway.

"Evening, Cousin. My, you're looking mighty pretty!" He took both of her hands in his and looked at her for a long and searching moment. And for a moment there was a look of happiness between them, of joy in each other's friendship. It was a friendship made up of a backlog of old memories and particularly dear because the world had changed so for them both. For a moment she was the girl who had lived in a big house on Laura Street, where a vine of yellow roses grew to the second story and framed her bedroom window. George had tried to climb it once, only succeeding in tearing the vine from the house, and it had taken three darkies an hour to pull all of the thorns from him. The house was gone now, even the trees around it, felled as barricades.

As though she were following his thoughts, Crockett leaned towards her cousin and whispered, "We had to walk back from Baldwin, Cousin. There were nigger troops in the house. I'm glad it burned. We walked along the broken tracks. Momma kept crying about Tom. I'm glad Tom died, and Poppa too, I am glad——"

"Crockett!" her mother cried.

"There, there." Her cousin patted her hand and drew her gently towards a chair. "It's all over now, Cousin," he said. "You must forget it."

"It's not over!" The girl allowed herself to be seated. "The [illegible]

a man finely built and the lines of his face were drawn with disillusion. Crockett looked at him and loved him, but she did not know what the harsh unhappy feeling in her was.

They sat there in silence for a while. Crockett soon looked away from her cousin, but though he leaned back indolently in his seat he never took his eyes from her. In the garden a whippoorwill sang his plaintive evening song and a river breeze moved the porch vines and brought with it the heavy sweetness of night jasmine.

"What have you done with yourself today?" Miss Janey asked at last.

George Morgan shrugged. "I came in from Mandarin this morning. We're having a time getting help. We've got three niggers out there, under contract, and they won't work. We've got to pay and feed them but there's no way to make them hold up their end. It beats me how Michael Bourne can't get help."

"It beats me," Miss Janey said scornfully, "how that carpet-bagger can have the son of Alphonse Morgan to run his place for him."

George Morgan laughed. "Bourne is all right," he said. "He's the only Yankee who admits he's a knave, and he's the only one who isn't."

"You put too much store in him."

"I know him, Cousin, believe me. You don't work for a

man without knowing him. He's got a reputation, but he fosters it. The last thing he'd stomach would be any one accusing him of ideals. But he's a man of ideals just the same. You should ask some of the fellows at Mandarin what they think of him. Any down-at-the-heel, hungry, sick fellow in a gray uniform gets a bed at Mandarin, and work if he wants it. No questions asked. They get the respect he wants for himself. They're soldiers down on their luck and it doesn't matter to him that he was in a different army."

"Charity——" Miss Janey said coldly, but her cousin shook his head.

"It's not charity. It's not the way he talks about it, but the way he acts about it that makes it something else."

Morgan laughed. "He is like the gnome in the fable who does something nice for you and then if you thank him disappears in a huff. Except that Michael is no gnome. He is a rowdy, blasphemous Irishman quite willing to pick a fight with the whole world at once!"

"It's still not right for you to work for him," Miss Janey said flatly.

Morgan shrugged. "Why not?" he said. "We both get something we want. Michael is too busy right now to watch his own interests. I want to be on the land and I want to be at Mandarin. Some day I'm going to get Valhalla back. There are things worth watching at Mandarin, and that's going to help."

Crockett said quietly but with a venom that sat strangely on her soft voice, "You should burn it over his head."

"Hains or Bourne?" Morgan smiled at her, trying to make her words a jest.

"You know who I mean. He stole your land. You should burn him right to the ground."

"Crockett!" her mother scolded, and then said illogically, "Anyway Hains is not at home."

Cousin George laughed. "Gentle ladies," he said at last, "with you in the fore we should not have lost a single battle." Suddenly he was sober again. "I go up to meet Michael tonight.

He is bringing down a load of fools. I want to help him trans-ship them at Savannah. He's on the *City of Florida* and I hear the new commissioner is aboard too."

"They say Hains Tolliver got him his appointment." Miss [illegible]

[illegible] have to buy them and the State don't have a sick nickel," he shrugged. "With all that, he can't be expected to help a private citizen."

"Why don't your friend Bourne do something, now he's going to be District Attorney?"

"It's not his bailiwick. It's the Governor or no one, and some doubt that he can do anything. God alone knows where the papers are. Who authorized the confiscation of Valhalla? How much was asked and who got the money? Maybe there are no papers. After all, Tolliver took over during the first occupation. With all the confusion and the fires and the lack of any central responsibility, there's no one left who knows anything. By Gad! if he didn't own every office in the State I could sue!"

"Oh, the viper," Miss Janey cried, "the asp!"

Mason laughed shortly and lopped off a vine tendril with his riding crop. "At least, the Governor's an honest man," he said.

"Honest!" Miss Janey scoffed indignantly. "Governor Reed is from Wisconsin. What's he doing as governor of Florida? He's got six Yankees in his Cabinet and they do say he's given out posts to five hundred darkies can't even read or write!"

George Morgan shook his head. "Those are things he had to do," he said, "they have nothing to do with his honesty."

"There's no such thing as an honest Yankee," Miss Janey

said firmly, looking up; "no such thing, as you very well know."

"Maybe there is," Crockett said in a suddenly clear voice, and she clasped her hands tightly, for they trembled. "But why would one come to Florida, or stay here either? There are only bones to pick here, Cousin George. Can't you forget Florida, Cousin!" Her voice had risen almost to a cry, some piteous rational being trying to be heard from a black pit. Her mother paid her no attention, but George Morgan came to her side quickly and took her hands.

"No, Crockett, no, I can't," he said. "But don't you worry. Please, you forget things. I'll have Valhalla back in the end, and you'll——" he looked at her helplessly, as though there were things that he could not say to comfort her, "you'll be glad, will you not?"

His voice seemed to answer some question in her and they were silent on the porch. Miss Janey's rocker creaked steadily and a whippoorwill called from the redberry tree. Now and again the horse tethered there moved restlessly. Soon after, George Morgan took his leave. He was going by train to Savannah and he had first to stable his horse.

The two women sat alone in the dark. Crockett clutched at the arms of her chair, a frail creature among the heavy shadows. Long after the sound of horse's hoofs had faded to gentle thuds in the distance she stirred and went into the house without speaking again to her mother.

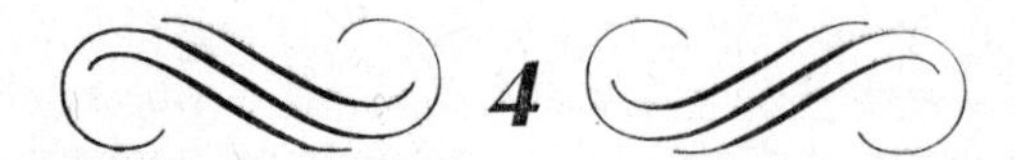

"NO evil can happen to a good man, either in life or after death." Archibald Rider stood upon the bridge and listened with half an ear to his own inner voice and half to Tolliver's gallantries and Kate's prattle. Cypress and water oak swarmed on the lea and the small town of Savannah was already in sight. The day was clear and bright and an excitement welled up in his breast. Like a snake who has shed his dead skin and left its dull stiff husk by the way, to writhe and flash his new beauty in the mirror of the sun, Archibold Rider made formal discard of the past. "No evil can happen to a good man." He had been weak, but he was a good man.

[illegible]

on the river; and Messelinni the black fiddler who had attended every bride or belle and enlivened every route.

"Today we are sober in the South," he said, "but we shall learn to laugh and sing again if the North continues to send us such charming examples."

Kate sighed. "I should like to go to a ball," she said.

"And so you shall," her father put his hand on hers, "if we have to give one ourselves."

"Hark!" Hains Tolliver said softly; "if you are quite still for a moment you should be able to hear the darkies singing on the deck. They are welcoming you to the South, Miss Kate."

Kate blushed at the gallantry, but she listened for the song, and in her heart she knew already that she would love the South, that this would be her home. Even Mr. Tolliver, who wore always an air of boredom, or perhaps was too old to feel excitement, listened, Kate thought, with pleasure. When he said, smiling down at her, "You are an enthusiastic little lady," she realized, exasperated, that her own expression must have run away with her.

"It looks to be a monstrous pretty country," she said primly. Tolliver was old enough to be her father at least. But still he was handsome and a great gentleman and she would not like him to take her for an uncouth child. She pretended a little yawn and said, "I must finish packing, if you will excuse me, sir." She patted her father's hand and curtsied to Tolliver and went sedately down the deck.

Tolliver watched her go with an amused smile. His trip North had been expedient. He wanted the new commissioner to be of his choice, and indebted to him. But Kate had lent a charm to the otherwise tedious trip. He found her delightful.

At Savannah, the passengers from the *City of Florida* transshipped to the *Georgia* which was to carry them down to Jacksonville. The *Georgia* was smaller than the *City of Florida* and the accommodations not so desirable, but neither was the trip long.

Miss Ferguesson, knowing that she must share her cabin with any other females who were travelling, made sure to set foot in it first. Once there, she directed the disposition of her effects and chose for herself the lower bunk farthest from the port-hole, for she mistrusted any seepage of water or of moist air. When this was done, she let the boy go. There was no stewardess aboard, and she sat down to await the arrival of the other passenger. It was her custom, when travelling, to retire before the boat left dock in order that the motion should not send her staggering immodestly about when she was trying to get out of her stays. However, she could not get into her nightclothes when any moment might bring the cabin boy with Miss Kate Rider's baggage. She could not even put her hair up in rags.

So it was that Kate found her, sitting stiffly on a stool with her hands folded neatly in her lap. She wore a green velvet dress that had seen good service and she wore neither a hoop nor sufficient petticoats to hide the shape of her knees. Kate thought that her papa would find this creature horrifying. Papa was always horrified at homely females. And Miss Ferguesson, with her gaunt features, her stiff brown curls lying like a row of pokers along her shoulders, her knees protruding like great velvet door knobs, was a very homely female.

"Good afternoon, young woman. Have the boy put your things there, that is your bunk." Miss Ferguesson took over immediately.

Kate said, "Good afternoon, ma'am," and curtsied. She disposed of her things as instructed and let the boy go, though she had planned to have him show where her father could be found when he came aboard. For he had gone off with [illegible]

"I am Miss Emma Ferguesson," she introduced herself to Kate and hung her bonnet upon a wall hook from which a large and unfeminine black sunshade was already suspended. "You are of course Miss Kate Rider. I am very glad to know you, my dear."

Kate curtsied again and said that she was pleased too.

"Make yourself at home," Miss Ferguesson said graciously, as though Kate were there by her invitation. "You will excuse me if I prepare myself for the journey," and she slipped over her head the tentlike sleeping garment. Beneath these yards of modesty her arms went to work like a small wind struggling to fill a heavy sail.

At this grotesque sight, Kate's small hand flew to her mouth. "I must look for my papa," she choked, and fled from the cabin lest she lose control of herself and laugh aloud.

She sauntered aimlessly about the deck, wondering when her papa would come and gnawed by the secret anxiety lest he might, led on by the other gentlemen, partake of intoxicating refreshment. Mr. Tolliver drank an inordinate great deal himself, though not having her papa's warm nature he was in no visible way affected. Perhaps he would influence her papa—but she feared that he would not. It was not a thing that a gentleman would concern himself to do.

On the dock she saw Michael Bourne talking to a handsome young man in a gray suit that looked to have been a uniform though there was no brass or braid on it, to be sure. It was not a fine suit, but even from the distance it had about it a look of military neatness and cleanliness. The young man carried a book and he kept referring to it and pointing to boxes that were being loaded onto the ship. Kate rubbed mittened fingers along the smooth oak rail. The young man was remarkably handsome, in a fine, frail way. Beside him, Bourne looked big and rough; beside him, even Hains Tolliver would look less polished, for all of his handsomeness——

"It is a uniform," Kate decided. "He is too poor to buy clothes, but he is an aristocrat, there is no doubt."

As she stood watching them count their boxes, Bourne caught sight of her and shouted to her, and she waved back, calling out, "Hello!"

Bourne stood on the dock with his feet apart and an easy grin on his face, and Kate thought wildly, "He makes me behave like a child and a fool. It's not hard to be a lady with Mr. Tolliver!" She turned away, blushing. Her heart was beating with a strange excitement. Another thing that didn't happen to her with Tolliver. Michael Bourne and his friend were about to come on board, and Kate hurried down the deck away from them. When Michael Bourne was not around, Kate found herself impelled by an inexplicable desire to go and find him. And when he was there all she wanted to do was to run and hide. She went to the end of the deck and stood there for a while, and then she continued the circuit of the deck. By the time that she came back to the gangplank the two men had disappeared. She stopped there disconsolately awaiting the return of her father, and wishing that Michael Bourne would come again, and that she herself had not been so foolish.

The boat was loaded and ready to sail long before her father and Tolliver, with two other men, appeared at the end of the dock. In the meantime she had been joined by Bourne and his friend, whom he presented to her as Mr. George Morgan. Morgan bowed with the grace of a courtier, but he had little to say for himself. Kate watched him from beneath her lashes and thought that she had never seen anyone so thin and so sad. He made her feel shy and quiet, as though she were in a sickroom. Bourne talked for both of them, ignoring their silence, and gradually imbuing them with his gaiety. He told them about his [illegible]

[illegible] and Morgan said, "You're quite right, Miss Rider. But don't let Mr. Bourne mislead you, he has no admiration for the gambler, I think."

"Suppose you let me do my own admiring," Bourne grumbled. "You just snuggle up smugly with your molly-coddling past and leave me to figure things my own way."

Kate looked from one to the other in amazement. "What past?" she asked simply.

"The past!" Bourne roared, as though he had been hurt. "Ask George here. He can tell you when the Spaniards first sighted the river and what they said, and every bloody deed that has been done since. And the St. Johns is a river of blood, never doubt; you'll see the old brown stains tomorrow! It's a fine thing, I suppose, to be a gentleman born, with your grandparents tied to your tail like an old tin can and the future a most ungenteel thing to be after!"

He was laughing at Morgan now. Kate felt the blood in her cheeks, but George Morgan only smiled.

"Mr. Bourne," he said easily, "is scolding me for a little story I have been telling him."

"A story, Mr. Morgan?"

"Called 'Paradise Regained.' Mr. Bourne claims it a sorry ambition. It is better to build a new paradise."

Kate looked from one to the other. She did not understand what they were saying, any more than she understood the strange current of friendship that ran between them. For they were as different as day is from night. And to make the simile literal, she thought Bourne was all of the harsh bright contours of day, with the sun laying bare every corner, while the Southerner had the mellow beauty of night. There was something infinitely sad about him and infinitely moving.

The Irishman saw her look of bewilderment. "You've completely baffled the little lady! I always said the King's English was no language for a man to talk in!" He grinned at them.

Morgan took immediate pity on her discomfort. "In the South," he said, "many of us have lost our homes." He gestured, a half shrugging gesture, dismissing in this way the cause of the loss. "The question is whether to go to a new place and build a new home, or to remain where you were born and bred and make every effort to regain what you have lost."

"Oh," Kate cried softly, "remain, of course."

Morgan smiled. "Mr. Bourne does not agree with you. And, indeed, many Southerners are with him, but for a different reason. Mr. Bourne believes that to recreate the past is a waste of energy. 'When a tree is past its prime'—he looked across at his friend, quoting him—'don't keep pruning and doctoring, dig it out and put in a young one.' In fruit-growing it makes sense."

"And the Southerners who agree with—this?"

"Agree only because they no longer believe in success. But here," he said suddenly, "are your friends," and the brief moment of friendliness was over as though a shutter had been slipped into place. Kate turned from him quickly. Four men had crossed the end of the dock, Tolliver a little in advance, walking easily, like a big cat too bored to hurry. Even at a distance, Kate could see that her father was more than slightly intoxicated. He walked behind Tolliver between two men, one big and red-faced and the other small and thin. The big man was roaring with laughter, while her father swung his cane and staggered a little. Kate felt the blood rush to her face.

At that moment a voice rang out from the bridge above their heads. "Blast you, Tolliver!" it bellowed, "we're in half an hour to missing the tide. Come aboard, sir, and step lively!"

Hains Tolliver did not increase his pace, but when he had reached the foot of the gangplank he acknowledged the irate captain with a wave of his hand. "Your pardon, Captain," he called, and you could see that [illegible]

[illegible]

[illegible]

[illegible] again, but he did not go before Kate had seen him direct upon her father a look of contempt and bitterness that was not to be mistaken. Kate commenced to tremble. How could he! He did not know her father, he had no right to criticise him; he had none, how did he dare! She clutched the railing with both her hands. She wished that Michael Bourne would go away too. She was afraid to look at him, for fear that he too was looking at her father.

Hains Tolliver came aboard first, he nodded to the lawyer and bowed to her. "Good afternoon, Miss Kate," he said. "My apologies for keeping you waiting. We've had a little difficulty," he explained vaguely, "and I am afraid that you have been anxious."

Kate looked past him to where her father was struggling up the gangplank, and she wished that everyone would go away.

"Miss Kate," Tolliver insisted, and something in his voice compelled her to look at him, "your father is not very well; pray let me see you to your cabin."

"Come!" he said impatiently as she did not move. "Mr. Bourne will be glad of the opportunity to attend Mr. Rider, I am sure."

"A pleasure!" Michael Bourne smiled at her reassuringly.

Kate put a reluctant hand on Tolliver's arm. She knew instinctively that however she might feel it would not do to let others see. So she thanked Bourne and turned her back upon her father.

"A turn about the deck, Miss Kate"—Hains Tolliver drew her arm through his—"or do you prefer to go to your cabin?"

"My cabin, I think."

"You must not feel distressed," her companion said, and his voice was as soft as a woman's. "It was hot in town today, and when one is unaccustomed to the heat——" he left the statement unfinished, a suggestion on the air.

Kate wanted to snatch her hand away and scream at this quiet man, "My papa is drunk! You know it and that Irish immigrant knows it, and Mr. Morgan knows it and the Captain and the sailors, though they don't matter, and I hate you all, all of you, all of you!" She felt tears flood her eyes and her throat was dry and tight, so that she could not say a word.

At the door of her cabin, Hains Tolliver put his hand suddenly to her chin and tilted her face towards him. He looked down at her for a moment, his gray eyes penetrating and a half smile on his lips. "Your father is a lucky man," he said gently. "Not many of us have a lovely young woman to weep for us." He let her go and said in his accustomed voice, "I will have the steward bring you a tray. If you care for a breath of air after you have supper, I shall be on deck myself and honored, ma'am, if you will allow me to escort you."

Kate nodded quickly and slipped into her cabin. It was dark inside, a curtain having been pulled across the port-hole. From the sounds of heavy breathing she knew that Miss Ferguesson was asleep. She sat down on her bunk; now that she was alone her eyes were dry, but her hands were cold and she rubbed them together. It was silly to feel cold on a warm day. She was confused and strangely frightened. Papa was intoxicated and she was alone. The tears came quickly back to her eyes, spilling down her cheeks. Suddenly she seemed again to feel Hains Tolliver's hand on her chin and hear again his voice calling her a woman. Something about it frightened her, though she half wished that she were still with him. She caught her breath in a sob. At least he was a friend, and she had not really minded his hand, she had liked it—well, a little. She thought hopelessly of her father and of the house she wanted and how far away

Florida was and how full of strangers. By this time she was on her bunk sobbing wildly. She was alone, she was after all not so very grown up. She would never know how to be a real lady, and probably all [illegible] Miss Ferguesson seemed to possess this sort of genius, for she immediately tried another tack.

"We are moving," she cried, "I can feel it. I must have slept." She moaned once or twice and Kate sat up upon her berth. "You must pull the curtain, young woman, and find my salts and my plaster."

At this obvious emergency Kate, still sobbing, but now catching every breath before it could quite run away, rose and felt her way to the port-hole and drew back the curtain. A distorted sun was setting in the sea, while water from the churning side wheel washed the glass with a careless rain of rubies and sapphires.

Kate stood for a moment looking at it. It was very beautiful, but it made her feel lonely. She turned back to the room to find Miss Ferguesson's medicines. The school teacher accepted her ministrations without questioning her again about her tears.

"Did you see anything of Savannah?" she asked brightly, and when Kate looked as though she were about to burst into tears again, "my, it was warm today." Even this seemed to bring a flood of memory to Kate and the teacher said, "Who came aboard today? Or perhaps you would not know names yet?"

Kate said, her voice still shuddering unhappily, "there were two gentlemen with Mr. Tolliver, and a Mr. Morgan."

"George Morgan!"

"Yes, ma'am."

"I'll warrant he wasn't with Hains Tolliver."

"No, ma'am. I don't think he knows Mr. Tolliver. At least, he didn't stay to speak with him."

"That is not wonderful," Miss Ferguesson said. "It would, on the contrary, be wonderful if a gentleman like George Morgan stayed to speak to a scallawag like Hains Tolliver."

"A scallawag!" Kate cried, suddenly indignant. "Why, Mr. Tolliver is a fine man and a great man. My papa says that he has risen above defeat and adversity as only a great man could. Why, I think it's monstrous to say——"

"He certainly has risen above defeat."

"Well, then!"

"Before the war," Miss Ferguesson said with unexpected gentleness, "Mr. Tolliver's family were not acceptable in Jacksonville. I don't know why but something had happened to make people turn their backs. Hains Tolliver and his father lived abroad much; they had some money. I've heard that they had pine tracts in Georgia but had lost a good deal through forest fires. They had a newly built house at Mandarin, and some land. Mandarin was the place that old Tolliver had his heart set upon, as his family had originally settled there. You'll find that a family as old as his is a rare thing in Florida. But you can't live in a wild country, as Jacksonville and Mandarin were then, when your neighbors ostracize you. The river country was run by two men and they wouldn't let him in. So now," Miss Ferguesson concluded, folding her lips primly, "his son owns pretty near all of it, all that's any good anyway!"

Kate said stubbornly, "I think that's fine!"

The older woman smiled. "Perhaps. But you can't be surprised that George Morgan does not."

"George Morgan?"

"Valhalla belonged to him."

Kate looked at the school teacher in surprise. "Why, that's the name of Mr. Tolliver's place!" she said.

"That is what I was telling you. George Morgan returned from the war, walked, miss, from Antietam to Florida, to find his father dead and his lands confiscated and sold to an old neighbor—a neighbor his father had tried to drive away."

"Oh," Kate said softly, her loyalties torn between her father's friend and the [illegible]

[illegible]

"Neither of them. Crockett Wilson wouldn't have been permitted to look at Hains Tolliver before the war. Her people were rich but provincial. And now, well, she's a loyal Southern girl. Hains Tolliver's richer than her family were at their richest, and owns more land, but he's a scallawag!"

Kate frowned, but she was too curious to interrupt. When the other did not go on at once, she said, "And Mr. Morgan?"

"He is still a benedict," Miss Ferguesson said concisely, "but he calls on Miss Crockett regularly."

"I should think they would marry—if they care for each other."

"They say Miss Crockett is not well. I reckon she went through enough to spoil any young female's health." The teacher paused, but Kate's eyes were as wide and intense as though she were being told a fairy tale. Miss Ferguesson said with pedantic enthusiasm, "She was reared in cotton batting. Florida was never like the other States, though it's older than any of them. From Virginia, right down to Georgia, wealth meant an aristocratic family. In Florida it was more likely to mean a clever thief from the North, or from some other country. There were few aristocratic families, and if you were one of them it meant there was no one around you quite good enough for you. The Wilsons were from Georgia, so were the Morgans. They kept pretty well to theirselves. You can imagine that when the men all went to war the ladies who were used to so much care did not have an easy time. They peeked out of their windows and discovered that there was a world full of people, most of them strange, and most of them mighty ugly. Jacksonville is full of stories. You hear them even though the folks don't tell on theirselves; they've seeped out."

"What happened to them, the Wilsons?"

"The Colonel, Miss Crockett's papa, was killed right off. Miss Crockett and her momma stayed right on in Jacksonville as long as they could. . . . There were bad stories. The colored folks began to feel their freedom, and the minute they ran off from their homes they were without food or places to sleep, and they weren't reared to think, so they just panicked; went about looting and even rape and murder happened. They say Miss Crockett and her momma finally pretended to go away, but really lived in their own attic, locked up. They were scared to stay, but worse than scared to go away. The Colonel was dead, but there was a boy, and they kept hoping he'd come home."

Kate said, "Poor things. That is terrible. But I should think that she'd be so relieved now that she'd marry Mr. Morgan right away. Was he away—too?"

"Of course he was. You didn't find a Southern gentleman buying himself out of going to war! But Miss Crockett, I guess she's just had too much trouble. When our troops came to Jacksonville, the last of the loyal people got out. Only people like Hains Tolliver came back, and they came to make a good thing of it. They got hold of confiscated property—likely saw to it that the property they wanted was confiscated. They began their rise above defeat and adversity right there."

Kate looked down at her hands. It was probably not true at all. Poppa said you should never believe everything that you heard, and Mr. Tolliver was his friend and nobody ever heard of Miss Ferguesson. Still, it was hard not to believe her, she was such a truthful-looking person. In fact, she was not unlike Aunt Enid, except that Aunt Enid never talked so much. Kate said slowly, "So, did they, I mean Miss Crockett and her mother, did they run away?"

"I don't know that you can call it 'run'! They stayed right through the fighting. Saw their own trees felled to barricade their own Confederate cavalry. When it was all over, Miss Crockett and her mother went up to Bald[illegible]

[illegible]

all over now. I should think she'd want to get married."

"Fiddlesticks!" Miss Ferguesson snorted. "Marriage is not everything and the things Miss Crockett has been through are never 'all over.'" The school teacher looked over the rim of her spectacles at Kate. There were no signs of the recent flood of tears. The young erased them easily. If *she* were to weep, her eyes would be red and swollen for a week!

Kate, on her part, was looking at Miss Ferguesson in amazement. "Why, marriage is most important," she cried. "I shall certainly marry."

Miss Ferguesson studied her little companion appraisingly. "And well, I have no doubt," she said at last. "You are young, you will be happy in Florida, Miss Kate. In a way, you are not unlike Florida, even if you are from the North—Florida has come out of the North, in any case. Today it is young and struggling and full of sorrow. Tomorrow it will have its place in the world, a useful and a prosperous one."

Kate looked at her with pleasure; would her life be like that? Yes, perhaps it would. She tilted back her chair, her hands clasped around her knees, her head thrown back and her eyes wide and dreamy. Perhaps she would marry a Southerner, someone like Mr. Morgan. A proud handsome aristocrat who had suffered a great tragedy. She would be rich and beautiful, silks and satins and velours swirled about her and she wore live flowers in her hair. Her great love would wipe out the tragedy in his life, they would be gay, they would do great things and they would be envied. She did not at first stop to think from whence the great wealth would come, but some tiny germ of realism in her made the dream not quite satisfactory. Certainly Mr. Morgan was very poor.

The cabin boy interrupted her reverie with a tray. Miss Ferguesson refused the offer of food and drew her bunk curtain in order that she might avoid the sight of it.

"You are fortunate, Miss Kate, to escape the affliction from which most ladies suffer," she said from behind her curtain.

Kate laughed, she was suddenly overwhelmingly hungry and feeling very much better. It was, after all, a very exciting adventure and, once they had a house, she and her papa would be wildly happy. Beneath the napkin on the tray she found a squab served with rice, a watercress salad and a small carafe of red wine. She ate hungrily and then, at Miss Ferguesson's request, put the tray outside the door so that no odor of food might remain on the air.

"Thank you, my dear," Miss Ferguesson said, reappearing from behind her curtain. She watched Kate wander aimlessly from the door to the port-hole and back, and at last she said, "Why don't you go out and take a little air? Your papa will doubtless be with the gentlemen, and glad to escort you."

Kate bit her lip, "Papa is not feeling well," she said, and was reminded of her Aunt Enid. "But Mr. Tolliver did ask me to come out on deck."

The school teacher folded her lips, but then she said, surprisingly, "Well, I should not care to walk with him, but you will certainly be safe with him, and I do believe a bit of air is what you need—after eating, you know," she added quickly.

"I believe I will," Kate decided gratefully, and she took down her cloak and bonnet, all at once in a hurry to be out of the small cabin. Miss Ferguesson was very kind, and Kate felt as though she had found a friend, but she was suddenly eager and curious to see the Mr. Morgan again.

Miss Ferguesson moaned. "My salts," she said; "then run along."

Kate found the salts and, when the older lady had been attended to, she slipped out of the cabin and made her way to the deck.

It was a cool evening and a breeze whipped at her skirts. [illegible]

[illegible]

He was a good-looking man, while you surely must admit that Michael Bourne was homely. Still, Mr. Bourne had a strong hard look to him that made his homeliness good to look at, while Mr. Tolliver looked too arrogant to be concerned with brawn. Well, handsome is as handsome does, she reminded herself, and thought with a little inner twinkle that for once she had thought in a way that Aunt Enid would approve.

"You will doubtless hear things about me, Miss Kate," Hains Tolliver was saying softly, "but I have in truth struggled for my country."

"Oh, Mr. Tolliver, surely nobody could say, or indeed think, anything——" Kate started, thinking guiltily of Miss Ferguesson.

"But, indeed, they could and do. Florida has been quite decimated by the war. I have tried, in my poor way, by recovering my own lands, by helping the blacks to a new way of work and of living—for, believe me, the poor dogs do not know how to go about it of themselves—and by co-operating with the Government, who only want to help us now. I have tried, as I say, to show fellow land-owners how to save themselves. And, incidentally, to save the State."

He had spoken slowly, as though he were addressing a child, and his eyes pierced the twilight to watch her reaction.

Kate drew in a breath. This was the truth, she thought fiercely, and not the school teacher's unlikely story. "How grateful they must be to you," she said.

He laughed shortly. "It is quite the other way, quite 'round about. It is almost as though they do not wish to be helped, as though they wish to be left with the visible signs of war about them to remind them of hatred and bitterness, or perhaps, as some say, it is jealousy."

"Oh, but how could they be jealous of you if they will not even try for themselves."

"Jealousy is a natural emotion, ma'am. In trying to re-awaken the industry of the State I have brought great material gains to myself." Kate found herself for no good reason pitying him and wondering what manner of person Miss Crockett Wilson was so to misread a great man.

"In Florida," Mr. Tolliver said slowly, "we have two kinds of men to contend with: the Southerner who won't take his hands out of his own pockets, and the Northerner who won't take his hands out of his neighbor's pockets"—he bowed to Kate; "for unfortunately they are not all like your father, my dear Miss Kate."

"Oh, I know," Kate cried indignantly. "Mr. Bourne was telling me."

"Well, now," Hains Tolliver turned towards her, as though better to read her expression in the twilight, "Mr. Bourne is a case in point. Not that there is proof of anything against him. Not a thing, I can promise you! Still, he has been burned out twice."

"Burned!"

"Indeed, burned! Nobody knows by whom, or why. Probably irate farmers. Also, probably he had been guilty of nothing worse than being misjudged. His groves are near my own at Mandarin, and I certainly have never heard of any misbehavior on his part. But he is the kind of a man to take justice into his own hands and he may have made enemies. In any case, I think that the Northerner is not so bad as many of our own Southern men. You take George Morgan. I believe that I saw him with you today."

"Mr. Bourne presented him." Something strangely physical

and unfamiliar stirred in Kate at the memory of the Irishman. "Mr. Morgan talked much more like a Southerner than you do, Mr. Tolliver."

"He is a good deal younger, and the war interfered with [illegible]

have been much older than herself at the time, going out to fight for what he considered his country and his right. Kate thought that he must have looked very beautiful and, perversely, she resented what her own side had done to him.

"He walked back, walked from Antietam to Florida," Mr. Tolliver said. "Even if he had had money, money could not have bought a ride. Both the horses he had taken with him had been killed, so he walked, and it took him a year."

Kate shuddered, though the words themselves could mean nothing to her, who had never walked more than a pleasant distance in her life, or felt either hunger or pain. But defeat was a sorry thing that had touched the fringe of her experience, for she had seen it in her father's eyes, and some sensitivity within her was alive to the story of George Morgan.

"How anxious his family must have been!" she said.

"He had none, by then. He was half orphan in any case and during the war his father died. None of us were sorry, for he was a proud arrogant fool of a man; a prince, the ladies would say, but I say fool advisedly. He disliked our modern age and, because he had the wealth and power to do so, he turned history backwards. Within his not inconsiderable domain he was a despot, if a benevolent one. Such a man could not have borne the end of the war. Even George could not regret his father's death."

"How tragic for him, still!"

"Yes, and then his father's lands were confiscated. With his arrogance, he had been a poor politician and he was a natural person to sacrifice, to make an example of. Even though he was already dead. The lands were offered for sale and, well, George had not been heard of. We thought him dead too. I myself bought the plantation at Mandarin and added it to my own groves."

Kate opened her mouth to speak but the words would not be found and her companion turned at the little sound of indignation that escaped her.

"Ah, Miss Kate," he said, taking her hand, "you will hear a great deal about this business. It has happened all over the South. Those few of us who have the will to rebuild have had to seize the means as they came to our hand. And then, with George, it is as well—for he would have wasted the land. He is the weakling I fear his father's despotism made him. A soldier, yes; for that I respect him. A poet, too. But there is no room for those in Florida today. A man must be a worker, and George Morgan is only a trouble-maker."

"How?" Kate asked, glad that he had relinquished her hands. His were surprisingly lean and strong and he held hers as though they did not belong to her at all but were some toy of his. A little tremor ran through her at the thought.

"He wants his land back. That is natural. But he doesn't want to pay for it. He had land at Osceola, which he has allowed to go to grass without lifting a finger to reclaim it. He will tell you that the Mandarin land is more valuable. But he will not tell you that it would have been quite overgrown by now if I had not poured money and work and great care into it."

"That is too bad of him," Kate said, but she did not really see any blame, for she thought, "Mr. Tolliver is right, but I'm sure I wouldn't let anyone at all keep *my* land without making a fuss."

The ship plunged on through the night and the wheel churned up the black waters and tossed them into the path of the moon. Timbers in the hulk creaked with the regularity of an old lady rocking on a sleepy afternoon. Somewhere a sailor was playing an accordion and by the aft rail two cigars glowed [illegible]

"How about it?" Tolliver asked softly, not attempting to hide the contempt in his voice.

Samuel Hess laughed. Cutler, whose features in the light of the kerosene lamp were as pointed as though the bones beneath the flesh had been whittled with a sharp knife, looked up and indicated the green bottle. "Everything under control," he said. "Morgan and Bourne came in to see if he had rested sufficient to have a chat, but he hadn't!"

"They won't come back tonight." Tolliver looked about him distastefully. "Governor Reed has appealed to Washington for guns," he said. "We'll have to talk about it later. Tomorrow I go straight to Mandarin. Get Mr. Rider settled in his office. He is going to board at Le Fèvres'. You'd better move over there and keep an eye on him until things get straightened out. I'll be in town next week and we will have a talk then. I think I have said sufficient about Bourne to make him distrustful, but watch him just the same."

Hess waved his cigar towards the bunks. "You coming back?" he asked.

Tolliver took a cloak from his bunk without answering and went out of the cabin, closing the door softly.

"God-damn haughty," James Cutler said under his breath.

His companion said, "Huh!"

Cutler shrugged and commenced to re-deal the cards.

5

JACKSONVILLE unfolded slowly to Kate, like a rose, a great perfumed rose with a worm at its heart. A gleaming cabriolet drawn by a well-groomed chestnut carried them from the station to Madame Le Fèvre's boarding-house. It rumbled up Newnan Street, which was plank-paved, and raised a cloud of dust when it whirled around the corner onto Caroline Street. Kate's eyes were everywhere and she held herself with a graceful consciousness of her pretty costume and of her newness. The streets were full of men, many of them in the blue uniform. In Hartford, the war, now three years done with, had never been so apparent, and Kate stared at the uniforms with a woman's delight and a child's lack of manners.

The sun was hot and it fell between the branches of water oak and the redberry trees on Caroline Street, and around the corners on Julia and Hogan, where sad frame houses stood in their grass-grown gardens. Across their long-unpainted piazzas the shadows of Spanish moss floated at the slightest stir of air, a million weeping, sorrowing banners at half-mast upon the town. On the shaded side of these houses, shutters were open and sounds of quiet living contradicted the empty piazzas and gardens. A door closed, dishes rattled or a pump was wielded, a piano tinkled a disciplined scale, the instrument sadly in need of tuning.

Now and again Miss Ferguesson, who sat at Kate's side, would bow primly to some black-clad woman on the boardwalk. Michael Bourne, who shared with Archibold Rider the small seat facing, grinned sardonically at the older lady. Once he said, "They never return the courtesy, do they, ma'am? They just ain't so well bred as we Yankees."

Kate looked at him quickly, astonished at his rudeness, but Miss Ferguesson nodded, agreeing with him. "Florida," she explained to Kate, "is not like the other Southern States. It is more like a Western frontier. Even though it was settled before any other land in America, culture never took hold. The French and the Spaniards and the English left nothing. They developed nothing and they abandoned what they started. The people here [illegible]

[illegible] held herself haughtily. She didn't want or need sympathy. Kate was just conscious enough of Bourne's attraction for her to resent it. For she did not forget her father's words. The man was an immigrant and a ruffian! She tilted her small nose a fraction. What if the ladies in Florida would not receive such a person, indeed neither would the ladies in Hartford! It would soon be seen that Kate and her father were a different breed. Miss Ferguesson was another matter. Kate felt the blood rush to her face as the older lady received, without change of expression or manner, one snub after another.

Her father, who either ignored or refused the implications of the conversation beyond his one quick expression of sympathy for a defeated people, cleared his throat and said with a certain pedantic enthusiasm, "The State was admitted to the Union only in 1845. Its population has doubled since then and its resources coined wealth for those who have taken the trouble to employ them——" He paused suddenly. "But I find Jacksonville a surprise," he tapped his cane on the floor of the carriage for emphasis, "a river town, access to the sea, transportation—and so poor-looking."

The coachman pulled up his horses in front of a two-storied white building, entirely surrounded by a vine-covered piazza. Michael Bourne got down and stood by to assist the ladies. "I am glad, for one," he said, "that Madam's is not an old house, for I myself am enamored of modern plumbing."

Kate blushed. Michael Bourne, she thought, was proving himself very coarse. Miss Fergueson allowed herself to be assisted and caused Kate to suffer another moment of discomfort by saying firmly, "I do not like a bathroom that gentlemen use. Madam should not permit it. I have my own tub." She turned to Kate. "If you have not brought one you are welcome to use mine."

Kate gasped audibly, then she said, "Thank you, Ma'am," dropped a stiff and graceless curtsy as though to terminate their acquaintanceship, and fled up the walk after her father. She heard Bourne laughing behind her.

Madame Le Fèvre insisted upon the "Madam," but Le Fèvre, had become Lefeever to all Jacksonville, and no amount of insistence could correct the pronunciation. She had come South at the close of the war in search of her husband. In her corset she had carried the two hundred dollars for which, she explained, he had sold his body in the draft market. Mr. Le Fèvre had preferred to say "rented," though Madam had since come to doubt that he had done either. Certainly not a single word had been received from him. After two years' search, Madam invested in a house in Jacksonville and put out a board. "Let him find me," she decided, writing him off her books. For the thought had come to her that he had not travelled farther than Danny's bar in Hoboken, and she begrudged the tears with which she had parted from him.

It was with Madam that many of the Government men boarded and with her that Miss Fergueson always stayed.

"If by chance you are ever called away," the latter explained to Mr. Rider, "your girl here will be as safe with Madam, and as respected, as she would be in a convent."

And Kate, dropping her curtsy to Madam, found it unpleasantly easy to believe. For Madam, despite her great and easy-going contours, had an air of command and inflexibility. It would have been difficult to imagine anyone so bold as to dare affront her. She was a short woman, but so grotesquely built that Kate found herself wondering at her great agility. Madam hurried up the broad stairs ahead of them, scolding, expostulating and welcoming with each step. She railed at the small black boy who trotted along, half buried beneath their bags; she expostulated upon the unseasonable weather and an influx to Jacksonville of most heathen tourists; she welcomed, [illegible] size only by pushing its bulk into other positions, and her breasts rose with each breath, like tubs of yeasted dough.

Dear, dear Papa, Kate prayed passionately, don't ever go and leave me with this—this mountain.

For the first time since she had left Hartford, a surge of uncertainty swept over Kate. The house at home would fit into a few rooms of this great rambling place. Neatly and sweetly. And Aunt Enid would not greatly approve this fat, strident woman.

"Put those bags down and get the door open, Matt," Madam shrilled, as they arrived in front of a shuttered door.

The boy, denuded of his bags, was slim as a bone. His big eyes rolled, but he flung open the door with a flourish and he grinned unabashed.

"Ces noirs," Madam complained, "ces sont des imbéciles. Quel dommage de leur avoir émancipé. Ils leur manquent le fouet." She turned to Mr. Rider. "I put your girl here with Miss Ferguesson, hein!" "Michel here gonna take you. Same room, Michel," she said to Bourne. "I save him for you. Whan the tourist he vamoose, I give you a fine suite for you and the girl, hein, Mr. Rider?" she rolled her r's and snapped her a's like rubber bands, caught between her mother tongue and a Hoboken twang.

The men went off with Matt and their baggage. Kate,

pouting angrily, followed Madam and Miss Ferguesson into the bedroom. Well, it would be a day or two until they found a house. Then they were going to move, but *tout de suite,* Madam, thank you!

The room was large and comfortable. Standing in the center and surmounted by a canopy of mosquito netting was a large brass bed which, Kate learned with dismay, she and Miss Ferguesson were to share. A wardrobe towered against the far wall and by the window were a table and two wicker chairs.

"Now, my friends, I go," cried Madam, but only after she had raised and closed the windows, tried the latches, fussed for an instant over the curtains, the bedding, and the rack of towels. Then she went to the door and called loudly for Matt, who ran to her, muttering, "Yes'm, yes'm, I is coming."

"I will send you wine to rest you from your journey," Madam told them, "and as soon as the baggage arrives, Matt will bring up your tub and water," and she finally bustled off with Matt at her heels like a bit of fluff caught in the machinery of a rip tide.

Miss Ferguesson commenced immediately to put her things away and make herself comfortable, chattering somewhat tersely as she did so. Kate went first to the window, where she stood looking down on the kitchen courtyard. A grape arbor formed a roof over the court, hiding most of it. But the path between the house and the cook house was in clear view and a stream of darkies were coming and going, carrying baskets covered with white napkins or trays of dishes and shining glassware.

"It's gone suppertime," she heard Miss Ferguesson say; "will you go downstairs with your papa, or have a basket up here with me?"

Kate said, "Downstairs," quickly, and turned back into the room. She went over to the bed and felt it, and then sat down on it. Miss Ferguesson frowned and pursed her lips. Kate smiled and dropped her eyelashes demurely. Miss Ferguesson was easy to understand. But when she did not speak, Kate got up and smoothed the bed.

Suddenly the older woman said, "What are your plans?"

"Oh, eat with my papa and go for a stroll, I expect."

"I mean, what will you do with yourself in Florida?"

"Oh," Kate brightened, "we'll look for a house at once. I shall keep house for papa."

[illegible]

Kate said, "Doubtless," and an anger that she did not try to account for choked her so that she could not say more.

"In the meantime," Miss Ferguesson said, "why don't you help me with my school? I need help and you need occupation."

Kate stood up quickly. "I don't at all," she said; "I'm no schoolmarm and I don't intend to be one."

"No, I guess not. But keep it in mind. And if you're going downstairs, miss, I shall be indebted if you will look to my tub. That boy should have been here by now."

Kate said, "Yes'm," and fled. Downstairs she "looked to the tub" and, finding that it had not arrived, she sent Matt to tell Miss Ferguesson while she went onto the piazza to await her father.

At each end of the piazza a wooden swing was suspended by chains from the ceiling, while a battalion of rockers was lined up against the house wall. Seeing at a glance that every seat was occupied by a gentleman, while others stood about in groups, Kate retreated to the hall, where she paused irresolutely, wondering what she should do next and where she would find her father. As she stood there, twisting her handkerchief, the door of the dining-room swung open and Madam sailed out upon her like a galleon before the wind.

"Ah now, petite," she cried, taking Kate by the arm. "Your papa has gone for a short stroll with two gentlemen, but come and I introduce you to my friends here."

Kate shrank visibly, but the French woman herded her onto the porch, quite oblivious of the girl's reluctance.

"Come, gentlemen, I want to present my little friend."

The men rose, and Kate was whisked from one group to another. Madam bellowed and laughed and the red blood swept up Kate's throat and her body was stiff with distaste.

"Mademoiselle of the South she turn up her nose at you, hein?" Madam cried to the men. "But Madam she find you a little lady of your own. Straight from the North! What a belle!"

Kate was young and bred to politeness. You submitted to an older woman, you dipped and curtsied and yes'm'd. Rudeness was the unforgivable sin, however you might suffer. And then Kate had never seen a woman like Madam before, so that she did not know how to classify her separately or behave to her differently. She submitted, but even as she did so a new consciousness of herself was born within her. Not the "I am looking pretty, my dress is fresh and gay and new and I am a grown lady" consciousness, but a new sense of her own being. "I am Kate Rider. I don't have to put up with this. I don't have to be polite. I don't care what anybody thinks of me."

When a gentleman in a green-sprigged waistcoat seized the hand that she had not proffered and pressed it, Madam rapped him sharply with her fan. "None of that," she cried aloud. "You may take your dandy tricks elsewhere, Bill Williams. Not on my piazza!"

Kate clutched stiffly at the sides of her skirts. The overwhelming desire to assert herself battled with the terror of making a spectacle of herself. The chatter of voices around her, and the host of faces, merged into a jumble of sight and sound and, for a moment, she could neither focus her eyes nor attend with her ears.

In despair, she turned to Madam. "I must find my papa," she said; "he will be awaiting me." And she walked hastily down the piazza, "like a horse at a fair," she thought angrily, "like a pig at the market." Every step, so publicly taken, was an agony. Suddenly she stopped. The Southerner, George Morgan, stood in the doorway with Michael Bourne. They had been watching her: the slender disdainful aristocrat with the sad look that made Kate yearn over him, and the big Irishman, his eyes warm and laughing. At the sight of him, Kate wanted to stamp her foot, to throw something, to scream at him. Then a [illegible]

Soon after, Bourne, on his way to his own room, found Kate standing in the hall, outside her door, looking forlorn and helpless. At sight of him, she lifted her small chin and turned away. The Irishman hesitated, then he said, "Is anything wrong?" in such a kind voice that Kate's defenses crumbled.

She gestured towards the room. "She's having a bath!" she wailed, and the picture of the gaunt lady sitting in her tin tub in the middle of the room, her nakedness modestly protected by a sopping wet under-garment, overwhelmed her. She giggled sharply and then the tears welled up and poured down her small, pinched face. Shame and confusion choked her. Her dreams and high expectations were tumbling about her and she didn't know where to go for a second's privacy.

Michael Bourne put an arm about her quickly. "There, there, little one," he said, as though he were talking to a baby, "you need a bit of rest, I guess. It's hard on a girl like you." He led her down the hall. "You shall have my room, and I'll tell the old harridan to send you up a basket."

Kate hesitated but only for an instant. It was that or the hall for all who chanced to see her.

"My papa," she said, catching her breath convulsively.

"I'll tell him you're resting. Now." He lifted her chin and wiped the small face with a large handkerchief. It was an immaculately white handkerchief and Kate noticed with a sense of surprise that the nails on his hard, square hands were also immaculately cared for. Somehow this daintiness in the big man lent him a new strength.

She said softly, "Will you forgive me? I was very rude."

"Sure now, forget it. You have to be tough to be a carpetbagger. I don't hurt easy," and he pushed her into his room and left her there.

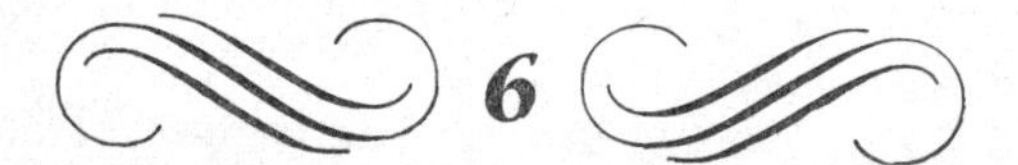

6

FOR a few days, Kate thought kindly of Michael Bourne. He had been good to her, and he had been strong and gentle. And, however the girl Kate dreamed of organdies and flowers and lantern-lit gardens with handsome beaux about her like bees about a rose, she had a great inner admiration for strength in any form. And she had seen it in the Irishman. What if he was an immigrant, perhaps that made him stronger. It took courage and endurance to come to a new country and start life all over again. He had fought in the war too. Though he did not talk, Miss Ferguesson knew a great deal about him. She said, and Kate giggled at the memory, "I should have been a man! I would have been very like Michael Bourne, save that I would not have been so slow."

Kate herself could see nothing slow about him. "Papa," she told the teacher, "says that Mr. Bourne is very quick and determined." She could not remember what her father had meant. She had not listened carefully. Papa was always storming about one thing or another, one person or another, and his words would often come back to her half remembered, without inflection. Papa did not like Governor Reed, but she did not know why. Papa said that Carse was a mugwump. Papa said that, if Seymour got in, there would be the biggest depression the country had ever known, maybe even another war. But Kate never remembered why her father held these opinions. Miss Ferguesson was a good deal easier to follow. Miss Ferguesson concerned herself with personalities, for the most part. Miss Ferguesson said, "There are some scallawags about who need horse-whipping. Michael Bourne bothers himself for proof—which he will never get! I should not wait an instant, not one instant if I were a man!" And she spoke feelingly, [illegible]

Kate discovered early what her life in Jacksonville was to be. There was no such thing as another Northern girl to keep her company, and there was no such thing as a Southern girl who would even meet her eye as they passed on the street. From the first morning, the people who had surrounded her on the trip had gone each about his particular business and she was left to pass the time as best she could. Miss Ferguesson, despite the season, opened her school. Her pupils had had a two-months' holiday and she was prepared to see to it that they studied through the summer. The company of men whom Kate had christened "the Louts" came and went at mealtime, and Madam bustled about like a whip at the heels of her black servants. Archibold Rider was swallowed up by his office as though he had stepped into the belly of a mammoth. Hains Tolliver and George Morgan returned to their respective groves. Both Valhalla and Bourne's place were at Mandarin on the St. Johns, a half day's ride away from Jacksonville. And Michael Bourne, to whom Kate was ready to give friendship, had turned his man's back upon her to concern himself with his man's world. By day she went for long walks, half to give herself something to do and half to discover the town, but always with an eye out for the house that she wanted. In the evening she would walk again with her father, or sit on the piazza with Miss Ferguesson and Madam while he talked with "the Louts" about the affairs of the nation. It was not the life that she had pictured, but she promised herself that it would not always be like this.

Somehow she did not miss the attentions of any of her former companions as much as she did those of Michael Bourne. He lived in the same house, for his work did not permit him to stay at Mandarin. But the work that kept him near at hand, also took up his time. He seemed to be at it nights as well as days. Occasionally he would stop by the swing and talk to Madam and Miss Ferguesson and tease Kate, and occasionally go into the parlor for an evening of poker. Twice he returned to the house too late for dinner and went straight to his room. It made Kate cross and at the same time disappointed her. He could have stopped to speak. Madam got up at once. "He kill himself with work," she grumbled. "If I don't get him some food queek I'm gonna find him asleep. He hardly take off his boots before he gonna be asleep. Et il dort comme un ours, celui-là!" The idea of fatigue bored Kate. She watched Madam go without sympathy. Miss Ferguesson clucked her tongue and shook her head.

They had arrived in town on the tail of a riot, which if not under Bourne's immediate jurisdiction had resulted in a suspected murder which fell to his lot. Federal troops garrisoned in the town had for some time been nurturing a grudge against the Negroes whom they were there to protect. The war had caused perhaps a too abrupt turning of the tables. Certainly the colored children were putting the "bottom rail on top" with a complete lack of grace. They were rude, they were arrogant, they took, with no reference to ownership. The country owed them a living! It was what they were led to believe, and they believed with an enthusiasm that did nothing but lose them friends. So one fine night the rank and file of their staunch defenders, with the aid of a pair of drunken subalterns, broke out upon the town and fired on every black man to be found. The black men being fleet of foot, there were soon not any to be found. The soldiers, well pleased with their work, imbibed here and there, called upon certain houses on the waterfront and went back to their barracks to sleep it off. The following day they proclaimed loudly that their cartridges had been blank, throughout. But a black man with a bullet through his heart was found on Newnan Street and, as the soldiery disclaimed any knowledge of the tragedy, Bourne [illegible]

[illegible] respectable white population to bar their doors and "doubtless," he shrugged, "hide under their beds." The less respectable whites did not trouble to leave their glasses and cards. The blacks were too busy running to note to whom the next pair of heels belonged, and the soldiers were as innocent as unborn lambs.

While Bourne was busy with his witnesses Archibald Rider was progressing from amazement to confusion. The morning of his entry into office a queue of colored people had met him at the door. They had risen early, for they formed a long line stretching from the street, up the stairs, and to the door of the Bureau. Cutler and Hess would have turned them away, complaining that they themselves could not very well show Rider the ropes while a city full of niggers demanded attention. But Rider was firm.

"We are here to minister to the freedmen, Mr. Cutler. Let us hear what they have to say."

Hess grumbled audibly, but Cutler only shrugged and unlocked the door.

The offices, Rider discovered to his surprise, were anything but adequate to attend to the morning's callers. Three doors opened on a narrow hall. One room took care of Hess, in the capacity of cleric, and a black boy to run errands. James Cutler, as assistant commissioner, had a room to himself. His walls were lined with file cases and a safe stood in a corner of the room. Rider's office was grimy with dust and the look of disuse.

He put his hat and cane on the wall rack, wiped his chair with a large handkerchief and sat down at his desk. "Let them in, Mr. Hess," he said, "let them in. The first thing we shall have to do is hire someone to clean this place!"

James Cutler stood at the door, looking somber and undecided. Finally he said, "You must do what you think best, sir, but I should advise you strongly to give these people a kind word and turn them away. It will take time to find out just what the resources of the office are. And I would not hire any help, you'll only make the rest of 'em jealous. There's a boy here—Jeff—who will come and clean up. He should have done it. I'll get after him."

With which words Cutler retreated to his own room. At a sign from him, Hess had gone to open the outer door and to regulate the flow of colored supplicants.

Archibold Rider trimmed and lighted a cigar and sat back in his chair. His work had started. He felt instinctively that his assistant was right. He could scarcely do any good by seeing these people, but they had come to greet him, or ask his help, and he could not bring himself to turn them away. His primary concern was not with facts and figures, he told himself, but with people.

The first to whom he talked was a woman, carrying a baby and flanked by two boys, who had been born in slavery. She said, "How'do," and curtsied clumsily. She had been a field nigger, she said. Her story was long, for the most part pointless and hard to understand. She came from Georgia, from a plantation called Upvalley, but she didn't know where it was. Her man, who was her "proper husband, 'cause the folks at Upvalley didn't 'low no loose carryings-on," had taken his family onto the road to see the world since he was free to do it. Now he had left her and she wanted him back.

Archibold Rider looked at the woman helplessly. "What is your name?" he asked.

"May."

"And your last name, May?"

She shook her head, "Ain't never had none."

"You have to have one, May. What did your husband call himself?"

"Tom."

[illegible] and wrote the two names down. "And your address?" The woman looked at him blankly. "Where do you live?" he asked patiently.

"Out dar." The woman gestured vaguely.

Archibald Rider drew a circle on the pad, then he drew a square, darkening the corners geometrically. "Come back tomorrow," he said at last. "I'll see if anyone knows anything about your husband."

"Yo ain't goin' t' find him today?" the woman stated dourly.

"It will take a little time, May. Come back tomorrow."

"What us'n goin' ter eat meanwhile?"

Archibold Rider looked at the group before him, shocked. They were certainly thin and sickly-looking. But it had not occurred to him—— He looked helplessly towards the door that led to Cutler's office. Cutler had spoken of the resources of the office and Rider realized that he did not in truth know what they were.

"De ol' Marst' ain't never let no one go hungry," the woman was complaining, "an' he ain't never let no man run offen his woman. He done brung 'um right home!"

Rider pulled his wallet from his coat and extracted a dollar. He held this out and said, "Get yourself something to eat and come back tomorrow."

"Bless de Lawd!" the woman cried, snatching at the money.

The two little boys grinned, their black eyes sparkling, and the baby, hugged too tightly, emitted a weak scream.

The next in line was a young man. He was big and strong and angry. The Government had promised him a mule and forty acres and he wanted to know where they were. No, he wasn't working. He was free! Nobody could make him work. He stuck out an aggressive chin and wanted to see anyone try. Archibold Rider said that he had not heard about the mule and forty acres himself, but he would look into it. He took the young man's name and told him to come back.

The next was a middle-aged woman. Her shoulders were thick and bent and she looked tired and out of humor. She announced in a voice that was thin and singing that she had been robbed.

"Ma home, ma chil'ren, ma clothes, ma vittels, all gone an' ain't nothin' in de place ob dem."

Rider blinked at the comprehensiveness of this catastrophe. In any case, he thought with some relief, it was a problem for Michael Bourne and not for him. "This is terrible," he cried. "When did this happen? Who could have done such a thing to you, my poor woman?"

"De Govn'ment," the woman said stolidly, "done tuk ebery-ting. Ma home, ma chil'ren, ma clothes, ma vittels. Promised us we is goin' ter be free, an' jess luk! Is dey given us a house? Is dey given us food? An' all ma chil'ren done run off a-lukin' for better freedom dan what we got hiar."

"Now that you are free," Rider said, clearing his throat and wishing that he had listened to Cutler, "you will have to take a job. You will be paid money, and with the money you can buy the house and food and clothes. And they will be yours —not what someone else gives you."

The woman shook her head. "Ain't we free, nowhow?" she grumbled.

"You come in tomorrow and we will see about work for you."

Few of his visitors wanted work. They wanted money, they wanted farms, they wanted clothes.

When the fifteenth said that he was going to see the President and wanted a ticket to Washington, Rider gave up and called Hess to him. “You'll have to turn them away,” he said; “I can't talk to any more until I see what the situation is. Tell them to come back.”

[illegible] were already allocated almost entirely to the colored in outlying districts and there was not enough to distribute in Jacksonville itself. As to money, there didn't seem to be any.

“It's all on paper,” Cutler said. “We get our salaries and enough for the overhead of the office. If you have to travel, you take it out of your own pocket.”

By the end of the week, Archibald Rider was looking justifiably dazed. By the end of two weeks, he was ready to give up. Hains Tolliver, calling on him for the second time at his request, protested. “You want miracles,” he said. “But I told you that things here were not easy. You are handicapped by funds and politicians. You will not, you may be sure, get more funds if the politicians can prevent it. And they can.”

“But then what can I do? What is the use of my being here? I am besieged daily by the most outlandish and outrageous demands. They want land mostly, but they also want money and comforts; they want to travel; and a girl came in today saying that she was with child and wanted a husband!”

Tolliver laughed. “She probably came from a good home where her master would have seen to it that the boy to blame married her.”

“So she said.” Rider shook his head.

“They prize their freedom, but they don't understand it. Why should they? They have been told that freedom is a wonderful thing. But they haven't been told about the responsibilities, and if they had they would not have understood."

"But what can I do?"

"Administer the office. You can't play Santa Claus to these people. Stop worrying about it. Try to get them to take jobs, and to pay their own way. See that they are represented if there are any civil actions against them. Advise them to vote and who to vote for——"

"But——" Rider raised his eyebrows, "how can I, a Government office-holder, advise them whom to vote for?"

"Better put it this way: How can they, ignorant children, know whom to vote for?"

"Still——"

Tolliver shrugged, suddenly impatient. "My dear sir, I ask you! You are here as mentor to these creatures. They can't be expected, after a lifetime of slavery, to know how to vote. They have a great voice too. And if they vote for a party inimical to their welfare, as the Democrats are, their progress will be put back another generation, I promise you."

Archibold Rider nodded. "Of course," he said, "of course." And a wave of relief came over him. This was a straightforward answer to his problem. This, then, was his work.

Tolliver stood up. "You are in good hands," he said. "Cutler knows the ropes. He will bring you papers that need signing. He has, in the past, administered the finances of the office and I should be inclined to let him continue. There is not much and he knows where every penny goes. It will save you a boring task."

Rider agreed easily.

"There is the question of the convicts at Valhalla. They are leased to me by the State. They live on the property and work there under State guard. I feed and house them and pay the State. They are not really under your jurisdiction, but as they are black the prison authorities like to have your signature."

"Of course, gladly."

"I shall tell them to send the papers to you. Now, perhaps you will honor me with your company for a drink. The Saint James House lies on your way."

For the first time, Archibold Rider left his office early, and was glad to do so.

Another week passed, and another. With the colored people [illegible]

[illegible] evenings to his daughter. He would take her hand on his arm and they would go down to the river to watch the boats. It was cool on the waterfront and it made a pleasant walk. Sometimes they went to the bridge on Pond Street, to see if there were any alligators in the swampy run. They saw none, but they often saw heron fishing, and Kate was satisfied that she was seeing the tropics. When the evenings were too warm for walking they stayed on the piazza and Rider talked to the other boarders.

The evening Rider joined a card game in the parlor Kate pouted unhappily. But then a man must sometimes play at cards, she thought resignedly, and contented herself with the company of the two older women on the porch, listening to their almost constant gossip. Madam, surprisingly, was not so much a gossip as she was a receptive listener. But Miss Ferguesson's active tongue still amazed Kate. The teacher was so gaunt and upright a person, so like Aunt Enid, who would rather her tongue be cut out than heard! But Kate felt she had commenced in those days to understand Miss Ferguesson, who often looked as though she did not quite approve of herself but had gone too far ever to return to her true nature. Florida, with its loneliness, would make a gossip of the very Sphinx. What was there for her to do but sit upon the piazza and talk to Madam! Miss Ferguesson had been here two years, and the ladies of the town must know that she was eminently respectable and a good person, yet they would not speak to her. As for men, she despised most of the Northern men. In any case, no man was going to concern himself with Miss Ferguesson. Nor with Miss Kate Rider, it would seem. Kate's thoughts drifted unhappily.

She had seen Hains Tolliver twice since she had come to Jacksonville. George Morgan came into town every ten days, and once he had brought her flowers from Mandarin. Michael Bourne worked, she thought, like a cyclone. He was all over the town, except at Madam's, and he was often away for days on end. Jacksonville was the kind of place where everything seemed to happen. She heard that Bourne worked too hard, and she heard that he neglected his duty. She heard that he bothered himself with the activities of the Klan and with some colored benevolent society, and that he questioned the leasing of convicts by the State. Things that seemed intangibly to irritate "the Louts." She had heard one of them say, "He hangs around like the itch. Some day something will happen to him." And another "Lout" had said, "Maybe he doesn't have enough business to take up his time."

And, as though his words had been overheard by some grimly playful fate, "business" had commenced to shower upon Bourne. The body of a woman was found in the river. A man came into town with a string of horses, sold them the same day, took his money and melted away. Two days later the true owner of the horses arrived, wanting blood as well as his horses. A fire-bug set fire to a pile of mattresses in a loft on the waterfront and started a blaze that threatened the town. Bourne took trouble over the dead woman, scowling blackly when he could find out nothing about her. The other matters he tossed to the sheriff. "Give me someone to prosecute and don't be bothering me with this trash in the meanwhile!" he stormed. The sheriff complained: he had handed him the murderer of the mystery woman, and Bourne had turned the man loose. There should be an investigation! Michael shrugged, "The man had nothing to do with it, I am convinced. He's a Negro and he'd never get a fair trial. A thing you can't always help—but I could help it, this time." It was said that he had helped the man over the border, and there were complaints and whispers.

Kate had asked him about it, but he only laughed at her. He would not talk about his work. "Would you be asking me, if I were a street-car conductor, how I liked punching tickets?"

[illegible]

one thing or another. It got to be too much. So one night I went out with a spade and dug up his whole estate and carted it off to the Irish Sea. When he woke in the morning, there wasn't a tree or a blade of grass to be seen. It put him in a tizzy, I can tell you!"

Kate laughed helplessly.

When Michael was busy she hated him for leaving her alone. When he stopped off to tease her she loved him and wished that he would stay. He made her laugh. He made her forget how dull the day had been, how dull the next day would be. She understood that his work was important to him, and, though she had no patience with fatigue, she realized that he must sometimes be tired. Later, when Michael, too, went into the parlor to play cards with the table of sharply whittled men, Kate let anger seethe within her, and she commenced to hate the very sight of the parlor.

Her father played spasmodically at first, and though she did not like it she did not protest. He would say, "Amuse yourself, m'dear, I will come presently," meaning to walk with her. But "presently" it was time for bed, and he had not come. When he went into the parlor the third night in succession, Kate fled to her room where she threw herself weeping upon the bed. For two nights after that, as though he had sensed something, her father accompanied her again, and the night following he played écarté with her. But the next night he excused himself apologetically and went back to the parlor.

Kate watched him go without protest. On the piazza she could hear the swing scream as it received Madam's great weight. From the parlor there was the clink of glasses. The big stupid man, Hess, was laughing loudly, and she could hear Bourne's voice telling some story. Kate grabbed her skirts in two tight fists and ran up the stairs to her room. There were no tears in her now, only a great anger. She stamped her small foot until it hurt, and pounded her fists upon the mantel. It was monstrous unfair. And, perversely, she hated, not her father, but Michael Bourne.

Kate was in the midst of such a tantrum when Miss Ferguesson came into the room, which they still shared.

"Look here, my girl," the older woman cried, "what ever has come over you!"

Kate whirled on her, her fists clenched and her eyes blazing. "Get out!" she spat, "get out, and leave me alone!"

Miss Ferguesson, who in any case carried herself like a soldier at drill, put an extra inch upon her being. "Mind your manners, miss," she said tartly, "and take control of yourself. I do not know what has happened, but there is no excuse for such behavior."

But Kate was too far gone to draw back. "Shut up," she cried at the older woman. "And you get out. Leave me alone, I tell you!"

In two strides, Miss Ferguesson had Kate by the arm and was half pulling, half jerking her across the room to the wash-basin.

"Leave me! Leave me alone!" Kate panted, struggling against the teacher, but Miss Ferguesson had the strength of a man in her hard thin arms, and in the midst of the girl's cries she took her by the back of her neck and thrust her head down into the pail of water. Then she let go, and Kate came up gasping and sputtering.

"There," Miss Ferguesson said, standing off, "dry yourself and fix your hair. If you want to tell me your trouble, I shall be glad to hear. If you don't want to, I'm sure you are welcome to keep it to yourself. But mind you get hold of your temper, miss, or you're going to see a peck of trouble in your day."

Kate wiped the water from her face and looked at the school teacher with new respect. But she could not bring herself to apologize yet, so she turned her back and went to the dressing-table. Her hair was like coiled seaweed on her head. [illegible] but it marks you. You may think a person unfortunate who has a dark skin, but his misfortune is merely on the surface, whereas a person who is ill-bred is tainted right through to the heart. Now, temper is another thing. I will not have temper around me, and you may make up your mind to it as long as you share this room with me."

Kate said, "Yes'm," meekly and commenced to work on her hair. And there the subject dropped. Though Miss Ferguesson waited for a while in silence, Kate could not bring herself to explain that she was in despair because her papa was gambling and drinking and leaving her alone, and that she could find no house for them, and that Mr. Bourne annoyed her intensely, and that she was in fact extremely lonely.

The very first day after her arrival, when everyone had departed so earnestly about their business, Kate had set out to find a house. Madam and Miss Ferguesson had laughed at her inquiries, but Kate had only put on her bonnet and gone out into the town by herself. There was no real-estate office and the newspaper carried no advertisements of houses to let. So Kate walked up and down the streets and when she saw a house that she liked she walked up to the door and knocked. Sometimes the door was opened, only to be slammed in her face; more often a shutter above her head moved and her knock was left unanswered. Kate would go home half angry and half ready to weep.

Her father would pat her hand and say, "It's to be expected, m'dear, it's only to be expected." Once, Michael Bourne said over her head to Madam, "It's a lot of walking about for a young lady alone. Jacksonville's not so pretty right now."

He had frowned as he said it, being very serious, the Irishman! Kate could have screamed with exasperation. "And who am I to go with, pray?" she said tartly.

Then he smiled. "Well, if you're looking for a house you won't be down by the waterfront, or up Nigger Hill. So you're safe enough, I guess."

Kate could scarcely wait for morning to go down to the waterfront and up Nigger Hill. The Hill depressed her and she came away ready to weep. The colored people had been given freedom but nothing else, it would seem. She had never seen or dreamed of such poverty or such want. And what she had seen was like a seed in her mind, which she buried for a while but did not forget. The waterfront she was to regret immediately. There were no women here at all and only the roughest sort of men, and a great quantity of Negroes. She felt as though every eye was on her. The street smelled of fish and sour bodies and rank mud, and there was nothing here that she cared to see, but she kept stubbornly upon her way. Suddenly a group of drunken men burst out of a gaudily painted door immediately into her path. Kate started back and when one of the men lurched against his fellows and said, with a gallant attempt to swallow a belch, "There ain't nothing so pretty in there, missy, not for no price," she turned and bolted down the street, her face crimson and her heart in her mouth. A bellow of laughter followed her and everywhere there were eyes and wide-open smiles.

It was after her adventure by the waterfront that Kate first had the feeling that she was being followed. Most of her walks took her over quiet streets, where the house that she looked for might be found. Once she picked her way through the charred ruins of the Wilsons' place, and once she walked down along the King's Road to watch the new buildings that were going up. And always there was the same black girl behind her like a shadow. The first time that Kate noticed her, she could not remember where she had seen her before. The next time, she knew that she recognized the girl because she was always going the same way, always turning down the same streets. The girl was young and nice-looking, she never tried to approach Kate [illegible]

[illegible], in so many words, but she was already at odds with the other Kate—the Kate who worried about the stiffness of a dress that nobody was going to look at, who did not want to be seen talking to "Louts," though there was nobody to see or care, and who was torn between wistful dreams and angry thoughts of the Irishman who teased her and then forgot her so easily.

"Niminy piminy!" she told herself, which was neither answer nor comfort, but was all that she could think of to contribute to the situation.

Miss Ferguesson asked her again to come to the school, and Michael Bourne warned her father against allowing her to roam about town alone. He had, it seemed, learned something about her headlong flight down Bay Street.

Her father fumed at her and tugged at his mustache and quoted Bourne liberally. "It's not safe, girlie! Michael says——"

Kate let her father talk, feeling angrily that as long as there was nothing else for her to do she would at least go where she pleased.

Then, one day, she made another trip to the colored village and her shadow suddenly materialized, darting up to Kate as she commenced to climb the hill.

"Don't go dar, missy," the girl cried, tugging at her skirt. "Marse' say don't go up dar."

Kate swung about and scowled at the girl. "Who are you?

And what do you mean by speaking to me?" she demanded. She jerked her skirt loose and examined the girl closely. It was the same girl, without a doubt, slender and black, with straight fine features and a pretty body. "Who are you?" Kate stamped her foot, all of a month's unhappiness coming out in anger, but the girl would not speak and, presently, Kate shrugged and, turning about, continued up the hill. And the girl followed behind her.

The road was dusty and, on either side, clustered tents and cabins made up of every kind of derelict material. Here and there a man slept, stretched out in the shade of his porch. Beside one tent a woman beat her clothes on a wooden board and, even from the road, her fists looked big and swollen. A young woman in a patched black silk dress pushed open her cabin door and threw slops into the road. The chickens and razorbacks came screaming and, from under the porch, a yellow hound shot out, cursing in ugly dog-language at the intruders.

As they went, the black girl had shortened the distance between them and suddenly Kate stopped in her tracks, whirled about and, caught the girl tightly by her wrist. "What did you say about Master?" Kate cried, the meaning of the girl's words reaching her at last. "Who do you mean?" She stamped her foot.

"Marse' Michael," the girl said quickly, "he says Vronnie watch little missy. Little missy no go up hiar."

Kate drew back her hand and slapped the girl hard in the face before she realized what she was doing. "Go back to your Marse' and tell him missy can take care of herself," she stormed. "Now git. And tell him to mind his own business."

The girl backed away slowly, tears in her eyes, and then she turned and ran down the hill. Kate watched her go and her anger burned in her like an excitement. She looked down at her mittened hand. She had never in her life struck or been struck. A feeling of horror swept over her. "I liked it," she thought. "I should like to do it again."

Presently she became aware that the people on the hill were watching her. Nobody spoke, nobody approached her. No small black child had a smile for her. The hound had chased the other animals away and was nosing through the slops by himself. Kate turned and followed the black girl down the hill. She wondered where she had gone and whether she still wept. It had been a shameful [illegible]

[illegible]

[illegible] House and looked thoughtfully across at his visitor. James Cutler would carry out orders; of that Tolliver was sure. But he was also sure that Cutler was beginning to resent the orders. The other's face was dark with frustration. Tolliver frowned. An empire, he thought, was built on a living network—certainly his was. There were, here and there, in posts of which he wanted the control, men like Archibold Rider. Men whose actions were predictable. Men honest enough and innocent enough to be dupes. And there were the paid employees, like James Cutler, who held State posts, but were paid by him. There were documents at Valhalla that served to control the Cutlers. There was no question about the trustworthiness of such a person: he would think twice before he put a noose around his own neck. A human tool had perforce to be a knave or a fool, and Tolliver had use for both. But he thought that the fool had to be completely fooled, and the knave at his mercy. James Cutler's surge of resentment was actually of no moment, but it came at a bad time.

"Reed," Cutler said abruptly, "is playing in with Saunders, you can bet."

Tolliver fingered his chin. "Reed," he said, "is not playing in with anyone."

He had backed Reed for Governor, feeling sure that when the time came Reed would be of use to him. Instead of that the Governor had proved difficult from the word go. He had vetoed the establishment of a State bank, the issuance of State scrip, and the sale of lands at specified prices. He had vetoed salary raises; he was working against bonuses. He had appointed to receiverships men of his own choosing instead of those he had been asked, or told, to appoint. He had gone over the head of local advice and appealed to Washington. He was costing Tolliver money instead of adding to his fortune, as the latter had intended he should.

"Reed," Tolliver went on, "was willing to use any means to get in. Now that he is in, he is trying to be his own man. He will have to learn. If he doesn't learn, he will have to go."

"You mean——"

Tolliver smiled. This little man thought that he could get something on him! Something to trade on. "A governor can be impeached," he said softly and watched the other's face close down. "Mr. Reed is at present being plagued by trouble in Jackson county. I think the trouble will grow. Reed has already asked for secret police. People ought to be told about it."

"But he didn't get them."

"Of course not. Still people must be told. Tell your Brothers, Cutler, tell them, sir. It will get around."

"And it won't make Reed popular."

"Exactly."

"But I don't see that it will get him impeached."

"Patience! We shall have to wait and see a few things. Perhaps Reed will come along by the end of summer. Then there is the question of those guns. He won't get them from Washington. I can see to that. If he buys them, there is the question of putting the State into debt for military supplies which have been refused him by his own legislature and by Washington. Something can be done. But I think that that trouble in Jackson needs your attention!"

Cutler stood up. "I'll have to be out of town. What about Rider?"

"Did you see that Rider got a bonus?"

"Yes, he got it."

"What did he have to say?"

"He was amazed! Didn't know that the Government was so generous."

"But he took it?"

Cutler grinned. "He took it. He may be wet behind the [illegible]

[illegible] gray top of Cutler's beaver appear from beneath the piazza roof and the carpetbagger walked quickly down the street. He frowned thoughtfully and, turning, paced across the room and back again. Someday Cutler would have to go. Perhaps he was going now. But Tolliver thought not. There were enough elements in Jackson County to make things difficult for a stranger, and dangerous for an interfering stranger. But Cutler, he thought, had a rat's instinct for self-preservation. He would come back. He would walk immune through the warring Negro clubs and the Regulators and the Ku Klux. Even Colonel Dickinson would not touch him. Not this time.

He thought of Dickinson, sorry that he was in Jackson. And then he shrugged impatiently. Dickinson asked for trouble, with his Regulators and his refusal to give up the fight. Tolliver knew him. He had fought with him. A gallant soldier, but a hothead and a fool. A good man to have by you in trouble, but one who did not know when to give up. None of which he could have said about himself. He smiled bleakly. No, there had been nothing wrong with his record. It had even been called brilliant. But he knew that it had been so out of his own making, not out of a passion for patriotism.

He had been in France at the outbreak of war and he had chosen his side with his mind, not with his heart. He was of the South. His best interests were served by the South. It had been a bitter campaign. He thought of Dickinson sitting on his horse in the rain, with a bloody bandage around his throat. A more sensible man would have been dead, but he was still fighting! He himself had seen that the war was at an end before the last grim battle had been fought. And he had given up, having no intention that the last bit of blood shed be his. Nobody could have called him a coward, but he held himself too intelligent a man to be one of heroic temper. He disbanded his men, ignored the insults flung at him by a lot of hotheaded fools, and went home. He had done his piece for the South and now there was something that he had to do for Hains Tolliver. Colonel Dickinson in the rain, with his bloody bandage, made it plain what he thought. In Jackson county, Dickinson was still at it. Fighting the carpetbaggers. Fighting abuses by Negroes, protecting landowners and women and children on remote plantations. Now he was going to have more trouble.

Why the devil should he Hains Tolliver care! He shrugged at himself. Belated patriotism? He had no use for the quixotic fools. Let them lick their wounds. They had thrown him out long ago; so be it. He stopped again by the window and looked down on the busy street. When he was a boy, it had been nothing but a planter's highway. Yet he had always thought of it as a very gay, very grand place. He could remember coming in on the front of his father's saddle, and the throngs of riders and wagons and oxcarts and, now and again, a high Concord coach that made this gathering of barnlike inns its stopping place before crossing the river. A rough piece of country to have cast out one so polished as Stephen Tolliver! Now it was a thriving city and Stephen Tolliver's son held the whip over it. He turned away from the window; it was no longer a very grand place.

Miss Ferguesson's information was, like most gossip, only half true. Hains Tolliver had been born at Mandarin, at the outset of the Seminole wars. It was also the year of the great frost, when the temperature dropped overnight to eight degrees and the river was coated with ice. The young Georgian, Rosaleen Hains, who had come to visit relatives and stayed to marry Stephen Tolliver, committed suicide in the first year of her marriage, after the birth of her son. Stephen Tolliver would not explain her death, and the long river community, outraged and suspicious, turned its back on him. The frost had killed the oranges all up [illegible] of them. The elder Tolliver boarded up his house and left Mandarin. He left two hundred acres of dead trees and an empty house.

Stephen Tolliver made money in Georgia, but his old neighbors, instead of forgetting their suspicion, had let it grow. Once, he brought his son to the old house, redecorated it and filled it with slaves. But the river had no hospitality for him, and a house in the country without friends is a poor place—as it proved, a tomb for old memories and hatreds. So Stephen Tolliver took his son away. He left the slaves in the house as a denial of retreat, and he took with him the memories and the hatreds. Father and son went back to Georgia, and finally to France, where the elder Tolliver died some time before the outbreak of the war. And now Alphonse Morgan was dead, and Zephaniah Kingsley. While Stephen Tolliver's son owned Valhalla! And not, he thought, because he was a noble Southern gentleman, or a great soldier, but because he was a man of reason.

He had done what any man of reason should have done, would have done. Only that was his, he had known, which he could save for himself. He left the battlefield to the victor, determined to use the victor to his own advantage. For if there were not many intelligent Southerners, there were as few intelligent Yankees. He took the Iron Clad Oath and when some finger pointed, at the right moment, to the treasonable affairs of the now dead Alphonse Morgan, Hains Tolliver was on hand to buy up confiscated Valhalla. With French and English securities at his command, if not in great quantity at least of unquestionable stability, he bought also several thousand acres of turpentine tracts at a few cents the acre, and he assured himself of labor by renting convicts from the State. In Tallahassee he watched the struggle of a constitutional government to establish itself and saw at once how the new citizens could be used to his advantage.

The State capital was crowded with pompous and foolish black people who could neither read nor write but who were enthusiastically occupying big chairs. The big chairs meant votes. Votes meant money. In the early days, the black people did not sell their votes. They had still to learn that from their white brothers. But they did go happily in the direction that a flattering, or sufficiently threatening, hand pushed them. And there were plenty of Yankees to trade with. Hains Tolliver prospered rapidly and if his fellow Southerners looked down on him, it was no more than he did upon them. For to say, like a spoiled child, "If you let that black man vote, you'll not get me to go to the polls," was not his way. Let the fools sulk! It would get them no forwarder and he, for one, was not with them.

Under the slave system, few had worried about the black man's mind—he was a beast of burden, that was all there was to it. Now he was a free laborer, but by an astute man his untrained mind could be used to advantage. There were more black voters than white voters in Florida. Hains Tolliver shrugged, "Then let them vote to my advantage." There were men from the North who would pay money for their vote, would get great profit from their posts, and would continue to pay money afterwards.

Tolliver drew out a watch and snapped open the cover. In a half hour his carriage would be ready. His gloves and cane and hat were on the table, and his satchel on the floor beside them. He was always glad to get out to the country. Valhalla had been the dream he was reared on and, strangely—for many dreams, when fulfilled, do not satisfy—it did satisfy everything in him. Though the price was always with him. His had been a hard struggle and a bitter one. Even now, perhaps the wealthiest and most powerful man in Florida, he had practically to sleep with his eyes open.

He thought of Rider and smiled. There was one tool that didn't need watching, in fact that hardly [illegible]

[illegible]

[illegible] bitions. He dismissed Kate from his mind, as he had dismissed the momentary qualm about Colonel Dickinson. The matter was closed because it was useless to him, and impractical. But in the back of his mind was the reservation that in Kate's case there was, after all, no need for an immediate decision.

On the precise minute of the half hour he took up his hat, cane and gloves and, leaving his satchel for a servant to bring, went downstairs to his carriage.

The summer in Jacksonville was as hot as Michael Bourne had predicted to Kate that it would be. But the evenings were pleasant with breezes from the river. On the land side, the big trees threw deep, moss-draped shadows, and in the river the waters were a murky brown or gray and cool to look upon. Kate dreamed through the summer stillness. She did not mind the heat, but she minded the loneliness. On Caroline Street, Crockett Wilson, too, watched the summer slip by. She worked spasmodically on a luncheon set to be sold at the parish bazaar at election time. Miss Janey rocked by her side, now silent, now chattering of the old days, or warning her daughter of the early decay attendant upon her unmarried state. In a cabin at the foot of Nigger Hill, Miss Ferguesson led her flock in alphabet and prayer. A hundred black souls looked humbly into New England's stern eyes, chanting in their soft voices New England's stern prayers.

At Mandarin, hard green fruit covered the trees. George

Morgan spent himself on the grove, with only one colored man and the vagrant soldiers whom Michael befriended, to help him. At Valhalla, strange people came and went. They came from Savannah; they came from Tallahassee; they came even from Washington. From them Tolliver learned about the affairs of the State. He listened and he gave advice that sometimes sounded more like commands. He rode the boundaries of Valhalla daily. A hundred convicts slept in the huts that had once housed slaves, and his groves were pregnant with their care.

The summer was active with the political fight for control of the State, for, though the Radicals had seemed to gain control in putting Reed into the Capitol, the Governor had displayed his disposition towards conservatism by using the veto heavily. As a result, he divided his own party and won but few friends among the Democrats or Southern whites. The State trembled with meetings and processions, torch-lit or sun-lit, and the streets were gaudy with boxes on sticks, painted on all four sides: "No Compromise with the Carpetbaggers." "Freedman's Bureau and Robbery." "300 Ticks in the Ballot-Box and Count Out 500." "Democrats Grantless and See-more in November." And Governor Reed was busy losing friends. Jackson County was in the grip of a reign of terror, and Reed asked his legislature again for a law allowing him to employ secret police to protect his government from the outrages which were daily growing. He vetoed a bill which meant money in the pockets of men who had put him in office, and he vetoed another which would have put Negroes in trains and hotels with whites, and certain politicians in pocket.

Michael Bourne left the functioning of his own office to his staff and followed the scent of political rot to Osceola, to Tallahassee and even to Washington, where he conferred with Senator Osborne. But the scent only led him back to Jacksonville, there deserting him as neatly as though it had been laid by the able servant of a drag hunt.

On the hall table at Madam's, Mr. Cutler laid his yellow gloves, while Mr. Hess carried a cane with a gold knob intricately worked with his initials. Mr. Cutler and Mr. Hess were clerics, presumably paid by the Government and enjoying the accustomed salaries of clerics. In two short months Archibold Rider found unexpected wealth in bonuses flowing into his pockets, and he sent to Hartford for Kate's piano and took a sitting-room, as well as two bedrooms, at Madam's [illegible]

[illegible] Morgan would call upon her. He would bring her fruit from the country, or flowers, or fresh eggs packed in Spanish moss and tied to his saddlehorn. Sometimes he would sit on the piazza swing and talk with her. He was always serious, and Kate, try as she would, found it hard to be gay with him. Once, he lifted her up like a doll and took her for a canter across town and out along the King's Road.

When they had slowed to a walk beyond the edge of town, where the oaks were giant groves edging the narrow road and plank paving had given way to dirt, he slid down and led the horse, the bridle looped loosely over his arm and Kate sitting sideways with her little feet dangling just below his shoulder.

She caught her breath and sighed with pleasure. "That was lovely," she said. "I do like going fast through town. It's exciting and, why, hardly anybody canters in town! It sounds lovely on the planks, doesn't it?"

Morgan laughed. "It does, at that," he said. "About ten years ago we used to race horses through the streets. The Aldermen were always trying to stop it. But people liked it too much. I doubt there's an ordinance to this day to prevent it."

"Oh then, why—it would be such fun!" Kate cried.

He shrugged and said shortly, "There are no horses left that could run and no sports who would want to. We're a sorry lot, Miss Kate."

Kate looked down at him in distress. He was not easy to

talk to, almost any subject was likely to end this way, with George Morgan bitter and she feeling unhappily as though she were somehow to blame.

"It's horrible for you," she said gently. "Please believe me—I—and papa too——" she left the sentence floundering and Morgan smiled up at her quickly and said:

"Apologies! Miss Kate, I am wicked to torment you. And do you know, I am not at all sure that we in the South have the right to complain so much. I speak from the heart, for I am one of the top complainers."

"Oh," Kate cried, "but you do—indeed——"

"No, don't misunderstand me. We have cause. I only question the right. We lost the war. That had to happen to one side, did it not? A soldier doesn't like losing, but then he doesn't mind in the same way that a civilian does. At home, they are bitter and hate the enemy, because he is really a creature of the imagination and it's therefore quite possible for him to be an inhuman creature. Southern women think that their men were murdered by fiends. But on the battlefield, a soldier is a soldier, whatever uniform he wears. He gets hungry, the same rain soaks him through and wets his ammunition, he's liable to get wounded or killed, he's sometimes a poltroon. But mostly he is courageous, a fellow you can respect, in blue or in gray. No, a soldier doesn't hate the enemy, and he can accept defeat from the enemy. It's the occupation that is hard to bear."

Kate said, "Of course," in a small uncomfortable voice.

Morgan switched his boot with his riding crop and cried out tensely, "Not at all 'of course,' Miss Kate, it should not be so. We're beaten. The slaves are free—the economic back of the entire South is broken. We cannot now secede. So what purpose is served by grinding us under? The North went to war to preserve a united nation—yet it behaves as though it wanted instead a subservient state—a plunder field."

"But papa says that we want to help the South back on its feet so that we can be one nation again, and a bigger one too."

Morgan shrugged and his mood veered abruptly to good humor. "Well, Miss Kate, as you will discover one day, your father is not a realist. You have met Messrs. Cutler and Hess. You have met some of the so-called gentlemen at Madam's." He used the word gentlemen with a sarcasm that comforted Kate, for this put them in another street from the Riders, though they [illegible]

could not vote. That left about eleven thousand Crackers free to vote, and fifteen thousand niggers. None of them fit to render a thoughtful vote with the welfare of the State in mind. So that has been patched up with the Reconstruction Act and the Freedman's Bureau! It means that we don't have a vote worth mentioning, Miss Kate. The niggers are being told how to vote, and anyone with the energy and the instincts of a leech can get a job with the Government."

Kate tossed her head at his words, but she said nothing.

"There now"—Morgan was at once contrite—"I've offended you. Your papa is a different sort, Miss Kate. Anyone can see that at once. Still, he made a mistake to come South with Hains Tolliver. It ties him in with the wrong people. Believe me."

"Indeed!" Kate cried warmly. "I've heard of the jealousy that is directed against Mr. Tolliver, and I think it quite unworthy. He, at least, is doing something about rebuilding." She was sorry at once, and said so, bending down from the saddle towards her companion.

"Never mind, Miss Kate," he said easily, "you and I should not talk of politics." He took the stirrup and swung gracefully into the saddle behind her. "If you're not in a hurry to go home, I'll show you an Indian hill. We used to picnic there when I was a boy. It should be covered with pock-marks where we dug for treasure."

"Did you ever find any?"

"Yes—the very best sort. Golden hours and days. Fabulous treasures, Miss Kate. I only wish we could have saved some."

Kate knew that hers were not the only flowers George Morgan brought to town, the only honey or eggs. And if he spent an hour with her, he spent the rest of his time with the girl Crockett. Kate had heard that she was very beautiful. She pictured her as having everything that she could possibly want of life. Not wealth, of course, not any more. And Kate did not underestimate wealth. It was important. But Crockett had friends and a handsome man in love with her. Kate would think, she is, after all, very poor, church-mouse poor. Papa is much richer and I have finer clothes, and we are going to be even richer still! But the thought was without comfort for longer than the time it took to think it. Kate wished with all her heart that she might be taken to call on Crockett. Every time she saw Morgan she would think eagerly, This time he will ask me if I'd care to call. "Would you care to call on some friends of mine," he might say, "Mrs. Wilson and her daughter? I believe that you two would like each other." But he never asked her.

With Bourne, her rival was not another girl, but his work. Upon the rare occasions that he forgot it long enough to remember her, even a child would have resented the contrast of being picked up and dropped at random. Kate swore to herself each time that she would have no more to do with Michael Bourne. When he was busy or occupied with some man—Mr. Cutler or Mr. Hess, Mr. Murchman or General Sprague, or General Houston, or her father, or Mr. Denny at the bank—Michael Bourne never seemed to see her. He would neither raise his hat to her nor stand up should she chance to come into the room. And if he was with a companion who was more punctilious, he would follow suit impatiently, as though he resented her intrusion. Kate would want to scream with anger, "I'll never, never, never speak to you again, sir, indeed!"

Then a lull would come in his work and Bourne would stride jauntily up the piazza towards her, or knock on her door, an Irish ditty on his tongue, his wide mouth stretched in a warm and friendly grin.

"The Topsy and the Fanny Fern are leaving for Palatka," he'd say. "It's going to be a rare race, and there's music and singing down at the dock. Will you come?"

Kate would frown angrily, and then his grin and her lone- [illegible]

[illegible]

not be serious with Kate. He treated her like a great lady and a silly doll, making fun of himself even as he did so, delighting her with his attentions. And when an afternoon or an evening was done and he went back to his man's world, anger at herself would add fuel to her anger at him, and Kate would swear that it should never happen again.

If the women in town had shown her any friendship it would have been easy for Kate to forget her angers, relegate Bourne to his proper inferno and leave him there without again considering him. But she was too alone, and during that period when she was moving from girlhood into womanhood she was so beset with frustrated dreams and rages that they were to become a part of her new character.

Then, one Sunday after church, the minister's wife, Mrs. Matthew Bornson, asked her to tea.

"Tuesday, if you will do me the honor," she said, bowing stiffly and without the smallest evidence of pleasure.

In Hartford, tea at the Rectory had been an important and a regular occasion. Though never a jolly affair, it seethed with ladies who knew Aunt Enid and who knew Kate's papa. And however he may have been rumored to have behaved the night before at the club or in some bar, they considered him a man of great charm and courted Aunt Enid for her widower brother. To Kate, tea at the Rectory had meant a function of social importance. Had decorum permitted, she would have skipped for joy. She would meet the ladies of Jacksonville at Mrs. Matthew Bornson's, after which they would no longer look through her as though she were a piece of glass.

When Tuesday came, she put a hoop on under her prettiest dress. Her blue organdy parasol matched the dress and her white mittens showed off her little hands to their daintiest advantage.

She went alone, half gay, half frightened, down the street, the palms of her hands damp and her heart beating quickly. Perhaps Miss Crockett Wilson would be there. Kate had seen the Wilsons' house and knew that it was small and shabby. But in her heart she always saw Miss Crockett in flowered skirts dancing on a marquee by the riverside. Gallant gentlemen attended her and oranges and oleander, jasmine and magnolia, blossomed in every direction. It was the South, like a blossom itself, that Kate had unrequited visions of.

Mrs. Bornson received Kate stiffly. Despite the heat, she wore a black alpaca garment that covered her thin frame from chin to toe. Her hair was a soft brown, quite colorless. It was carefully arranged, having been optimistically brushed forward and then bent back to a knot on top of her head. It had neither the body nor the life to hold this position, and Kate's first impression of this structure was that it should have been built up with rats or surrendered to a wig.

Kate sat on the edge of her chair as erect as her hostess. She did not miss the thin expression that was directed upon her gay clothes. She folded her hands primly and watched her tea being poured. She was the first to arrive, and began at once to feel that it was a monstrous thing to have done. Without seeming to take her eyes from the tea urn, she examined the parlor in which they sat and the small dark dining-room separated from it by a curtained archway. The curtains were magenta and hung at either side in dusty-looking folds. Kate dismissed them at once as being quite innocent of any speck, for Mrs. Bornson was no person to tolerate dust and everywhere else her mahogany and black horsehair, her glass-covered bookcases, surmounted by a large glass bell of roses, shone dustless and cared for.

"I expect that you are finding the weather trying," Mrs.

Bornson said, holding Kate's cup out to her. Kate took it and sat down again.

"It is cooler at home this time of year, but I like it here."

"That is good. Northerners are adaptable, I always say."

[illegible]

The ladies were arriving. She smoothed her skirt and lowered her lashes. Too much excitement was not well bred and she, Kate Rider, was not going to be found wanting. The fat old darky who had opened the door for her came padding softly down the hall. They heard her querulous voice at the door.

"What you want, Miss Bessie? You done been told not to come hiar today. Miss Effie's busy."

Miss Bessie's answer was inaudible but the darky's voice rose again. "You skat right along, else you want I should tell your mammy on you," and the door closed firmly.

Kate's fingertips tingled as though they had been asleep, and for a moment she could not move. For the first time now she noticed the tea-tray; with her own cup and Mrs. Bornson's removed from the tray, there were none left. No other ladies were expected. The minister's wife merely executed a duty in asking her to tea. She was not acceptable to the ladies of Jacksonville. Indeed, they had been warned to stay away! Kate's face was gray, and suddenly she became acutely aware that her stays were too tight.

Mrs. Bornson leaned forward quickly and her own face was mottled.

"I am so ashamed," she cried in her tight high voice. "It is terrible, terrible. But, you see, they don't want to meet a Northerner—it's not you, my dear, believe me. And Miss Bessie is a very curious young woman, and a gossip. She did not come kindly. I told her to stay away. I wouldn't have had this happen for worlds. Dear me, I wouldn't. But it was better that she should be turned away."

Kate stood up, the color returning to her face. "It is all right," she said. "It was nice of you to receive me. Good day, Mrs. Bornson."

Mrs. Bornson twisted her fingers nervously, and came towards Kate. "Please stay, Miss Rider. I am—oh dear, what will Mr. Bornson say! That black girl needs a whipping! She does indeed."

Kate had turned her back but now she whirled upon her hostess, her hurt transformed into a trembling rage. "Your black soul needs a whipping," she cried, scarcely knowing her own voice, "and all the rest of you black-souled ladies too. What makes you think you're too good to receive a Northerner? Because your men gave their lives for the cause of money in their pockets and human slaves at their call? Our men died too, but they died for somebody else, and the church I grew up in says 'greater love hath no man.' Good day to you, ma'am," and Kate whirled out of the house, leaving Mrs. Bornson with mouth open and wordless.

Kate went down the street like a small tornado, her anger burning in her and her young body upright with pride. This time she did not hold her skirts away from the dust, mincing daintily, but let them swing free among the eddies that her quick steps scuffed up. Once in her own room, she tore off her dress and hoop and flung them upon the floor, where her parasol and bonnet already lay. In her haste she had ripped the seed-pearl buttons from the gown, and now she stamped upon the garments, the pink ribbons in her stays bouncing grotesquely. Her small sharp heels ripped and stamped and crushed. Her eyes burned and her throat swelled, so that each breath became a gasp, but she was tearless. Suddenly nausea descended like a hood over her eyes and she stumbled to the slop pail. Her fingers were nerveless and clammy as she clutched it and coughed up a bitter mouthful of bile. The tears came then and she lay on the floor by the pail and wept violently. When she had done weeping, she straightened up her room, putting the broken parasol and the torn garments in the bottom of her wardrobe. Then she pinned a message on her door telling her father that she had a headache [illegible]

like that again. Never. Because she would never be a fool again. Moonlight on the river, magnolias and Southern courtiers!

"Niminy piminy snivelling pip-squeak!" she said aloud and, slipping out of her nightgown, she commenced to wash herself energetically.

Aunt Enid was a sew-a-fine-seam lady, but Kate had always known that she herself was different. Until now, her experience had not been such as to show her in what way. Aunt Enid would have understood the Jacksonville ladies and been crushed by them. Kate was going over them, beyond them. That she had determined somehow in her sleep, awakening to a full sense of that determination.

She scrubbed her teeth with powder, spitting the white grit into the slop pail. "I'll give them something to be mean about," she thought. "I'll make them crawl with envy, and hate too, if that's what they want—but I'm going to be on top with papa. I don't know how, but I'm going to!" she muttered.

She breakfasted with her father in the dining-room. When they had disposed of the matter of the head, which no longer ached, her health and her good night's sleep, Kate said, "Papa, when will you take me to Valhalla?"

Her father looked at her in surprise. "Why, some day, when it can be planned."

"Mr. Tolliver has asked us, and I should like to see Mr. Bourne's place."

Archibold Rider dragged on his mustache and looked across the table at his daughter.

"Soon, please, Papa."

"Well, my dear, it's a long drive, five hours each way. Frankly, it makes no sense unless we stay the night."

"Then let us stay the night."

"There are no ladies there; really, Kate!"

"I am not interested in ladies," Kate said with sudden venom. "Please, Papa, I want to go."

"Well now, and what would your Aunt Enid think?"

"Perhaps she won't know. In any case, I don't care."

Her father stared at her, scandalized. "Well, Miss!" he said, sternly.

"Well, Papa!" Suddenly Kate smiled, her small face lit up and her eyes twinkled at her father. "Fix it up and take me," she said, "and I will do something that you want. I will try out, for a few weeks, working for Miss Ferguesson."

"There, there, girlie," he said, his eyes softening at once, "you don't have to bribe your papa. I expect you know only too well you will get your own way. And I don't want you to work for Miss Ferguesson unless you choose to. It is just that I feel you are alone a lot. Michael thought that you might enjoy the work and be less lonely."

"Oh, he did!" A hard calculating look flickered deep in Kate's eyes. "Well, as a matter of fact, it is a good idea, despite Mr. Bourne. It will give me time to think things out, and it is boring doing nothing."

"Think things out?" her father said, bewildered.

Kate leaned across the table and patted his hand. "I have to think, Papa," she said, and she smiled. "And you will fix up the trip to Valhalla?"

"Yes, yes. After all, your own father ought to be sufficient chaperon." He folded his napkin precisely and waited for Kate to finish her tea. And Kate smiled into her cup and drank slowly. I'll put us on top, Papa, somehow, she thought, and she pictured her father riding down the street in a glistening equipage drawn by a pair of the finest-matched chestnuts in the country. He'd have a gold-headed cane and she would sit beside him, like a princess, in an ermine cloak with a fringe of little black tails about her throat. She pouted. It was hot in Florida for ermine. The dream dissipated and she looked up and smiled at her [illegible]

[illegible]

[illegible] she combed about the long beak of her glove-stretcher each stiff curl that was to stand in pokersmooth clusters about her neck. This done, she removed the towel which she had placed across her shoulders to protect her dress, smoothed the ruching at her throat and stood up. From a hook in the high wardrobe she took down a bonnet fashioned of dark-green alpaca to match her dress. This she coaxed feelingly into place on top of her headdress, smoothed and patted her skirt and viewed her gaunt person in the mirror with a satisfaction in itself somewhat gaunt. She was neat, she was orderly. More, though God had left her unrewarded in the coin of her sex, she still did her duty by it. Curl nor ruffle nor ribbon was neglected that could advertise her otherwise negligible femininity. A parcel of books under one arm and the umbrella fit for sun or rain crooked over the other, Miss Emma Fergues-son set out to interview the Board of Education.

She walked the short blocks to the center of town. The Board was housed wherever it felt like meeting. She had seen them as many times in Madam's parlor as elsewhere. Today they met at the District Attorney's office because Bourne was leaving for Tallahassee and had no time to see them elsewhere. By virtue of his position, he was an important member of the Board and no major decision could be made without him.

Michael Bourne met her at the door and led her to a seat. Tolliver was there and Murchman, surrogate for the supervisor.

They waited for the Reverend Pierce. After ten minutes, when he did not come, Mr. Murchman, who had consulted his watch twice in the interval, voted that the meeting be brought to order.

Michael Bourne slipped his pencil through his fingers, tapping first one end and then the other. He spoke without looking up. "I've been hearing things about Pierce," he said.

The others were silent, waiting. Miss Ferguesson looked quickly from the pad on which she was preparing to take notes. The surrogate fingered his watch nervously and almost visibly bent his ear towards Hains Tolliver. The latter, having waited his fill, said easily, "Well, Bourne, are we to guess?"

Michael's eyes were cold and hard and level now, and made no pretense of interest in anyone except the speaker.

"Now maybe I thought you wouldn't have to," he said. "It seems Pierce don't show up for any official meeting he's due to attend, when it's known you're to attend."

Tolliver smiled and his soft lips seemed to twist rather than to expand. "Extraordinary," he said, "now that you mention it——" he made a quick mock-helpless gesture with his left hand, "what would it mean—to you, Bourne?"

"I don't make guesses."

"Ah, then supposing you ask Pierce."

"Yes, since you have no answer, it would be the thing to do."

Murchman tapped his watch and said, "The time, gentlemen."

Hains Tolliver looked across at Bourne with a sudden intensity, and then the intensity slipped from his expression leaving an almost pitying look in its place. "His black soul has probably never thrown off the shackles," he said softly. "Pierce used to belong to me," he laughed. "You Yankees! You don't free a slave, not ever. Unless he stick a knife between his owner's ribs. Till then he's branded where you can't see but where he never stops feeling it."

"You know who should be branded?" Miss Ferguesson cried, as though she could contain herself no longer—she leaned forward in her seat, clutching the handle of her umbrella—"Every Southern mother's son of you, who dared to fly in the face of God and own a fellow human!"

Murchman cried, "Miss Fergusson, gentlemen, the time!"

Tolliver smiled unexpectedly. "Well, then, to Miss Fergues-

[illegible]

[illegible] women won't teach blacks and no Northern teacher, save a fool like me, is coming South for any four-dollars-a-week salary, and no respect paid her either."

Michael Bourne spread his hands flat on the table. "There is a bid in for an appropriation for education," he said. "So far they seem to see no reason to grant it."

"At the moment it is not the money I am coming to you about. Miss Kate Rider has offered to work with me for a term, and I am interested in having her passed by the Board without examination."

There was a moment's silence and then Michael Bourne slapped the table, leaning forward on his hand and grinning at the school teacher. "So the little lady's illiterate." He leaned back and laughed, a hard, friendly laugh. "Sure and she does put on a show!"

Miss Ferguesson tucked her thin lips away, as though for safekeeping. "Keep your laughter to yourself, Michael Bourne. Miss Kate is a nicely accomplished lady. She was not reared to teach. I was, and I fancy I can guide her sufficiently well."

Hains Tolliver said smoothly, "No offense, Miss Ferguesson. I'm sure Bourne meant nothing. And the situation is amusing. Miss Kate is a child. But then, I'm not against it."

"Nor I," Michael said heartily. "In fact, I had suggested to her father that the girl should do this very thing."

"But the examinations!" Murchman cried. "We are a Board,

gentlemen, and responsible; we can't take the matter so lightly."

"Fiddlesticks," said Miss Ferguesson. "You take lightly what you choose so to take. Do I so much as speak of funds or supplies and I find little enough attention paid me."

"Now, now, ma'am."

"Well, sirs!"

Mr. Tolliver said, "I'm sure Miss Ferguesson will vouch for Miss Rider's abilities."

"Indeed I will. She is an intelligent girl and, what is more, a little aristocrat."

Michael Bourne laughed again. "Then she has my vote," he cried. "If there's one thing the niggers need it's an aristocratic education! If you've any earls or princes up your sleeve, bring them on too." The others laughed, and he said, "For all of me, she can be superintendent." He grinned at Murchman. "Until there's a will in Tallahassee to do something about educating the freedman it's nothing but a sop to Congress and I'm not interested in how it's run. Get children in to teach!"

Murchman cleared his throat. "Gentlemen!" he protested, "this is unduly frivolous."

"It's settled," Michael said, and looked across at Miss Ferguesson. "Would you like me to dictate the minutes, ma'am?"

"Dictate, indeed! I'll thank you to worry about your own duties, sir, and leave me to worry about mine." The school teacher's voice was tart but there lurked in her eye a certain sympathetic understanding of his meaning. "Do you think I have been composing poesy as I sat here?"

"Heaven forbid, ma'am! But you have yourself made certain unorthodox suggestions, to which we have most unorthodoxly agreed. I'm sure that our fellow members will agree that a good deal of this should be considered off the record."

Murchman nodded; Tolliver merely smiled his twisted smile.

Bourne noted their assent, and went on. He spoke smoothly, with a hint of mockery in his voice. "We made note of the absence of brother Pierce and discussed the business of Miss Rider's acceptability to the Board as assistant to Miss Ferguesson in the colored school. Miss Ferguesson has vouched for her ability to fill the position. We also noted that funds, as usual, are needed by the school. The Board is in agreement in all matters, including the fact that Michael Bourne is going to look into the matter of brother Pierce's neglect of his duties"—the Irishman rose abruptly [illegible] give me the pleasure."

Miss Ferguesson rose, almost as tall as the Southerner. "It is not five blocks, sir," she said ungraciously, "and my feet are waiting right here." Her tone indicated that she would not like to be seen dead riding about in Tolliver's carriage.

Tolliver accepted the rebuff without apparent hurt. "As you wish, my dear lady," he sighed, "as you wish, but I am on my way to the St. James and Madam's is not over a block out of my way. Mr. Murchman, sir——?" he raised his eyebrows, bowing towards the surrogate. Mr. Murchman was small of stature and owned to so protruding a set of viscera that each step he took was a masterpiece of balance. He wore a yellow waistcoat snugly buttoned down the front and he had a habit of pulling at the points of this garment as though he hoped to correct their quite incorrigible habit of jutting forward. He bounded up now, ruefully displaying a small foot clad, as with a second skin, in patent leather. "Delighted, sir, delighted," he cried. "I never miss an opportunity of giving my own feet a rest." He tittered at his jest.

Bourne interrupted him quickly. "Perhaps, Mr. Murchman, you will wait for Tolliver downstairs, then. I have only a short time left me and I had hoped for a word with him." He glanced at Tolliver, who nodded briefly.

When they were alone, every sign of pleasantry left Bourne's face. He came back from the door and leaned against his desk. "I have a piece of information for you," he said. "Reed has succeeded in getting his hands on a shipment of arms."

"Can it be, sir," Tolliver said easily, "that you consider this of any interest to me? Governor Reed's trouble is in Jackson County."

"Would you pretend that the trouble in Jackson has sprung up independently? That there is even sufficient money to warrant or run an independent revolt there?"

"Even so?"

"Look here, Tolliver," Bourne said slowly; "I know a lot about your activities. I know that you take a 'paternal interest' in the Brotherhood of Lincoln. I know that when any agent connected with my own bureau comes from another section he calls on you before he comes to report to me. We all know that the Brotherhood is supposed to be back of the trouble in Jackson. Barns and houses have been burnt and murder has been done, yet in not one instance has a black man profited."

"Knowing the blacks, does that seem strange to you?"

"Yes, I'm afraid it does."

"Well, sir, your job is to worry about them. You are seriously mistaken if you think the matter is of concern to me. Now, may I remind you that Mr. Murchman is waiting?"

Bourne gestured quickly and Tolliver, who had been in the act of rising, sat back in his chair. He was dressed somberly in black and as he sat there, with his broad-brimmed felt on his knee, he looked more like a parson than the reputed wealthiest man in Florida. Sideburns molded his face, but otherwise he was smooth-shaven. He bent his head with a slight impatient gesture, as though he were ready to listen but not unaware of the time.

"The point, sir, is simply this," Michael Bourne went on quickly. "Your friends, the Brotherhood, are the implement; they do the burning, destroy crops, they are the labor that refuses at the last minute to carry out its contract."

Tolliver shrugged. "What do you expect? Freed slaves, one step from Africa! It is all very well for sentimental Northern women to weep in their ignorance and send their husbands and sons out to free their poor enslaved brothers—they have done nothing but give license to savages——"

Bourne grinned. "Save it, sir. Save it for a better audience. [illegible] I only want you [illegible]

[illegible]

"Land made valueless [illegible] of terror that is directed against them."

"And you tie this up to me?" Tolliver asked.

The other shook his head. "I make no statements of any sort now, I merely show you what I know. Governor Reed was refused help in Washington. When he applied for the State's allotment of arms he was blocked, when he went to Massachusetts for help someone was there before him. However, he has managed to buy arms in New York. They will be shipped through Jacksonville. If anything should happen in Jacksonville to stop their going on to Tallahassee I shall have the proof I want that there is a connection between Jackson County and Jacksonville. The rest will not be too difficult."

"Don't you rather weaken your case, sir?" Tolliver smiled coldly.

Bourne shook his head and grinned again, but no shadow of good humor lurked in his eyes. "Six of one and half a dozen of the other," he said. "I am interested in seeing the arms go through —but I am also interested in an inquiry into your affairs. Either the one happens—or, if there is trouble in Jacksonville or Duval County at all, I intend to rip down your little structure, Mr. Tolliver, and examine its component parts."

"Dear me," Tolliver said, "I do think you are violent, sir, as well as abusive. But I suppose that one must forgive you for the commendable interest you take in your work. I only wish that you did not have such an erroneous set of ideas about me, but, well, well——" He stood up, and now the commissioner did not detain him. "Poor Mr. Murchman, I hope that he has not given me up. Good day, sir, good day and a pleasant journey to you."

He went down the long corridor that connected Bourne's office with the offices of the Freedman's Bureau. James Cutler stood in his door but Tolliver went by, barely touching the brim of his felt in acknowledgment of the other's greeting. At his carriage he apologized to Murchman with a swift gesture that dismissed the apology. As he was about to step into his carriage he hesitated, drew from his breast pocket a heavy silver card-case and a silver pencil. On the back of a calling-card he wrote "A. Rider, Esq." in a script which, even with the handicaps under which he labored, was thin and precise. On the face of the card he wrote again rapidly and, when he had done, he looked about. A small colored boy squatted by the side of the building. Tolliver drew a copper from his pocket and signalled with it. The boy rose with a graceful lack of speed and came grinning towards the coin.

"Do you know Mr. Rider, boy?" Tolliver asked.

The boy ducked his head towards the Freedman's building. Tolliver nodded and handed him the card and the coin. "Take this to him without getting it dirty, and perhaps he will match your penny."

The boy pocketed his coin with enthusiasm and held the card gingerly in front of him, as though it were a poisoned barb.

"It occurred to me," Tolliver said, stepping into his carriage, "that it was time I asked Rider and that girl of his to take a cup of tea." He didn't say more but gave directions to his groom. And he did not suggest that Mr. Murchman should join his little tea-party.

At the St. James, where he proceeded immediately upon the delivery of Mr. Murchman's person at his own door, Hains Tolliver repaired to his room. He removed his hat, coat, collar and tie, laid them with fastidious neatness upon a chair. Thus prepared, he set about removing the filth of Jacksonville from his face, hands, neck and ears with the hot and cold running water which the St. James supplied in an enamel plumber's basin to every room. Cleansed to his satisfaction, he rubbed himself with a smooth towel and anointed his hair with cologne. Then he put on a fresh shirt and, taking from the satchel that stood by his [illegible] Byron ever penned.

He was interrupted once by a house servant with a message from Mr. Rider, and he took the opportunity to order tea to be served at five o'clock on the east piazza.

Tolliver's tea was, in a sense, the beginning of a new life for Kate. Like the embowered Lady of Shalott, she ceased looking at shadows and looked boldly down to Camelot.

She came with her father, having first dumped upon her bed the batch of books Miss Ferguesson had pressed upon her. Each was neatly marked with a slip of paper. There was a prayer to memorize, and certain indicated pages to be studied in order to refresh her memory on the subject of numbers and the various and sundry uses of a grammar book. Kate had not so much as glanced at the school teacher's flowing script. Tea was more important and, with her blue organdy ruined, she had the hard choice to make between the ginger frock in which she had travelled, a white eyelet and a Christmas green trimmed with red fringe. She held the eyelet before her for a wistful moment, and saw hereself quite charming in it. But it was a garden or an evening frock, and she put it away firmly. The ginger, she decided, was tired, and the green looked wintry. Still she had only worn it twice and the green straw sailor that went with it became her. Her aunt had made the dress for her from a *Godey's* pattern and it was smart and very grown up, though Kate did not realize that the sailor undid the art of the dress and made her look half her age instead of twice it.

They rode to the St. James in Hains Tolliver's carriage and Kate sat very primly, with her hands in her lap and excitement burning in her cheeks and eyes. At the hotel her father helped her down and she walked ahead of him up the steps of the piazza, suddenly diffident and frightened, but holding herself as stiff as a poker to hide it. The front piazza was crowded with a rich assemblage of Federal officers and expensively clad civilians. There were even a few Northern women come South in the wake of Harriet Beecher Stowe. They were obviously Northern by the wealth of their dress and accouterment and the gaiety of their tone and, obviously also, by the frequency and loudness with which they used her name, they were admirers of Mrs. Stowe. Overhearing them, Kate felt suddenly native and angry at these aliens in her land. With the help of anger her poise returned like the flow of blood coming back into a sleeping limb. She held out her hand to Tolliver, who was coming through the crowd to them, and when he had greeted her father she let him take her hand again; and, tucking it in the crook of his arm, he led them to a quiet end of the east piazza where a tea-table was laid out.

Her father eyed the tea askance, as though he did not quite believe in it. Tolliver laughed, not missing his look, and when he had seated Kate behind the tea urn, he signalled a boy and suggested that Rider and himself might find more enjoyment in something stronger.

But, first, he accepted a mild cup of tea from Kate.

"Tea should be weak," he said, "and unadorned."

"Like a beautiful woman," Archibold Rider added, heroically refusing a cup. "Now I myself am afraid of beautiful women. I admit to it. Their very weakness puts me in a ferment of terror."

Kate bent her head over the tea lest they see her blush. A beautiful woman unadorned was an indelicate topic for conversation in her presence. Her father was not always predictable in the matter. Her aunt had often to correct him for this very fault. She remembered his saying once in a solemn lecturing way, tossing out his hands like the Reverend White in his pulpit,

"They do say that women marry for two reasons, for love and for money. But I give it to you that they marry for a third. That they shall have somebody to do up their stays for them." Aunt [illegible]

She turned to her host. "It must be lovely at [illegible] Morgan tells me that it is the prettiest time of the year."

It sounded obvious, but she didn't mind that. She wanted to visit Mandarin, and her father was too slow for her.

Hains Tolliver smiled. "It is lovely indeed, my dear Miss Kate. I have so wanted you to see my home. I had thought to wait for the first school holiday, so that Miss Ferguesson could accompany you."

"Miss Ferguesson!" Kate cried quickly. "Oh, but I don't think she'd even want to come."

"Kate," her father admonished gently.

Kate dropped her eyes to hide the expression in them: I'm being rude and yet I enjoyed it. Like the day I slapped that girl. Something happens to me.

"I am sorry," she said demurely. "But Miss Ferguesson is very set in her ways and I do so want to go."

"And come you shall, my dear little lady," Tolliver said with a smile, having seen the flash in her eyes before she dropped them. "Surely, sir, you're chaperon enough for your daughter. And then there is Halla."

"Who is Halla?" Kate's eyes were boldly up again.

"An old servant. She wouldn't leave me for all the emancipation proclamations in the world. Oh, it's not devotion," he laughed. "Halla is smart. She knows she's mistress, always has been; and she doesn't ask better than to run me!"

Kate laughed too, crediting him with modesty.

"Of course," he said easily, guiding the conversation, "there is always a certain amount of devotion. A slave who was treated with consideration doesn't forget. He may go wild with the idea of freedom and start wandering. Nearly all of them have done that. But you don't find the trouble around the plantations at Mandarin, for example, that you find in some sections. Jackson County, for one."

Archibold Rider let the boy refill his glass. "Shocking," he said. "I hear that Permann was fired upon, wounded."

"Yes, it is shocking. But then the situation is not without cause. Here, we are noticeably peaceful."

Archibold Rider looked at his host in some surprise. "Well, sir, we do have the Federals," he gestured.

"And colored troops garrisoned at La Villa, and, if you will pardon the term, the town seething with carpetbaggers, and the townspeople petrified with hatred and fear. There's room for trouble, sir. In fact, there is something definite that I am worried about. Something that I believe you can handle."

Kate put her cup down, as though holding it impeded her hearing. Her father had merely nodded without speaking.

Hains Tolliver said, "Governor Reed is going to handle the trouble in Jackson County in the only way he can, with the State militia. Arms are being shipped South and are due to go through Jacksonville. The date doesn't matter. What does matter is that this shipment will undoubtedly be protected by Federal guard from the moment it comes into Duval County until the moment it reaches its destination. And a Federal guard will attract the notice of the interests which do not want the guns to arrive safely. I put it to you, sir, that there will be fighting in Jacksonville, fighting of the worst sort, against the Federals. By good behavior we have almost won our release from occupation—such a struggle would put the cause of freedom back indefinitely—and then there is the honor of the city."

Archibold Rider had leaned forward during this speech; now he said, "And what would you advise? A shipment of that size can't get to Tallahassee without coming through Jacksonville."

"True. But it can come quietly. In the back door, so to speak. No guard, no fanfare. Just in and out of Jacksonville, as though it were a shipment of cotton. Secretly and expeditiously. The Governor gets his guns and Jacksonville retains her honor and, what is more important, I am not ashamed to say it, having been [illegible]

"How you can help?" Hains Tolliver smiled. "As commissioner for the Freedmen, you have the respect and the ear of General Houstoun. I should not say that we had discussed the matter. The army is, I find, prejudiced to the opinions of a Southerner, however he may have the welfare of his city at heart. But the General should be advised, sir; he should indeed."

Archibold Rider pulled at his mustache. "I don't see it so simple an issue, sir. The shipment itself would certainly be safer if guarded, and the town is so alive with soldiers that it would surely take a larger force than the troublemakers can have at their command to so much as make a feint at an attack."

A look of impatience flashed in Tolliver's eyes. He shrugged. "Logic," he said coldly, "does not always follow the path of fact. There will be serious trouble, I feel, if that shipment is brought in bristling with Federal guard. It is perhaps hard for you of the North to understand, but we still suffer from our defeat and any honest Southerner will go far to prevent even a small skirmish. We have had too much."

"Yes, I can understand your anxiety. Perhaps it would be well to discuss the matter with General Houstoun."

"You mistake me, sir."

Kate looked from one to the other. There was a smear of excited red in either cheek and her eyes made open surmise of what she heard. Mr. Tolliver wanted something and her father was being over-cautious.

"I am in a position to know things, let us say to hear things that would not normally come to your ears. Do you grant me that, sir?"

Her father nodded quickly. "Believe me——" he started, but Tolliver interrupted with a certain gentle peremptoriness.

"You might almost say that I brought you South. I certainly sought you out, because I knew of the position that was to be filled and, as an interested citizen, I wanted to make sure it was filled by a man of integrity."

"Sir!" Rider cried, but Tolliver went on, holding out his hand.

"Your success in the South is important to me—and, believe me, sir, I would not advise you ill."

"Indeed, but I should never question that."

"Then it is settled. In your position as commissioner I should brook no discussion; put your advice to the General strongly and let it go at that. He will make up his own mind. But the army are not people to discuss things with. They are bred on orders. Although you cannot order the General, you can put it to him in language that he will understand."

He turned to Kate and smiled, his eyes cold, as they were indeed at all times, but his smile was friendly. "To pleasanter matters," he cried gaily. "Let us plan our little trip. And your pardon, Miss Kate, for so serious a conversation."

Kate's own smile came slowly. Like the fabled Lady of Shalott she had looked down to Camelot and, if curse there was to be, it had come upon her. For she had seen in the tense conversation something that her father had not, something she was sure that Hains Tolliver would not have chosen to have her see. She thought that Hains Tolliver wanted his advice taken for other reasons than he had given. And she thought that he did not want her father to think this. She was surprised to find herself neither shocked nor displeased but, on the contrary, only full of expectancy.

"Oh, but you mustn't ask my pardon," she cried, "political talk is so interesting."

Her father smiled. "That was scarcely political talk, child," he said indulgently.

Both of the men laughed and Kate smiled demurely, but in her heart she was thinking, "Men are very simple indeed."

That evening, after supper, she took the mess of school books from her bed and made her way to Miss Fergusson's room. [illegible]

Kate opened a grammar at random. In a few minutes she said: "Do my children know their alphabet?"

"Children! They are, of course, but you'd best remember that most of your pupils are, in years at least, older than yourself. As to their alphabet—some do, some don't!"

"Oh, well, what shall I do first?"

The teacher looked at her thoughtfully. "Best try them out for a week, get used to them, see what you think yourself. That's always the best way to teach, by understanding what your pupils are going to be able to learn!"

"Oh, very well." Kate studied her book for a few moments, then she lifted her head abruptly. "Would you say that Mr. Tolliver is a friend of Governor Reed's?" she asked.

"Humph!" Miss Fergusson was startled. "I should say that he will be glad enough if someone can think up a good way of sending Reed to Halifax!"

"What is wrong with Governor Reed?" Kate asked simply.

"Good Heavens, girl," the teacher scolded, "better ask what is wrong with your fine Mr. Tolliver."

"He is a very clever and a very distinguished gentleman," Kate answered with angry vehemence, and the teacher smiled and said nothing. It was a point of argument between them, in which neither had any hope of convincing the other.

For a while Kate turned the pages of the grammar with a concentration which was satisfactory to the school teacher, and when she was ready to go to her room for the night Miss Ferguesson smiled upon her.

"Eight in the morning, then, Miss Kate, and pleasant dreams to you."

Kate went soberly. Something was wrong. Mr. Tolliver did not love the Governor and the little bits of the puzzle did not say that he worried overly much about the honor of Jacksonville. She thought wistfully of Mr. Morgan. He was the kind who worried about honor.

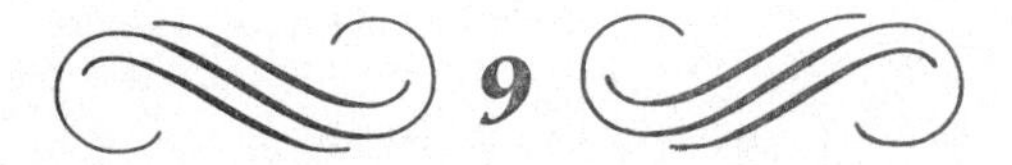

9

ON Thursday evenings, the colored children were put to bed early and the women went into their cabins and pulled the shutters to and barred the doors. And on Caroline Street and Church and Duval, white children were put to bed early and the window shutters were pulled to and barred. In this house and that, yellow strips of light showed through. Some women sat in the dark, those who had no man in the house. Others sat by their lamps and sewed quick, tight little stitches, and they cast anxious glances, from time to time, at the angry pacing men whom they were still blessed to have by them. It was not a day when you could count your blessings as durable things to be hidden away, like family silver, from the looters. An angry man was a vulnerable man and you could never know what would happen next.

Miss Janey Wilson was unable to bear Thursday evenings in a manless house. When George Morgan could not come in to spend the night with them, she would have Crockett pack a satchel and they would go to spend the night with Colonel Morney and his daughters, who were, in any case, kinsfolk and owed them shelter. She and Crockett would help the Morney girls with the bedspread they were making. They would talk softly of the small news of the town and the up-river plantations. Now and then some word would drop that would lay bare their thoughts and feelings. And, across the hall, in his study with his son-in-law, the Colonel would pace back and forth, fingering his gray mustache and eying fiercely the shadows on the wall, where a fine collection of firearms had once hung.

"Colonel MacKenney and one of his daughters was killed [illegible]

drive 'em crazy, to boot."

"This Thursday night business! By Gad, sir, it'll end in massacre, mark me."

The men were silent, suddenly aware that the women no longer chattered at their work. The Colonel cleared his throat with a long rumbling, grating sound and laughed harshly.

"I had a letter from Anthony today," he said loudly, as though wilfully to erase with his voice the alarming words he had been guilty of. "The Governor has been called upon to let the niggers into first-class carriages, hotels and boarding-houses. They'll try to get him on that one. He daren't say yes, and if he says no they'll call him a slaver and accuse him of discrimination against enfranchised citizens."

The women commenced to chatter again, quickly and nervously. Later, when they had put out their light and retired to bed, Colonel Morney leaned close to his son-in-law's ear and said in a deep whisper.

"Reed's got his guns."

The younger man lit a fresh cigarette from the one which he already held between yellow-stained fingers. The Colonel scowled. His son-in-law smiled sourly. "Better an effeminate cigarette than a cheap cigar, Colonel," he said.

The other shrugged. "Since you can't get a good cigar, much less afford one, you can give up smoking."

"About these guns. Who would you say they are going to be used against?"

"Reed means well, but he is in the thick of thieves. I should say that the guns will only make things worse."

The younger man said impatiently, "He should license every home-owner to use a gun on his own land. As it is, every scallawag and carpetbagger has a gun and there's going to be a militia to protect them."

The Colonel pulled at his mustaches and said softly, "The guns haven't been delivered yet, now, have they?"

Across town, down black streets that were empty and silent, the dust packed hard by a hundred bare foot-marks, the Methodist colored church was dimly lit. The sentinels were at their posts and President James Cutler glared through the slits of his black hood at a sea of frightened faces.

"They're bringing guns in," he shouted at them. "What for! Do you want to know! It's to put you back into slavery!"

A moan rocked the room.

"You know what they call you? Animals! That's what. Animals in the form of men! Savages! That's what. They say you need to be beaten. To be made into slaves again. Remember that, when they come talking pretty about votes. Governor Reed is no friend of yours. No sir, he's the one is bringing in the guns. The Brotherhood of Lincoln is the only friend you have in the world, and why is that? Why, now," he screamed at them, "because the brotherhood was started by the President himself, and he's your true friend. Now that it's getting time to vote, he sends word to you what he wants you to do. Vote! Is that much for a friend to ask! Vote—get out there and vote Republican!"

The brothers cried out and waved their naked arms in assent.

"Now then," the President said, rapping his gavel for order, "there's some work open, out in the fields. Nobody's asking you to break your backs; just go take it easy like. Anyone who wants to work go around to the Freedman's Bureau tomorrow. Bring fifty cents with you. Fifty cents a job. You'll get good salaries.

And the bank needs more subscribers. It's your bank. You niggers got to support it, see. You ain't good Republicans if you don't put money in the bank regular. It's your own Freedman's bank. And what makes a good Republican is money in the bank. [illegible]

[illegible] let a nigger go to [illegible] quaking in their breeches and yelling murder!"

"I hear Reed's bringing guns down. Got thrown out of the Ordnance Department, and Governor Andrew of Massachusetts and Fenton of New York both turned him down. But he's got them just the same. Some firm in New York."

"The war'll start all over, and I want to get out of this hell-hole. Hasn't a girl spoken to me in two years."

"Two thousand stands of muskets and Enfields and four thousand rounds. Not a war!"

"No, by God, but trouble. Someone ought to blow the shipment up."

"Hell! Let the Governor have his round of trouble. There are a few he could shoot down with impunity, a little bloodletting I'd like to join in myself."

"Sure, you don't like women anyway. What's it to you if we get stuck here another four years!"

A bottle flew across the table, knocking the speaker hard on the side of the head. There were shouts and jeers and laughter, and a lively medley of bodies and furniture being pushed aside.

"Clear the way, clear the way."

"Give them space."

"Make it fair, sir."

"Gentlemen, gentlemen, no fighting. Please, gentlemen!"

Somebody threw a bottle at the big swinging lamp in the

center of the room, and the bar of one of the most expensive hotels in town presently became a shambles. The bartender crept out a back door and went around the building to an entrance that admitted straight to the office of the proprietor. The proprietor was a small dark man with a large dark mustache. He was quietly ensconced behind his desk and quietly busy cutting a large cigar. He heard the bartender enter and looked up.

"The bar!" the man cried in distress, and he gestured excitedly. "They're tearing it to pieces."

"Soldiers?" the proprietor asked. It made a difference. You couldn't get anything out of civilians. But the Government always paid. When his man nodded, he said briefly, "Send a boy around to the barracks for help and go fix up that cut on your head."

"But they'll break everything in the place!"

"What do you expect me to do? Go in there and ask them to be careful? What started it?"

"I dunno. Something about Reed. He's bringing down a shipment of arms."

"That so? Did you hear when? Or how many?"

"Hell, I didn't listen. They're always talking about something."

"It sometimes pays to listen. Get on with it now. Keep your ears clean in future."

The bartender went out and the proprietor sat rubbing the back of his neck thoughtfully. Jacksonville was a good place in which to keep informed. There was sometimes a price for information. And even if there were not, there were friends to be won.

10

MICHAEL BOURNE looked around him, his blue eyes narrow and keen. His horse ambled, seemingly without direction, the reins knotted on his neck. They were twenty miles north of Jacksonville on a path that ran high and dry, like a causeway, through the cypress swamp. The trees straggled out of the swamp in careless giant fashion and there was little or no underbrush. Three hundred yards beyond the nearest tree, their ranks closed in and the eye could not penetrate.

[illegible]

interested. And then, at the last minute, he had mentioned this time and this place. If the Colonel should change his mind he would come here, and now. If!

Bourne turned in his saddle and swept the track behind him, and the swamp and the jungle, with experienced eyes. He had fought over this land. He had pursued over this very causeway the man he hoped to meet. But he knew that you didn't learn the swamps so easily. Dying, or close to dying in them, was not enough. You had to be born within their wet boundaries to know them. So he was not surprised when he turned back and saw, on the path ahead of him, the figure of a man leading a horse. He had come out of the swamp at some point where passage was possible, though the ignorant eye would never have advised it. Bourne dismounted and walked towards the man, studying him curiously. Colonel Dickinson was becoming a legend—this slight dark man, with his stiff leg and his weak eyes. He wore a uniform that, despite stains, was clean and neatly mended.

Neither man spoke until they were upon each other and then the Colonel said abruptly, "What do you want?" ignoring the hand that Michael offered.

"Your help, Colonel—and I think to be of help." Michael thrust his hands into his pockets. He didn't blame the Southerner. He had made a gesture, but he had expected the rebuff.

"There is nothing I can do to help you. And the only thing

you could do for me would be to get out of Florida—with your friends."

"That wouldn't help you as much as you may think."

Dickinson shrugged. "What do you want of me? Jackson county is no concern of yours."

"I asked you to come because I think it is. I've talked to Saunders up there. He thinks with you." Bourne grinned. Dickinson was not likely to want to be found in agreement with the carpetbag District Attorney of Jackson county. "But things are too bad to be segregated into little areas. There is a disease running wild in this State, Colonel, and it's going to set Florida back a hundred years unless we all get together and stop it. Wait!" he cried as the other would have interrupted. "I fully understand that you think that you are fighting it yourself. But Hell's bloody delight! You are fighting blind, without discrimination, without knowing who your enemy is."

"It does not take a brilliant man to know who the enemy is, Bourne," the soldier said bitterly.

"I put it to you, Colonel, that you are being used by your own enemy."

"I think that I am the best judge of that."

"I don't think that you are. Certainly I cannot know all of your problems or your aims. But I can, from where I sit, see a great deal that goes on that you cannot see. How would you like to hear that Hains Tolliver sent Cutler up to Jackson two weeks ago? The Lyons place was burned down immediately after, was it not? A black preacher was hanged. Saunders lays that at your door. It would be more convincing if it hadn't been a preacher. The preacher was a fellow by the name of Pierce. He comes from my yard, so I went up to look around. I don't know what he was doing in Jackson. I think he was taken there. The Lincoln Brotherhood didn't like him. They also don't like you."

"I didn't hang him."

"I didn't think so."

Dickinson looked up sharply, as though something in the other's voice were a warning to him. "I have a long way to go,

Bourne," he said, "and I want to get there before morning."

"I understand. I didn't come to talk about Pierce. I merely wanted to point out that a lot of your trouble up there comes from Jacksonville. When you get a packet of money, or a wagon-

[illegible]

Jackson and I will keep away from you. If you come looking around there, it will be your last trip!" He bit his words off, lending them an added violence.

Bourne shrugged, and now his own face was hard. "I would ask you to go to Governor Reed and offer him your services. He needs a militia. He needs coöperation. I believe he would take you on and that you could do a great service to the State. But you would have to work with Saunders. You could not ride around meting out your own justice. With coöperation like that we can clean up county by county. The State will have a chance to get back on its feet."

"You have already talked to Reed?"

"I have. He agrees with me."

"Then you may tell him from me to go to hell or Wisconsin. He'll never get a Southerner to work for him."

Bourne looked at the other helplessly. This was a man he would have liked to have on his side. A fine soldier and a rarely true human being. But he had let a hard unreasoning core of bitterness grow up in him. A posse would get him some day, if he didn't die first of starvation, or of snakebite in the swamps.

"I am sorry," he said. "I had hoped that we could bring an end to this."

"And I," Dickinson said quickly, as though he were sorry himself, and surprised at his own emotion. "I am sorry. Under other circumstances, Bourne, you are the sort of man who might have worn the gray. Under different—but there is only one way for the thing to end." And he held out his hand as abruptly as he had offered his words. The two men shook hands and then swung into their saddles and turned their horses, the one to the north and the other to the south, without further speech.

Michael did not look behind him. He knew that he was being watched. That, however the Colonel might trust him, there would be men with rifles, ready and perhaps even aiming at him. He had expected that at least. He had also expected the failure of his mission, and yet he was bitterly disappointed. Wherever he turned, he met defeat. If he tried to line up the new elements, men who had come to Florida, as he had, after the war, they slapped him on the back, swore that they were with him and went their own way. Which was whatever way money was to be picked up the quickest. But at least they never disappointed him. He had, he thought, to try them, but he never expected anything of them. A man like Dickinson was another thing.

Bourne was, and he knew it himself, both too big for his job and not big enough for it. To discover why a woman's body was floating in the river, or to track down and prosecute a horse thief was work that he would not be bothered with. If the sheriff could not do it, then to hell with it! At the moment he was not interested in crime, either in preventing it or in cleaning up after it. He was interested in seeing a certain unity of purpose in the State. With the judges and the D. A.s sticking together, the sheriffs could be forced into line. At that point the prosecution of crime became reasonable, and only then. And, at that point, crimes against the State would be on the decline. Men like Tolliver would probably always find ways to draw the blood of the country, but men like Cutler and Hess would be behind bars before they could tip their hats.

Bourne pushed his own hat to the back of his head and gathered up the reins. It wasn't ideal. He wanted Tolliver. He knew that, even without help he could get Cutler and Hess. But he knew also that they would be replaced as long as there was a Tolliver. Without help, he would never get Tolliver. Or if he got the man, he would still not get the system. It would take another form of civilization to wipe out human leeches. Yet he was not asking for the impossible. He wanted only to win the battles of his own day. A man like Dickinson could have made it at least closer to possible that Hains Tolliver should some day [illegible]

a few others like him. As to Rider, perhaps he could warn Rider in time. For the little commissioner was obviously a dupe, obviously innocent, and obviously getting himself deeply involved.

Bourne thought of Kate and swore softly. Her piano had just arrived from Hartford—an expense which Rider could not have honestly earned. Bourne knew that Kate was lonely, blocked every way she might turn. She had given up looking for her house, admitting to herself that it could not be found. And now she was teaching for Miss Ferguesson. It could be, for her, nothing but an unpleasant occupation. Her days spent in a close room crowded with sweating blacks. They would not understand her and she would not understand them. But it would take up her time. Without willing it, he pictured her standing before his cabin at Mandarin. The grass ran down to the river and the big trees stood like kindly umbrellas in the way of the sun. Kate had her sleeves rolled high and she was smiling. As quickly as it had come the picture faded, running like water-mist into the steaming swamp.

Michael Bourne knew about women. Enough, he thought, to know that he was not in love. But there was something about Kate Rider that made him want to give her what she wanted. She wanted a house, and he had a house. But away out in the country. It was no place for her. She also wanted companionship. It would be good to give her that. He was a fool, Christ and was he not! Where was the time coming from to give her companionship? Some day, he thought, some fellow is going to grab her up in his arms and he won't be worrying about whether he has time or not. Not with that girl! He frowned at the tuft of hair between his horse's ears. "It's time I took her out a bit. She's lonely, that's what, and I am a selfish hulk!" And he grinned, not deceiving himself a bit, and he kicked his horse up and set him to cantering down the causeway. He would not get back till late. But there was tomorrow. Tomorrow would be a good day in which to relax.

The next day, when he asked for Kate, it was to learn that she had gone to Valhalla and would not be back till the end of the week.

"You'd think she was going to Heaven!" Madam said; "all stars and champagne, la petite."

"Good," said Bourne, but he scowled blackly and he did not take the day to relax.

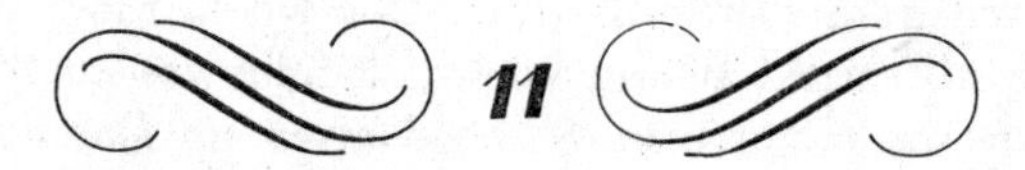

11

MISS MAMIE DELAHANTY parted the porch vines cautiously and stared at the passing carriage of Archibold Rider.

"Humph!" she said, "I'll bet that fellow didn't have two cents to rub together, back where he come from. And just look at that girl of his, sittin' up like she owned the air."

Miss Mamie's hands were thin and yellowed and the skin covered her bones loosely like an over-sized glove. Behind her Crockett Wilson said suddenly:

"They're not freckles, they're liver spots."

Her voice was loud and clear, and the small company on her mother's porch turned to her in surprise.

Ossian Delahanty said, "Come now, Cousin Crockett, give the devil his due; that gal has the finest complexion I've ever seen excepting your own, Cousin."

Crockett was silent, her eyes riveted on Miss Mamie's yellow-spotted hands. Miss Mamie started back, and an angry flush crept into her sallow skin.

"Well!" she said under her breath, and turned her back on Crockett. "I'm going," she said tartly, taking up her mittens and

[illegible]

food he got now didn't seem just right for him and he was downright flabby. Miss Mamie shook her head; she liked big men but she liked them firm-fleshed and ruddy. Mr. Delahanty had been firm-fleshed and ruddy. Miss Mamie could bring back the memory of the feel of his body till, if she wasn't careful, she'd start blushing. Not the sort of thing you should think about in public, but, once the thought came, there it was. A man with great, firm, ruddy flesh had the power to make a woman feel mastered, and that was something Ossian would never do. Poor boy, it wasn't his fault. She watched with tight lips as he ogled his cousin. He had always adored Crockett, and for no good reason as far as his mother could see. Crockett had never been kind to him, of that she was sure. Not that she wasn't up to spooning with a beau in the garden or down by the river. But Crockett hadn't seemed to care much for Ossian. Well, look at her now, crazy as a coot. Let Miss Janey say what she pleased about the girl tippling, Miss Mamie had her own opinion. Where would she get anything to tipple, ask yourself! The girl was crazy. Maybe she *had* been raped. There had been dark days and no one would ever know just what had happened, excepting Miss Janey and she'd not tell. Maybe there'd been a baby. Maybe, right now, there was some little mulatto toddling about with Crockett's fine eyes in its head. Miss Mamie could feel herself shudder, from the inside out. They said if you had a black child any child you ever had would be marked, tainted. She wished

Ossian would stop ogling. It made him look like a fool. And then, with the girl so crazy, she might take him.

Miss Janey rocked her fat body easily too and fro and watched Miss Mamie with a little smile tucking up the corner of her lips. "Bothering 'bout Ossian and Crockett," she thought. "If she only knew!" Ossian looked so like a barnyard pig, not a rangy razorback but the kind that got larded up proper. Miss Janey never looked at him without picturing him standing, at the age of three, at his mother's breast. He didn't look much different now, only bigger. Likely, Crockett had the same thought.

"It's warm," Miss Janey complained, fanning at her open throat. "I'll be glad to see the rain."

Miss Mamie nodded. "The gardens are burnt to a crisp."

"Humph. With the care they get, it wouldn't matter much."

Miss Mamie pursed her lips. "That carpetbagger's girl had twenty-seven blacks fixing up a garden alongside of the school. That's her idea of how to teach. She'll have flowers and greens the year round."

"So I hear," Miss Janey said. And, leaning forward, she went on, "There's Cousin George now. Cousin Ossian, go help him, he's got packages, seems like."

Ossian Delahanty got up reluctantly. Crockett had been murmuring to him in an inaudible but soothing undertone all of the time, stroking his hand with her frail fingertips. Ossian helped George tether the horse and take his packages into the house and then he came back onto the porch and stood sullenly by while his seat on the swing was taken.

"You're that good to us, Cousin George," Miss Janey was saying. "Looks like you've brought a might."

"Eggs and some greens and a piece of pork. There's more than you can use, Cousin, but likely Miss Mamie would care for some."

"Indeed and I would!" cried that lady, bringing her thin hands down upon her knees in emphasis. And she beamed upon the company with lips surprisingly full for so angular a person.

"That's fine, Miss Mamie." George turned from her and took Crockett's limp hand in his. "Are you feeling the heat, Cousin?" he asked softly.

The girl didn't answer but looked at him from beneath half- [illegible]

The people on the porch were silent, making no effort to cover up their thoughts. George Morgan said, "They are going out to visit Hains Tolliver, so they tell me."

Miss Mamie sniffed. "I didn't see any lady in the carriage to act as chaperon. But, then, I reckon they don't know better in the North."

Crockett said quietly, "Mr. Hains has still got Halla out there, he told me."

"That witch. She'd know more about running a disorderly house than chaperoning a lady." Her mother stopped abruptly and stared at Crockett. "Crockett," she said, "when did you see Hains?"

"I saw him." Crockett smiled.

"Did he—give you anything?"

"What, Momma? What would he give me?"

Miss Mamie stirred uncomfortably. Ossian had an ugly red swollen look about the throat. It made him look aggressive. She said, "Ossian, come take your poor little ole momma home, she's right tired."

Miss Janey got up quickly, too quickly. "I'll get the things for you." She went into the house and came back in a few minutes with a fiber basket. Ossian took it and said good-by to Crockett, who smiled up at him silently and patted his hand.

Miss Janey took Miss Mamie's arm and walked with her towards the steps. "Better send Ossian up-country for a bit," she said quietly. "He's been over three times in the past week and, well, I told you about Crockett."

Miss Mamie stiffened, and her friend said quickly, "It's just for Ossian's sake." Well, it was her duty to say that much. She didn't have to say more. Not "Crockett is contemptuous of Ossian, just as she is of herself—so she is comfortable with him. She doesn't have to pretend. She does, with George, because she loves him; she doesn't want him to see what has happened to her."

When the Delahantys had gone, Miss Janey went into the house. Crockett was all right with George and she liked to leave them alone a bit. There'd be no spooning with George, no quick trips to the hall closet only to stagger back to Ossian's fat pattings, and in broad daylight too! Miss Janey shuddered. She stood for a stealthy instant by the hall closet and peered into its neat hideyhole. She could not see anything, but she knew it was there, somewhere. Take away the liquor, and Crockett would drink cologne; take away the cologne, and she would drink spirits. Take everything away, and she'd likely go crazy. Miss Janey closed the door softly and went to put up the food George had brought with him.

Back on the porch, she found George and Crockett still side by side but silent. George had a hard, drawn look about his mouth and he no longer held Crockett's hand.

"Well, Cousin," Miss Janey said brightly, "what's new with you?"

Morgan shrugged. "I came in to see Rider. Looks as though I should have stayed at home. Still, there are always things I can do. Michael's got an order of tobacco plants coming down and I want to inquire about them."

"Tobacco, at Mandarin!"

"No, he's bought up some land at Madison."

"Humph!" Miss Janey snorted. "For taxes, I expect."

"Well, at least he didn't order the sale. And as long as somebody is buying——!"

Crockett said, "It's a shame, a shame," and two large tears glistened in her eyes without falling.

"Now, Crockett," her mother said quickly, "you better go in and lie down a spell."

"Yes, Momma." Crockett got up quickly and went without speaking to her cousin, though he held the door for her and

[illegible]

"But why would he? Miss Janey, it doesn't make sense. It's weakness, and Tolliver, for my money, has no weakness."

"He's fond of her!" Miss Janey shook her head and rocked in silence for a bit. Then she said slowly, "Aunt Bessie used to say his mother was like that, after Hains came along. She was only fifteen. Well, lots of girls marry and get their children young, but they say Rosaleen was frail and a pure-minded girl and not in love. They gave her alcohol to help kill the pain, and after that she came to depend on it. She never liked her baby and couldn't stand her husband. She was a quiet one and, first off, they just thought she was ailing from child-birth. When her husband caught on, he had every bit of wine in his cellar destroyed and when she still found ways to get it he locked her in her room."

"So she killed herself," George Morgan said softly. "I never heard why."

"Yes. You see, I keep remembering all that."

"Miss Janey," her companion said, looking down at her, "how did Miss Crockett—why——?"

Miss Janey's soft face was cold and stiff for an instant and then she gave a lost little shrug that disturbed her fat shoulders like a ripple breaking on a swollen sea. "Some people," she said, "can't accept life. Crockett was splendid when things were bad, but I reckon she never quite faced what was happening. Later, she had to face things, and she couldn't. She used to talk in her sleep a lot. You couldn't tell much what it was but I think she was trying to go back. To go back to before the war and have it all happen different. You couldn't blame her for that."

"No. No, you couldn't," her cousin said in a slow, dissatisfied voice. Hard little muscles jumped in the side of his cheek. "Miss Janey, do you think it would help Miss Crockett if we were married soon."

"I don't know. I don't, really. And then there are other things to consider."

"Yes, of course. I haven't much to offer a wife." He turned and paced angrily down the porch and back again. "If only I could get somewhere about Valhalla. They're going to try to impeach Reed, I've heard. It means he'll be too busy to do anything. I tried to talk to Rider—it's not his department but he's honest and he has influence. But he's been warned off!"

"Another bunco," Miss Janey said. "I always knew he'd turn out that way."

George shrugged. "He's not a bad sort, really, but he's swamped. He doesn't know what it's all about. In any case, he's not an active man by nature, but he has a fine hand with words. 'We in the North are alive to our responsibilities, sir,'" he mimicked, putting his hands behind him and teetering on his toes. "'Our hearts bleed, bleed, sir, at the injustices which are the natural wake of war.'" Morgan was silent suddenly. He went to the swing and sat down, leaning forward and resting his arms on his knees.

"And——"

He shrugged. "He thought he was being kind. I told him that I had heard it before. Not very diplomatic but, Hell, he and his North are likely to bleed to death, and they don't take care! All I want is to see those papers of condemnation. You wouldn't think that was asking too much. I've every right to see them."

"Maybe he has been bribed."

"I doubt it. Still, Tolliver got him his post. Rider is the kind who would rather believe his friends than someone else, regardless of where the truth lies. Besides, I've an idea he doesn't know what to think. I'm sure his heart does bleed! But when you try to pin him down, he brays about like a wounded ass. I've broken the law and I'm not willing to pay the penalty! My land was confiscated by due process of law, and that cannot be reversed. If it was done in my absence, I am reminded that [illegible] liked to have brought Miss Kate to call."

"George Morgan!" Miss Janey cried.

"She is lonely and, then, it has occurred to me that she might prove a salutary companion for Miss Crockett."

"Well, I will not have a Northerner under this roof. Not even in the garden," Miss Janey said pettishly.

"I suppose not," her cousin said, taking up his gray hat and twirling it on the head of his cane.

"Indeed not! I do not understand you, young man. You forget."

"No," he said, getting up, "I don't forget a thing." Not Valhalla! Not a single flower in his mother's garden, not a horse in his father's stables! Not the stately *Morgana,* which carried their lumber North to market, and, loaned to the Confederate navy, was sunk in the Battle of Jacksonville. "Looking back," he said, "is part of our lives today. But it is not good enough unless you go back."

Miss Janey's rocker was still. "It is not a question of looking back," she said; "it is a question of looking around you."

When he would have spoken, she raised her hand. "Now, no more of this. It is a subject which I will not have discussed on my porch, Cousin."

"My apologies, Cousin." He smiled, and Miss Janey said, "Granted, Cousin, granted"—with a hurt little sigh. "We will think no more of it."

But she did. Long after he had gone, she sat on the porch and thought of her husband and of her son and her daughter, of the rotting remnants of char that had been her house and of the sawed stumps of once green trees. "I scarcely blame Crockett," she murmured at last, "I scarcely do. With none to choose between but a lover who all but licks the Northern boot and a fat parasite who sits on his mother's porch and complains."

She got up and went to the porch steps and looked up and down the street. No one was in sight, and presently she sighed and went back into the house and the chair that she had recently left rocked for a moment with the energy of her going.

12

ON the day when Miss Mamie Delahanty parted the vines to see Kate Rider and her father go by, Kate had been teaching for nearly a month. Miss Ferguesson doubted that it could be called teaching. Their two classrooms were log cabins covered with boarding and set face to face across a dirt yard at the edge of Nigger Hill. Children and grown pupils mingled in both classes, separated only according to their degree of knowledge or the lack of it. Miss Ferguesson's pupils sat with punctilious stiffness upon their benches and recited the wisdom of the Bible, and McGuffey's Reader, or chanted upon request their tables, weights, and measures or such rules of grammar as made a memorable bit of poesy. In Miss Ferguesson's class, school opened with a prayer and closed with a prayer or a psalm read aloud. It might be said that, in Miss Ferguesson's class, order preceded learning, and the switch more than the book set the standard for each day.

The first day at school, still shy and nervous, Kate put upon the board an alphabet that was somewhat irregular and wrote, beneath, a list of words in capital print, all rather too close together. Then she went and sat at her table, which faced the rows of backless benches her pupils were to occupy. When they came, she heard them in the distance, whooping and singing, but as they approached the cabin their noise died down, and then they were there, crowding about the door and peering in at her shyly.

[illegible]

She was their book learning. She was putting the old bottom rail on top! And they were like children pleased at a pretty sight. But their greetings went over her like waves, and she could find no words to answer.

"Sit down," she said at last, and prayed for Miss Ferguesson to hurry, for the older woman had promised to settle her own class and then to come and start her off. Miss Ferguesson was apparently equally anxious, for she came soon, her skirts hurrying about her feet like leaves before a busy wind.

The giggling and chattering in the room was stilled at once. Miss Ferguesson frowned on Kate and the room alike. "Stand up," she said with some asperity. Kate and the class rose as a man, Kate blushing and suddenly angry, the colored people shuffling and hanging their heads. Against the far wall, a big Negro lounged. His head was tilted to one side, showing a purple welt where one ear had been trimmed close to the bone. Miss Ferguesson's eye went straight to him.

"What's your name, you, over by the wall?" she snapped.

He put his hand to his chest and the teacher nodded, "Yes, you."

"John," he said.

"John what? And say 'ma'am' to me."

"John," the black man said sullenly, "is all I is gwine ter tell you."

"All right, John," said Miss Ferguesson, "out you go. Right

out of this school. If you don't have better manners at your age, there's nothing we can teach you."

"Make me!" John said arrogantly. "This here school is a free g'ment school fo' us, an' you has gotter teach all us as wants lernin'."

Miss Ferguesson's face was red and hard with anger but, before she could move or speak, Kate had snatched up the pointer from her desk and descended upon the black man. "Get out," she said, her voice low and tense, and she brought the stick down on his shoulder and neck with a force that whistled upon the air.

The big man threw up his arms to defend himself, and cried out once. But he made no other effort to avoid the beating he was getting, and when Kate stopped, he let his arms drop and stared down at her a moment. Then, slowly, he grinned and said,

"I is John Bever, ma'am, and I 'pologize."

Kate looked at him for a long minute, then she shook her head and said, almost reluctantly, "I am sorry, John Bever. But you will have to go." The tips of her fingers tingled and her face was white with excitement and fear, not of the black man, but of herself. For the second time in her life she had struck a human being and had liked it. "Anyway," she said, "you're a big man, you should be working."

A flicker of his old arrogance shot through John Bever's eyes. "I is free," he said, "I doesn't have to work never no mo'."

"Well, then you don't have to eat either," Miss Ferguesson said from the platform, and she came down the aisle towards them. "Enough of this. Out you go, John Bever, before I call the soldiers."

John Bever went reluctantly. But he went, having first startled the older teacher by sticking his chin out at her with a sudden threatening gesture. Then, with a sheepish grin at Kate's raised stick, he ambled out of the room. Miss Ferguesson hurried back to the platform, Kate thoughtful in her wake.

"Does anybody wish to leave now?" Miss Ferguesson snapped.

Nobody did.

"Well, then, I want all the children out here in front." She turned to Kate. "Get them seated according to height, then try and get names from them. This has taken me from my class too long already. It's going to take you the rest of the morning to [illegible]

did not know how to sort themselves out. She thought a moment, and then she rapped on the desk. The room was instantly quiet.

"All the children out in the yard and play, until I call you," she ordered. When they had gone, she separated the men and women and then went down among them herself, sorting out the tall and the short and seating them. There were fifteen adults in the class, and seventeen children, and she spent the day coaxing names and approximate birth-dates from them and making them memorize their places, go out of the room, form lines, come back to their places, children alone, women alone, men alone, and all together. It was a day of confusion. In three days' time, they could come into the room in orderly line and take their proper places without fuss or noise. On the fourth day, Kate turned to the blackboard and with a sweeping gesture erased every word and letter she had written on it.

"You all know where school is," she said. "You know how to behave in school. Your names are on the roll. Now, every one of you, go home, and bathe, and wash your clothes. I'm not teaching animals." And she marched her bewildered class out of the cabin and locked the door.

Miss Ferguesson had no complaint to make about this procedure. But when August ended and most of the adults had left Kate's class, complaining that they had to work too hard to stay in it, while those who remained knew more about hygiene than they did about the alphabet, she shook her head. Michael

Bourne was pleased with Kate's work and would not let the teacher complain.

"She can't spell," Miss Ferguesson told him. "She counts on her fingers, and her grammar is almost as bad as theirs."

But Bourne only laughed at her. "You knew she wasn't a schoolmarm, now, did you not! And sure, ma'am, it's not school learning is needed by the poor benighted creatures so much as learning how to live."

He had heard of Kate's victory over the big black man, John Bever, with great amusement, and that a week later she had taken him back into her fold. Miss Ferguesson did not like it. "That big brute!" she protested. "It is dangerous, and bad for discipline too." But Michael shrugged and Kate would not listen. The so-called victory over John Bever had left her with a sense of dissatisfaction. The way that he had taken his whipping had haunted her. So one day she had gone up the hill to find him. "Come back to school, John Bever," she said; "I like you and I will teach you." And he followed her down the hill with such a look of pleasure and humility that Kate felt herself burn with shame for her share of throwing him out of school.

Jacksonville turned its back neatly on Miss Ferguesson, an outcast, not by virtue of her calling but by virtue of having lowered it by teaching black people. Upon Miss Kate they stared aghast. All the pent up energy of her months of idleness and loneliness found vent in the need she saw before her. She worked her pupils until they said that she was driving them like slaves. Certainly she had no mercy upon their constant fatigues and miseries. At school they made gardens and kept the cabin in repair, cut out patterns and mended clothes. And in the morning they brought their homework down from the hill, a carding of cotton, a length of stuff or a dress finished and on the worker. Most of the adults did drop out, but those who stayed were rewarded with a smile and a lesson, their alphabet, or a few words spelled with at least phonetic accuracy, a few numbers added up with the help of ten fingers. And those who stayed away were repaid by a visit from their teacher. She would trudge up the hill, find out their cabin and go through it like a small cyclone.

"Open those shutters!

"Throw out those mattresses! Burn them!"

"Here, John." And the big black man, John Bever, who [illegible]

landed running, its hard little hoofs tearing at the earth and its high child-like voice screaming iniquity. The black man roared with big short cough-like laughter, and the owner of the pig scolded helplessly.

For, with John's loyal bulk to back her up, the hill people were helpless in Kate's determined hands. She made them scrub and burn and air. When she would at last go down the hill, she left them in a state of reluctant order and great discomfort. John Bever, her guardian angel, would retire with a grunt of satisfaction to a hammock slung beneath his own porch. From here he would watch through half-closed lids the sullen glances, listen to the mutterings directed at him. He would push idly with a big pink-soled foot, having removed the shoes that Kate had given him, and grin at his black girl down in the yard stirring at a pot of pork and grits.

It was in the midst of these activities that Kate closed the school for three days and went with her father to Mandarin. It was her first visit and one which she had been looking forward to ever since her arrival in Jacksonville. Miss Ferguesson protested feebly. "A school is a serious business, miss," she said, though she doubted whether Kate's class could be called a school.

Kate shrugged and went. "I've left them plenty of homework," she said, and turned her back on the older lady's look of prim disapproval.

Tolliver sent a carriage to take them to Mandarin, and they

left Jacksonville at a smart clip. But, once the ferry was well behind them, the pace slowed to a fast walk. They had twenty miles to go and the groom saved his horses for the home stretch. Madam had sent a lunch basket with them, while Archibold had thought to bring a little flagon along, "to relieve fatigue, m'dear."

His fatigue was well relieved before they came into sight of the white gate-posts of Valhalla and Kate could barely arouse him.

"Papa," she whispered urgently, shaking his arm, "Papa, do wake up. Do look, Papa, we're there."

Archibold Rider opened his eyes reluctantly, closed them, opened them again and shook himself with one long-sustained shudder that brought him upright in his seat.

"Ahumph, m'dear, yes indeed," he brought his voice back into use with these simple words and looked sideways at his daughter. "Little snooze," he said.

Kate looked at him reprovingly, and then she smiled and immediately her father smiled back at her. "Fine-looking groves," he said, encouraging her to forget the matter.

The drive was straight, from the gates to the house in the distance, and on either side stretched acre upon acre of orange trees. The trees grew in precisely planted lines, each tree carefully pruned up the middle and falling, on every side, close to the ground like a leafy umbrella. All about, the ground had a loose combed look, with not a tuft of grass to be seen. Kate grew dizzy watching trees go by, and looked ahead eagerly to see what the house would be like. When they came to it she was disappointed, for, though it was an imposing structure, it was ugly and harsh. It crouched like a monster in the center of the groves and there was not even a border of lawn to soften or brighten its appearance. It was a large house, and square, with two stories of porch on all four sides and a railed deck in the center of the roof. The tops of two or more large oaks showed beyond the deck, and Kate hoped that on the far side of the house there would be flowers and a lawn.

They were met in the hall by a black woman whose gaunt

body was covered from throat to toe in the stiffest of black taffeta. She had on a white turban and, when Kate's eyes had become accustomed to the dim light of the hall, she saw with a sense of surprise that the colored woman wore at her throat a heart-shaped brooch of [illegible]

[illegible]

sir. If you will come this way, I will apprise the master."

She led them into a large reception room which must originally have been intended for a ballroom, for it took up an entire side of the house, and the floors, which were inlaid with four different kinds of wood, were hard and smooth as marble. Halla left them here, and Kate sat down on a horsehair sofa and, suddenly and unexpectedly, she smiled. Her father went to the fire which, despite the warmth of the air out-of-doors, was needed in this room. And in all of the high cool room, only the fire gave a living touch. The walls were an old purple and the woodwork polished oak. There was gold damask at the windows and there were ancient Chinese rugs on the floor. Over the mantel, the white face of a Spanish or Italian gentleman stood out from a dark, almost undecipherable canvas, one hand resting at his side and the other on the hilt of his sword.

"It's lovely," Kate said aloud, "it's lovely."

In a moment, their host was with them and Kate saw with quick delight that he had dressed himself to resemble as closely as possible the portrait over the mantel. But with his clothes any resemblance ended, for he bore no slightest likeness to the hawklike man who dominated his reception room. Hains Tolliver's face was white enough but soft, and where the man in the portrait had hot eyes in his sharp face, Tolliver's eyes were gray and passionless.

Halla came behind him, bringing a tray of decanters and small glasses.

"Welcome, my friends, welcome," he said, and he held out his hands to Kate and took hers persuasively as though, instead of hands, they were little frightened animals. "I hope that you had a pleasant journey," he said, "and that George brought you at a considerate pace."

"Indeed, sir, indeed," her father cried heartily, and Kate listened with amazement as he discoursed about a journey through which he had slept almost entirely.

"Papa," she said pertly, "was quite overcome, I assure you, sir."

Halla served a sweet wine to them as they talked, and then she went out of the room. But, later, she came back and stood in the door.

"If Miss cares to come, I will show her to her room," she said.

"Miss Kate," her master corrected, looking across at the colored woman, with a strange expression in his eyes. Half wilful, half cruel, like a child, Kate thought, who is about to pull the legs off a fly, and knows that he should not.

"Miss Kate," the colored woman repeated, but Kate never heard her use the name again. Halla never again addressed her in her master's presence, and behind his back Kate remained Miss and knew that she was being insulted without knowing how or why.

She followed Halla reluctantly. In the room prepared for her, she found her things unpacked and put away, and her white dress, already freshly pressed, hung on the wardrobe door. An empty tin bath stood before the hearth. There were no windows in the room but four tall glass doors, now shrouded in blue and silver brocade. Kate would have pulled the curtains back but Halla's cold voice stopped her.

"The curtains will keep out the late sun," she said. "If Miss will rest, I will bring her bath later," and she put Kate's bonnet and gloves away and commenced to unbutton her dress. Not until she had seen Kate on the bed, with a coverlet over her, did she go out of the room, closing the door carefully behind her.

Kate sat up at once, threw back the cover and, making a face at the door, flew across the room to pull back the curtains. Her room opened onto the second-story piazza and from it she could see the lawn that she had hoped for [illegible] her petticoat, and she tiptoed quickly back to her bedroom. It was a dainty room; the mahogany bed was hung and covered in the same blue brocade that draped the glass doors, while a pale Aubusson covered the floor. Kate forgot Halla and went back to bed. She was tired and it was pleasant to lie back and look at the room.

It's a lady's room, she thought, a queen's room, and she wondered about the rest of the house and longed to explore it alone, with no one watching her. While she thought of it she fell asleep and, sleeping, she dreamed. She was a bride, a beautiful bride dressed in yards and yards of billowing blue-and-silver brocade. She was going to marry George Morgan, and all of Jacksonville was there to see her married. The aisle that she walked up was green and interminably long and when she came to the end of it, Hains Tolliver and not George Morgan awaited her. All of the joy in her changed to sudden terror, and she turned from him to flee down the aisle, only to find Halla blocking her way, with her arms crossed and her lips thin and hard. She was Halla and yet Kate seemed to know that she was someone else. She was saying loudly, "My curtains, my curtains!" when, as suddenly as she had fallen asleep, Kate awakened to see the black woman standing by her.

Kate sat up. "Oh, I've been sleeping," she said, filled with elation at finding her dream a dream only.

"And dreaming?" Halla said, unexpectedly. "It is a room of dreams. The master's mother dreamed of her death here, on this bed."

Kate shuddered, and then looked crossly at the colored woman. "I don't believe in dreams," she said firmly. And she thought with sudden surprise: Now she does look like somebody and I should know who!

Halla did not answer her. "Your bath is ready, Miss," she said.

"Well, then," Kate said, "if you will leave me I shall have my bath."

But Halla made no move to go. "The master sent me to attend you, Miss," she said calmly, and once more Kate felt her skin prickle, as though a spider with cold little feet had crept across the nape of her neck. She looked at the black woman, no longer shy but all at once hard and clear in her mind. Abruptly, the memory of slapping the colored girl on the hill came back to her. What was her name! She couldn't think. Her eyes on Halla, she knew that she would never dare slap her. Kate stood up. "Very well," she said coldly, "attend me," and as the woman approached her to unfasten her petticoat, Kate said:

"Unfasten my petticoat!"

Halla's eyes glittered sharply, but she undid the petticoat with deft fingers.

"Undo my stays," Kate said coldly, and she stood with her hands at her side and allowed herself to be undressed, forestalling with an order every step that she could think of until she felt that she could see the colored woman tremble with rage.

She hated me the minute she laid eyes on me! Kate speculated idly, and wondered why. Then she dismissed Halla from her mind and concentrated fiercely on the house, so ugly outside and so beautiful within. It was a house, Kate thought, of which she should like to be mistress. Later, she stood midway on the circular stair, quite still for a moment, in the grip of a desire stronger than anything she had ever felt in her life. Instead of the white eyelet gown that she wore she saw herself in a purple velvet evening gown, created to harmonize with the reception room. Her hair was piled high on her head and she wore a diamond pendant at her throat. The picture changed in a flash, and she was crossing the hall in a green riding habit. The front door was open and lawns now stretched down among the groves, and a groom waited patiently with her horse. She [illegible]

[illegible] arm and wished that he were Bourne or Morgan, and then she remembered her dream and shuddered.

"You are cold, my dear young lady," he said, "the fire will warm you," and he led her into a small room at the end of the hall, where her father awaited them, a glass in his hand that glittered in the firelight like liquid rubies. A piano stood at one end of the room and over the mantel, flanked by mirrored candelabra, was the portrait of a young girl. She wore the dress and coiffure fashionable forty years earlier and she was as frail and transparent as though she were painted in wax. At her throat she wore a brooch which, Kate saw with quick amazement, was either the replica or the very one now worn by Halla.

"My mother," Tolliver said, misreading her expression.

"A lovely woman," Archibold Rider said, twirling his glass slowly and looking first at the frail girl in the portrait and then at his daughter. Excitement had heightened the color in Kate's cheeks and, though she was by no means so beautiful a creature as the painted woman, she looked in every way a richer, warmer and more desirable companion.

"She was very delicate," Hains Tolliver explained. "She came from Georgia. My father built this house for her, modelling it after her own home."

"She must have loved it," Kate said softly.

"She would have, yes, she would have, my dear Miss Kate, but she never lived to enjoy it. She died at the age of sixteen."

Kate looked back quickly at the portrait. So this was the master's mother, who had dreamed of her own death in the brocade bedroom. Nonsense! Kate told herself firmly. Halla was an evil skulking witch trying to frighten her away.

"I hope," Tolliver was saying, "that you will play for us after dinner, Miss Kate."

Kate accepted a glass of cordial and glanced towards the piano. Candles stood at either end and there was music on the rack. "It will give me great pleasure," she said. "Do you play, sir?"

He nodded. "Sometimes I, sometimes Halla. Halla sings also, though her voice is overlow for a woman."

"Amazing woman, sir," Archibold Rider said, his face looking round and surprised. "Ahem, for a colored woman, that is."

"Yes, but then my father bred Halla up for a special purpose, and the result is not in truth so amazing. He needed a housekeeper and some entertainment, and he saw no good reason to import some harsh spinster relative to make his life miserable for him."

"Still, there must have been years——"

"Indeed, but then he travelled. Halla was sent to a school for quadroons, in New Orleans. She is a highly bred race of Negro. She was twelve when she came home to take over her duties, and she has never been away since. Perhaps I should not say never, for once, she came to France with us. Certainly her education has been exceptional."

Kate wanted to say, "And your father gave her your mother's brooch, and she resents guests in your—her house."

"By the way, Tolliver," her father said suddenly, "I had intended to tell you, I talked to General Houstoun——"

Kate drew a grateful breath, for in the instant Halla was expelled from the room like a wraith before holy water.

"I'm inclined to believe that he agrees with us. The less fanfare attached to the travels of those guns the better."

Tolliver nodded. "I'll be interested to hear his final decision. I think, myself, that he is wise."

Kate sat down and smiled sideways into the fire. Hains Tolliver was making it look as though the thing were of little concern to him, as though indeed it were not his idea at all. Her father already half believed himself responsible. Papa was the honest type, he was not clever like Hains Tolliver, but Kate [illegible]

B[illegible] with Spartan promptness if not Spartan fare. There were oranges on the table, and mandarins, sour cherries, and bananas imported from the south. There were hot cakes and sausages, hominy and pork gravy, and biscuits served with sweet butter, and orange honey.

"It is a shame to get you up so early," their host apologized, "but the day on a plantation starts early. I had thought that you might care to drive about the place, Miss Kate, while your papa and I talk business."

"I should like to," Kate said.

"Good, then, Halla will go with you." He turned to the servant who stood by the sideboard. "Tell Halla to prepare herself."

Kate drummed unconscious fingers on the table and Hains Tolliver smiled as though he were answering her unspoken protest. "It would not do to have you ride alone."

Her father nodded, and Kate said quietly, "It will be a pleasure, I'm sure."

She took a long time in preparing herself, because she knew that Halla was ready. Then, having behaved badly, she was sorry and went quickly to the carriage, intending to make it up to the black woman. "I've imagined things about her," she decided, "that couldn't really be." After all, to be born a slave and raised like a lady, practically, and then suddenly to find yourself free, with no home and no people unless you're willing to remain a slave! It would be hard. Kate was full of repentance that disappeared by degrees as she rode along with the colored woman opposite her, her commanding shadow falling upon Kate like a pall.

"Come and sit beside me," the girl cried at last. "I cannot see a thing."

But Halla shook her head. "It would not do," she said, and was silent.

Kate turned her head away and studied the groves through which they were passing. They had come upon a swarm of half-naked black men who were working among the trees. A solitary white stood with his back to the road and a gun held low and easy but looking as though he was aware of it and might at any moment use it. A round of rope hung loosely from his belt. Kate said softly, "I thought there were no more slaves."

"There will always be slaves," Halla answered unexpectedly. "These are convicts, they're slaves of the State. The State rents them, but the State is not to blame for them. They are slaves because they are not strong enough to be masters."

For a moment the black woman's face had been harsh with passion, but in an instant it was still and cold and she said, "Where would you like to drive, Miss? We are coming to the end of the line."

Kate was sorry. She wanted to hear Halla talk, but she was half afraid to question her. "Could we go to the old Valhalla?" she said, "I have heard of it." But Halla shook her head. "It's boarded up, the master would not like us to go there."

"Well, then, let us drive to Mr. Bourne's place."

Halla looked at Kate for a moment and, whatever she intended to say, she said, "Yes, Miss," and directed the driver to take them to the Irishman's place.

The Bourne place was up the river and across two fords that bridged a span of swampy land. With Valhalla's groves behind them, the growth was thick and the land uncared for on either side of the road, and Kate felt as though they were driving into the wilderness. A pile of whitewashed stones marked the beginning of Michael Bourne's grove. There was no fence here, and no gate posts. A dirt road bent in among the trees and, though these were well cared for, there was not a single black man in sight at work on them. Halfway to the house they found George Morgan completing the binding of a [illegible] sweep her whole being.

"The house is just a cabin," George Morgan said, "a working camp. It could not please you, Miss Kate. Let me show you the new trees instead."

But Kate waved the trees aside. "I have seen nothing but trees for two days, and I should dearly love to see your house."

Her companion was silent and Kate, who had gained confidence from her firmness with Halla, commenced to feel less sure of herself as his silence progressed.

"If you mind——" she said at last, almost timidly.

Morgan laughed. "Your pardon, Miss Kate, I was thinking of another matter."

"Oh."

"You should not go riding with that woman. Halla Tolliver is not a fit attendant for you."

"Tolliver!" Kate cried. "Is that her name!"

"Her given name. That's not unusual. But she is not just the usual servant."

"Yes, Mr. Tolliver told us."

"He told you?" The young man frowned.

"And he sent Halla to accompany me, and Papa thought it best too."

"Well, then," he shrugged.

"What is it?" Kate asked.

"Nothing more than a matter of taste, I imagine."

Kate frowned, uncomfortably aware that she agreed with him. "Are you working here all by yourself?" she asked brightly, to change a subject that she had no answer for.

He shook his head. "Too close to it, Miss Kate, but not quite. We are in a way, an old soldiers' home—confederates," he said shortly, as though he did not like to speak of it. And then, with a burst of generosity, he added, "Michael takes in any sick, down-at-heel fellow in gray who comes by. They work if they can—and they stay as long as they want. There are a couple in the grove now. But here we are. How do you like our house?"

They had come to the end of the trees. Some hundred feet away, a small brown cabin stood beneath a sheltering roof of oaks. Where the grove ended, a meadow of coarse thick grass grew up to, and past, the cabin, down to the river's edge.

It was a lovely piece of country and Kate caught her breath, but at the same time she was disappointed. He should have a house like Valhalla. He belonged to something big and grand. What was it Mr. Tolliver had said of George Morgan's father, "—a prince—" George Morgan was a prince himself. The grace with which he wore his shabby clothes and did his laborer's work made her want to weep. She said gently, "This was part of your old home, was it not?"

"Yes, the original homestead was not far from here." He pointed up the river. Beyond the acres of oranges sitting upon the land as precisely as though they were a thousand giant heads, their green locks neatly coiffured by some gigantic hand, rose a tangled mass of green. Cypress and oak and pine were knit together with suckers and vines, and the place looked impenetrable.

"My great-grandfather put his cabin there. It was not unlike this. It was his wife who named it Valhalla."

"What happened?"

"The Indians. It was burned. My grandfather built the present Valhalla. No, not Hains' place—that was called Hains House in the old days."

"Oh," Kate said softly. Her companion frowned at the pity in her voice.

"Hains bought Valhalla; he had the right to use the name as he would." He turned his back on the river and faced the girl.

Behind them, the wheels of the carriage [illegible]

[illegible] must have been a lovely house and a lovely life.

The carriage was not yet in sight, and Kate said impetuously, putting her hand out to Morgan, "I wish I could stay here. I could keep house for you!"

He laughed at her. "You would get a bad name!" he said.

"It wouldn't be ladylike, I suppose!" Kate stamped her foot. "I'm sick of being ladylike, and I don't care what people think." She was as angry now as she had a moment ago been sorry. Perhaps *because* a moment ago she had been sorry. And because, too, she had said something very young and they both knew it.

George Morgan took her hand. "You shouldn't have come, Miss Kate," he said. "This is no place for you."

"It could be." But the moment she had said it she was sorry. She did care what he thought, and he would think her very bold. She withdrew her hand, blushing. The carriage had turned the bend and was upon them, and Halla was watching.

"This piece of Valhalla," he said gently, "is Michael Bourne's. Over there it is Tolliver's. I have nothing, Miss Kate, except a memory. People with memories are old, and not good company."

Kate's chin went up. What had come over her! She had come close to throwing herself at him, at this gentle, hurt Southerner whom she didn't really want at all. And who, apparently, wanted none of her. She said quickly, as though she would ignore the whole strange conversation, "Won't you show me your house?"

But he shook his head. "It is not a house that I can invite you into. We have only one room." He smiled at her, undoing the shortness of his apology.

If Michael Bourne were here, Kate thought with sudden clarity, he would ask me in, no matter how his house looked, or how small it was. And if Mr. Tolliver were here, he would whisk me away. Isn't it funny!

She gave him her hand and murmured conventionally. The warm and sudden impulse to go hide with him, to pity him perhaps, was gratefully replaced by clear cold logic. She did not belong here, it was true.

Kate climbed hastily into the carriage and all the way home she held herself stiffly, almost scowling at Halla. She could not rid herself of the impression that her visit had done some subtle harm. There was no visible sign of it, only the contempt in the eyes of the Negress, and the proud young man reduced to an apologetic smile.

He'll go back to his trees and forget that I came. Probably he was just annoyed at being interrupted, she told herself firmly. But she thought of him still, as the carriage had turned away, standing among his lonely trees, so thin, so intense, and somehow, she was sure, so hurt. And she thought of that surprising Yankee Irish immigrant, who gave hospitality to his old enemy. And the next day, when she was driving home with her father, she surprised him by saying suddenly, "Isn't it funny, in Hartford I didn't know any men at all, and now I know three."

"Why, you know more than three, baby," her father answered, and Kate let it go without trying to explain, not quite understanding what she herself meant.

Kate and her father stayed two nights at Valhalla, but they came back again within the month. Hains Tolliver talked for long hours with the father, but he found a great deal of time to give to the daughter, without seeming to single her out. He discovered her interest in her black pupils and heard about the man John Bever. He consulted her about a garden for Valhalla and showed her the walled hollow, now a grazing plot for sheep, where his father had started a garden for young Rosaleen Hains, whom he had married so far from her own home. And, walking or talking with her, Hains Tolliver was always watching Kate, quietly, as a trainer will [illegible]

[illegible]

in Florida, the only fine house, Michael Bourne had said, that was left in Florida.

There were convicts in the groves and black people in the house who were somehow too dependent to take advantage of their freedom. Well, why should there not be? Certainly there was nothing about them that was not legitimate. Her own father had twice signed for the release of county prisoners to Mr. Tolliver's groves. And the house servants were free. Once, she had asked why they stayed, when everywhere else former slaves had left even good homes. Hains Tolliver had shrugged and said in an indifferent voice:

"They know when they are well off. They must work anyway; they are paid well, and this is their home."

"Have none of them ever left?" she had asked, still curious, and he had said, "Yes," watching her now. "Once or twice we have lost house servants, if fools who do not know what is good for them can be called a loss. They were well dressed and fed and housed, and they were paid. They went out of weakness, they didn't want to work—and so of course they came sooner or later to trouble. And, strangely enough, they all came back with the work gangs—the only three who ever went. They didn't like it. House people don't like to work on the land."

"Did you take them back into the house?" Kate asked, but her host shook his head:

"It was the price for their actions. I am not a man to set myself up as God, Miss Kate, to reward and to punish. It was a philosophy forced upon us in the days of slavery. In this new world, a black man is no slave to be guided and protected but a free man who must make his own decisions and abide by the outcome of his own actions."

Kate was puzzled, but she still admired the man who had made wealth out of a condition that had spelled poverty to his fellow Southerners, and she knew that though he denounced slavery his freed and paid servants at least were aware of the dangers of freedom.

Kate didn't attempt to repeat her visit to Michael Bourne's place. She knew that she had been ashamed in front of Halla, and she resented her own smallness. That Halla, for all of her veneer, could not appreciate the spirit of pioneering men, or the beauty of a pioneer cabin, was after all understandable. The true humiliation had come in the realization that Kate Rider and Halla shared the same taste. Kate would have been pleased to have heard that George Morgan had won back his Valhalla, that he had torn down the shutters and wrenched out the bars that closed the old place to him, and taken it over as his right. Once, she would have asked her father to help him, but she had changed since she had come South. She had commenced to recognize the dream quality in her longing over the old South. If this Southerner could not take what he wanted, she might be sorry, but she would not help and, however she felt, she could not but admire the big indolent-looking man who had wrested Valhalla away and who looked as if he were going to keep it.

14

JOHN BEVER had not come to school for a week when he appeared, late one afternoon, just as Kate was preparing to go home. Her pupils had already gone. She was putting on her bonnet when she heard the door click, and looked up to find him standing there, his hand still on the latch.

"Now, John Bever," she cried with some asperity, for she had missed the big man, "where have you been, and how do you expect to learn anything if you don't come to school?"

The colored man shuffled uncomfortably. "Missy," he said, coming towards her [illegible]

[illegible]

how to find the next word.

"Work's not going to bring you any trouble, John."

"No'm. Hit's like this, ma'am. A white man's bin comin' around a-talkin'. They is sendin' down guns to shoot us up with. Gonna put us back in slavery, seems like."

"Nonsense," Kate snapped, but she sat down and stared up at him, her face as serious as his. She had heard talk of guns, and here it was again. "Who is 'they' supposed to be, John?" she asked.

"I don' know, ma'am. But they is sending them guns to the gob'ner."

"Look, John Bever, do you know how the governor got to be governor?"

"Yes, ma'am."

"Did you vote? Well, you see most of you colored people did vote. Now, why do you think a governor you voted for would get guns to put you back into slavery?"

"Missy," John Bever looked down at his frail little teacher and said earnestly, "John Bever ain't never bin no fool. Massa used ter say effen John warn't so big an' useful on account o' bein' so strong, likely he'd a bin a minister on account o' not bein' no fool. We bin hearin' laterly how de gob'ner has lowed we ain't good enuff to git on trains or go in no public places with white folks. All us niggers is good fo' is fo' to vote. Dis fellow down ter de depot wants us to take them guns and trow 'em off de train soon's we hit outta Duval County."

"He is lying to you," Kate said, "but if you believe him—why did you come to tell me?"

"Hit's like this, ma'am. I believes him, an' I don't believes him nohow."

Kate smiled. "That makes it hard."

"If he's talkin' true, whyfor he wants to pay us?"

"So, you are going to be paid—to save your own hide?"

"Yes, ma'am."

Kate looked down at her hands. In her ears she could hear the echo of Hains Tolliver's words: ". . . let it come quietly—no guard, no fanfare! Just in and out of Jacksonville, as though it were a shipment of cotton!"

He should be warned, and at once. Abruptly she drew a notebook towards her and, dipping her pen in the inkwell, she wrote quickly. When she had done, she tore out the sheet, folded and addressed it, and handed it to John Bever.

"Take this to Mr. Tolliver, John. He is in town tonight and you can find him at the St. James House."

The colored man took the note doubtfully, shaking his head but not saying anything. When he did move, Kate said with a sudden surge of fear, "John, did you know the white man—who talked to you? Had you ever seen him before?"

But John Bever shook his head and Kate drew a breath of relief. "Well, get on, then," she said, "and hurry!"

He went then. His footsteps shuffled on the boards, the door opened and closed and he was swallowed up in the silence of a black man's going. Kate stared so long and so hard at the door through which he had gone that she commenced to see a silver silhouette of the big man out of the corner of her eye. Despite John Bever's assurance, the doubt that had crept into her mind remained. That John Bever hadn't recognized the white man did not, after all, mean anything. The town was full of strange white men. And Mr. Tolliver had not, she had thought at the time and she thought it still, wanted Governor Reed to get those guns.

Kate locked up her small classroom and walked slowly across the yard. Not until she was halfway home did she remember that she was expected to walk home with Miss Ferguesson.

[illegible] not belong to the Irishman who strode about with a chip on his shoulder and talked of the future as though the present were merely a dirty place to clean up as one went through it. Valhalla belonged to a man who lived in the present; and whether he did or did not want something, Kate was quite willing to believe him right.

All about her, where bushes and trees invited, the evening was falling in uneven pools of shadow. John Bever had gone swiftly and there was not any sign of him. Two darkies hurried by her, going towards the Hill, and on Caroline Street a shabbily dressed white woman turned her shoulder. Only one thing troubled Kate, and as the evening wore on she became increasingly aware of it. If Tolliver did not care to see the guns go through, how was he going to persuade John Bever not to say anything? The black man had a native honesty that would not be easily appeased, and if he thought he was being made a fool of he was not likely to sit back and take it. So what was going to happen? For Hains Tolliver, on his side, was not going to be balked by a colored man.

When Archibold Rider returned that evening he found Kate sitting in the darkened sitting-room, a small lace handkerchief worried into a knot in her lap. "What's this, what's this!" he cried, coming into the room and rubbing his plump hands together. "Are you ill, Kate? Is anything amiss?" Kate's moods ran from gaiety to temper and she was rarely morose.

"I'm all right, Papa," she said, and got up to light the lamp. "I'm just tired, I guess."

But her father was still doubtful. "Then the work is too hard for you," he said wrathfully. "I've never seen you tired before, baby."

Kate smiled. "Perhaps I'm getting old, Papa."

"Perhaps you're coming down with something. Go to bed, Miss. We'll have Madam send up a basket from the cook house."

"Now, Papa!" Kate went to him with a sudden graceful movement and drew him to a chair; "you're the one who is fretting; I'm fine." And she smoothed his forehead and rubbed his temples and said artfully, "Tell me about your day." Then before he could say a thing she said, "Papa, would you say that Mr. Tolliver was a good man?"

"Good Heavens, Kate," her father protested, but he relaxed under her hand.

"Well, Papa!"

"Well, Miss, first tell me what you mean by good."

"Don't tease, Papa. You know! Miss Ferguesson says he is a scallawag!"

"Miss Ferguesson," her father censured, "is a very homely woman."

"But Papa . . . " Kate wailed.

"There is a saying, Miss, 'There is so much good in the worst of us, and so much bad in the best of us, that it doesn't——,"

" 'Behoove any of us to speak ill of the rest of us!' " Kate finished indignantly. "Papa, you're just no use, you won't answer anything."

"Hains Tolliver is a fine man and a loyal friend, Kate," her father said sententiously. "I don't know what has come over you."

What had come over her, indeed! To spend a whole evening fretting about a colored man who could take perfectly good care of himself. She dismissed the worry from her mind as firmly and relentlessly as she would have sent a disorderly child from the classroom. But for some reason not quite clear to herself she said nothing to her father.

That evening, Michael Bourne came pounding on her door.

"The *Fanny Fern* is going out at midnight," he called, "and there is dancing aboard. Madam says she will come with us if you would like to go."

Kate had pulled the door open, intent upon snubbing him this time. But [illegible] with him, and she got little enough gaiety. "I wish I could go myself," he said, but when they urged him he would not, pleading papers to attend to.

On the boat, Kate completely forgot John Bever and her worry. Michael Bourne was not accomplished in the waltz but when he whirled her in a reel she gave herself up to his hard arms and felt like a feather in the wind. He was surprisingly light on his feet for so broad a man, and Kate thought that she would never again be whirled so wildly and so gaily. Now and again he would leave her and say: "Now stay there and be good!" and look as though he doubted that she would.

Then he would catch Madam about the waist and whirl her and twirl her and prance her and dance her until the great piece of a woman was shaking with mirth and the tears running out of her eyes. Like Miss Ferguesson, Madam had an enormous liking for the Irishman, though her reasons were quite different. To be practical rather than to be principled was her ideal, and she found Michael both of these. *"Plus que ça,"* she would say. "He has the humors lusty, clear-cut and verrry masculine. And what more could you want of a man?"

Kate tapped her foot and clapped her hands and laughed with them and with the laughing, singing, shouting people about her. It was not a genteel gathering. Anyone who had a mind to pay his tick and come aboard was welcome. Even as she laughed, Kate contrasted this gathering and the stately flowing pace of Valhalla. Then she saw Bourne deposit Madam in the arms of a florid seafaring man, slap them both on the back, and come striding towards her, and she was acutely aware of a surge of excitement that turned her feet to lead. But in his arms she found wings again.

Bourne swung her into the heart of the dancers and then deftly away to the edge and around a corner. "That will confuse the old lady," he laughed, "—now she sees us, now she don't!"

"But——"

"No buts!" He took her hand and led her along a corridor until their passage was barricaded. "My friend the Captain," he said, "he thinks he can keep the people out, and this a free country!" And before Kate could protest he had lifted her over the railing and vaulted easily after her.

"Are we going to see the Captain?"

"We are going to the pilot house, from where we can watch him dancing with Madam. It will be a pretty sight, I promise you."

Kate giggled, and when he took her hand again her fingers curled unconsciously about his.

The bridge was deserted and in semi-darkness. Paper lanterns were strung across the deck below, and laughter and music were everywhere. On the near shore were the small yellow lights of Jacksonville. There was no light from the far shore, but on the river bright specks bobbed everywhere, night lights on ships at anchor and their own gay lanterns and jumping reflections in the water. A moon was rising, big and red, and Kate turned to Michael and said almost breathlessly, "Thank you for bringing me."

For answer he caught her to him and kissed her young lips, and Kate clung to him afire with a strange and wild happiness. His hands were tender on her shoulders and her neck, and he pushed the hair from her forehead and looked down into her eyes. She looked back at him with such solemnity that he smiled.

"You are growing up, little one," he said gently.

Kate thought: I should say, How dare you! and slap him

soundly and walk away. Instead, she just stared, and when he laughed softly and took her into his arms again she could feel her head whirl and her feet sink into the floor of the deck as though she were taking root. And when the whirling stopped, she found that she [illegible]

He grinned at her, and Kate stamped her foot. He was teasing her. You could not trust him for one minute. "I hate you," she said, meaning the words to be firm and clear. Instead, they came out in a broken whisper and she had to clear her throat ignominiously.

"As a matter of fact," Bourne said, leaning with one elbow on the railing and looking at her with startled seriousness, "it is just what I shall do! It's time I took a wife. I shouldn't be surprised if it made all the difference. The Southern branch of my troubles may still despise me, but if they see I'm settling down to stay with a nice respectable little wife . . . ! I don't know why I didn't think of it before!"

"Oh!" Kate cried inarticulately, and she whirled past him and fled down the stairs.

At the barrier he caught up with her. "Better let me help you over," he said, and he swung her up. But instead of depositing her on the far side, he held her, laughing at her. "Such an impetuous child!" he said. "Didn't they teach you that it is good manners to hear a man out?"

"Let me down at once!"

"You didn't let me tell you that I love you."

"You don't."

"Don't interrupt. I was going to tell you how our marriage would benefit me and how it would benefit you, and then I should have told you that I love you."

Kate struggled helplessly. "It would not benefit me at all!" she muttered. "You put me down this minute."

"I had forgotten how vain women are. It's amazing. No matter how young, the worst always comes out in them the very first thing!"

"My papa would horsewhip you, sir!"

Bourne laughed. "For proposing marriage to his daughter? Do you want to remain a spinster!"

"I won't, I promise you!" Kate cried.

He put her suddenly over the barrier but, holding her still, leaned over and kissed her. With a surge of venomous pleasure, Kate bit him.

"Christ, girl!" he bellowed, letting her go.

Kate giggled and started to run, but in a minute she heard his voice behind her. "Better wait, you're going to look a fool when you pop out on deck!" She stopped as abruptly as though she had run into a wall. Bourne was sitting on the barricade, not even trying to come after her. He got down and walked towards her slowly.

"Don't you touch me!" she said.

"My heartfelt promise! I wouldn't even marry you now. Not with your wicked ways. No man in his senses would!"

"I wouldn't marry you, Mr. Michael Bourne," Kate snapped, "and you needn't go pretending that it's you who wouldn't marry me!"

"So you think I would marry you!"

"I don't know and I don't care. I want to go straight home."

Michael walked by her side, surprisingly silent. And he did not tease her again.

When they found Madam she made no comment either on their absence or their expression. But she wagged a broad and playful finger at them and winked, and Kate wished ardently that the finger and its owner were at the bottom of the high brown river.

The next morning, over breakfast, her father told her that Hains Tolliver had called to see her. Kate smiled, feeling mysteriously pleased. She had come home the night before angry enough to throw things. And she had awakened remembering

Bourne's kisses and feeling very much the mistress of any situation that might arise. It didn't stand to reason, perhaps, but there it was. She wondered how it would feel to have Mr. Tolliver take the same liberty. He would not be rough and passionate, [illegible]

[illegible] offered to drive Kate home. He did not come into the room but stood in the doorway looking at her, with a fastidious expression, across the heads of her pupils. Kate dismissed her class at once. It never occurred to her to ask him to wait. As soon as the last of her colored people had gone, she locked up the room and came away with him.

Tolliver rode on his horse beside the carriage he had brought for her. "I am restless," he excused himself, "you will forgive me for not sitting with you." He rode close to the carriage, however, and conversed as easily as though he had been sitting beside her. "I hear you went aboard the *Fanny Fern* last night," he said. "I trust you enjoyed yourself."

"Oh, it was lovely!" Kate cried, and then, inexplicably, she blushed, and looked over at her companion. He was riding with an easy hand on the rein, but his expression showed no interest in her pleasures aboard the *Fanny Fern*. Kate dropped her eyes and, as though they were a signal, her spirits dropped with them. Just because a stupid immigrant chose to flirt with her it did not mean that a man like Hains Tolliver would find her of any interest.

She was silent for a while, and then she said quietly, "Did you talk to John Bever?"

Tolliver turned towards her with a little frown. "John Bever?" he asked. "Who is John Bever?"

"Didn't he bring you my note?"

"A note for me, Miss Kate? I am flattered that you should have chosen to send me a note, but I have not had one."

Now Kate frowned. "But—are you sure! I mean, of course, you must be. Still, it is so strange."

"Supposing you tell me about it."

Kate tried to explain, floundering a little because Tolliver continued to look at her with a half-quizzical, half-tolerant expression. As though she had been guilty of sending him a love-note and were now trying to explain her way out. It did sound far-fetched. Told by broad daylight, it sounded too dramatic. When she finally finished, he was smiling.

"These darkies, Miss Kate! It takes a Southerner to understand them. They love dramatics, the best of them. Your John Bever has been inventing things and, when faced with explaining himself to a man, he slinked off."

"Undoubtedly you are right," Kate said primly, feeling as though she had made a fool of herself. At least she had not gone as far as to explain to him her later fears and worries. What would he have made of them!

Hains Tolliver, on his part, was watching her shrewdly, for all of his careless pose. She is smart enough to be worried, he thought, but too innocent still to give her mind credit. Some day this would be an exceptional woman. She was not just a pretty little Yankee. In any case, she had never *been* pretty. He did not see why he always thought of her in connection with such words as *pretty,* or *lovely*—when she was alive, or touching, or interesting, but never the first two more acceptable words. He thought of her, not for the first time, as a mistress for Valhalla. She had been attractive to him from the first instant he had laid eyes on her, and once he had thought of her as a plaything, dismissing the idea as impractical rather than as ungallant. The idea that she might serve him as mistress of Valhalla, though it had occurred to him vaguely before, was now for the first time a full-fledged and practical thought. He looked over at her.

"Have you discussed the matter with your papa?"

Kate shook her head, but she did not say anything, unable to explain her silence even to herself.

"Perhaps it would be as well not to trouble him, Miss Kate. If the matter worries you, I will see what I can find out. But he has a good deal on his hands——"

"If you think so——," Kate agreed readily. It was no longer her problem, and she was [illegible] said, leaning [illegible] her from his saddle:

"When do you come to Valhalla again? We have missed you, Miss Kate."

Kate did not look at him. He had managed by his manner, almost more than by his words, to make her feel very foolish and small. Now he apologized, making her feel only the more foolish. She had started the day feeling very smart and important. She had even thought of Hains Tolliver—well, she had certainly been silly.

"I am sure that Halla does not miss me," she said tartly, and would gladly have bitten her tongue out to have the words back. For Hains Tolliver, Kate thought, must be monstrously amused at her words, and small wonder!

Tolliver, however, did not smile. "Has Halla been—rude to you?" he asked, his brows drawn together angrily. "If she has dared!"

"Oh, no!" Kate cried, startled at his look, "indeed not, sir. I don't know why I said such a thing. I sometimes have the impression that Halla does not like company, that is all," she explained lamely.

"Perhaps she does not. But it is not her place to give that impression."

"She has been there a long time—she must feel that it is her house almost——"

"I should not be surprised! Still, it is not." Tolliver looked over at Kate: she had forgotten her pique and was listening to him eagerly, as though she were a gay and curious child. "Unlike the blacks farther north," he said, "most of those in Florida are not more than a generation from Africa. It makes them more primitive."

"I can't think of Halla as primitive."

"But I can assure you she is. Polish has brought out nothing soft and civilized in her, I promise you. And then, Halla is different in other ways. Her grandmother was the daughter of a king and married, in her father's land, the biggest and wickedest slave-trader of all time. It was a marriage that you might have expected would mean nothing. But she must have been an exceptional woman, Anna Madagigine Jai. For Zephaniah Kingsley brought her to Florida and kept her by his side for the rest of her days."

"Then Halla is his daughter!"

"Her mother was his daughter. My father bought her. It is a strange story in itself. I must tell you about it some time."

"Tell me now!"

He shook his head. "There is too much to go with it. In a way, it is the history of my life." He shrugged. "Too long a story, Miss Kate. Compared with you, I am an old man—and we have come to your door."

Kate protested politely. She let herself be handed down from the carriage. She could not bring herself to say with any great enthusiasm, "Oh, but you're not old, sir, not a bit of it." For she was inclined to think that he was.

"You must come soon," he said, taking leave of her, "I shall make arrangements with your father."

Later, thinking over their conversation, Kate had a tantalizing sense of dissatisfaction. It was as though she were always on the brink of, but never quite arriving at, an understanding of Hains Tolliver. Something in the way he spoke to her, more than the things he said, should have meaning for her, and did not.

[illegible] organized sedition.

Miss Ferguesson brought the news to Kate, her austere face set in hard lines. "Murdered in our beds next!" she said. "It comes back to that namby-pamby man in the White House! What we need is a soldier at the helm!" She whirled on the class, "You Negroes, get out there and vote for Grant, do you understand! Vote for Grant, if you value your lives—just as likely to be tarred and feathered and run out of town——" and, having pronounced this grim piece of incoherence, she stalked out leaving a room full of rolling eyes and frightened faces. Kate stared after her, fascinated; she had never seen the older woman show such emotion. Suddenly she turned and erased with a stroke the small list of misspelled words which she had put on the board for her pupils to copy.

"It is a holiday," she pronounced. "Go home. Be sure you're on time tomorrow."

And she put on her bonnet, locked up the cabin and started off across town to her father's office. John Bever had not been wrong. Then where was he? Why had he not come back and why had he not gone to Mr. Tolliver with her note? She was puzzled and worried. She went quickly, driven by an anxiety for her father. She should have told him about John Bever. He had advised the general to let the guns go through Jacksonville without guard, and he was going to be badly upset at this news.

Across town, in the commissioner's office, Hains Tolliver sat at ease, his knees crossed and his long slender fingers brought thoughtfully tip to tip. From his desk, Archibold Rider stared at his friend. The muscles of the lawyer's face hung like wreaths at some unfortunate's door.

"It was bad advice," he said, and he looked away from his visitor, down at his littered desk. Too littered, he thought, and he looked up again. On the far wall was a large picture of Lincoln and, beneath, were bookcases filled with the dusty, rusty books that were the mold into which the Law was poured to jell.

"I feel that I should call upon the General."

"Perhaps you feel that you should send in your resignation!"

Rider let his fingers run over the wooden handle of a desk drawer. Inside, was a small flat bottle. It was not a time to think of such a thing. "It would be the honorable thing to do," he said, "the only honorable thing."

The other laughed. "Come, come, Rider," he said, "is your honor such a Spartan thing that it cannot permit a mistake?"

Archibold Rider looked up, suddenly hopeful. "Was it a mistake?"

"Call it bad judgment, if you wish. You acted for the good of Jacksonville. I am as much to blame as you," he said with a generous flourish of his hand. "But somewhere the news leaked out. Probably from the General's office. You know what the army is, my dear sir; an order must be handed from one person to another. A very hard thing to hush up!"

"Then why did you insist——"

Hains Tolliver leaned forward and said in a crisp voice, not at all his usual easy way of speech, "I have been over-patient, sir, over-patient! Your doubts become insinuations which I will ask you to withdraw. You remind me that I gave certain advice. Now I will ask you"—and abruptly he shrugged and smiled wryly—"could I have benefited by the poor advice I seem to have given you? I am not in arms against the Governor and my interests lie far from his bailiwick."

Archibold Rider's face grew red and he breathed deeply. "I have been a boor, sir!" he cried, jumping up and taking his friend's hand, "a boor and a fool, sir! The responsibility has quite undone me, I cannot quite—I beg your consideration, my friend!" The lagging muscles were back in place and his face was foolish with relief.

"Well then, it is done. [illegible]

[illegible] of surprise. [illegible] he said at last, "my daughter, I—she is over-young."

"Young, sir, but not, I think, over-young."

"This is very unexpected. The child is all that I have."

"She must marry some day. I can offer her a becoming position." Tolliver smiled as though he had decided upon a step and had no doubt as to its outcome. "Valhalla will become her. And, for my part, it is time I took a wife."

Archibold Rider looked at his friend curiously. Not a word of love or even of esteem. A man did not make such an offer without implying such a state of affairs. Southerners were supposed to be expressive on these subjects, and Rider found his friend's lack of ardor both surprising and unattractive.

"Perhaps you had in mind a different—perhaps, a younger son-in-law?"

Archibold Rider started at the other's voice. "Sir," he cried out with distress, "I am not a father of the old school. I shall make no choice for my daughter. It is a thing that Kate must decide for herself."

Neither of them heard the door open or, for a moment, noticed the girl standing in the doorway. "Papa!" Kate said softly, and the two men turned to face her. "I am sorry. I should have knocked," she said; "I did not know that Mr. Tolliver was here." She dropped a quick curtsy. "Forgive me, please."

"Come in, my dear, come in," her father urged nervously, and quite unnecessarily, since she was already in and the door pushed to behind her.

"You are looking very charming, Miss Kate," Tolliver said gallantly, and pulled up a chair for her.

Archibold Rider looked from one to the other. "Well, sir," he said at last, "will you call on us this evening, perhaps?"

But Tolliver shook his head, smiling. "Unfortunately, I cannot. Unless, of course, I must! I have business at Valhalla. And then, I think that Miss Kate is already at least halfway to our confidence! I suggest there is no time so auspicious as the present —and these stark walls, they lend a touch of honesty now, do they not!"

Archibold Rider closed his lips. To cheat a girl of her moonlight and roses for honesty's sake seemed to him a poor sort of honesty. But, at least, Kate would understand just what she was being offered. To his daughter's puzzled frown he said, "Mr. Tolliver has something to discuss with you, and I have an appointment with the General."

"The General!" Kate cried in alarm, jumping up and clasping her hands. "Why, Papa?"

"Why? my girl." In her father's face astonishment and outrage mixed.

"Miss Kate has probably heard the bad news, and is quite unnerved."

Kate looked over at Tolliver. His voice was slow and his manner, half smiling, half indolent, seemed almost bored with the turn the conversation had taken, but for a moment his eyes held her in hard, cold speculation, as though he were trying to warn her of something.

Kate dropped her eyes. "I am," she said nervously. "I apologize, Papa. That sounded very rude. But it has been such a worrying day. I don't understand anything." She pulled a lace-bordered handkerchief from her sleeve and put it to her eye. "Miss Fergusson has been quite out of her mind with anxiety. We're all going to be murdered in our beds! And the Negroes are afraid of something, though they won't say what.

And then you go rushing off to see the General, and I don't understand." She was frankly weeping now, though she had commenced with no more than a pretense.

Hains Tolliver turned his back on the two and stood in the window, a small smile [illegible] He watched the [illegible] cart traffic below and the busy streams of people. The tops of beavers were round and shiny in the sun and the women's hats were big and cast ungainly shadows. Out of the air, the scream of a rusty wheel came and a big voice yelled "Get. Get!" A rider trotted neatly by, raising small pocket-size billows of dust, and an urgent sparrow voice shrilled, "Paper, paper, paa-per!"

"There's been a shocking leak in the General's office," Archibold Rider was saying, his voice loud and indignant. "It is my duty to point it out. Investigation—the army—shocking behavior!"

A woman on the street below struck a black boy with her umbrella and the boy ran, screaming as though the whole Ku Klux were after him. The heat and dust and sounds of the street engulfed the window. Hains Tolliver swung about when he heard the door close. His friend was gone and Kate sat primly in her father's chair, her handkerchief tucked once more into her sleeve. Her father had left the desk drawer open and she peered into it, wrinkled her nose angrily, and pushed it to with a little slap.

He came to her, smiling, and sat upon a corner of the desk. "Well, Miss Kate!"

"Well, sir!" She looked at him squarely and solemnly. "Your guns did not get delivered, did they?"

"My guns?" He raised an eyebrow. "You have a pretty imagination, Miss. What would I do with a train-load of guns? Do you picture that I want to start a revolution?"

"I don't know."

"Then let us talk of things that you do know." He was silent for a moment, watching the girl. "Did you hear what we discussed when you came in, Miss Kate?"

Kate shook her head. "That I am to decide something," she said.

"And so you are." He reached down and took her hand from her lap as though it were some possession that he had mislaid. "I want you for my wife, Kate," he said.

"For your wife!" Kate looked up at him blankly. "Oh, no," she said quickly, and pulled her hand away.

Hains Tolliver looked at the girl in amazement, his brows drawn together in a long dark scowl. Abruptly he got up and took a step across the room, then turned back to her. "You are young, Kate," he said, "and ignorant. Shall I explain your heart to you?"

Kate's cheeks were pink, but before she could protest he pulled her to her feet and close to him. "Not long ago something happened that worried you. You did not understand it, but you thought that some dishonest intrigue was in question. You should, of course, have taken your information to your father. Instead, by your own story, you took it—or sent it—to the person whom you thought to be the arch intriguer! Do you know why, little Kate?" His voice was soft but there was a ring of triumph in it that bore no element of kindness. "Because you love me." He kissed her then, with a cold possessiveness that left out of consideration any thought or feeling that she might have.

With his lips still on hers, Kate thought of Michael Bourne, and she commenced to struggle wildly. But Tolliver did not let her go at once. "I want you for mistress of Valhalla," he said, his mouth against her ear.

As abruptly as he had taken her, he let her go, and the moment his hands were removed Kate ceased wishing for Michael Bourne. What was he to her! Telling her that she must either marry him or be a spinster. She would show him. The greatest gentleman in Florida had asked her to be his wife, mistress of the finest house in Florida! And she would too. The devil take Mr. Bourne and his rough kisses. And she sat down and burst at once into tears.

[illegible] the problem [illegible], without a thought of going to anyone else, and there were more logical people to have gone to. What conceivable reason could she have had, unless in truth she loved him?

"I am a great deal older than you," he said. "You will understand your own heart in time. In the meanwhile, trust it to me and believe that I am better equipped to defend it than you are!"

Kate dried her eyes slowly. Perhaps I could be engaged! she thought. Perhaps I *am* in love. I'd find out that way. An engagement can be broken, it's not final. And a little voice in her said, "Won't this show Mr. Michael Bourne!" She looked up. "I will marry you, sir," she said. The minute she had said it she was afraid. It didn't sound like just being engaged.

"Well, then!" Hains Tolliver smiled. He took her in his arms and kissed her upon her hard young lips. She would learn, without a doubt; those lips would not always be so hard.

Kate protested when her engagement was announced immediately. But Hains Tolliver was not a man to bargain. "We must be married before Christmas," he said. "We are in for a heavy orange harvest at home and a riot of political trouble in the State. Reed is going to be impeached and a new governor must be found. I have my hands full, Kate, and I want my personal affairs settled. I will not wait."

"You don't have to wait," she said quickly and, she thought,

You're the one who wants to marry! but she hadn't the courage to say it.

He was quick to placate her, as though he read her thoughts. "You are a woman now, Kate. And these are a man's problems that I have brought you. Don't disappoint me."

So Kate agreed to the short engagement. And, having agreed, she knew that she would marry, that she wanted to marry Hains Tolliver. Her thought of a broken engagement had been a childish play. It had had something to do with Michael Bourne. She dismissed it finally. Certainly she would never have considered marrying the Irishman!

Her wedding was set for the week before Christmas. Her aunt was to travel South to be with her, and Madam promised to turn her house over to the wedding. Her big bosom heaved and she wept with joyful sentiment. "Marrying from my house," she cried, "like my own daughter," and the tears spouted like water from her little brown eyes.

Only Michael Bourne did not like the news. He went to Kate at once. "I've come to ask you," he said, "for I don't believe——"

"You don't believe what?" Kate could feel her cheeks hot. She was glad that she was alone, that he had not come when there was anyone to hear him.

"—That you should do such a thing! You cannot be going to marry Hains Tolliver." He took her hand, but there was no ring on it yet and his face cleared. "I knew——" he said softly.

"You know nothing, Michael Bourne," Kate said and pulled her hand away. "And how dare you come here and talk to me like this!"

"Because I love you myself," he said, and he swept her up and kissed her until Kate felt as though the very heart were being drawn out of her breast. When he let her down he said, "And I think you love me too."

Kate's small hand flew up to slap him, but Michael caught her wrist and held her fast. "Don't admit it if you won't, Little One. I know when a kiss is welcome," he laughed. "Even a dead man would have known then that you had kissed him."

Kate pulled herself free and stamped her foot. "I did not," she stormed angrily. "I did no such thing!" She was confused, for she knew that she had liked Michael Bourne's kiss, that she came to life in his arms, wildly and weakly. Certainly she did not feel this with [illegible]

[illegible] Love is not a thing to have to think about."

"I am engaged."

"Then you must break it."

"Oh," Kate cried, "you don't understand anything."

He came and stood over her. "If you are afraid to face the music," he said, and the tenderness in his voice atoned for the insult of his words, "I will face it with you."

"Face what?"

"Look, Little One," Michael said quickly, taking her unresisting hands in his, "from the day I saw you standing in the sunset in your pretty ginger frock, you were the girl for me. I have nothing to offer you but doubt and neglect. I've hard work to do and no time to play games. But I will make it up to you one day; by the Saints, I will."

Kate's hands lay in his like little mesmerized birds, no slightest flutter left in them. Her eyes, on Bourne's, were mesmerized too, for he was giving her his heart.

"There's not much to begin with," he went on. "I've a house, it's small, but it will be your own——"

Kate pulled at her hands, suddenly awake. "I've seen it," she said breathlessly. "I'm not like that. I'm no pioneer. I can't —I don't want to live like that."

"You don't know what you're like," Bourne said sternly, and then his voice was gentle again. "You're too young to know yourself. But I know you. You and that school of yours! It doesn't hide you well. You and your love for your papa! You haven't learned to think yet, perhaps not even to work. But you will. And I——"

At his words, Kate felt a sudden furious rebellion. Was everybody going to tell her that she was too young to know anything, either her own mind or her own feelings? A defiance that she had been too bewildered to recognize when Hains Tolliver had addressed the same words to her took hold of her now. With Michael Bourne she had none of the diffidence that she had with Tolliver, and she took out on him her sense of outrage with them both.

"I am not so young as not to know my own mind, Mr. Michael Bourne. I will thank you to remember that I am sixteen, and—well, an offer of marriage is an honor, so I will forget your impertinence. Thank you and good day to you, sir."

Bourne pushed his hands deep in his pockets. He scowled blackly at her. "You love me," he said flatly.

"I do not!" Kate almost screamed. She stamped her foot but managed to control her voice, so that it was low again even if it trembled. "Get out of here," she said, "get out of my sight. I never want to see you again."

Michael was suddenly meek. "I am going," he said. "But I'll be around. I know you don't love anyone but me, and you can't be happy married to a thousand acres. What do you know of this man you say you will marry?"

"What do you mean?"

"There is a man here in Jacksonville," Bourne said slowly, his voice quite expressionless, "who is head of an organization called the Brotherhood of Lincoln. It is set up to terrify the blacks and get money out of them. But also, and primarily, to influence their vote. Incidentally, it instigates them to rape and to murder and to burn and, less dramatically, to break working contracts so that a man's land or his business goes to pieces for lack of labor."

Disarmed by this suddenly impersonal shift in the conversation, and interested despite herself, Kate said, "But—I don't understand——"

"These things scare away the owners of the land—if the owner is particularly hardy he may be driven into impossible debt—or killed. When he is gone, his land is then bought up—cheap."

"Why do you tell me this?"

[illegible] out of my jurisdiction."

Kate stared at him, white to the lips. "What has this to do with me?" she said, her voice scarcely more than a whisper.

"Only this. Everything that happens seems to lead back to, or indicate, one man—one central figure. The State is full of crooks, but only this man counts."

He was silent at last and Kate said, after a moment, "You have a very big job, Mr. Bourne." Her heart was racing and she could feel the blood surging up her throat. "The Governor lost his guns. The Governor lost his guns!" beat in her mind like a pulse.

Bourne shook his head impatiently. "I am not telling you this to show you what a big job I have. I want you to know that there is such a man. I believe that he is the man you plan to marry. If you loved him, I couldn't tell you this. But you don't, and so you had better know."

"It's a lie." Kate said.

"I have no actual proof, but it is all true enough."

"Please go," Kate said. "I—I have to think."

This time he left her, hesitating only a second. When he was gone Kate turned and paced the room in agitation, kicking at a footstool as she went. It couldn't be true. But if it were! Oh, not a word of it, not a word. Would she listen to a rough no-account? But Michael Bourne was not no-account! Kate came to a standstill by the window. But he was wrong. It was not difficult to be wrong, with all the problems that he had. And he had said he had no proof. Kate conceded this. Besides, she thought deliberately, it doesn't matter. I don't care!

She thought abruptly of her father. "Golden apples!" he had said, teetering back and forth on his toes, and fingering and jingling the silver in his pockets. They stood among the groves of Valhalla, looking across the miles of orange trees. Hains Tolliver had picked an orange for her and had said, "They are golden apples, and they make possible a whole golden kingdom."

Michael Bourne would like her to think that the golden kingdom was something else. Suddenly Kate found herself hating Michael Bourne. It was unfair! And what did he know? Mr. Tolliver was an intelligent man and a big man. She would not question his methods of handling his own affairs. He was too wise for her, or any one else, to sit in judgment on him.

She threw a book on the floor and kicked it. She remembered Michael's cabin and curled her lip. A fine life for a woman! A fine house for children to grow up in—and things! She remembered his kisses and fled through the connecting door to her bedroom to stifle wildly excited sobs in the goose-down bosom of her bed.

16

IT was early morning and a dew-laden mist was upon Jacksonville, suspended at knee-height from the ground and covering everything it touched with a sparkling moisture. It was Sunday morning and Miss Janey Wilson had gone to early Communion. Crockett stayed home, pleading a headache. For a full five minutes she stood at the parlor window, peering from behind the slats of the shutter. Her mother had gone slowly, almost reluctantly down the street, her black serge glistening in the fog and gradually and gently disappearing into it. Crockett continued to watch the street. When the older woman didn't turn back her daughter left the window, sighing a little and smiling a little. She sat down and commenced to rock, and she thought of the hall closet. In another minute! Though she could hardly wait, she continued to rock, clasping her moist hands tightly together. She felt ill [illegible] wasn't decent to hate your own daughter. And Crockett would have to be a hypocrite too, because it just wasn't decent to hate your own mother.

"I won't be touched," Crockett said aloud; "I won't"; and she stood up and went towards the hall door.

Halfway down the hall she stopped. A scraping sound was coming from the kitchen. Crockett frowned. It sounded as though a sack of potatoes was being dragged across the floor. Crockett tiptoed down the hall. I'm being very brave, she thought, but she was not frightened. Whatever she might have been, or should have been, she was not frightened. The dragging sound had ceased and all the house was quiet excepting for the small tip-tip of Crockett's muffled footsteps. Crockett pushed the kitchen door open, still not frightened, but holding on to the knob in case she might want to pull it to. That there was someone on the other side of the door she was sure. A sensitive person can almost always tell if a house is empty. Crockett was sensitive and she was quite sure that she was not alone in the house. There was little light in the kitchen. Every corner was black, and the center of the room gray with shadow. Miss Janey had done up the dishes the night before and they hung in a rack over the sink, dry by now and ready for use. As she was taking Communion she had had no breakfast, but two places were set at the kitchen table. The cups and saucers glistened whitely, while on the stove a kettle steamed. Crockett's eyes were accustomed to the half light, but it was a moment before she saw what she was looking for.

"Who are you?" she asked in a whisper. She had not meant to whisper, but somehow her voice came out that way. "What do you want?"

On the far side of the kitchen table crouched a colored man. From where Crockett stood only the top of his head was visible, round and black and moving just a little with each breath.

"I have a gun here," she lied. "I could blow you to pieces in a second."

"Miss Crockett," a voice said in a quick whisper, "is 'at you?"

"Yes, but who are you?"

"Don' you shoot, Miss Crockett. Dis here's John Bever. I'se sick enuff like it is."

Crockett let go of the door and came into the room. "John Bever?" she said. "I don't remember."

"Jes' John, Missy. I hadda have a name, so I hooked onto Bever. I is yo' pappy's boy, before he solt me."

John Bever still crouched on the far side of the table, but now his head no longer showed above it. Crockett said, "John, John!" puzzled, but eager, as though an old, old friend had walked into the room, bringing all of the past with him. She fumbled anxiously for a match, but as she struck one the black man cried out, "No light, Missy! I'se gwine to get kilt!" and he collapsed onto his side, with a thud that shook the room.

Crockett shook out the match that she had struck, then at once struck another and lit the candle that sat in the center of the table. She held the light over the black man for an instant, but he was half turned towards the floor and she could not see his features. She hesitated. Then she went quickly to the back door and pushed home the bolt that her mother had left undone. The one window looked out over the back yard and a small alley that ran back of the houses on Caroline Street. Day was gaining on the land in strides and, though the sun was low on the horizon still, the fog had drifted out to the corners of town and every object stood out clearly. Satisfied that there was no one in sight, Crockett turned back to the black man. She put her candle on the table and leaned down to see if she could move him. When she touched him he moaned and turned his head slowly towards her, and then she sat back on her heels and cried out, for John Bever's face was a swollen [illegible]

[illegible] won't let anyone come in. Tell me what happened."

John Bever opened his mouth but when he tried to talk only a grunt came and the blood spilt out over his lips. He turned his head slowly and spit onto the floor and then he said, his voice clear and urgent, as though he knew he hadn't many words, "I tolt Miss—schoolma'am—eve'ting——" after the first two words his voice had grown thick again. Crockett leaned close to him.

"What was it; what, John?"

But the black man had fainted and this time he did not revive when she touched him.

Water, a basin, clothes, brandy! Crockett went with surprising efficiency about the task of nursing the black man. She found a cushion for his head and a blanket to cover him with; she bathed his cuts with water and kerosene, and put bread and milk poultices on his eyes. She propped his mouth open with a spoon and tried to pour brandy down his throat, but John Bever did not waken and the brandy came up reddened with blood. She was still kneeling helplessly by him, watching his slow and heavy breathing, when her mother returned.

She heard the door-knob turn, first gently once or twice, and then with a hard, firm thrust. Crockett jumped up. She had forgotten the bolt. "Quiet, Momma!" she said urgently, pulling her into the room. "I don't think there's anyone around to hear, but there might be."

"Crockett, whatever——" Miss Janey pushed at her daughter, who stood in her path unexpectedly strange and firm. And then, looking past her, she saw the black man and gave a squeal immediately smothered in Crockett's hand.

"The Regulators must have gotten him, or something," Crockett said. "He's terrible. We've got to get a doctor."

"Doctor Bob is sick himself," her mother said.

"There's that new doctor."

"Crockett!" Miss Janey cried.

"Go get him, Momma. There's no time to wait."

"Bring a Yankee into this house? You must be mad!"

Crockett pushed her mother towards the door. "You must be mad," her mother said again, resisting her.

"I don't care, you've got to get a doctor. This nigger's dying, Momma, and he was Poppa's boy."

Miss Janey gasped, then she turned and almost ran from the house. It was an hour before she came back, and she came back alone, every muscle of her fat face tucked tightly up with pride and rage, and her eyes red and wet with tears. Crockett sat at the kitchen table, the brandy bottle that she had brought out for John Bever was empty now, and the black man on the floor was dead.

"That Yankee doctor's wife wouldn't even let me see him," Miss Janey cried to Crockett's back. "He'd been up all night and she wasn't going to disturb him for any dirty nigger. His health was too important! Wouldn't even tell him. I walked right down to Dr. Bob. He tried to come, got right out of bed, white as a ghost, and fainted dead away. What are we to do, Crockett? Crockett?" For the first time she looked down and saw that the figure on the floor lay gauntly, with a blanket pulled up over its face.

"Crockett," she whispered. She looked from her daughter to the tall bottle beside her. On the table the candle still burned, its yellow flame flickered across the dark glass and Miss Janey could see that the bottle was empty. The cups and saucers were pushed into the center of the table and on the stove the kettle sang noisily. Miss Janey sat down opposite her daughter and commenced to cry into her soft fat hands.

Crockett watched her mother weep. Once, her lips moved as though she would speak, but she did not. It was morning now and sunlight lay on the floor, and across the table, in warm bright panels. Presently Miss Janey got up and went to the sink. Crockett raised her head, still watching. [illegible]

[illegible]

"There's no point to cry, Momma," she said. "John's dead. We've got to get him out." Crockett stood up. "And I've got to dress." Her robe was soiled and spotted with blood and her hair hung in a tangle down her back, for she had not plaited it the night before and she had not used the brush that morning.

Miss Janey continued to cry, "But what are we going to do, honey, what are we going to do, poor li'l us with no man to help us?"

"We'll have to get help."

"No——" Miss Janey drew a deep breath. "People will think —Crockett, do you know what people will think! That we did it—that he came here to—to—and we——"

"Stop it, Momma," Crockett cried. "Anyway, I don't care what people think."

"But, Crockett, the soldiers will come. They're just lookin' for a chance to dishonor Southern women. You know it—you should, Crockett."

"Now, Momma!"

"We've got to get help."

"We'll send Ossian out to get Cousin George."

Her mother looked at her shrewdly. "Honey," she asked, "will you tell Ossian? Honey, I wouldn't."

Crockett moved her shoulder impatiently. "Ossian is all right, Momma. Ossian is a gentleman."

"Well," her mother said reluctantly. "But if you think so, why send for Cousin George at all?"

"Ossian is soft! Momma, we ought to eat something. Could you fix a dish of something? Do you mind?"

"Of course not," Miss Janey said brightly, her tears forgotten for the moment; "you go right upstairs and dress," and she bustled over to the cupboard, taking the long way around and being careful not to glance at the blanket-covered figure on the floor.

All day long the body of the colored man lay in the small kitchen on Caroline Street. Even after Ossian Delahanty came back from Mandarin, bringing George Morgan with him, the body was not touched.

"You can do him the honor of letting him be until it's time to take him right out of the house," Crockett said.

"Oh, but, honey," Miss Janey wailed, "I can't go in there and cook, I just can't. And it's not necessary to leave him there—and we've got to eat!"

"He's not a dead cat," Crockett said. "Leave him."

Ossian, obviously of a mind with her mother, said, "Miss Crockett, honey!" and he reached out and patted her hand. He wore a suit that had belonged to his father, and it became neither the wearer nor the age. A black velvet watch-band stretched across the full expanse of his abdomen. And if his clothes did not fit, or become him, still they lent him an air of great gravity.

"Ossian," Crockett said, succumbing to a sudden impulse, "you ought to be an undertaker, really you ought."

Miss Janey cried out and Ossian's big face grew crimson. "Really! There's only a Yankee undertaker in town, and who's to lay us all out! I'm sure Momma'd haunt me if I ever let him touch her! Why, Cousin Ossian, you would quite recover the family fortune."

George Morgan, who had at first met her words with a surprised frown, suddenly commenced to laugh. "Not laying out Southern gentlefolk, he wouldn't! It would have to be undertaking for undertaking's sweet sake!"

Crockett laughed and in a moment Miss Janey and Ossian were laughing too, Ossian's big ha-ha drowning them all out. The four of them sat and rocked and laughed, and the day fell away and the parlor grew dark with evening. No one spoke again of taking the body of John Bever [illegible]

[illegible] a spot we picked out and muss it up good—maybe have to kill a chicken. If they ask, we'll be able to show where he was found."

Miss Janey pressed a little fat hand to her throat. "But, Cousin, the Regulators! Better bury him and say nothing."

"The Regulators didn't do this, Cousin, you know they didn't." George Morgan frowned heavily. "They shoot a man when he needs shooting, and they hang a man when he needs hanging, and they'll whip a nigger when he needs whipping, but no one's ever been beat to death. A man's got a right to protect his women and his property. But torture's another thing. That nigger's got broken bones."

"The Ku Klux!"

"They ain't come south of Jackson—not yet. It's murder—and something's got to be done about it."

"Yes, something has." Crockett had said nothing about John Bever's words to her, and now she said, frowning, "He said something about the schoolma'am——" she shook her head. "It doesn't sound right. He told her something, or I was to tell her something. Do you know her?"

"Miss Ferguesson?" George Morgan said, in a puzzled voice. "That's funny. I'll ask her tomorrow."

"Will you come and tell me what you learn?"

Her cousin nodded. "I will come."

Later, when night had darkened the sky, he and Ossian

brought the wagon to the kitchen door and took away the body of John Bever. Miss Janey remained in the parlor, rocking and sighing, but Crockett went to the kitchen.

"Thank you, Ossian," she said, when the thing was done, and she let him pat her hand. She didn't give her hand to George Morgan, but said in a stiff, breathless little voice, "Be careful," and he looked down at her without smiling at all and said, "God grant you get some sleep tonight, Cousin; you need it," and for a moment they looked at each other warmly, and almost as though in these strange words they had declared their love for each other. Then the men were gone and Crockett was bolting the door and feeling on the shelf for the matches and lamp. She would have to fix some supper now, if only a dish of porridge. But first the floor had to be scrubbed.

17

WHEN Crockett Wilson awakened the following morning her head was heavy and soon commenced to ache, while her heart was beating with a sickening and insistent thud. When she got out of bed to get herself a drink of water, her hand shook so that she could scarcely hold the glass. Something had happened, something portentous and evil hung over her with, however, some faint and haunting hope emerging from beneath it all. She sat on the side of her bed and remembered, and the horror that had been too real and too close to feel it, the day before, grew upon her. "It's always that way," she thought; "you never do know what's happening to you until it's over, and then you have to live with it the rest of your life." She remembered too her Cousin George's expression and wished that she had shown him more warmth. It was so easy to be warm with Ossian because he was fat and young, and because he didn't matter a hoot. But it seemed she could never be herself with George.

A bottle of corn, with the cork put in tight, was submerged

in the wash pitcher. Crockett pulled it out and sat on the bed again. She slept on a tester bed in a room so small that only a narrow aisle ran down between the bed and washstand to the window at the foot of the bed. Miss Janey called it a closet bed- [illegible]

and away. The pillow, the mahogany headboard, the wall, disintegrated like feathers under a wind, while her head slipped backwards. Crockett groaned and clutched at the side of the bed and fell asleep. When she awakened again, the headache had gone and so had the trembling. She got up slowly, trying herself out, and then she smiled, got dressed and went downstairs.

Miss Janey was in the kitchen. The door to the back yard was wide open and the sun poured into the room. A bowl of flowers was on the table, and Miss Janey herself was shelling peas, having made sure to sit as far as she could from the spot where the colored man had lain.

"Well, dear, there you are!" Miss Janey looked up and smiled a wan smile. "And hungry, I'll just bet."

"Yes. No, I'm not hungry, Momma." Crockett was staring at the flowers. "Where did they come from?"

"Cousin George has been."

"When did he come?"

"About noon. He wouldn't let me waken you." Miss Janey continued to smile fatuously.

"Noon!" Crockett could feel the corners of her mouth droop and she pulled them so that they were straight and secret. She wouldn't let her mother know that she was disappointed. It made her look sullen. Her head commenced to ache again. "I didn't know it was so late," she said. "What did he say, Cousin

George?" She turned her back as though the question didn't interest her and went to the cupboard.

"Oh," her mother said brightly, "the court's going to make a big fuss. Everyone's sure it's murder. That Mr. Bourne is going to make a big case out of it. Not that he'll ever find out anything!"

"How can he?" Crockett agreed morosely. "He can't even know the truth about where John Bever died."

"Well now, Crockett. You've no count to put it like that. Where he died had nothing to do with it." Her mother broke open a pea pod and shelled out the peas with nervous emphasis. Crockett looked to be starting a difficult spell.

Crockett brought a plate of bread and cheese to the table. Then she took a mug from a hook over the sink and went out on the back porch and down the stairs to the root cellar. She returned in a few minutes with the mug full of milk and put it down beside the plate on the table. "You don't care what happened to that boy, do you, so long as people don't think bad of us?"

"Crockett," her mother said, watching her, "I don't understand you."

Crockett shrugged impatiently, her mother had a way of making her feel smothered.

"You change so," her mother said and, seeing the shrug, she said plaintively, "Oh, Crockett, Crockett!"

"I'm sorry, Momma." Crockett looked quickly across the table, but Miss Janey had gone back to her pea pods with renewed energy and, though her ample bosom heaved once or twice, she did not look up again. She had sounded suddenly pathetic in her daughter's ears and Crockett was remembering how often she wished, after a moment was over, to be able to go back and speak or act differently. "Did Cousin George say anything else?" she said, in the way of offering an olive branch.

"Oh, why, yes, he did." Miss Janey looked up quickly, accepting the branch. "I most forgot. He went to see the teacher."

Crockett frowned, her head was throbbing now. She drank the milk, but her gorge rose at the thought of the bread and cheese. Then she remembered, and the frown cleared. "What was it?" she said. "What did she say?"

"She knew him all right. Said he was a bad sort. But she knew nothing personal about him. He was going to the other school class, the [illegible]

[illegible] in a low monotone.

He won't come back today, Crockett thought, and she wished that the day were over. "I've got a headache," she said suddenly and she got up and went out of the room without moving her dishes or replacing her chair. Miss Janey looked after her and sighed, and then she looked at the bowl of flowers and her lips tucked up tight and angry. "Drat!" she said aloud. She broke open the last pod and spilled the peas into the bowl on her knee. "Your son's your son till he gets him a wife," her mind sang, "but your daughter's your daughter all your life." And she thought, And me feeling puny, too. I could cry. I could just cry.

A few blocks away at the St. James House the desk clerk said, "Mr. Tolliver is not in town, ma'am," and he looked curiously at Kate Rider. Her face was white and set, and her hands on the counter were clenched.

"Is there some place else he could be staying?" she asked.

The clerk shook his head. "We keep a room for him. We would know if he were in town." His voice was coolly regal. Kate turned and ran from the crowded lobby, careless of the stares and smiles that followed her. On the boardwalk she stopped. She didn't know what to do. She had to see Tolliver. She had to see him at once. She clutched her fingers nervously, and abruptly she became conscious of his ring and, wrenching it off, she thrust it into her pocket. She wouldn't wear it. He should never have her. Unless——! Oh, she had to know!

When George Morgan had walked out of her classroom that morning Kate's first reaction had been one of horror and of self-blame. John Bever was dead and it was her fault, she knew it was her fault. Miss Ferguesson, who had come with George to tell her the news, had said:

"I told you not to take that brute back into your class. He's got himself into some murdering fight and you're lucky it didn't happen right here in this room."

"John Bever wasn't a brute," Kate had cried, and she snatched a piece of chalk from her desk and wrote hastily on the board.

"*School,*" Miss Ferguesson said coldly, "is not spelled *scule* and *tomorrow* is not spelled *tumorro*. By the grace of God you have spelled *no* correctly."

Kate slapped the chalk into a drawer with a medley of papers. "Class dismissed," she said to the frightened faces before her. She pointed to the board. "Come back, day after tomorrow."

Miss Ferguesson said "humph," but the black people were glad to go. The older teacher stood staring at Kate. "It's not right," she said.

But Kate didn't care, and she didn't care what Miss Ferguesson thought. She grabbed her bonnet from the hook, and fled. Miss Ferguesson could lock up. Kate had to find Hains Tolliver. She had sent John Bever to him. And John Bever was dead. Beaten to death! He had been her friend. He had been good to her. She thought of him as she had first seen him, standing so truculently at the end of the room. She had switched him. And he had just stood still and taken it, and then smiled at her and been polite ever after. Kate felt tears, hard and painful, behind her eyes. But they didn't come. She was not going to cry. She was going to do something. She was going to make someone pay. It wasn't her fault. It couldn't be! Oh, perhaps he had got into a fight. But she couldn't believe it. What he had taken from her he wouldn't have taken from another nigger. He was too big and strong.

Kate walked slowly away from the St. James towards her

father's office. There was a livery stable next to the Freedman's building. She didn't know what she would say if she met her father. She couldn't speak to him now. She couldn't speak to anyone. She was a murderess. Anger boiled up in her. She was not a murderess. She should have been [illegible]

[illegible] season had come late, but the past two weeks had made up for that lateness and the St. Johns was swollen and brown. To the east, the river widened and there was a give and take between it and the ocean. Oak and pine cut her off from the river, but here and there it came into view and, gray or brown, sparkled in the sun. Once, out where the water was deep, she saw a school of porpoise dipping and clowning and, where the light struck their bodies, they glistened fleetingly.

For a way, Kate let her horse walk. He could not gallop for hours. She sat with the reins loose in her lap and watched his rump moving. The pace was torture to her. She kept remembering the big black man. He had been a good friend. He had almost been her slave! Following her about like a big black avenging angel to see that no harm came to her, and that she got her way with his people. She remembered his throwing the pig over the fence. "Trash," he grumbled. "It ain't fitten'." He was still a slave really, for all his arrogance about freedom and how the government belonged to the Negroes. Not a slave as some used the word, to mean a lowly person without spirit or soul, but a very personal person. He needed to devote himself. All the freedom in the world couldn't take the place of having someone to belong to who, by the same bond, belonged to him. She had heard him talk about his former masters and it was there in his voice, the pride and the love. "The boss solt me," he told her once, and when she said, "My poor John," he shook his head.

"It was more like a fiancement present," he said, "on account of Mass' Tom were financed to Miss Callie. Only Miss Callie's pappy wouldn't have no offerments ontil the financials bin celebrated. So he done paid for me. Howbeever, I was solt and I come to drive the carritch for Miss Callie an'——"

"And you didn't mind, John?"

"It's lak this, Missy," he said patiently. "Miss Callie was fianced to Mass' Tom. When they married I would 'a' bin back with Mass' Tom agin, wouldn't I? Only they never did marry up on account of Mass' Tom went away for to study and Miss Callie took a spishun on how he'd found another sweetheart up No'th, an' Miss Callie took to bed and never got out, an' then the war come an' Mass' Tom got kilt, an' now, I reckon, Miss Callie ain't never gonna get up for sure."

"You mean she went to bed and stayed there—and she's still there?"

"Yes, ma'am, Missy."

"In the same bed, in the same room, all these years, for no reason? I don't believe it."

"Lawd Jesus, look at me, I is speakin' true," John Bever swore. "Only time Miss Callie done git up otta dat bed was once when the Yankee sold'ers come an' burnt the house down, an' she wouldn't git outta bed, an' the Captain done ordered her, an' she done said there war only one captain in the world could order her an', him being daid, murdered by a murderin' thief of a Yankee, she was settin' right war she war. Yes'm."

Kate remembered, thinking that John had looked as though he approved. He said, "Yes'm," and closed up his big mouth tight, as though to say, "that'll teach 'em."

"So what happened?" she had asked.

"The Capt'n tolt his sold'ers, 'Tek up thet bed an' walk it plumb otta hiar',' an' they did, an' Miss Callie fainted plumb daid when the sold'ers come into her room, an' Mammy Lina she run along side a thet bed raisin' hell, an' all the sold'ers a-yellin' 'You is free nigger, git outen de way!' An' Mammy Lina a-shakin' her fist an' a hollerin' back at 'em, 'You sassy aig-sukkin', roguish varmints, I wisht yo' innerds was full ob a'snic an' ox-vomit an' blue vitrul, so's 'twould cut yo' inter'ls to chitluns! To be molestin' of a fine lady lik yo' is!' She carried on somethin', but they jes' done tote thet bed [illegible]

[illegible] house an' now I've bu'nt thern.' An' she went down an' set up the bed in Mammy Lina's cabin, an' tha' she is yet." And he had looked pleased again.

Kate crossed Black Creek and turned inland and then back towards the river again, though now she could not see it, for the growth was heavy on either side. From here the road was straight, running for six miles under pine and oak all draped with the million gray-green beards of Spanish moss. Kate was thinking, Some place here, some place along here it must have been. She shuddered. It was a lonely far-away spot in which to be set upon. Even by day, with the sun and the bright blue sky and the clear pure air, it was a secret hidden place. The moss made the trees seem to bend too low, as though they were trying to touch their giant toes. Suddenly, not three yards ahead of the carriage, a snake dropped with a thud onto the roadbed and instantly slithered away. Kate drew a frightened breath and held the reins hard as her horse shied to the side, pawing at the dirt in his fear, and then with a bound started running down the road. The carriage skittered and bounced after the frightened animal like a balloon on a string. Kate shoved her feet against the buckboard and threw every ounce of her slight weight backwards, hauling on the reins, but the horse ran only the faster. She had driven only the gentlest animal at the gentlest pace before, but she had heard that a runaway can be stopped if he is unbalanced soon enough. If the road were long enough, and she was not thrown out of the carriage, or the carriage tipped over, the horse must sooner or later tire. But the road was not long enough, for there was still McGirth's creek to be forded, and when the road dipped into it they were bound to be wrecked. She had to unbalance her horse, and that quickly. Kate knew how it was done, but she had no experience in trying it out, and little strength. With a sudden thrusting motion she let the reins slack; then she threw herself back again, pulling them in with all of her strength, only to let them go once more, so suddenly that the horse almost stumbled. Surprisingly, she was succeeding. The flow of terror fell back like a tide and a sense of power and excitement grew in her. Within a quarter of a mile they were cantering, with a rollick of fatigue to the pace; and before a mile was run, Kate had brought her animal to a standstill. He shuddered and tossed his head once or twice and then dropped his nose to his knees while Kate, with the reins clutched tight in her lap, burst into tears. It was too much to bear! John Bever's death was, for Kate, the first sorrow of her life and it found out every root of feeling in her being. Combined with the way of his death it had shocked her into a passion of self-blame soon diverted into the more bearable channel of blaming Hains Tolliver. She wept with a frenzy of abandon. The horse hung his head and his flesh jumped nervously, and the long road was empty and lonely. Finally she dried her eyes, and blew her nose. I wish I'd died, she thought. I wish the carriage had turned over and killed me. Tears rose in her eyes again. But she took up the reins and slapped them together a couple of times and shook her head.

It was noon when Kate arrived at Valhalla. The trip had been too long and her passion was spent in fear and tears. But she was there—she would say what she had come to say. She got down from the carriage, limp with exhaustion. She was unhappy and depressed. She would get nowhere. She would do no good.

Tolliver met her in the hall. He had watched her from his window and sensed at once that, whatever spirit she had started out in, its back was already broken. It was no little thing for her to come all this way by herself. But he knew that she had never left Jacksonville in this state. "My dear," he said, taking her bonnet and giving it to a young black woman. Kate gestured helplessly, as though the act had interfered with her thoughts.

"I must talk to you," she said.

"Of course. But won't you rest first? [illegible] fatigue."

[illegible]

[illegible] the moment the door was closed, and she turned upon him, clasping her hands with a return of anguish, "John Bever is dead!"

"John Bever?" Tolliver looked at her questioningly.

"He has been murdered."

"Who"—he started, and then his face cleared and an unexpected look of pity came into his eyes. "My poor child," he said softly. "It is that darky you were so fond of. Tell me what happened."

"Oh, I don't know. They found him. He was beaten. Mr. Morgan said he had been beaten to death!"

"Ah, Kate, poor little girl! I am afraid it sounds as though he had got into a fight. Though it could have been murder." He drew her to him and held her in his arms tenderly. She didn't resist, but he could feel the doubt and reluctance in her.

"I am proud of you, Kate," he said. "There are not many Yankee girls who would feel for a black man as you have. You are a pure-bred little lady. But I can't have you worrying like this. Be logical. What could have happened to the man?"

"He was worried about those guns—and—and they did disappear. The last words he spoke were to ask for me."

"He was devoted to you. And probably delirious too. As to the guns—the State is certainly full of a lot of thieving carpetbaggers, who would not stop at murdering anyone who stood in their way. If he did——" Tolliver's voice was suddenly black and hard and she could feel his body stiffen. "They didn't have to beat him," he said. "By Christ, they go too far!"

"But the guns!" Kate almost wept. It was Hains Tolliver who had not wanted the guns to go through.

"I imagine," he said, as though he could read her thoughts, "that there are a good many elements who might have tried to have the guns stopped."

Kate buried her head in his shoulder and gave herself up. What a fool she had been! He was good to his colored people. How could she think that he would have anything to do with a thing like this! Oh, he was right, she thought, he was quite right. She hadn't betrayed her friend at all.

Tolliver turned her face to him and kissed her, and Kate clung to him, her whole being alive with relief. He was strong and wise and tender and for the first time she experienced a sense of wild happiness that she was going to marry him.

"Go upstairs and wash for lunch," he said, putting her away from him at last and smiling at her as though she were a child. "Dilsey is there. She will see to anything you need."

He held the door for her and watched her go slowly up the long staircase, her fingers sweeping the banister with a gesture that was like a caress.

18

"I RODE on the sky,
Quite ondestified I,
And the moon it was under my feet."

Kate sang clearly and gaily and she cocked her head and looked over her handwork at her father. "I'll make a good Southerner, won't I, Papa?" she said.

Her father smiled. "You'll make a good anything you care to be, baby," he said. "It's too bad your poppa ain't got some of the same stuff in him."

"Oh, Papa," Kate frowned, "that's not at all right. Just look at you! Head of the Freedman's Bureau and getting rich as Croesus—think how poor we were at home!"

It was approaching evening, three days following Kate's ride to Valhalla. She and her father [illegible]

[illegible] come to nought?"

"Because there is nought for it to come to. Miss Ferguesson has given her deposition that John Bever was an ugly customer, and you have had to admit that he was a boaster and a trouble-maker."

Kate's needle was still, as she listened to her father. It was a Judas-sounding thing, put that way. There was no one, it seemed, to say good of John Bever, and she wasn't going to be allowed to! Well, he *was* a boaster, that was no lie. What had he said once, coming into school with a cap on the side of his head and his shirt open clean down to his waist? "I done likked thet nigger Bob Hatches what said he warn't a comin' back to scule no more. He'll be down terrectly he kin walk agin, an' it ain't likely anyone else'll quit, ma'am, Missy, on account I is the strongest critter on the whole hill. Likely, in the whole State." There hadn't been a mark on him and he had grinned, as pleased as a baby, or, as they say, "as sassy as a Confedrit quartermaster."

"Oh dear," Kate cried in genuine distress, but when her father looked up, surprised at her vehemence, she said, "Nothing, I've pricked my finger," and she bent over her work. In a little while, she said, "Papa."

"Yes, m'dear."

"Papa, do look."

Her father put down the paper that he was reading, and looked.

"I don't mean look, I mean listen. Papa, what else will there be at the trial?"

"Hearing. Nothing. Now stop fretting yourself, Kate. The man was in your class and now he's dead. There's nothing you can do about it. I declare, I don't know that it's good for you to continue with that work."

"Now, Papa, it's nothing to do with that. I want to continue. I love—well, I'm fond of those poor black souls. They're like children. But I just wanted to know about the trial, and you won't tell me. It's not asking much, is it?"

Archibold Rider sighed. "Women!" he said helplessly. "The man was murdered, m'dear, so they'll find that he was murdered. In fact, they will say so. They will then try to discover why he was murdered, and by whom. They will decide that he deserved to be murdered. They will also find that he was murdered by persons unknown. Unless this little twerp from the depot proves to know more than he has said so far."

"Who, Papa!"

"A cracker who has been overseeing a job of work down at the depot. It seems John Bever worked for him for several days last week. He is maybe the last person known to have conversed with him."

Kate put her work down. "Papa," she said, "you've got to take me. It sounds so—exciting—it does. And you've just got to."

"No such thing, young woman." Archibold Rider was firm, and for once he was cross with his daughter. "You're not going nigh that session, do you hear?" He raised his voice as though he thought her hearing might be defective.

"Yes, Papa," Kate said meekly. The following day she went to the hearing. But she went discreetly after everyone was seated, slipping in quietly and taking the nearest seat. Her neighbor was a gaunt old man whose clothes looked to be rotting on him and who smelled unbearably stale. Kate put her handkerchief to her nose and her mind to the proceedings. She found them long drawn out and dull, repetitions of things that she already knew. But there was still the little man from the depot to give his testimony. Kate waited impatiently. She had to hear him and she was going to stay in the smelly, awful room until she did. Her father was there, and George Morgan, who testified that he had found the body. Michael Bourne did the questioning, scowling like a thousand thunderstorms and making everyone who opened his mouth look like a [illegible]

[illegible]

"[illegible]," the witness said in a voice that sounded as though his tongue had been put through a colander. Kate leaned forward in her seat and scowled. Some of her colored pupils talked like this, but she had never learned to understand them when they did, and had to call others to translate, "just as though it were a foreign language," she had complained to her father.

Michael Bourne was patient. "I am not asking you, for myself," he said. "I want you to tell the court. Now, what is your name?"

The witness digested this and then he said, "Bill Arp." He was a small man, dressed in a suit that might have been fifty years old but showed little signs of wear. His beard was grizzled and he allowed it to grow untrimmed, but the hair on his head was cut at neat angles by a careful if inexperienced hand. He had an air of dignity that was quite destroyed by the way in which he grinned at the people in the courtroom.

"Very well, Bill Arp," Bourne proceeded. "Now, Mr. Arp, what do you do?"

Mr. Arp gaped.

"Let me put it this way, how do you make a living?"

"Ah," said the witness, "good enuff 'times. 'Tother times po'ly."

"You are a farmer, are you not?" Tolliver asked, unexpectedly.

Bourne frowned. Arp said, "Could be." Tolliver rubbed a finger along the back of his ear and smiled.

Bourne took a breath and said, "You're also overseer of loading operations down at the depot?"

Bill Arp nodded.

"Well, say so, man, say so," Bourne cried. "This has to go on record. If we just write down, 'the witness nodded,' who's to say he hadn't just spotted an acquaintance in the court!"

A titter went round the room, and Bill Arp said with unexpected loquacity, "Ah've a fa'm, but Ah've bin wo'kin to the depot."

"Now we're getting somewhere! You've been working at the depot. As you know, Mr. Arp, we are interested in a colored man who worked for you, one John Bever."

"Ah re'kollects."

"Perhaps we shall get this matter straightened out best if you will tell us about Wednesday last. Wednesday was the last day that John Bever worked at the depot. It was also the last day of John Bever's life. So anything you can remember may prove an invaluable help."

The witness batted his eyes, cleared his throat and heaved his shoulders with a gesture of resignation. "Well then," he began, "it's lak this. Captin Rice, he gin a treat, an' Cousin Sally Dilliard she come over to our house an' axed me if my wife she mout'n't go. I told Cousin Sally Dilliard that my wife was po'ly, being as how she had a touch of the rheumatics in the hip, an' the big swamp was in the road, an' the big swamp was up on account of all the rain laterly; but howsomever, being it was she, Cousin Sally Dilliard, my wife she mout go. Well, Cousin Sally Dilliard then axed me if Mose he mout'n't go. I tolt Cousin Sally Dilliard that he was foreman of the crap, an' the crap was smartly in the grass; but howsomever, as it was she, Cousin Sally Dilliard, Mose he mout go——"

Michael Bourne had been staring at the man incredulously. "In the name of God, Mr. Arp," he broke in at last, "what is this?"

The witness pulled at his beard and frowned. "Captin Rice,

he gin a treat," he said patiently, "an' Cousin Sally Dilliard she come over to our house and axed me if my wife she mout'n't go. I tolt Cousin Sally Dilliard——"

"You are not here to tell us about your Cousin Sally Dilliard and your wife," Bourne [illegible]

[illegible] though he had got hold of a hot poker.

Tolliver smiled openly and the witness looked frightened. "Ah di'n' ax to come hiar," he said with dignity. "You axed——"

"Hell's bloody delight, man!" Bourne turned to Tolliver but he turned back at once and said, in a tone of forced patience, "Your story is irrelevant, sir. Now, it don't seem so hard a problem to me. Do you know anything about the last day of John Bever?"

Hains Tolliver said suddenly, "Mr. Attorney, the court is of the opinion that we may save time by telling the witness to go on in his own way. Proceed, Mr. Arp, with your story."

In the back of the room, Kate held her handkerchief to her mouth and laughed. Bill Arp's voice had commenced to make sense to her, and Michael Bourne's confusion was delicious. Tolliver did not look greatly displeased and Kate thought, with her father, that the whole thing was coming to nought. The witness said, "Yes, sir," but he gripped the arms of his chair and cast a frightened look at Bourne.

"I'm not going to hit you, Mr. Arp!" the latter said, and he pulled up a chair for himself and sat down with a look of resignation. "Let's hear about your Cousin Sally Dilliard."

"Yes, sir. Well, Captin Rice he gin a treat, an' Cousin Sally Dilliard she come over to our house an' axed me if my wife she mout'n't go. I tolt Cousin Sally Dilliard that my wife she was po'ly, being how she had the rheumatics in the hip, an' the big swamp being up; but howsomever, being it was she, Cousin Sally Dilliard, my wife mout go. Well, Cousin Sally Dilliard she axed me if Mose he mout'n't go. I tolt Cousin Sally Dilliard as how Mose—he was foreman of the crap, an' the crap hit was smartly in the grass—but howsomever, Mose he mout go. So they goes together, Mose, my wife an' Cousin Sally Dilliard, an' they come to the big swamp, an' it was up, lak I done tolt you; but bein' as how there was a log across the swamp, Cousin Sally Dilliard an' Mose, lak genteel folks, they walked the log; but my wife, lak a durned fool, she hoists her coats an' wades through."

Bill Arp stopped, overcome with indignation. A loud guffaw shook the room, and Michael Bourne grinned helplessly. When there was quiet enough for his words to be heard he asked ominously, "When did John Bever come into all of this? In case you care to mention. Perhaps, now that your wife and Mose and Cousin Sally Dilliard are out of the way, you can tell us."

Bill Arp said, "My wife, the durned fool, gittin' herself all wet, she warn't to Captin Rice's a hour afore a rheumatic spell come on her that lak' to carry her plumb outen her mind. Captin Rice sent Mose to fotch back my wife, and the carry-all hit got stuck in the big swamp an'——"

"What about John Bever?" Bourne thundered, slamming his fist down on the judge's desk.

Bill Arp started anxiously from his seat and his own voice rose in alarm. "Mose an' me we was all day a-gittin' thet carry-all outen the swamp," he cried. "An' so I never did git to the depot that day. Not the nex', neither, what with my wife hollerin' sick."

Michael Bourne drew a deep breath. A shocked silence was followed by a roar of laughter that swept the entire court. "By God, sir," Bourne said at last, "a man has been murdered and you fool around—! You said that you knew about——"

He scowled, grinned and shrugged helplessly. "By damn, I don't even know myself what you did say."

"You axed me about last Wednesday an' John Bever an' Ah bin a-tellin' you how come I didn't git to see John Bever on thet pertic'lar day."

"Well, witness, you may step down."

Bourne turned to Tolliver. "Seeing there isn't another soul who knows even as much as this man, I see no reason to proceed with the case. But I promise you if I ever find out——"

"Yes, Mr. B[illegible]"

[illegible] would not admit that she had had, certainly now they were dispelled. He had been all dignity and infallibility on the bench and his parting words had been spoken with feeling. Michael Bourne had, she thought, looked furious enough to do murder himself! At the memory of his anger a surge of excitement swept her. She was glad that she had gone to the hearing. As she climbed the steps of Madam's she was singing aloud:

"I rode on the sky,
Quite ondestified I,
And the moon it was under my feet!"

THE first time that Michael Bourne saw Hains Tolliver's ring on Kate's finger his mouth set in a grim hard line and his blue eyes on hers were implacable. But he did not go near her, or try to speak to her again. Kate saw him throw himself into his work with renewed vigor, and her momentary sense of victory over him died in disappointment.

"Thought you didn't want any of him," her heart said spitefully. "And I didn't," her mind answered, "the lumbering

Irishman with his one-room shack and his boarding-house manners!"

Whatever her heart might have answered, she had no time now to listen. Christmas was coming on wings and there was much to do in preparation for her wedding. Her aunt, who should already have been with her, had been taken with a severe kidney ailment and it was not known whether she would be able to attend the wedding at all. Rider would have liked the ceremony postponed, for he had in any case never been greatly in favor of it. But Tolliver had his plans set and was not of a mind to change them and Kate found herself swept up in his strong will. Though she scarcely understood her own mind these days, she was in a hysteria to have the thing behind her.

She closed school the end of November and Miss Ferguesson took back into her own class as many as she could crowd in. Kate hoped to open a school at Valhalla, though Tolliver did not encourage her in thinking that she could teach in it herself.

"I have asked you to be my wife," he said. "If I had wanted a school teacher, I should have hired one."

He let Billy drive her to the village that had grown up about his dock, and he let her prattle about a cabin and plans. But he forbade her going into the little church or the plantation store.

"Give your chosen people a little privacy," he said, smiling at her, "and you'll get on with them a sight better."

Kate pouted, but she let it go for the moment. The church was, in any case, nothing but a shabby lean-to and the store, so called, was a warehouse cabin, without even windows. No one would know it was a store unless he was told.

As she had promised to do, Madam joined in the preparations so that the wedding might be from her house. The groom would have liked to give a reception at Valhalla, but this Archibold Rider would not hear of.

"You'll marry from your own—well, what is closest to your own home, Kate. And that is all there is to it. Your mother would turn over in her grave if I permitted anything else."

From her sick-bed in Hartford, Aunt Enid dispatched a

variety of linens and laces as well as, carefully wrapped in black paper, her mother's wedding dress. Though Kate was not a big girl, the dress was small for her and certain adroit alterations were necessary. On that and on other items for her trousseau. two dressmakers were employed [illegible] the county [illegible] had been reared in the greatest luxury. But they were too unromantic in their persons and too lacking in either character or color to hold Kate's interest. She only wished they would finish in a hurry and get out of her life.

For Kate's life was full of bright, gay promise that lurked around a very immediate corner and she was in haste to be upon it. During those busy days she never saw Michael Bourne, for he had removed himself to St. James House, while George Morgan, if he came to town, did not come to see her.

A week before the wedding, Mrs. Bornson called upon Kate. It was the first time that Kate had seen her since the horrible afternoon of the tea party. She considered for a moment refusing her. However, as the Reverend Bornson was to officiate at her marriage and as she had already, in any case, left this lady far in her wake, she shrugged, made a face and instructed that she be shown up. Mrs. Bornson had a gray complexion with a wen on one high thin cheek-bone and a thin gray line of down on her upper lip. A victory over a Mrs. Bornson was not very exciting.

Mrs. Bornson fluttered in, holding her hands as though she were afraid they might do something foolish if she did not control them.

Kate curtsied and showed her a seat and Mrs. Bornson twittered with such obvious discomfort that Kate was quite put to it not to smile.

Felicitations were in order and received, the weather was discussed, Miss Kate's trousseau came into line and the two gifted sisters who were at work upon it.

"Such ladies," Mrs. Bornson simpered, "such dear ladies. And now, my dear," the minister's wife said nervously, "I do feel—you here alone; I mean, without a mother to advise you—so distressing, but a duty. Yes, a duty," she said firmly and then went on, as though the word alone obliged her, "I shall be glad to instruct you, if you have not been instructed."

Kate said, "Instruct? I don't understand what you're talking about, ma'am."

Mrs. Bornson's complexion commenced to assume a healthier hue. "You are about to marry, my dear!"

"Yes, ma'am."

"But don't you understand," the good woman whispered loudly and unhappily, "gentlemen and ladies are not at all alike," and she added hastily, "that is, to be sure, quite correct and as God intended!"

Kate, suddenly understanding the gist of the conversation, jumped to her feet. "Oh no!" she cried. "Please, Mrs. Bornson! I don't care to talk about it at all!"

Mrs. Bornson stood up, her face was mottled but her eyes were quick with relief. "A duty, my dear Miss Kate, but as long as you know," and she looked at Kate with such unaffected sympathy that Kate felt as though she were being farewelled upon a journey that the other knew to be long and graceless.

"Thank you," she said simply. "It was kind of you just the same."

Mrs. Bornson seemed to hesitate. "There is another thing, Miss Rider——"

"Yes, Mrs. Bornson?"

The minister's wife looked at Kate uncertainly. "It is—well ——" she said, "I could not but tell you. The plans for the church are—they are lovely!"

"Oh, thank you." Kate smiled.

"But that's not all—you see, Miss Rider, the ladies of Jacksonville are in deep trouble from the war. Mr. Tolliver——"

"Has made the mistake of being successful——" Kate said stonily.

"Oh, dear! Give them time—that's all. It does take time."

Kate nodded. It wasn't a matter of giving them time—people took what time they wanted [illegible]

[illegible]

[illegible], to see the end of her visitor.

But Mrs. Bornson's departure was not enough to erase her words from her mind. The fact that the ladies of Jacksonville would not attend her wedding might, under other circumstances, have distressed her, but in conjunction with the earlier topic of conversation they faded into insignificance. Kate went nervously to the window, where she stood and watched for Mrs. Bornson to appear. When she had emerged from the house and bustled down the boardwalk Kate turned her back on her.

"Horrid old hag!" she shuddered. "Still, I shall have to speak to Papa, for it doesn't look as if he was going to speak to me!"

Nor did he. And Kate could not bring herself to go to him. "There's time," she thought, and she waited. The days slipped by, and still there was time. She became nervous and irritable and flew into rages at the smallest cause until everyone who had any cause to be near her wished that she might marry and settle down in a great hurry indeed.

The evening before her wedding, Kate recognized that she could no longer delay and she came in to her father, who was preparing to dine with the groom.

"Papa," she said, and smiled at him. He looked very dashing in his dove-gray trousers, a white satin vest and a dark cutaway.

"Yes, baby?" he brushed an imaginary layer of dust from his

lapel and then took her face in his hands. "It's going to be hard for the old man, baby."

"Why, Papa! we're going to be together, just as soon as we're settled."

"Of course, girlie. I'm being sentimental. Don't like some one else ordering you about in place of me—not that I got anywhere when I did!"

"Now, Papa!" They smiled at each other.

"Papa," Kate said shyly, "is there anything—I ought to know?"

Archibald Rider looked startled. He cleared his throat. "I hadn't thought," he said. He looked at Kate searchingly. Kate blushed and stood her ground.

"You're getting married," he said slowly, and then he brightened almost perceptibly. "There's nothing for you to worry about, girlie. Your husband will take care of you. It's all in the way of nature. Like a beautiful song. And God intended it so," and unconsciously he quoted the minister's wife.

"Very well, Papa," Kate said primly, and if her voice was unhappy her father didn't hear it.

"It's getting late, baby." He kissed her and took up his beaver, his gloves and his cane and went off looking gay and bright. Kate swallowed her disappointment and prepared to have supper with Miss Ferguesson and Madam.

It was a sad supper for a bride-to-be, though Madam had exerted herself to make it rich and gay. Kate had no friends but the two older women and she was lonely enough at the sight of her father's departing back to consider them even closer to her than they actually were.

"To your happiness, little one!" Madam toasted her in white wine and red wine, and in champagne as the meal progressed. "Though I think you've chosen the wrong man," she said loudly as the wine loosened her tongue.

Kate drank with her and smiled, not caring what she said. "Her husband was going to take care of her." It made her tremble to think of it. But it was precisely what her father would have said, and she should have known it.

Miss Fergüesson drank more sparingly, but a little of everything. Once or twice she hiccoughed and excused herself primly.

Madam said, rolling her r's and snapping her a's, "Men are brrutes, brrutes, ma mie! The Irishman would have been betterr for you. Though," she shrugged, "a cold [illegible]
verry ardent, [illegible]

[illegible] told
[illegible] through her honeymoon without ceasing. And when she did settle down, she never addressed Papa again. Not as long as she lived."

"She didn't speak to him?" Kate cried.

"Not directly. Always through some other person. She would say to the maid, 'Ask Mr. Fergüesson does he mind if I attend Aunt Agatha's tea,' or whatever it was that she had to say. Until the children started coming along, and then she used us."

"Well, it sounds intolerable!"

"Peculiar, cerrtainly," Madam agreed.

Miss Fergüesson nodded wisely. "Gentlemen are—trying," she pronounced. "Still, my parents had a long and happy life together. In later years, perhaps, Momma would have spoken to Papa, but I think she did not know how to begin."

"Would you treat your husband like that, ma'am?" Kate asked curiously.

Miss Fergüesson snorted. "I," she said firmly, "would not marry, never," and she looked as though the mere idea shocked her profoundly.

Supper was over and the ladies were sitting on the piazza in a state very close to inebriation, when they heard a horse come down the road at a gallop. Madam was telling a rollicking tale of her adventures in search of M'sieu Le Fèvre and Miss Fergüesson was hiccoughing politely and pulling at her stiff curls as though she would have liked them longer. Only Kate paid attention to the galloping.

When the horse was pulled to a snorting pawing stop at the steps of the piazza, she commenced to laugh riotously. "Oh, Madam," she cried, "that is delicious, it truly is," and she thought, with her heart in her throat, "it's Michael Bourne, come to say good-by to me."

It proved in fact to be he, but if Kate thought that he came to bid her a sweet farewell, she was wrong. He strode onto the porch and, seeing the three of them, he came and stood astride before Kate.

"The little bride!" he saluted her, and Madam said to her friend later that his breath, even from a distance, was what the captain from Indiana intended when he preached on "The Harp of a Thousand Strings—sperits of just men made perfect."

"Thar's a great many kinds of sperits in the world. In the fust place, thar's the sperits as some folks call ghosts; then thar's the sperits of turpentine; and then thar's the sperits as some folks call liquor, an' I've got as good artikel uv them kind uv sperits on my flatboat as ever was fotched down the river——" the captain preacher had bellowed, some ten years earlier. It was apparent to the three ladies on the piazza that Michael Bourne had not left his 'sperits' on any flatboat!

"You're drunk, sir!" Kate cried indignantly.

"Inebriated!" the Irishman sneered. "We're goin' to be a lady now, must learn to talk like one."

Miss Ferguesson rose, flushed with wine and indignation. "Miss Kate," she cried, "you must retire! This indignity—this——"

"No, no, my friend." Madam took the spinster's arm. "We retire. We leave the young one alone, hein! It is good, hein?" And by pure superiority of bulk she propelled Miss Ferguesson and her moral backbone into the house.

Kate said, "I've nothing to say to Mr. Bourne!" and would have gone with them, but the Irishman said, "Wait, please," so humbly that she turned an immediately forgiving countenance upon him.

"Well, if you will promise to behave."

But Bourne did not wait for the ladies' skirts to swish about the corner of the door, to break his promise, but so gently and so sweetly that Kate could at first say nothing.

"I suppose," he said gloomily, "that [illegible]

[illegible] He leaned down and kissed her angrily.

Kate, who was in any case in an emotional state from excitement and fear, from red wine and white wine and champagne, and the disquieting conversations of one dismayed spinster and one over-natural Latin, reacted as she would never have had the courage to have done at another time. For a moment she lay against him like a spineless wax doll; then she threw her arms around him and clung to him, returning his angry kisses, while breathless sobs commenced to shake her whole being. All the while a crazy fire swept through her from her toes to the icy cold roots of her curly hair, filling her with pleasure and fear and a delicious sense of abandon. And, had she wanted, she could not have moved an inch from where she was.

"My beauty," he whispered at last, smoothing her hair with his big hands and kissing the tip of her ear, "—my lovely little one."

"Take me away," she cried. "Oh, Michael, take me away."

He held her at arm's length, and he shook his head, not at her but as at some inner thought. "There's no question you'll always be the weak one of the family," he said gently. "Which is as it should be; but this is something we can't be weak about!"

"What do you mean?"

"We're going to face Tolliver, you and I."

"Oh, no!"

"Oh, yes! After a decent period we'll be married, right here in Jacksonville."

Kate pulled herself free. "You're mad," she said. "You don't know what you're talking about."

"I'm talking about honesty."

Kate tried to pull away. She was coming to her senses. She was both horrified and frightened at what she had done, though at the same time aware that she would still run away with him, if he would take her. In the dim light that shone out from the parlor he looked enormously big and strong, and the light and shadow emphasized his rather homely features in an exciting way. Kate looked at him silently, wanting to bury her hands in his dark hair, to see the stern eyes turn tender again or fiercely passionate. Her eyes caressed the fine line of his nose, but when they reached his wide mouth, now so firm and determined, she dropped them quickly and pulled away again. But he held her with his strong hands and she could not free herself.

"You are a fool, Mr. Bourne," she said almost inaudibly. "Please forget all of this and let me go."

Michael Bourne stared down at her. "You love me," he said, "but you would marry another man just because you haven't the courage to tell him. Or is it Valhalla? Do you go to his arms because he can bed you in silken sheets!"

"Oh!" Kate cried. "Oh, you boor! Sir, do you hear! And I do not love you. On the contrary, I abhor the very sight of you, sir!" Anger, once let loose, mounted in her, submerging all other emotions.

Michael Bourne grinned, but not kindly. "And I thought it was love," he said. " 'Tis an interesting emotion, your brand of abhorrence!"

Kate aimed a furious slap at him, but she was too far away and Bourne caught her hand and held her out of reach. "It is getting to be a habit," he said, "and bad habits make bad wives. My sympathy is with Tolliver, the poor fellow. He won't have my advantage, as I've no doubt he's too much the gentleman to understand your shrewish way!"

Then, abruptly, he put his hand to her chin and turned her

so that the light from the parlor shone on her face. "I thought so," he said, at once gentle and contrite. "You're crying. Miss Kate——?"

"Please! Go and leave me!"

He looked [illegible] not so ignorant as not even to know what you're about."

He left and she remained standing there, too tired to feel anything but a horrible wave of loneliness.

20

MISS JANEY faced her daughter. Her big bosom heaved with indignation. "You can't go," she said.

Crockett shook her head. "I don't see why not, Mama. I'd be sorry to marry away from my home and my own people with not a single friendly face to see me."

"Your father and your brother died"—the older woman struggled with her emotions—"and Cousin George——" she said at last, "look what *they* did to him—he'll never get over it. He'll never marry you, Crockett. Can you forgive *them* that?"

"Maybe he will."

"No—he'll spend his life, set on giving you all the things he's lost. And those things will always be tomorrow."

Crockett turned away from her mother. She said, "I'm going to Kate Rider's wedding."

Miss Janey watched her go. Her chin trembled. She put a hand up to her face. "Oh, Mr. Wilson!" her heart cried, "why aren't you here to help me. Oh, Mr. Wilson, oh Tom!"

Crockett turned in the door, hearing some little sound. "What is it, Mama?" she asked anxiously. Her mother had broken in the instant. Her old flesh crinkled helplessly, like a baby's.

"I'm puny, Crockett. Stay with me."

Her daughter helped her to her bed. "You're not puny," she said firmly. "And I'm not going to stay away from that girl's wedding just because you want to be mean. No, it's not mean. I am sorry. But she's not to blame for all the North, and you aren't being reasonable."

Miss Janey lay down and turned her head away. Tears scalded her eyes but she did not speak again.

On the piazza, Ossian Delahanty slapped George Morgan on the back, and admired his costume. "Hi, old Stud!" he cried. "Regular old Jack-o'-hearts, aren't you!"

Morgan said, "Don't be a fool. Where's Miss Crockett?"

"She'll be down. And since you've stopped by, you may take up the pleasure of escortin' her to the weddin'."

"You don't want to go?"

Ossian shrugged. "I'd as soon, if I had to. But there's no use a-courtin' trouble. Miss Janey's fit to be tied, an' Ma's back home prostrate."

"Scared you'll breathe poison air!"

"No point fetchin' up trouble. I'll escort Miss Crockett if necessary. If it ain't, I'll go comfet the old lady."

Crockett pushed open the door. She looked fresh and frail as a wood flower in her home-dyed black dress.

"Afternoon, gentlemen," she said. "I'm glad you've come, Cousin George." She took Ossian's arm and offered the other to George.

Ossian said, "I'll see you to the corner. I'm goin' home."

Crockett frowned. "Seems to me the sperit of the South is really dead if we can let a stranger in our gates go marry without one kind look or word. I'd be sorry to be in her shoes."

Ossian slammed his hand into his pocket. "You're soft, Miss Crockett," he accused, "like Ma says."

Crockett only smiled. When the corner was reached and

Ossian turned from them she let him go without further protest.

"He's only half grown," she said to George, "a little boy. I shudder to think on what will become of him when his momma dies."

"You are soft, Cousin! if [illegible]

[illegible]

[illegible] to be a gentleman."

Crockett laughed. "You are probably right, Cousin. In any case, here we are."

Madam and Miss Ferguesson were already at the church, sitting in the front pew with Mrs. Bornson. Halla, and a handful of servants from Valhalla, sat by themselves in the rear and the rest of the small church was empty. Morgan hesitated, looking at his cousin.

"Well, ma'am, what now?" he whispered.

"We'll go up front, as long as we're here," she said, and she sailed up the aisle, bowed graciously to the three ladies and, opening the small paneled gate marked with her family name, she entered the pew and knelt for a moment of prayer.

In the vestry, Kate wept. Her father patted her hand unhappily. "It's not too late, baby," he said. "You're not married yet."

But Kate shook her head. "It's all right, Papa. I'm just being silly."

"Well, as long as you're not unhappy. I won't have you unhappy!" He cleared his throat. "Always considered it fiddle-faddle, crying at weddings," he said, blowing his nose and pouring himself a stimulant at the same time. "Fiddle-faddle! And here I am bellowing like a baby!" He downed the brandy, patted Kate's bent head and said, "Drink your brandy, baby. It's almost time."

In the cloak-room, Hains Tolliver talked to Mr. Bornson. His manner was bored and he listened impatiently for the organ to grind out its prelude. Prelude to a new life. Kate at the foot of his table, Kate in his house, Kate in his arms. She was a child, but all the promise was there for him. She would turn into a woman before his eyes . . . a woman for his every need. There would be no limits to Kate. She would be a man to his mind and a woman for his body. Hains Tolliver did not think in terms of heart. But he did think of a cradle and of an heir to all his labors and ambitions.

A loud whistling and breathing came at last from the organ, followed by the promised peal of music. Kate started, her heart beating in her throat. She would throw herself on her father's mercy and beg him to take her away! Her father smiled at her a trifle wetly. "I am proud, baby, proud this day!" He wiped his eyes and Kate put down her glass and smiled back. "We'd better go," she said and they went out of the vestry and up the aisle.

Kate had known that they would not be in step with the music. Papa was tone-deaf. But she had not counted on the fact that she would not care. Every now and then Archibold Rider took a little extra step to make up for his deficiencies. But Kate never noticed. "I am marrying," her heart cried, "I am marrying. How can I, oh, how can I!" She hated Hains Tolliver with a burning hatred. And she wished that she might die there at the altar before she must speak words to tie herself to him for the remainder of her life.

"Dearly Beloved——" Mr. Bornson's voice was deep and quieting. Dearly beloved, dearly beloved! Kate listened and the hate and fear drained out of her. This was her wedding, this strong poetry. She lifted her head and the beauty and promise entered into her. When the words were spoken, she turned with her new-found pride and joy to her husband only to see, with a sense of cold shock, that he was bored. Bored at their wedding! Doubt rushed back upon Kate and, with it, a strange knowledge of guilt. As though she should not have brought him here. "But he wanted to marry me!" her mind protested. And then he kissed her and the feeling dropped away into the realm of half-registered thought.

Mr. Bornson stepped down from the altar and deposited a musty salute upon Kate's cheek. And at once she [illegible]

[illegible] and looked at her curiously. She is beautiful! she thought. How nice it would be to have her for a friend. But I can't. She came only because she is sorry for me. Kate looked across at Miss Ferguesson and remembered something the teacher had told her long ago. I have married the man Crockett Wilson turned down!

"You were very kind to come," she said stiffly.

"I hope you will be very happy," Crockett said, "and I know that you will."

"Thank you." I will, too, she wanted to cry, I will, I will. She put her hand on her husband's arm. She wanted terribly to be taken away. To be alone. Never to have to face people again.

Crockett watched Kate go down the aisle. "I might have stayed and made Mama happy," she said. "It didn't help Miss Rider—Mrs. Tolliver—my coming."

"She was cold," Morgan agreed. "But I don't think she meant it. She was confused, no doubt." They went out of the church and turned towards Caroline Street.

"She's not pretty," Crockett said unexpectedly, "but she's so full of life and strength!"

"I would say that the strength remains to be seen."

"No, I can see it. Only, I wonder, should she have married Hains?"

"She is young, perhaps——"

Crockett shrugged. "Tom was born before Mama was seventeen. Miss Rosaleen was fifteen when she married and so was your mama. It's different nowadays only because girls got old during the war, or their sweethearts got killed. I'm twenty, Cousin, and Mama says everyone in town is calling me a spinster!"

George took a quick step towards her. "Crockett!" he cried.

"I didn't mean that, Cousin!"

"I know, but you know how I feel. I love you dearly. But I have nothing to offer. And you have had so much trouble—I wish that I could ask you to marry me——"

"Why don't you, Cousin?"

He shook his head. "It's too hard," he said. "I can't have you leading the life that I am leading."

Crockett nodded and put her hand on his arm. "I understand," she said, "I do. But—oh, it seems so wrong. Out West it would be different. Out West the very best people live in cabins and do their own work—because they are building something. Here you can't get away from the past. Only listen to the way folks talk: Hains is a scallawag, Ossian is a gentleman, you are dishonoring your blood by working for a Yankee. If you make anything for yourself they will call you a scallawag too! Only look at Mama and Miss Mamie! Cousin George, couldn't you—we—go West!"

They had reached the steps of her mother's house and Crockett turned and looked into her cousin's eyes. Her cheeks were pink with exercise and her own lovely eyes were deep with longing.

But George Morgan shook his head. "This is where I belong," he said. "I'll give you a decent home here, or nothing!" She went up the stairs and he called softly after her, "I'll give you all the old beauties, Cousin, never doubt it."

Crockett turned and smiled, but she looked so sad and so in need of something more than promises that George's heart went out of him.

Maybe, he thought, she is right. Maybe a new country. Maybe going away is what Crockett needs. The West—— He settled the saddle on his horse and tightened the girth. Florida was his home, and he knew that he would never leave it. His grandfather had come here from England when Florida was a republic, a little country on its own. He had been [illegible] other way. So he went unhappily back to Mandarin. And in her cupboard bedroom Crockett stared out of the window and felt that she would never recover from the terrible fatigue that was creeping upon her.

I'm getting a headache, she thought unhappily, and she listened to the diminishing sound of a horse's hoofs on the dirt road.

21

A WEDDING journey might have made every difference in Kate's life, in her relationship to her husband and to her new home. To have gone away, immediately after the ceremony, to some unfamiliar place where both of them would have been strangers on an equal footing of strangeness, to have returned to Hains House its mistress in fact as well as in word, would have made every difference. But the wedding had been planned close to Christmas and Kate did not wish to be away over the holiday leaving her father alone. Travelling took time, and there was no time to go and come and still make preparations. And as for Tolliver, he had had to make his plans with a thought to the orange harvest, so that any other time for the wedding would not have suited him so well.

On the morning after her wedding, Kate awakened to find

herself alone. Her head was in the grip of a vise and it was as though she could feel the very shape of the ducts that ran from somewhere back of her ears to empty their streams of salty liquid into her mouth and throat. She struggled out of bed, shaking from head to foot with nausea. A slop pail of white porcelain, hand-decorated with forget-me-nots, stood by the side of the washstand. She relieved herself retchingly and then, cold and still trembling, she went back to bed. Her head hurt, but the nausea was gone and she was suddenly hungry and eager to be about.

Still she did not sit up. She pulled the covers over her and lay back. Across the piazza doors the blue brocade curtains blocked out the light of the day, at the same time having an aura of brilliance about them, as though they screened a great fire from the darkened room. This room, this blue-brocade and thread-of-silver room, was hers then, just as it had been that other bride's who had dreamed here of her own death. Kate shook her head, and then, because the shaking had awakened a spasm of pain, she put her hands quickly to her forehead. Then she slowly took one hand down and stared at it. The pearl engagement-ring was big on her small hand, but also graceful. Her wedding-ring was wide and heavy, like a golden shackle. In this bed she had dreamed of her wedding, and it had come to pass. She was married. She, Kate Rider, was a married woman with a house of her own, the handsomest house in the South, and perhaps the richest husband. On the dressing-table, if it had already been laid out, would be the silver toilet set that had been her mother's and, still safely threaded through her ears, the diamond earrings that had been her father's present to her. Her husband had presented her with a pearl necklace, while out in the stables was her Christmas present, a handsome chestnut and her own carriage. Marriage was lovely. She wondered shyly where Mr. Tolliver was. She knew that his room was at the front of the house, while hers was at the rear, facing the river, but she had never seen his room.

She thought, suddenly, I wish Papa were here! It would be

such fun to have gone over the house with him. She knew only a few of its rooms, and she was wild suddenly to see the rest. If only her head did not hurt her so. She had had too much wine the night before. In Jacksonville, everybody had had too much wine, and she herself had certainly had enough. She [illegible]

[illegible] had sat at the head of the table and imbibed heavily without once raising his voice or behaving badly. He had just sat there and never taken his eyes from her, and kept her glass full and had insisted that she dance in turn with every man there. But not once had he offered to dance with her himself.

Then the long drive home. For Valhalla was home. Five hours without exchanging a word! Once she had slept, her head dropping naturally to his shoulder as it would have done if he had been her father; she had been too sleepy and full of wine to remember her dignity. She had awakened to feel his hand on her. She had cried out. She should not have done so. She knew at once that she had no right to cry out. She had abandoned that right in the church, in the sight of God. Remembering, Kate commenced to tremble. Mr. Tolliver had been very tolerant, and had journeyed the remaining distance sitting aloofly by her side. He had made neither protest nor comment. Tears had come scorching to Kate's eyes and she had tried to say something to him—"It was just wakening so suddenly!" or "It was just that you startled me, sir," or, humbly, "Please don't be offended with me. I am not afraid, and I will be honest!" But she had had no voice to speak with.

Unbidden, one of Madam's raucous tales of the courtship of

M'sieu Le Fèvre came to her mind. Well, thank the Lord, Mr. Tolliver was not of that ilk! And yet what he was like Kate did not know. They had arrived at Hains House at midnight to find a blaze of light coming from the first floor, where lamps and candles decorated every room. Halla was there alone to welcome them, for the rest of the servants had been given a holiday and a barrel of wine. Kate tried to remember how she had felt seeing Halla standing there as though the house were hers and she were welcoming a guest, but it hadn't seemed to register strongly. Not even when her husband said, "Bring another glass, Halla. We are going to the music-room and you will drink with us."

In the music-room he had touched her again, but not when they stood there alone. He had waited until Halla came. Kate turned her head gingerly into the pillow and started to cry, her head hurt so. He had taken her bonnet and her coat and then, when he had poured the glasses himself and handed them to his bride and to his housekeeper, he had raised his own glass and said, bowing, "To my bride." He had finished his drink at a swallow and put down his glass. Then he had touched her with both his hands, caressing her throat and shoulders, even pushing her dress down a little, right there in front of the colored woman. Kate had felt shamed and frightened but she had made no protest, and then he had said, in a cold, peculiar voice, "Your dress is indecent, madam. Wear a kerchief with it in future," and he had turned his back on her and said to the Negress, "Play for us, Halla, it is my wedding night."

Halla's dark eyes had smoldered with anger.

But it was I who was insulted! Kate thought. He was punishing me, she understood suddenly, for my coldness in the carriage.

Halla played and, even to Kate's uneducated ears, Halla was a gifted, even a great musician. Kate sat stiffly in a French fauteuil on one side of the fireplace and Tolliver lounged on a similar piece of furniture opposite her. He had poured himself another drink, and his eyes were red and they were on her as his hands had been, caressing her throat and shoulders, pushing,

pushing at her dress. Once, Kate had started up to get her coat. He hadn't moved but his eyes had stopped her.

"Where are you going, madam?" he asked.

She told him, and he said, "No, stay as you are."

And then Halla's music had swept the room, big angry [illegible] she had ever heard. Suddenly, Mr. Tolliver had jumped up and cried out:

"Stop it! By God, woman, you'll feel the whip, and don't think any law can prevent me!" He had clutched the back of his chair, quite drunk. Halla hadn't moved but she had played, then, one sweet tune after another with a tinkling, pumping time as though she played upon a clavichord. Mr. Tolliver presently left them and Kate stayed on her stiff chair, like a child who has been put to face the corner, nervous with fear and overwhelmed with exhaustion. Then Halla had come and poured her a large glass of wine. Was it one? She hadn't wanted it, or them. Somehow, there the headache had commenced and the trembling and the nausea. And somehow there had been a soft voice saying, "She is intoxicated." Kate thought that somebody had laughed and laughed and she thought that it had been herself.

She slept again, and when she awakened the curtains were drawn and Dilsey was there to dress her. Her headache had disappeared and she was at once shy and excited, afraid of seeing her husband and eager to see her house. The first she need not have worried about, for Tolliver was in the groves. As soon as she learned that he was out of the house, excitement overcame every shyness and she put her wedding behind her as though it had been an unreal nightmare, best not dwelt upon. In the meantime, there was the house to be seen and she could not wait.

22

GEORGE MORGAN banked the fire, cocked the lids of the stove and went out into the evening to smoke. Bourne was already there, silhouetted against the sky, with only the red coming and going in his pipe bowl to give him life. In the distance, an alligator wept, and an owl screeched nearby as though it had caught, and were relaying, some message.

"They say it brings bad luck if you hear the screech-owl," Morgan said, coming to stand at his friend's side. "Reckon it was a good way to keep the darkies in at night, those that were bold enough to dare the 'patter rollers.'"

Michael smiled, and his smile was lost in the night. "Back North, they say you kept them in with shackles and heavy chains, or with the help of vicious dogs, or of guards with guns and whips!"

Morgan laughed. "They pictured a busier plantation than any I ever saw! Or my father, in his day, I think, though there was of course old Zeph Kingsley. I have heard that what he did not do to tame the blacks he brought in is also omitted from Dante's *Inferno*. He trained them, with whips and hot irons, how to run a plantation profitably, incidentally profiting by their labor; then he sold them at a large price because they were no longer savages but well-broken servants. He slept with the women and sold his own children, sometimes delivered, sometimes in the belly. But the South can scarcely be blamed for him, he was a Scot, a Northerner and a Loyalist!"

Michael Bourne drew on his pipe. "Mr. Kingsley," he said, "would recognize plenty of his ilk were he alive today."

"Slave-beaters?" Morgan protested.

"No—slavery has little to do with it—Kingsley was an opportunist; there will always be people who will climb up on other people's labor. In his day, it was slaves. Now slaves are done with—not because they were badly treated, but because the principle is wrong. The opportunist is still going to climb up by the aid of somebody else's sweat."

"So the institution of slavery is obliterated, and the principle goes on!"

Bourne nodded gloomily, and the two men walked slowly [illegible]

merely sweated and toiled for his master—and yet a good portion of my father's people spent their time working for themselves. Six hundred people, not counting children, had to eat and be housed and clothed. They had to weave and make strong, decent clothes; they had to grow their food, to prepare it—to butcher; to build and keep their cabins in repair; to tend their own sick. For every slave who worked for the master one also worked for the slaves, and all the materials thrown in! Show me a nigger today as well off!"

Michael shrugged again. "It's not a question of being well off," he said, "as you know, my friend. You would not want to be a slave, even if you were better off than you are today."

"You'll not compare me to a black man, I trust!" Morgan said angrily.

But Bourne only laughed at him. "I would that!" he said. "You and I, my friend, are albinos, as it were; peel us and I'll wager the inside meat is of a color with our dark brothers'."

"What of our generations of culture? What of our universities and libraries and churches, what of our arts and our sciences? Perhaps you can teach your black brother— it remains to be seen—but can you explain why, in his own free land, before he was captured and carried way, his mind—his *'equal' mind*—had not set itself a few of these engaging tasks?"

"Why, yes," Bourne said, "I think so. The land he came from

was too easy on him. No rigorous changes in climate to keep him on the jump and force him to develop a civilization. Now that he's transplanted he'll start to develop. It's too bad we can't watch, but it'll take more than a lifetime. It's not strange. Living conditions can make or unmake. They can degenerate the most cultured in a generation."

Morgan scoffed but Bourne said, "Only look at your Crackers—they say that some of them have the blood of kings in them, but they're certainly no addition to civilization."

They had reached the dock, where three wagon-loads of oranges stood ready for loading the following morning. The *Orange Maid* made five trips a week, loading at the small docks and sorting and packing aboard. Larger groves, like Tolliver's, had their own packing-houses and they loaded directly onto boats heading for Savannah.

Out on the river a float heaped with fat-pine loomed like a log cabin against the sky. It was fuel for the river boats, and one of many stops along the river. Michael stared at it for a moment. His friend had disdained to answer him and already his mind was on another matter. The two often argued violently on academic subjects, but in the actual treatment of life they were remarkably of one mind.

"If only we could get more labor," Michael said, expelling a furious cloud of smoke, "we could make something out of the wood lot, gradually clear it and then put in fruit."

George looked up the river to the line where a second growth of saplings towered over the grove. "It would do for fuel," he said; "it's not old enough for lumber. That's where my grandfather's house was, the first Valhalla, a cabin like this one. Michael," he added suddenly, "I have been intending to ask you—will you sell me that piece? I'd like to rebuild where the old cabin stood—if I can even find the spot!" He laughed shortly, as though to make little of his own sentimentality.

"You're sick of a partnership in which the other fellow doesn't do much!" Bourne said quickly. "Sure! I don't blame you."

"No, you wrong me," the other protested. "I am more than

content with our arrangements—you pay the bills and buy the trees and the tools and I do a little work and profit by your investments! But I should like to lay a foundation. You think that I try to go backwards, but you don't understand what it means to me. I have come to realize that I may not get Valhalla back. I [illegible]

They turned and went back, going around about in order to pass the small cluster of shacks where a family of fruit-pickers had battened themselves in for the night, taking every precaution against either screech-owl or evening air.

"If they'd take as many precautions for the hogs as they do for theirselves, I'd be content enough," George grumbled, trying a door that immediately proved to be swinging free. A cow and her calf were in this shack, and a company of hogs, while in another there were chickens. He bolted the doors, and the two men went back to their own cabin. "Every time a 'gator carries off a hog," he complained, "I seem to see an extra layer of fat on them niggers!"

"Alligator alibi!" Michael laughed. During the season of frost he came often to Mandarin, to help as he might. The nights were cold now, and they were trying to pick the fruit as fast as it ripened, with only the inadequate help of one black family. "I'd like to take a vacation," he said shortly, "and come out for a couple of months."

"Why not?"

"Two days away sees my work slip back so that I might just as well not have done a lick; a month would undermine it so that there'd be nothing to start with. I make little enough progress as it is."

"You do yourself an injustice."

"No. Only look at this business of John Bever. I have done everything that I can, and still I cannot find any shadow of evidence even that the man was murdered—except the very vivid evidence of a body!"

Morgan scowled. "You can't mean the black man?"

"Sure, it's what I do mean."

"But Michael," Morgan protested, "you can't waste your time worrying over that. It was a shocking crime—but—a black——"

"Just a shocking crime is the way I look at it. The color of the victim's skin don't matter a damn!"

George Morgan had never spoken of the true circumstances of John Bever's death. Now he looked at his friend with a perplexed frown. They were in the cabin, and the yellow lamplight filled the room like a welcome. "Look here," he said, "if you're still worrying. I think there is something that you should know—though it would do you no good, nor get you any further. I should have told you sooner if it would have——"

The two men faced each other. "You found the man," Bourne said, remembering.

"He came to Mrs. Wilson's house in Jacksonville. Crawled there somehow—from where, we—I—couldn't tell. He died there, on the floor of the kitchen. Miss Janey was upset enough and afraid they'd be blamed. She was sure it looked like he had come there to attack one of them and that they had killed him. If there'd been any point in putting those ladies through the ordeal they would have been put through, I'd have made them own up. But there was nothing to be gained. So I took him out and 'found' him."

Bourne had been staring at him throughout this discourse, with incredulous eyes. "Why, you bloody fool," he cried at last, "do you set yourself up as a tribunal all of your own! What——!" he ran a hand through his hair. "Oh, Jesus! Why, you could go to jail for what you've done! And I've a mind—no—your benighted Southern jury would, no doubt at all, approve of your gentlemanly behavior!" He sat down and took a deep breath. "Supposin' you tell me all about it now," he said, with a return of patience.

Morgan pulled up a chair to the stove, opened the oven door and, sitting down with his chair tilted backwards, put his feet in the oven. He told what he had to tell, and when he was done he spread out his hands: "There you are!" he said. "It's a mere confusement."

[illegible] to himself—the very last thing he wanted was to see her, in her silken gowns, on her husband's arm! He found it hard enough to see as much of her father as he did, though he liked the older man. They were very dull and lonely at Madam's, without the girl.

That night he avoided Archibold Rider, going straight to his own room despite the older man's eager welcome. "Let him gamble or get drunk!" he decided angrily. "Cutler's always willing to strip him." He was sorry at once, for Archibold Rider had seemed to him remarkably forlorn, more like a child who has lost a parent than a parent who has lost a child. Still, he did not go down. He did not want any more heavy arguments, with his opponent charmingly sure that the world was made of sugar and spice. Michael had once told him that he ran his Bureau like a Chinese tea-shop, with every unaromatic evidence of vice in the rear—only that he had never gone through the rear, so that he didn't know. Rider had stormed lustily, red in the face and outraged, finally petering out with an abortive—"If I thought you were right, sir, if I thought you were right!"

"Oh well, the poor fool!" Michael said under his breath, dropping his coat onto the floor. You could fight a knave but every time you aimed a blow at a fool a little bit of fluff popped out of a seam and the fool smiled back at you.

When he had washed and changed into fresh linen, he

relented and went down to find the older man, but Archibold Rider had given him up and was gone for one of his disconsolate walks.

THE Commissioner sat spooning the bubbles from the top of his coffee. Bubbles were money. The back of both his lapels were thick with the pins he had picked up. Pins were good luck. James Cutler came into the dining-room and sat beside him. Archibold Rider did not like the man, who was sharp and in some way unhealthy. He nodded and hurried through the rest of his breakfast.

"Come into my office when you get down," he said when he had finished, "one or two things have come up." He folded his napkin, rolled it and pushed it into its ring. Then he took his paper and went out.

At his office, Rider examined his reflection in a wall mirror and smoothed his hair. Then he went to his desk. A tray of papers was in the middle of the blotter. A note on the top of this pile read: "Ready for signature."

Rider sat down and commenced to apply a flourishing signature as directed. When he had completed the pile, he opened his right-hand drawer and took out the small flat bottle. When he had refreshed himself he replaced it, closed the drawer and rang a brass bell on his desk.

A colored boy opened the door and pushed his head into the room. "You ringing?" he asked.

"Take these to Mr. Cutler's office," Rider said with a show of dignity. "And when I ring, come all the way into the room and say 'yes, sir.' "

The colored boy came into the room now. "Yes, suh," he said, grinning, and he took the papers.

"When Mr. Cutler comes——" Rider commenced, but the colored boy interrupted him:

"He done come, plumb on top of you!"

"Well, remind him that I want to see him."

This time he did not have long to wait. Cutler rapped on the door almost immediately. But he made no apology for his delay. Rider swept him with a look, from his dove-gray spats to his satin tie. An apology would have made the interview [illegible]

[illegible], always had been, now that he thought of it. Maybe there was something in what Bourne said. Well, he intended to find out.

"I've been hearing things about the Bureau," he said at last, tossing the words out as though they were liable to burn his tongue.

Cutler sat more easily in his chair. "Like what?"

"Well, how many Freedmen have we placed in positions this last year? And has this office taken any—er—remuneration for this service?"

The other man stared at him. "You got all the figures," he said slowly, "Boss!"

"What do you mean?" There was that in the way the word "Boss" was used that he did not like.

"You're the boss, you sign the vouchers and the records and the reports."

"That doesn't answer my question."

"But there's nothing I can tell you——" The other spread his hands out in mock innocence and smiled an ingratiating smile. Or what purported to be an ingratiating smile. "I only follow orders," Cutler said. "You're the boss."

"Very well," Rider said weakly, only eager now to see the end of the fellow. "I thank you for your time, sir."

For a long time after James Cutler had left him he sat there staring at the dusty backs of his law books. You could find out what was in the book by opening its cover, but you could not so easily find out what was in a man. It did not seem likely at all that the man was doing anything dishonest right there in his, Archibold Rider's, own office. Just because he looked unpleasant did not have to mean that he was. Still, perhaps he had left too much to him in the past; he had been so well recommended. Better keep an eye on things. He lit a cigar and sat smoking and feeling bewildered and lonely. If it were not for Kate, he thought, I should return North. Well, another year, when she was more used to her new home. Perhaps she would have a baby by then, and he could go back to Enid's warm and narrow little house in Hartford.

He missed his daughter deeply, though she was only a few miles away and he could go to her at any time. He was lonely, and he had no one to greet him with enthusiasm and exchange with him the little happenings that made the day. And if Kate had seemed at times to wish him stronger or more ambitious than he actually was, still the quality of her love was like sun and rain and good earth to a plant. He hoped that Hains Tolliver knew how great was his good fortune. In the meantime, he, Archibold Rider, was merely suffering from being transplanted to sandier soil. Certainly he was not being neglected! Both Miss Ferguesson and Madam had bestowed upon him their solicitous attentions. But Miss Ferguesson was homely as sin and a spinster to boot, while Madam had a voluptuous way with a man, which charmed a man when his was not a voluptuous nature. Furthermore, Madam considered herself a widow.

In the meantime there was always the gaming table and the warming effects of liquor. The gaming table, to be sure, had lost some of its charms. Certainly not because Kate's disapproving eye had been withdrawn. But it was a strangely lonely game when there was nobody in the sitting-room upstairs to look forward to. And then, Michael Bourne rode out to his groves a good deal during the cold months and the remaining company seemed less pleasant to him, now that he was alone, than they had seemed when he had his daughter in the house. Mr. Cutler,

Mr. Hess, Captain Freeman, Mr. Gordon! As Miss Ferguesson had once said, "Every one a bunco man, excepting that he has a legitimate job—or at least the looks of one!"

He marvelled at himself that he had not been more astute about these people before, for his sudden distaste had nothing but loneliness as it [illegible] dismissed this thought at once. The bales would call for a tribe to move them, and a large cart, all of which would attract more attention than any thief dare risk.

It called for investigation, without doubt. He pulled his mustache and, crossing the street, went into the building. At the foot of the stairs, he listened. He could hear nothing, though a crack of light showed beneath the door at the head of the stairs. He took out his key and went up. He made no attempt to walk quietly, but his patent-leather shoes were soft on the wooden treads excepting that both they and the treads squeaked from time to time. Halfway up, he stopped; there were voices on the other side of the door but whose they were he could not yet distinguish. He put his key in the lock and pushed open the door, not stopping to think that if the intruders were indeed stealthy he was not pursuing the wisest course.

His own office was dark, and the small room that Hess and also Jeff occupied. The door to Cutler's office was open, and it was from this room that the voices came. A kerosene lamp hung from the center of the ceiling, spreading out its yellow brilliance. James Cutler himself sat at the desk directly beneath it, and it dropped a path of shiny light upon his dark head. He wore a pencil behind one ear and he had removed his collar and tie. With one hand he rubbed his neck and with the other he fingered the chewed stub of a cigar.

Archibold Rider stood there, fascinated by what he saw and heard, his faculties so occupied in listening that they made no thoughtful decisions for him. His eyes took in the occupants of the room and the old familiar furnishings, the mottled gray file boxes that lined a wall, their orange-and-black labels standing out dimly.

Leaning in the door and idly turning and twisting a short thick stick, stood Samuel Hess, while between him and the man at the desk was a large colored man, his hands at his side and his head bent slightly, as though to listen better.

"Now, friend Paul, you know what the Freedman's Bureau is for, don't you?" Cutler was saying, his voice empty of expression.

"Yes, suh," the black man nodded.

"It's to help you niggers, isn't it?"

"Yes, suh."

"It's to keep you from harm."

"Yes, suh."

"It's to teach you how to be free, isn't it? How to take care of yourselves, all alone and free in the world the way you are now."

"Yes, suh."

"Ebbet's farm is going to be auctioned Monday, I hear," Hess said from the door. "Any of you people planning to be there?"

"Yes, suh."

"It would not be safe."

James Cutler sucked at his cigar and looked through the smoke at Hess. "Almighty God would be tried to keep these niggers out of trouble," he complained. "You'd think they would know better than to try to buy land around Jacksonville right now. But if we're to write to Congress and tell them Senators that the niggers down here are still free and healthy, we have to spend our time saving their skin. Now, you git home and tell the folks; see, brother Paul? And next time you hear of a piece for sale you come tell us, and if it's safe we'll fix up the whole deal for you."

Brother Paul was silent and the stunned man in the hall was about to step into the room when Hess flicked the stick in his hand and said as softly as his big voice could manage, "It's good advice, brother."

"Is Mist' Rider to town?" the Negro asked unexpectedly. In the corridor Rid[illegible]

[illegible]

This was more than Archibold Rider could quietly stand. As though the words were a burr beneath his saddle, he cleared his throat with a loud grinding and cried out: "That will do, sir, that will do," and, pushing Hess aside with a show of violence quite alien to him, he thrust himself into the room. The colored man, in any case frightened and nervous, let out one terrified and despairing cry and bolted, sweeping Rider and Hess into each other's arms as he did so. Hess cursed loudly and long. Archibold Rider said, "Damn it, sir," once but with sufficient vehemence, and James Cutler, having recovered from his first surprise, commenced to laugh.

"By Christ, sir," he cried at last, "you certainly expedited matters for us. That nigger won't show up at Ebbet's—though I've lost the fifty cents I was going to charge for advising him."

"You were going to what!" Rider cried, sputtering with rage.

"You heard me," Cutler said, no longer pretending to defer to the Commissioner.

"Sir! This is shocking! Outrageous! I trust that you and Mr. Hess will be able to explain," Rider cried, for, despite the witness of his eyes and ears, he could not face the situation without a struggle.

"Sir," his assistant said coldly, "you pretend. There is no reason why we should explain."

"No reason! But, I assure you, I shall go to Washington with this. And my candid opinion is that you will go to jail!"

Hess said, "Say!" with inarticulate protest. Cutler raised an eyebrow. "The other day," he said, "I thought you were just filibustering, using up some of that excess of wind which you ain't got anyone to listen to now the girl's gone."

Purple blossomed in Rider's face and he made a sound that had no meaning, for his tongue lolled thick and useless in his mouth. Cutler signalled quickly to Hess, "Get him a chair, he looks about to have a stroke."

Archibold Rider took the chair with sudden meekness and, as though Hess's words had brought him to his senses, he said heavily, "I have been a great fool, it would seem. Now I should like to know what this is all about."

Cutler pulled open a drawer and withdrew a sheath of papers, which he handed across the table to the older man.

Rider frowned. "Vouchers!" he said. "What about them?"

"You signed them."

"Well?"

"With a note, in your hand, that the shipment vouched for be turned over to Hains Tolliver."

"Well?"

"Wake up, Mr. Archibold Rider! Those vouchers represent five hundred pounds of food and at least the same amount in clothing and medicines. It is sent down from the North as relief for the freedmen, who as slaves were taken care of all of their lives and are starving now because they don't know what the hell to do with theirselves. And you turned it over to Tolliver."

The Commissioner rubbed his chin, a shadow of anxiety crossing his face. "But he distributes it. There is a large community at Mandarin——"

"He sells it to niggers, who don't want to buy it, for a little more than the price of their labor. See! He pays his niggers as the law demands. Then they give the money back to him and remain always a little in his debt! It is slave labor, Mr. Commissioner, with the help of government supplies and a government official."

"It's not true! It's not true!" Archibold Rider whispered, his voice rising in the end almost to a scream.

"It's true enough, brother."

"I don't believe it. And I warn you [illegible] convicts continue to be released to Tolliver when their year is up."

"I have been a fool," Rider said at last, "but don't think that I am your man, Cutler. I shall tell the whole story and hand in my resignation."

Hess growled, but Cutler said with unexpected smoothness, "That's up to you. But just remember—it's no question of being 'my man.' This office is run by your son-in-law. He picked you out because you were just the sort of man he needed as a figurehead. And he had you tied in knots before you'd been down here a month. Now you want to plead ignorance— Well, sir, I put it to you—what court is going to take ignorance into consideration? You are of a responsible age and, to the world at least, head of this office."

Cutler looked at the older man shrewdly. "In any case, nobody south of the line is going to believe you. Tolliver's not popular, but he's a Southerner and you're a carpetbagger. Even back home they'll be glad to make an example that'll quiet a lot of the belly-aching they've been getting about carpetbag administration. You've got nothing to gain, and you've got a lot to lose—for that girl of yours, if it don't matter to you."

Archibold Rider got up and went out of the room without saying another word. In the corridor, he stood for a moment bewildered. He still held the office keys in one hand. He looked at the outer door. He pictured the long flight and the dark streets and Madam's porch with the two ladies in the sitting-room talking about the cool weather and the last boat in from the North and other trivial everyday topics. His knees commenced to tremble; and his hands, and then uncontrollably his jaw, while a sweat rose cold and sickening on the back of his neck. He turned to his own darkened office. He had to be alone. He went into the room, bolting the door behind him. At his desk he sank down, with his head on the blotter, and wept.

In the office that he had left, the two men looked at each other. They had heard the direction of the Commissioner's footsteps and the bolting of the door. "He's not going to shoot himself?" Hess said uncomfortably. His companion shook his head, but the big man shifted and said,

"I don't like it. I'm getting out of here."

"Scared?" Cutler jeered.

"Just careful."

"Well, we might as well go." Cutler adjusted his collar and Hess pulled the lamp down from the ceiling and waited to blow it out.

"O.K." Hess blew out the light and raised the lamp to its place. He struck a match, and the two men made their way out of the room and down the hall. Cutler hesitated for a moment, looking towards Rider's darkened office, then he followed his companion out. There was nothing that he could do. The old fool wasn't going to commit suicide, not while he had a bottle in that top drawer. The two men walked down the middle of the road-bed and neither of them spoke. Hess, now that he was free of the building and any possibilities that lurked there, dismissed anxiety from his mind and hummed a grating tune in a contented voice. But Cutler was nervous, not at all sure that it was such a good evening's work. Still, there had been nothing to do but tell him—once he walked in like that. He thought irritably, I'll have to go out and see Tolliver—he'll have to know before the old fool can get to him. "By Jesus!" he cursed under his breath. He, James Cutler, took all the risks and did all of the work, while Hains Tolliver sat out there on his silks and satins with his fine young wife and lapped up the gravy. Too bad his niggers didn't cut out his black heart and eat it, but who knows—maybe some day they would!—and leave James Cutler free for the gravy.

They had come in sight of the lights of the boarding-house, and they climbed onto the wooden [illegible]

[illegible] lay on his office floor dead drunk and snoring like a bull alligator in the swamps. For the moment, the situation was in hand. Still, Tolliver would have to be forewarned.

Cutler was not a natural horseman. He had rented a heavy nag from the livery stable next to the office on Bay Street, laying stress on the fact that he was not interested in speed. Not that he would have got it. The livery stable, like most of its kind, operated a line of hacks remarkable only for their lack of blood and spirit. No gentlemen would willingly rent a horse, and if such a person could not afford to keep his own, well then he took what there was and that was all there was to it.

At the cow ford a ferry was in, so that the rider went aboard at once. As he was late, the boat was already crowded and Cutler could not move up from the rear. Every traveller, every dray or ox cart moving from north to south overland, crossed at the cow ford, and the day set in early for the ferry business. Not seeing anyone aboard whom he knew, James Cutler knotted his reins and lit a cigar. Up and down the river, enough ships to have made up a navy were a-move in the choppy water and the air was pungent with the smell of pine smoke. It was a rich sight for a man whose mind was upon gains. Of all the South, this man was wont to congratulate himself, he could not have picked a better spot than Jacksonville.

But he could have picked a more equitable situation. I'm

clever enough myself, he thought, to do without a clever master. Today I know more than he does, I'm more valuable to him than he is to me.

The ride to Mandarin was tedious to one who had no eyes for beauty, for the rich growth of trees and underbrush or the river with its ships and its choppy waters sparkling in the sun, its leaping porpoises playing in the channel. Cutler, having found that his nag was not under any circumstances going to exert the energy necessary to bolt, proceeded to keep him kicked up to as much speed as was possible. In between these lumbering dashes, the horse would fall into a stubborn shamble, only indirectly resembling a walk. Cutler, seeing that he was bested beyond his power to improve the matter, would light another cigar and reflect on the choicest words to use on the liveryman in returning the creature. Glue was all the animal was good for, and he would make a strong, tenacious substance guaranteed to hold whatever it was applied to in one unmoving position for eternity. Mr. Cutler was moved to bitterness. A usually five-hour ride was going to take him seven.

And what for! He tortured himself, went through the greatest discomfort, to carry a warning to a man who was no friend of his. Indeed, who used him as a servant. I am given a salary, James Cutler thought, kicking his mount in the belly, and a bonus here and there, to line another man's pocket! Well, I'm a fool. And now I'm going out to do him a favor, and all I'll get is a kick in the pants, and he dug at the horse so sharply that the animal shook his head and commenced to canter with a ponderous rollicking motion, as though he were trying to move ahead without bending his knees.

James Cutler was not wrong about his reception. Tolliver took him to a small building that stood among the orange trees, where he carried on the business of the estate. There was neither pleasure nor welcome in his manner.

After six arduous hours in the saddle, to be given a drink and told to state your business as quickly as possible calls for a sweeter temper than James Cutler was in possession of. He stated his business as slowly as he could, watching the fury gather in Tolliver's cold gray eyes.

"You fool!" the latter cried.

"What could I do?" protested Cutler; "he walked in at a bad time!"

"Don't talk back to me, sir," the other lashed out at him as though he [illegible]

"I think," he said with a sudden return of softness to his voice, "that you are getting ideas, Mr. Cutler. I would not, sir!"

Cutler started to protest, but Tolliver held up his hand. "Remember, my man," he said with a cool insolence that brought out a scowl on the other's face, "if you wish to make difficulties—there is evidence that can be adroitly placed. If you just wish to leave me and go out on your own—I might decide to allow that—but not in Florida. Even if I did not place evidence, there is not a position in the State you can get against my direction."

"You think you own the bloody State," Cutler snarled.

"You might put it that way. Now"—Tolliver accepted the other's unspoken surrender; there was nothing the carpetbagger could do—"you can have dinner. Then go back to the office. As Rider has started drinking, it will be easy. Get him to the house, say he's had a stroke, but give Madam the wink. Lock him in his room and keep him supplied with liquor for a few days. About Thursday you can start easing him off. I'll come in and talk to him. If he doesn't take another attitude, he'll have to be sent back North. His only use to us was his obvious honesty and his innocence. I am afraid he'll prove a loss, Cutler, that I cannot overemphasize. Well, we'll undo it as well as we can." He pulled at a cord that hung by his desk. Wires attached to it ran through a pipe from the small office to the rear of the main house, where they set a-jangle a handful of tiny bells. While the two men waited, Tolliver poured another drink for his visitor, and when the black servant, Mose, came to the door, he said,

"Mr. Cutler will dine with me. Have Halla serve Miss Kate in her sitting-room."

Mose bowed and went out, and James Cutler downed his drink at a gulp, pale with rage. So, he was not good enough to sit at the table with the old fool's daughter! Miss Kate was somebody now, but James Cutler was just a servant, a menial who could not be received by his master's wife. He wanted to throw his glass in Tolliver's face and shout at him, "You can countermand that order, you fool. I won't eat the salt of a man I'm going to kill some day, so help me God!" But the thought chilled him even as it came to him, and he stayed meekly, and ate at his master's table. He ate largely, being ravenous with hunger, but he scarcely tasted what he ate, for he was cowed by his own thoughts.

Later, riding away through the miles of orange trees, so heavy a symbol of their owner's wealth, he let himself think again. He was no murderer, nor would he be! To kill a black man was bad, certainly, or to have any part in it—but sometimes a thing like that was unavoidable. But to kill a white man was murder. "I'll go," he thought. "I'll get him to let me go. There's plenty of money to be made farther north. Maybe all the way to New York. It'd be good not to see any more damn grovelling stinking coons!" He thought of the rich dinner he had eaten, cooked by a fat black slave of a woman no doubt, and served by three neat bowing black slaves. "But they don't even know they're slaves!" he shouted aloud, shaking his fist in the direction of the distant house. A flock of birds rose from a tree, frightened at his loud voice, and he laughed a short laugh that was more like a nervous cough. "Those niggers would cut his throat, if they knew," he thought. "They'd rise up in a body and hack him to pieces, if I know niggers, and I ought to. I'm their friend, aren't I?" He laughed again. "I'm their leader, I'm their friend." He kicked at his animal hopefully, but it had done its piece for that day, and a slow walk was all that he got the rest of the way to Jacksonville.

25

FEBRUARY [illegible] going Cracker will keep a Southerner in a town. And I, for one, have nothing against going Cracker."

"You would have," Crockett argued, "if you had children. As it is, you cannot really go Cracker. You can bud trees until your hands bleed, or hoe or weed or patch a leaking roof and still play the piano. You can call the hogs and sing arias, you can stand by the river where there's not a human being in miles to talk to, just you and the 'gators and cottonmouths and wild shoats, and you won't be alone. Because you haven't always lived like that. You have all the past, the intellectual and the spiritual companionship that you have had with other minds, to fall back on. You have meat to work on for the rest of your life. But with a Cracker's fare you wouldn't have time to hand any of that on to your children. They'd bud the trees and tend the hogs and be alone by the river. The few darkies left who'd work for you wouldn't come near your children, the little poor-white-trash."

"It's partly why I must have Valhalla back," he said. "Which, paradoxically, is why I'm not afraid of going Cracker. My sons could not go Cracker on Valhalla. And if any one of them was so poor in himself, so without strength or resource, he would still be better off."

"I don't understand you."

"You mean you don't agree. But that's because you don't like Valhalla, Crockett."

"No," she said slowly, and she looked at him so unhappily that he was tempted to take her in his arms. But he had nothing yet to show her, no security to give her. He had bought from Bourne the piece of land that he wanted. The piece where his great-grandfather's cabin had stood. When the harvest was done, he would start to clear it. In the meantime, he had nothing to his name but a bit of jungle. And it would be months before he could do anything about it. For they were in for a long harvest at Bourne's and a large one, with too much of their fruit rotting for lack of pickers as it was.

"It's a big country," he said at last, "a big and moving country. A man could get lost in it, without his land, without some meaning to his life. I know that you still think of the West, Cousin——" he shrugged. He could not say more than he had said.

"Your great-grandfather left the country he knew and came to a wild place. Are you sorry that he came? Are you lost here?"

"No, of course not. Too much time has gone by. But unless he was very different, he must have felt lost. I often think of it. What manner of house did he come from, back there? What was his father like? What kind of a woman his mother? What road ran up to their house? Was there sea there? Or forests? Were the pastures green and low or high and rocky? Did he love to remember how the land lay, every inch of it, and all of the boyhood happenings, along every inch of it? And yet however much it meant to him, however dear the price of his going, as far as his children were concerned it might never have happened. It is gone now. He lost it when he came here, and there is not a ripple left. Michael would say 'And to hell with it, good riddance!' But I can't."

"No, I don't think you can," and Crockett put her head back and closed her eyes. And Morgan went back to Mandarin, knowing once more that he had let her down. Knowing, despondently, that he always would.

At Valhalla, Kate was enjoying her home with the enthusiasm and the energy of a child who has been given a doll-house and a family of dolls. She was everywhere at once and, at first, attempted to direct everything. The realization that the household moved in its tracks smoothly despite, rather than because of, her came slowly. Halla was feared by every colored person on the place. They had no such awe of Kate, but were soon calling her "honey" and talking back to her if what she said did not [illegible]

[illegible]

suddenly Halla was there.

"Plant the seeds," she said, "where Madam wants them."

Three days later, Kate stepped out onto her piazza for a breath of air. It was afternoon, the sun was still high in the sky and the house was at rest. She leaned on the balustrade for a moment. Immediately beneath her Halla was moving along the edge of the lawn. She had a pitcher in her hand and she was pouring a white liquid into the newly planted beds. Kate frowned, suddenly frightened. Halla was not watering the seeds. She is seeing to it that the "sperits" don't let anything poke their heads up, Kate thought, and by broad day. She doesn't care a rap who sees her. Kate turned soundlessly and went back to her room.

Halla hated her, she had always known that. But, before, her hatred might have meant something. Now it was without meaning. Kate was mistress of Valhalla. I could have her sent away, she thought, and she could never have me sent away. Does she think me so silly that she can scare me away? But Kate was not ready to face Halla, though she knew that some day it must be done.

Later, the same afternoon, she met Halla again. Kate was in the kitchen and had asked whether they could not have liver sometime for dinner.

"Honey," fat Alma said, "ain't the boss gwine ter eat no liver?"

Kate didn't argue. She didn't know her husband's tastes well enough yet, but she protested just a little. "I used to see that Papa got it once a week," she said. "It's good for the blood."

"The boss ain't got that kind of blood," Alma grumbled, but goodnaturedly.

And, then again, Halla had been there ordering liver once a week and everyone yes'm'ing her. Kate fled, not wanting anything to do with Halla. Instinctively, she put the day of reckoning off again. She could not overcome the feeling that she might in some way be bested.

The liver was not a success. When it was offered to him, Hains Tolliver looked across at his wife and said firmly, but kindly, "Kate, you don't know my ways. I prefer to have you leave the planning of meals to Halla."

"Oh, dear!" she started to protest, but he stopped her at once.

"You have a housekeeper. Let her do her work, which is to keep house. Now really, Kate, I forbid you."

So that was that. When she pouted he smiled at her, tolerating her mood. "You've music and books and sewing. Later, when the trees are in blossom, we'll have a festival. Senator Osborn is coming down, and we will entertain the future governor."

That pleased her, and why not? Why be a rich lady without guests and entertainment? People came to Valhalla all the time, but not many of them were attractive. And the ladies of Jacksonville never came. Kate passed happy days planning the fête that they would have. She was going to ask Crockett Wilson, and she knew that she would come, too. Perhaps Miss Crockett would like the future governor and they would marry. Of course, she was supposed to be affianced to Mr. Morgan. But it was easy to see he was never going to have enough money to marry on. And, then, marriage was more than love. Marriage was like the land. All of life came out of it. No woman in her right senses could afford to marry a man; she married a safe way of living. Only look at me, she thought, with a closet full of clothes, a carriage of my own, with my own maid! She also had a house that made her heart turn over, every breath she drew in it. Uncounted servants, and uncounted acres of fertile land. She could have children and children and children. And they would have everything that was beautiful in the world, and all the world would adore them. Children she would have!

Though Kate still occupied the blue room, in the sense that her clothes were kept there, and her silver mirror and [illegible]

[illegible] she clung to the stranger and, though she screamed once, he never knew that she had suffered any feeling other than was wifely and pleasant. For they never spoke of what was between them, either then or at any other time. It was a hidden thing that belonged to night and must be robed in silence.

For a long time, Kate approached nightfall with renewal of terror, but she had too much pride to show it, and too much native honesty. Hains Tolliver had carried out his part of the bargain, he had a right to expect that she would come to him willingly, even gladly. Though the latter, Kate thought, was asking a great deal of any female. Once she closed her eyes and wondered, with a sense of guilt, whether she would have felt differently if it had been Michael. She hadn't been afraid of *his* kisses, or felt alone with him. A wild hot surge of feeling raced in her blood. She opened her eyes quickly to find her husband staring at her, and she blushed furiously. She was too experienced now not to read a new meaning into her thoughts, and a new shame.

Tolliver said, "Still being a little girl?" in a voice half bored, half amused, but kind. Though Kate was not always sure that the things he said were really kind. She did not always understand him. And she did not understand at all what he wanted of her, or how he felt about her. He was sometimes very tender. And he talked to her seriously when he felt like it, talked as though she were another man. Sometimes it was long drawn out and boring but even then it had an element of excitement about it. In those moments, Kate was a wife as she never was in his arms. She knew it instinctively, but she could not fathom it. He was never rude to her, in the sense of being impolite, but he not infrequently hurt her. And when he did his manner had an exquisite infallibility, as though he delighted in her pain.

Halla had always to be polite with her, always visibly humble. Yet he would sometimes, and in front of them both, prefer Halla's judgment or Halla's taste to hers. Once he told Kate that she must not play the piano while he was in the house.

"Amuse yourself while you're alone," he said. "You are no musician, m'dear. I did think of having Halla teach you. But even she would never be able to make anything of you. You haven't the touch."

As the months went by, Kate grew used to her married state. She was still without pleasure in her husband's love-making, but she ceased being afraid. An unpleasant duty, even a boring one, claimed her nights, but she complied as graciously as she knew how. Upon occasion, she found herself experiencing a certain maternal superiority over the strangely weakened creature who spent his strength on her and then fell sleeping at her side.

Kate never called her husband by his first name, though he had once laughingly invited her to do so. "Oh, I'm quite sure it isn't done, ma'am," he had laughed, pulling her onto his knee. "But we will set our own styles, and to the devil with the fashionable world, eh!"

But Kate would not. She tried out his name in her mind, but "Hains" seemed almost an impudence, and it did not suit him nearly so well as "Mr. Tolliver." And yet, she thought, if I were married to Michael—— But I'm not! Still, he was Michael to her and she thought that he always would be, and that it was natural so. She smiled at her husband and she continued to call him "Mr. Tolliver." Halla had watched this display of affection on the part of her master dourly. Kate wished her elsewhere, but Halla seemed always to be there. In the evenings, when they went to the music room, Halla played for them. Or if she did not play she sat, as though she were mistress of the house, in the French fauteuil across from Mr. Tolliver. Kate herself would sit on a stool at her husband's knee, and alternately watch the fire or the reflections that it sent dancing across Halla's skirts. Halla would work on a piece of [illegible]

still be called Valhalla. Kate had ridden that day to the colored village at the dock. The house servants lived there in a company of shacks and cabins. To the east, beyond an alley of oaks said to have been giants when the Spaniards christened the river River of May, was the old Valhalla, the house where George Morgan had grown up.

"I saw it today," Kate said, "the roof and chimneys struggling out of all that tangle. It will rot. You should let Mr. Morgan have it—or tear it down."

Halla bit off a thread. "There are cottonmouths in the wine-cellars, and wild cats in the ballroom," she said and for some perverse reason Hains Tolliver smiled.

"Why should I give it away?" he asked. "Your Mr. Morgan hasn't the strength to hold his own among men; what makes you think he could get the better of snakes and cats?"

"It must be a beautiful house," Kate said. "I shouldn't let it rot. I think it's a shame."

He pinched her cheek. "But I like to see it rot," he said. "It is a symbol to me. And it has, believe me, nothing to do with George Morgan, who is a weakling and of no interest to me."

"But then why? I don't understand——"

"My father loved this place. He wanted to live his life out here. But he was the kind of man who had to have friends. It is too bad that he was not more like me. Then, perhaps, I was not meant to be this way. Certainly I learned it in a hard school and I was not always happy about it. It is true nevertheless that he travels fastest who travels alone. And I have no room for friends." He looked across at Halla and said with a twisted smile, "Halla knows. Halla has no friends either!"

The black woman looked at him long and silently and he smoothed Kate's hair. "My father," he said softly, "met my mother at Alphonse Morgan's house. She was visiting there. When she went home to Georgia he followed her and married her. Morgan took it upon himself to object. He wrote my grandfather, said that he should never have introduced the two. Well, they were suspicious people in Florida in those days, and that in itself was not blameworthy. My father had come to Mandarin to buy land. He had money, but so had a lot of brigands, cutthroats and pirates. He said that he was descended from the Tagliaferros, but Morgan had no proof of it. When he brought my mother back to Mandarin, Morgan was relieved. God knows what he had thought was going to happen to her! He sold my father a piece of land, and this house was built. Halla was born here. That didn't disturb anyone, did it, Halla?" When she didn't answer he said, "But I was born here too, and that seems to have made all the difference. My mother killed herself."

Kate clutched her fingers together. He had never told her of this thing, though she knew it from others. She would have liked to say something to him, but she couldn't find a word to tell of her pity. She turned her cheek against his knee, feeling strangely dissatisfied, as though he needed her for once and she had nothing to give him.

"Alphonse Morgan chose to hold my father responsible. He would have hanged him if he could. What he did was worse. He drove him away. He turned every white man on the river against him. And when the frost ruined all of the groves on the river, Morgan had another weapon. My father got no loan or help to clear out the dead wood and replant. So perhaps you can see, m'dear, why I am glad that Alphonse Morgan's groves belong to me, that his land and his trees yield their fruit to me. And that his house rots at my pleasure."

"But it does you no good," Kate said. "In fact, I think, it hurts you."

"It's time you began to feel the same way. You are nothing now, Kate, and no one. You are in Limbo, you know! But one day you will give me a son and with his birth [illegible]

"Didn't you like living in France?" she asked, to dispel the feeling.

"I would have. But my father didn't. He kept coming back. He made money in Georgia and he replanted the grove here and filled the house with slaves. But he couldn't stay."

"I shouldn't have cared to stay," Kate said indignantly.

"But he did, Kate. It was in his blood. His forefathers came here with Menendez. At one time, half the State belonged to them. As," he said quietly, "it will to me, again."

"It could," Kate said. "Was your forefather Spanish?"

"Italian, and a natural colonizer. He married, so they say, an Indian princess. By living outside of the fort among her people he escaped the de Gourgues massacre, and he also inherited her lands."

"He must have been very rich."

Tolliver pulled a curl and laughed at her. "The land was wild, m'dear, swamp and jungle. But his sons did well. Then, in a hundred years, the English commenced to take an interest. The lands were raided, the trees cut down, the buildings burned and the family murdered, or most of it."

In the dying embers of the fire Kate saw dreamy shapes, burning orchards and fleeing women and dark-haired men with flaming swords. They could not have been like her husband; he belonged to a more sophisticated age, a cultured age, an age rubbed smooth with time. Those other men were strong and fierce and uncouth. Men like Michael. Men—— Kate looked away, ashamed of her thoughts. "How can you know?" she asked. "Or is this the way you think it was?"

"I can't know, of course. But the story lived. A daughter out of that generation lived. She had been raped by a British soldier. A missionary found her wandering in the woods and took her South where he placed her in a convent. She gave birth to a son to whom she gave the name Tagliaferro, though she spelled it Tallifero."

"Was he our—grandfather?"

"My dear child, his grandson was my grandfather."

Kate thought of the Tagliaferros often. They made Valhalla important. She began to understand her husband and his hatreds, and, strangely, she pitied him. At the same time she was sensitive enough to know that her pity would only enrage him, and she kept silent.

With her new knowledge her desire for a child was reawakened. A son first. After that it wouldn't matter. She would stand in front of the mirror in her bedroom and examine herself and prod her abdomen, but she never looked different one day from the next, and no mysterious and blissful knowingness descended upon her. Her desire became so all-consuming and intense that she even ceased to find her husband's possessive embrace unpleasant. And then, suddenly, Hains Tolliver turned from her.

It was as though he sensed a change in her that was outside of him, outside of his command. She was no longer the supine child responding to his will and his need, but a woman seeking an end of her own.

"You are over-eager," he told her once. "It is ill-bred." His voice was cold with disgust. Kate lay by his side, trembling, like a child who has been whipped. As though in expiation for his roughness, his passion seemed to return. But, soon after, he sent her back to occupy her own room.

Kate cried at first. Not because she was dismissed, but because she was not with child, and wondered whether she ever would be. The first morning that she awakened in the blue room Halla was there instead of Dilsey, and Kate's misery of the night before turned to rage.

The black woman seemed to tower triumphantly over her, her gaunt face hauntingly familiar. She just looks like herself, Kate thought angrily. But [illegible]

[illegible]

up. I have put magic against you. You will never give him a child. He will keep you here, like a doll, at the head of his house, to greet the fine people who are too fine to be welcomed by a Negress. But you will be no wife."

"Oh!" Kate cried inarticulately, and she snatched up the kerosene lamp by her bed and hurled it at Halla. But her aim was broken by her position and the lamp shattered against the marble mantel. "Mr. Tolliver shall hear of this," she cried, jumping out of bed. "Send him to me at once—at once, do you hear!"

"He has gone. He won't be back today or tomorrow, madam." Halla's voice was cold with hatred.

"Then get out and send me Dilsey. He shall still hear, and he will send you away."

Halla left without another word, but she was certainly not afraid. Kate dressed without waiting for Dilsey. She was alive from head to foot with anger. Mr. Tolliver should hear! This was more than she would put up with. She wished that she had not thrown the lamp—and she wished that her aim had been better.

When he did hear, Hains Tolliver scowled with fury, but the outcome of his fury was not what Kate had hoped for. He went to Halla at once, and when he came back he looked weary and depressed, and Kate was sorry, thinking, "He has had her here all of his life—I should have tried to make friends with her somehow."

"Will it be so bad," she asked, "without her?"

"Without her?"

"Halla. I can do everything that she does, and I shall like running the house——"

His expression stopped her. "You don't think that I would send Halla away, do you?" he asked, incredulously. "I've whipped her, that's enough. She won't be impertinent again."

"Oh no," Kate whispered, looking at him with horror.

What kind of a man was he, anyway? She found herself wondering about this increasingly, wondering increasingly just how much of a home she had won, how much of a growing home. She had always pictured the great golden groves as the heart of Valhalla, but she had come to see that Valhalla grew out of her husband much more than out of the land.

One day, towards the end of March, Kate ordered her carriage and drove to the village by the dock. She would no longer sit home and be lonely and dissatisfied, as during the past weeks. Her father made fewer and fewer trips to visit her and, when he came, he had little of the old companionship to give her. He had been lonely when she first married but interested in her life and her home, smiling at her and saying that her eagerness became her. Then he had not come for a long time and when he did, on the occasion of her birthday, he had been vague with her and more than once sharp to the point of rudeness with her husband. He said he was nervous, that the climate did not suit him. He kept saying that he wanted to go home, but he made no plans to do so. Now that her honeymoon was over and the delight in her new home was slightly dulled, Kate missed him keenly. People came and went at Valhalla, but none of them were friends and Kate rarely saw the same visitor twice. On the very day that she had ordered her carriage, she had decided she would open the school she had so often thought of. It was high time, and good time, that she did so.

The village by the dock was teeming with activity. Thanks to the lack of frost, the harvest had been unusually heavy and the warehouse was full of fruit, the packing-house and the long docks alive with convicts. Here and there, a white man stood with his gun ready, or moved upon some group of working men with shouted orders or a curse. There was no boat at the dock and the fruit was being sorted, crated and moved into the warehouse to await shipment. Behind the packing-house, where the cabins clustered, a flock of children [illegible] under a bed or a stove. There were evidences of well-being here that Kate had not seen anywhere on Nigger Hill, a place where a stove was unheard of. Not that all these houses had stoves, but two of them did and that was a beginning. She picked one of the cabins for her future school, pointing it out to Billy, her groom.

"See!" she cried, "the shack with the big oak by it. We can hang swings from the tree. That's my school."

The oak had a low branch almost as big around as the trunk itself. It jutted out like an arm, and then bent upwards to avoid the roof of the cabin.

"That's Alma's house," Billy protested. "She's got eleben chil'ren."

"We'll build Alma another, a better one."

"Not till harves' is done, no ma'am," said Billy emphatically, as though he knew a lot.

"Drat the harvest," she said. "Which is the store? No, I remember; it was boarded up. It must be down at the end."

"Ain't no one 'lowed to the store 'cept Wednesdays and Sat'days," said Billy, but Kate felt that that did not explain why it was kept boarded up.

They probably all steal, she thought, and she started to walk towards it. Billy left his horse and came with her, as though he hoped she'd open up the store immediately.

"Hit's everything in the world, in that store," he said. "Alma 'lows as she ain't gonna git outta debt to thet store long as she lives mebbe."

Kate frowned. The storekeeper shouldn't allow these people to get into debt. In Hartford, her father had sometimes handled collection cases and Aunt Enid used to say, "A business man who allows his clients to get into his debt is either a fool or a knave. If he's a fool, he does it out of kindness of heart and he will surely go bankrupt."

The store was boarded up, as it had been the first time that Kate had seen it. But today there was a wagon-load of crates standing out in front waiting to be unloaded.

Billy's eyes sparkled. "That's the stuff," he said vaguely but enthusiastically.

A stencil on one of the boxes attracted Kate's attention and she climbed up on the hub of a wheel to look more closely. She stood there for a moment and then she got down and, without a further attempt to examine the store or make friends with the village children, she said to Billy, "Take me home at once. I'm tired."

That night, Kate confronted her husband, taking Halla's empty seat in the music-room and saying:

"I have been to the village, Mr. Tolliver. I wanted to see where a school had best go."

"I've no intention of having you teaching," he told her, but she shrugged it away, and said,

"I went to the store and there was a wagon-load of cases there, clothes and food and things."

"Well, did they interest you so very much?"

"Mr. Tolliver, those are government supplies and relief bundles sent down by churches and charities, to be given free—they're not being sold? Oh, I was sure that couldn't be!"

"Then you were wrong, my dear, for that is just what is being done with them."

"But it's——"

"Dishonest? Ah, Kate, what a surprising child you are! You want the cream but you don't want to know how it is come by.

Success is a hard path. It is a rough world that we live in and success is not for those who preach and pray, it's only for people who will take it."

Kate said unhappily, "But the government——"

"The government!" her husband said softly. [illegible]

[illegible]

"But you pay your labor," Kate said, thoroughly puzzled.

"I rent convicts," he told her brutally. "By special arrangement, I rent them for their board and a present to one or two men in authority. The other labor I pay, to be sure. Then I sell to them more than they can afford. If they try to leave, I'll have them arrested for stealing. They know it."

"But it's you who are stealing," Kate cried. "It's terrible."

"I am taking the only means that the government allows me to reclaim what, you must admit, that government has stolen from me. We are all thieves, in a way. It is perhaps the most basic principle of life. To take what is necessary to you. It has always been that way. The other way is to sit back and be taken from. And I think"—he smiled at her coolly—"that if I were that kind of a man I should not have so charming a wife at my hearthside!"

Well, it was true enough. And, in any case, she could not complain of the outcome. The people at Valhalla were better off in every way than any colored people, however free, that she had seen since she had come from Hartford. So she looked at her husband solemnly and she said no more.

But the strange insecurity that she had found, in other ways, in her husband was gradually finding its way into her house, her lovely house. It seemed sometimes as though she lived in a golden palace built on top of a swamp. The thought was fleeting when it came and Kate did not encourage it to stay. Talk of the school was abandoned for the moment. Kate adopted the sunken place where the sheep pastured, and there she determined to have a garden. The white liquid that Halla had poured on her flower-beds had proved effective and nothing grew near the house. So she bowed to the "sperits" and moved farther afield. She had three gardeners, and Mr. Tolliver sent North for roses, and to Tallahassee for camellias and a quantity of other seeds and plants. Further, he promised to build her a tea-house which should be a precise copy of the one that stood on the grounds of the governor's mansion at Tallahassee. Kate was delighted.

The winter was over and everything looked better to her. She began to visit her husband's big, dark, oak-carved bed again, and to think again of childbearing. In the groves, most of the oranges were gone from the trees and the ever-busy black men were at work plowing up and harrowing the land. Flocks of passenger-pigeons winged over Valhalla now; having wintered in this temperate zone, they were headed for the brisk exciting spring of the North. The parakeets left too, and Kate missed their flashy brilliance, though she was glad enough to be rid of their chatter. It was undeniably spring. At Valhalla they were preparing for a festival as soon as the trees should blossom.

26

JAMES CUTLER sat in his high tribunal and looked down upon his black gathering. He had seen Tolliver a dozen times since his unhappy trip to Mandarin, and he had not on any one occasion found cause to change his mind. Rider was in hand, and there seemed to be no more danger from that quarter. Rider walked around like a man in a dream, signed what he was given and gave no more trouble. But James Cutler did not profit because a fool was made a fool of. James Cutler went to Madison and sold a hundred pieces of paper called land certificates to a hundred credulous blacks and Tolliver deducted the train fare from his bonus. James Cutler was being made a fool of now, and with his own connivance. He had received in that very day's post an invitation to Valhalla for tea. For tea! He was to ride half a day for tea. He had heard that Senator Osborn was to be staying there, and there would no doubt be a big dinner in [illegible]

the bottom rail's on top—but it can slip."

A high-pitched voice cried out indignantly, but Cutler raised his voice over it. "In the old slave days there were free niggers, weren't there? You remember?" A dozen heads nodded. "A nigger with a good master could work extra and buy himself, or he sometimes got freed because he was so good and his master was grateful to him!" He paused, then he shouted, "But the Law always thought of some reason to arrest him and put him back on the block again!"

A shout went up from the room and an old man started to scream, "Hear 'im, hear 'im!"

"Well, that's what's happening to you," their president shouted. "You've been freed! And if this monster gets his way, you're going to be set up again and sold." The old man was screaming hysterically now, and several others were shouting and yelling. Then Cutler rose, with his hands outstretched, so that he looked like a great black cross, and stood there until they quieted.

"I am your friend," he said at last, "I am your president, I am your savior." Some of them were shouting and most of them were moaning. "When the time comes, I will tell you what to do. I will let you save yourselves. I will tell you the name of the monster and you will go out and save yourselves."

They begged him, they yelled and screamed at him, but

he only held out his arms to them and said, "Soon, not yet."

He had worked out a perfect plan. He would get rid of the overwhelming burden that Tolliver had become to him. He could have all the money and the position, and without having to do fearful service to any man. And he, James Cutler, would be at cards at the St. James House and never have to lift his finger to do a wrong. He was waiting for Osborn's visit. After the Senator was back in Washington and there was no one here to look beyond the surface facts—that was the time. Bourne would be a nuisance, but there'd be nothing for him to prove. Just try to get testimony out of these creatures. Cutler wanted to laugh. He was being clever. The niggers had a bone to pick with Tolliver anyway. Well, let it be his bone. Who would need to look further?

He went solemnly on to the business of the day and then he whipped his people up a little more and let them go, out into the black night, with half the town crouched behind its shutters, afraid of them. James Cutler wanted to laugh.

On Caroline Street, Ossian Delahanty held yarn for Miss Janey to wind. He and his mother had come to spend the night so that the ladies should not be alone. Crockett had her eyes closed; in the yellow light you could see lines under her eyes. She looked tired. Miss Mamie was reading aloud from the *Du-Kesboro Tales* and she and Miss Janey would laugh over a thing until the tears would run out of their eyes. There was the story of Seaborn Bynes getting whipped. Ossian thought it was silly. Miss Crockett appeared not even to be listening, though now and then she'd smile, more as if she smiled because the older ladies laughed so hard.

Crockett had been different that winter; everyone had noticed it, though no one could tell whether it was a good or a bad way of being different. Miss Janey was sure, about half the time, that she was not drinking. And then Crockett would be silent and morose for such long spells that her mother was not at all sure that the girl was not better off drinking. Then she'd work about the house, doing what her mother thought was nigger work and not fitting for her to do. And once or twice Miss Janey had seen her daughter watch the Northern schoolteacher go by, with an expression that frightened her.

"Plumb scared me," she told Miss Mamie. "As though she was figgerin' on going right out in front of the house and speakin' to that female."

[illegible] you feel ashamed to complain of ours."

Miss Janey nodded with satisfaction and Miss Mamie said, "I went North when I was a girl. But I like to die and my momma took me home and wouldn't hear of our going up again."

"Now that the harvest is done, Cousin George will be about more," Miss Mamie said slyly. They all looked at Crockett. Crockett either did not hear or considered the question unneedful of an answer. She got up and smiled sleepily and said, "I'm going to retire, if you'll excuse me."

When she had gone, Miss Janey said anxiously, "Miss Mamie, did you get one of those——"

As though a special telepathy were set up between the ladies, Miss Mamie seemed at once to understand. "I did!" she said. "That Hains Tolliver surpasses impertinence."

Ossian, whose face had puckered with bewilderment, whistled softly and raised his eyebrows. "The fête!" he said, "Momma won't say whether she'll go."

Miss Mamie sighed. "Indeed, I won't go. But it's long since there's been a fête. It would be nice." She said the "nice" bigly.

Miss Janey looked scandalized. "You'd cross the threshold of that scallawag and his Northern creature just for a nice time?"

"Oh, no, no, Miss Janey. Of course not."

"Mr. Wilson would turn in his grave, turn!" Miss Janey

cried, "and my poor Tom! But of course you have a son still."

"Now, Miss Janey! No call to talk that way."

"No, I guess not. But I'm worried. I'm just that worried. That creature wrote a special note to Crockett and I'd not be at all surprised if Crockett up and went."

Her guests stared at her and Ossian whistled again. Miss Janey rocked for a moment without saying more; then she shook her head and got up. "She's been different lately. Well, I guess we better retire. It's getting late."

Wednesday, a week later, Michael Bourne stood in the hall of Valhalla and waited for its mistress to receive him. The muscles of his lean jaw were tense and he waited impatiently. Almost immediately, the big fierce Negress who had taken his name came back and he was shown into a sitting-room, where Kate Tolliver sat at a desk strewn with lists and cards and envelopes. She rose at once and gave him her hand.

"It's the nicest possible way to answer," she said. "You've come to tell me you'll be here. Mr. Tolliver will be delighted."

He took her hand and then stared at her, unable to say any of the things he had come to say. She had changed in these short months, and yet she had not. She was as vivid as ever, but she had a new quality almost of sweetness, as though something had rubbed away her sharp edges. He thought, I haven't said a word to her in five months and I'd like to take her and kiss her. And he wondered whether she would like it as, he well knew, she once had. It was no way to think of a married woman. But a wanton little gold-digger! He scowled, and Kate laughed at him.

"You still have the gift of looking angry nicely, Mr. Bourne. But you are coming to our fête, are you not?"

"The fête?" he said, enlightened. "For a moment, I didn't know what you were talking about."

Kate lifted one arched eyebrow. "You did not——?"

"I am sorry. I shouldn't have stopped in here for any but a serious reason. But I come out of friendship, Mrs. Tolliver. Sit down, will you not?"

Kate reached for the bell-rope. "I can offer you wine, though my husband is not here."

He stopped her with a gesture. "I knew that he was not at home," he said, "and I do not care for wine. Will you sit down, ma'am?"

Kate sat back obediently, frowning now.

[illegible]

"Tell him to go away," Bourne said, "without delay. In another twenty-four hours I am going to seize his office, and he had better be over the border when I do."

He left her then. He had not said he was sorry, or any other word that might be construed as kindness. But Kate had, in any case, no ears for verbal kindness. What he had done spoke for itself.

Long after the sound of his going had faded from her consciousness, Kate moved, but slowly, as though she were coming out of a dream. It had never occurred to her that the materials at the store were from her father. Now she saw that they must be. He had never known that they were being sold, of that she was sure! He was weak, in that he would always avoid trouble. But it was not in him to condone such a thing. It should not be in her. But, then, Mr. Tolliver was her husband. She had known, when she married him, that he was unscrupulous. And she had approved. That "unscrupulous" had been merely a word to her then, made no difference; she had no right to turn against her husband because the materialization of that word had made her squeamish. She looked down at her hands lying idly among the notes and invitations and lists that littered her desk. For all of this her father was sacrificed. In a week she would be standing at the foot of the circular stairs, receiving her husband's guests in an orange silk dress while her father was a fugitive from the law that he held in such high esteem. The dress had been made to order for the occasion: imported silk, dipped the color of ripe oranges. All the windows and doors would be open and the house would be full of blossoms, and all of the out-of-doors would be full of blossoms and sunshine, and there would be music and gay people and the clatter of horses and carriages, and an army of servants. The dining-room would be graceful with silver and sparkling crystal. There would be ham and beef and game and mousse and aspic, there would be cakes and wine and punch. In the hands of the myriad black people, the food would come pouring out of the kitchen and through the dining-room, into the reception rooms and gardens and groves, and all the time her father would be a fugitive. And all these people would shrug and say—"Carpetbagger! They're all alike."

Kate pounded the desk with her small fists. It wasn't true! Her father was different. He was not a carpetbagger—it was her husband who was dishonest, and herself! Her thoughts flew to her husband: he would be back for dinner and he would know what to do. Kate clutched at this hope—he could not have involved her father without having planned some way out for him. Suddenly she brightened; of course he could not have. She sat back with a sigh of relief. That was it, of course; it was certain! She glanced at the window. It was growing late and he should be home at any minute. Perhaps he had already come home and, as he often did, had gone to his office.

At the thought, Kate jumped up, unable to wait an instant longer than she need. She would go out and see. Nothing was really so bad. Mr. Tolliver would see to everything. In her return to good spirits she ran, slamming the front door behind her.

In the back of her mind was the wish that Halla might be near enough to hear the slam. Halla had a way of disapproving any show of spirits and this always set Kate's nerves on edge. If Kate so far forgot her new dignity as to skip, and she sometimes did, or to run and slide a step or two, at the invitation of a highly polished floor, Halla could be counted upon to appear instantly with a black girl who was instructed to repolish where her mistress had left an invisible scuff. Kate sometimes thought that she would end by running and sliding through every inch of the house just to see what would happen.

Tolliver was not, as Kate had quite made herself believe he must be, in his office. She turned away, her heart dropping from [illegible] looked directly down upon her father's flowery signature affixed to some sort of formal-looking document. Without stopping to consider, Kate lowered the lamp for greater light and sat down to read the uncomfortable print through. It took her a long time, for the wording was lengthy and legal and each statement seemed to have been repeated in every possible form in which it could be repeated in the English language. By the time that she came to the end of the document, Kate realized that, whatever else she had missed, there was no misunderstanding that the man who had signed this paper was solely responsible for the sale of the relief supplies, had in fact ordered such sale. Then her husband was not going to help her father. Whatever he was going to do, he was not going to help! Kate started to pull open the drawers and to search frantically through their contents. She would have to find every single one of these papers; if there was one, there would be others. They must be destroyed and that before her husband returned. She worked with frantic haste. At any moment he might come and find her going through his desk. Once, Kate thought that she heard a step and her fingers froze on the papers she held, but no second step followed and she went back to her search. Hains Tolliver was not a man to brook his wife's interference with his affairs, for whatever cause. She found the papers at last, neatly put away in a book in the bottom of the desk—a sheaf of papers like the one that lay on top of the desk—and with them she found, folded twice over and addressed to Mr. Tolliver in her own handwriting, a soiled sheet of foolscap. Kate turned it over, and then back again. It was familiar and it was not familiar. She stared at it. It meant nothing to her. And yet it must mean something, for it was in her own hand. She had been married half a year and she had never had occasion to write to her husband. No, once she had. Kate stared at the paper with growing horror. Her fingers were slow to open it out and she could feel herself growing cold, as though a door had been opened and icy air allowed to engulf her whole body. It was her paper, torn from her pad at school. The note read, "Dear Sir—The bearer of this note has a remarkable story to tell. I recommend him to you. I am your sincere friend, Kate Rider." It was the note she had given to John Bever.

But he had said he'd never had this note. He had never seen John Bever! He never had! He could not have lied to her! He had said, "John Bever? Ah, the nigger, a trouble-maker, yes, I know him! A poor rascal to trust with a message, Miss Kate. It is outrageous, but the days are past when you can pay a rascal with the thrashing he has earned. Was the message of moment, Miss Kate? Is there something——" All so smooth. But he had lied, for here was her note. She thought, with mounting hysteria, of what it meant. John Bever had gone to her husband. He had told Mr. Tolliver about the guns, and Mr. Tolliver had not wanted to save the guns. The guns were nothing to Kate. If her husband thought it best that they never be delivered to the Governor, well, he was wise, and he was clever, he knew best. But John Bever was a canny Negro, he would not have kept silent just because he had been told to keep silent. And John Bever was dead, beaten to a pulp.

There was a small sound behind Kate and with a frightened motion she thrust the note into her dress and swung about. Halla stood in the doorway and, for an instant, Kate thought that she had been smiling. She was not smiling now, her gaunt face was without expression of any kind. George Morgan's words echoed suddenly in Kate's memory, "That woman is not merely black, she is the materialization of all the shadows in the world." And she moves, Kate thought, as though she were still of the jungle.

"What do you want!" Kate cried, and her voice was shrill in her own ears. "What are you standing there for!"

Halla unexpectedly bowed her head, and said quietly, "The master has just come in the gate, and you are not yet dressed."

[illegible]

had touched her naked body. But if Halla had voodoo'd her, so that she could not bear Hains Tolliver a child, she had done her a favor. For Hains Tolliver, memory returned with a flash of agony, was no better than a murderer!

"I am not going to change tonight," Kate said slowly. "If Mr. Tolliver comes to the house first, kindly tell him that I am here."

For a moment Halla did not move and Kate thought, with an angry throbbing, "If she doesn't go quickly I'll, oh, I'll hit her." And then Halla was gone, as silently as she had come, and Kate was trembling like a frightened child, while something inside her wept. "Anybody who can want to strike another human the way I do, is wanting to kill. My husband is a murderer, and I am no better," and she promised herself, "I will never strike a human; I will never again, as long as I live, allow myself to want to strike a human." It would be hard to live with Halla for the rest of her life and not ever want to. The rest of her life!

Kate jumped out of her chair. It was not living with Halla that mattered. It was the rest of her life with a murderer! Sitting at the foot of his golden table with all its eight gilded feet sunk in the mud, sleeping by his side and receiving into her heart his body in order that she might one day give it back to the world as a new life. New life, with the oldest, blackest taint in its blood.

Hains Tolliver came in, to find her pacing the floor of his office. On the desk was the neat black book, and the drawer from which it came was still open. A batch of papers had fallen to the floor and others were on the desk in disarray. A glance was sufficient to explain her state. He looked from the desk to his wife, who had come to a sudden standstill at his entrance.

"I trust that you have some explanation, madam!" he said coldly.

Kate's heart turned over in her, but she could not speak. She had forgotten him, in her horror at his deed. She had forgotten what he was like. He stood before her, and Kate was afraid. She wished wildly that Michael Bourne had not gone. She wished from the deepest place in her soul that he were there to hide her and to face her husband for her.

And then she remembered, and the blood returned to her head. Her father was in great danger—John Bever's note would have to wait, she could decide about that later.

"Mr. Bourne came," she cried out, with a rush of words. "He is going to arrest Papa! I came here to find you." She waved her hands towards the desk but said no more.

Her husband said, "In my father's day a woman could have been whipped for going through her husband's papers!"

Kate drew a quick angry breath. So this was the way he would treat her anxiety and her fright.

"And I am sure that his son would be quite capable of taking this view also," she cried, her fear submerged in indignation. "Sir, I have told you that my father is to be arrested!" She pointed again to the desk. "I saw a paper on your desk that makes it plain why he should be arrested. That's why I looked through your desk, to find the others——" She drew a breath, remembering the note. "I should have burned them, if you had not come," she said slowly.

"It would have been most unwise, m'dear."

"Well, sir, what are you going to do?"

"Supposing, Kate, that you sit down and tell me more. I find all of this most confusing."

"Oh, it's not!" But she sat down obediently and, clasping her hands in her lap, she repeated word for word her conversation with Michael Bourne. When she had finished, her husband said with cold contempt:

"The Irishman is very fond of you, is he not?"

Kate shrugged. "Does it matter?"

"Yes, it matters. It matters that my wife should lower herself to attract the attentions of a common immigrant."

[illegible]

"[illegible] alone," he said. "I'll bring your father back. Afterwards, we'll see what's to be done." He smiled and touched her cheek, "Wait till I come home. And weep for me. You weep prettily, it's a shame to waste it." He went out and slammed the door.

Kate heard him shouting for his horse and she wiped away her tears, angry at herself. He should not see her weep again. But his passion, on top of her hours of distress and terror, had undone her. It gave the illusion of strength and mastery. And though Kate knew now that there was no strength there for her to lean on, nor ever could be, she still longed to have it, to pour everything into his lap and accept his word and his command, to know that what he said would be right, that what he did would be right.

She went slowly to the desk, gathered up the papers on it, and hesitated. She was afraid to burn them now—perhaps she had not understood them entirely. And then, her husband had to be placated until her father was safe. She put them back in the drawer and closed it. At least she knew where they were. She put out the light and went to tell Halla to have a room prepared for her father. It would be dawn before they could possibly be back and she found herself thinking that her husband would be dead with exhaustion.

KATE slept that night because she could not help herself, but she did not go to bed. She paced the floor of the music room and she sat before the fire in Halla's chair, for she would not even sit in her husband's, and presently, when midnight had passed, she relaxed within the stiff and unrelenting arms and slept. Her exhaustion being mental rather than physical, she slept heavily and did not hear her husband and her father come, or stir when her husband lifted her and carried her upstairs to bed. In the morning, she awakened at his side slowly to remember. She knew at once how she must have come there and she wondered at him, fatigued as he must have been, to have wanted her near him. What manner of comfort could she possibly mean to him, when he had ruined her father and knew that she knew it? In his sleep, as men often do, he looked young and seeing him so always made her feel old. Now she could not help but feel sorry. He hadn't had an easy life. He had grown up with no mother, and with a cold, bitter father whose heart was full of pride and revenge. She blamed him for John Bever. But she knew also that he would not understand her blame. He had been brought up to believe that black people were nothing but animals. He wouldn't kill a Negro unless he had to, but if he thought he had to he would not regard it as murder. Kate watched her sleeping husband and tried to understand herself.

Hains Tolliver did many things that he must know to be wrong, but he had said, "It is not an easy thing, life: 'To those who have shall be given, from those who have not shall be taken away even that which they have.' The Lord invites us to see to it that we have."

To Kate, such things were not wrong. Her husband had grown rich and successful. He was a power in the State. The letter of the law did not interest her. But he had killed, or brought about the death of, a black man. And here Kate knew instinctively that they differed radically, that he would never recognize that he had done wrong. She got up quietly and stood looking down upon him.

"I married [illegible]

[illegible] her skirts and walked quickly to her husband's room. For some reason that she did not trouble to understand, she must tell him first.

He awakened quickly, he always had this gift of sleeping soundly but coming into complete possession of his senses when sleep was done.

Kate gave him the message and was amazed to have him say, "Good! And good-morning to you, madam."

"Good?" she cried. "But the building's burned!"

"What a pity! But I've returned your papa safe to your arms. Are you pleased, madam?" He caught her wrist and pulled her towards him, but Kate jerked herself free and backed away.

"He didn't come to bring you news, that man, he came to report that your orders had been carried out!"

"Exactly."

"Oh," she said softly, "but you take too much on yourself—to burn a building! If anyone was killed!" But, then, he had already taken a life, why should another matter to him?

"You are hysterical," he said, suddenly cold. "Go say good-morning to your father and tell him that it is time to be up. There is still a good deal to see to."

She went obediently. She went without telling, as she had planned to tell him, that she knew of his guilt.

Her father, she saw at once with a deep sense of shock, was not well. In the past months she had been too preoccupied with her new life to see the changes in him. She felt sick with guilt. He had needed her and she had been too full of herself to know it. He was thin, so that his clothes seemed to hang on him from the shoulders, as though they hung on an empty hook. And he had the drawn look of one who has been ill for too long to remember the old gaieties of life. He smiled at her now and said almost wistfully, "Are you happy, baby?"

Kate kissed him quickly, "Oh yes, Papa." What else could she say, when he looked so hurt and sick. Surely not: My husband is a thief and a cheat and a murderer. I am not honest enough to care about the first two, but my gorge rises at the last. Some day he will be caught—perhaps not for this, but for some other crime—because he has no respect for the life of a black man or for the dignity of a black man's freedom. They will hang him and strip him of his wealth, Valhalla will fall to decay, and no one will have had an hour of love or true happiness out of the bad bargain!

"The groves are lovely, Papa," she said. "Oh, I do wish you came more often. I wish you lived right here. Now, hurry for breakfast, though it's really dinner! We've got orange-honey and cakes!" And she kissed him where his hair was getting thin, and hurried away from him for fear he would see how shaken she was.

When they had eaten, the two men went to the office in the groves and Kate was left to occupy herself as best she could. She went back to her invitations and finished these. Then she went to the grove, but the office door was still closed. She pulled weeds in the garden; she went to the kitchen to talk to old Alma; she went to the music room, where she executed two scales and one half of an arpeggio. She went onto the front piazza and walked up and down, and then she went down through the grove to the office and knocked on the door.

"You will have to let me come in and hear what you plan," Kate said with quiet dignity. "I cannot wait any longer."

The men looked up in surprise, but neither of them refused her. Tolliver had been to great lengths to explain his position to Archibold Rider, and the Northerner was too profoundly shocked to care now whether his daughter heard or not. In any case, happy or not, she could no longer remain here with such an unregenerate scoundrel. Unhappiness was better than dishonor. He cleared his throat, and said with unaccustomed simplicity, "I have known some of this [illegible]

[illegible]

Her husband said, "You are out of your mind, sir. Kate is going nowhere and, if you are wise, neither are you." He reached into a drawer and pulled out the book of papers that Kate had replaced the night before. He selected one and handed it to his father-in-law. "Bourne will have to have some satisfaction," he said. "Just because of the fire he is not going to give up the fight. He knows something. Now, this form which you have so frequently and so unwisely put your signature to, was printed in quantity by a small printer in Newark, New Jersey, for James Cutler."

"I thought it a bill of lading," her father said helplessly, knowing that the excuse, though the truth, would not help him in a court of law.

"Cutler designed it to look like a bill of lading, for that very reason. I have his original draft, in his own handwriting. We will hand that over to Mr. Bourne and he will be satisfied as to where the responsibility lies for the sale of the relief supplies. You can show it to him yourself, say that you just discovered it—give him an unsigned bill; he need never know that you put your signature to one of these papers. Cutler will have to take it. He will get a lighter sentence than one I could bring upon him, and he knows it."

Archibald Rider had listened to this plan with growing shame. His eyes were on the points of his toes and his heart was cold within him. "I have been a great fool," he said at last, "and guilty of the greatest carelessness and, in the past two months, of at least partially knowledgeable coöperation with your dishonest schemes. Now I am to be saved at the expense of another man—another man, however much a scoundrel!"

"Rot," Tolliver said with feeling. "All of your high-sounding sentiments have only landed you in a hole, sir. Now I advise you——"

Archibold Rider stood up. "Kate," he said, "will you come with me?"

"Watch what you say, Kate," her husband said softly. "I warn you."

Kate drew a deep breath and looked from one to the other. The little room was silent and they could hear a flock of parakeets chattering in the trees outside.

"You see," Tolliver said triumphantly, "she doesn't want to go home with you and be honest and poor and a fool to boot!" He held the printed bill out to his father-in-law. "Take it to Bourne and say that you found it on Cutler's desk."

Archibold Rider made no gesture to take it. "I ought to tell Michael Bourne quite another story, sir, if I had any honor left."

"Perhaps, but I should not, if I were you. Bourne would undoubtedly believe you. But there is still a court to be convinced, and a people. I have too much money, too much influence, I own too many people, to be harmed by you—and then I am a Southerner, while you are a carpetbagger! If I have undue wealth, I have groves and pine forests to explain it. But how does a commissioner make enough money to buy his daughter diamond ear-rings for her pretty ears?" Hains Tolliver was leaning forward and his face was cruel with the mathematical surety of what he was saying. "I could crush you, Mr. Archibold Rider, and I shall if you get in my way."

"No, you won't." Both men started at Kate's voice. Her face was white with passion. "You daren't hurt him." She held one hand hard against her breast, where she still carried the folded foolscap note. "If you don't get him away safely, and if you ever dare to say one thing against him, I shall go to Michael Bourne with what I know about John Bever!"

"And what, little fool, do you think that you know about John Bever?"

"You did not want the Governor to get his guns," Kate said breathlessly, "for some reason of your own. You asked Papa to see that they went through Jacksonville [illegible]

[illegible] husband said coldly, his eyes on hers.

But she shook her head. "I do," she said. "If it is not murder to you, it still is to the rest of the world."

"Are you saying that if I save your father you will remain with your murdering husband and never mention the subject again!"

Kate was white. "You are making a fool of me."

"You are making a fool of yourself, m'dear."

Rider, who had listened to them both with a growing look of horror, said, so slowly that he almost stuttered, "It is my fault that you are here at all, Kate. But I won't have you stay."

I am married, Kate thought—but murder—how can I stay and act as though murder were nothing! She could not, and yet in that instant she could not face all that going meant.

"You want to stay!" her father said, and his eyes on her were sick. "You can't, you can't, Kate. No daughter of mine——" he broke off, but Kate knew what he was trying to say and that he meant it. If she let him go alone, she would never see him again. Whatever happened, he would not want to see her. "I shall wait for you," he said, and he brushed past Kate and went out of the office without another look at his son-in-law.

Kate would have run after him but Tolliver caught her by the arm. "Let him go. He has a long ride, and he shall have a slow horse. He will cool off."

"No, you don't know him. He hides from things. I know. And you have done something to him and to me that he can never hide from. He—oh, let me go!"

"Not now, or ever."

With a sound that was half cry, half heartbroken sob, Kate wrenched a hand free and struck her husband in the face.

Hains Tolliver let Kate go and stared at her incredulously. Then, before she could move, he struck her twice, the second time catching her so hard on the ear that she staggered and fell. He did not stop to see whether she were badly hurt, but went out and locked the door behind him.

He stood on the porch and shouted for his groom. When the latter came running, he said, "Get over to the stable. Mr. Rider is going to want a horse. He is not to have one until I say so. Do you understand!"

"Yes, suh!"

"Don't make any mistake," Tolliver said harshly, and his eyes added, "or I'll break every bone in your body. Now, send me Tom."

Tom was the blacksmith, a short man, but big and hard, as though he had been shaped out of the pig iron he hammered and fired day after day.

"Get the shutters up on this office."

Inside the room, Kate was pounding on the door. "Papa, Papa," she cried; "oh, Papa!"

Tolliver frowned. "Stay here and see that nobody tries to get in," he said. And he strode off to find Halla.

28

HALLA stood upon the threshold and looked into Kate's room. Afternoon sun lay warmly on the floor and the room was quiet, but gay, as though its mistress had but lately been there and had left behind the memory of laughter, or a song. Halla's dark face was without expression. She pulled the door to and went down the stairs and out of the house. A carriage stood at the door. It would take her to Black Creek and wait for her there, all night if necessary. Though Halla did not expect to be that long. It was early afternoon and she was going across the swamp to Jacksonville. Both the road and the River were too slow for her mission. She hoped to reach town by [illegible]

[illegible] Within the circle of giant cypress and water-oak that crowded, dripping with moss, to their door, the ground was hard-packed and grass-free from the passage of many bare feet. Each day, before the sun went down the black people counted their razor-backs and their chickens and their children, and every living thing was closed up away from alligators and snakes. None but those in desperate need would travel the road by night. The path wound from creek to creek, from island to island, and yet, for all its deviousness, it was shorter by half than the highway. Halla carried a lantern for her return trip, and a pistol, both tied to her belt so that her arms would be unhampered. The swamps were used by the black people, who were in any case but a few generations removed from the jungle, but to the naked eye there was no path and even the traveller who knew his way must have the use of every part of his body.

Halla went swiftly. Before long, the Yankee would be given a horse, a heavy, plodding horse to carry him slowly but surely down the road to Jacksonville, or towards Jacksonville, for it was not intended that Archibold Rider should reach his destination.

"He cannot be trusted," the master had said. "I regret this intensely, but he cannot be trusted. And, since it must be, I think it an advisable season in which to put Cutler out of harm's way as well. He has been out of hand for some months now, and a man of his caliber does not learn the easy way."

Tolliver did not have to repeat his instructions to Halla and, if he explained them, it was because he thought aloud. For this woman, whom he had whipped only a month ago, had a mind as keen as his own, and his interests entirely at heart.

It was dusk when Halla reached Jacksonville and she went at once to the boarding-house where Cutler still lived. The piazza was empty, and from the dining-room the loud sound of men's voices and the clatter of dishes and cutlery announced that supper was being served. Halla put her hand on the cord that sounded the big bell, and at once withdrew it. That would attract too much attention. She must find someone to bring Cutler out for her. At the back of the building a stream of boys and women came and went, carrying their baskets and pails of steaming food and napkin-covered hot breads from the cook-house to the dining-room. Halla stood watching until she saw a short, thin boy come towards the house alone. "You, boy!" she called.

"Who dat?" he said distrustfully, for she was not a good sight to look at despite the fact that the dusk hid most of the tatters that now hung about her.

"H'it don't matter. Go in and find Mr. Cutler and tell him that there is an important message for him. I will wait on the piazza. Hurry!" and she tossed the boy a penny, and slipped quietly around the corner of the house, for the kitchen door had opened again with a burst of noise and laughter.

James Cutler came onto the piazza, with his napkin still tucked into his vest and his mouth full of food. When he saw who the messenger was, he swallowed and said, "I'll be damned!"

"If you'll come away from the door, sir," the black woman said politely. "It is urgent—and for your ears only. The master has sent me," she said, when she was satisfied that it was safe to speak. "Mr. Rider came to Valhalla. He has discovered how John Bever was killed."

Cutler scowled and even in the dusk the life seemed to drain from his face so that all of the hollows showed. "What does this mean!" he said in a hard voice. "What is Tolliver doing about it?"

"There was nothing he could do—out there. Mr. Rider is on his way to town now, to lay information against you. The master detained him as long as possible. He sent me to warn you. I came across the swamp. Mr. Rider will have been given a farm horse. He cannot have crossed McGirth's creek yet. You have plenty of time."

"Time for what?" Cutler said quickly, peering at the [illegible] I'll take care of everything."

"Yes, sir." Halla went quickly, leaving him standing there, the white napkin dangling at his waist and his thin fingers roaming nervously over his lips. Dark had come at last, as though the earth were a blotter drawing first daylight and then dusk away from the world. Halla did not go far. She had another message to deliver, but first she had to see the carpetbagger on his way. She went openly and with sufficient noise down the board-walk, and then she left it and came back to stand and wait, shrouded by the porch vines. James Cutler was still on the porch, but he was not alone. He had a colored boy with him and he was talking urgently.

"Get up the hill," she heard him say, "and let out there's a meeting. They're to get to the church, every man that wants to keep free and alive. And tell Jim Peter to go to the livery stable on Newman Street and get me a horse. But just pass on word about the meeting."

"But it ain't Thursday," the boy said, stupidly.

Cutler took a step towards him. "Ever seen a cat skinned?" he asked. The boy rolled his eyes and the whites glittered in the dark.

"I've seen a black boy skinned the same way," Cutler said. "Now git, and don't make any mistake." He gave the boy a shove, and he turned and went into the house. When he came out again, he had his hat and coat and his riding stick. And Halla followed him when he went down the street. She was puzzled and, though she had another message to deliver, she wanted to see what this meeting meant.

Cutler went down the side of the boardwalk. It had come too soon, but he was not entirely unprepared for it, and he had lived too many years by his wits not to recognize his moment when it came. He did not trust Tolliver, and he trusted even less the black witch. Her voice was too soft, her words too well chosen; she had, he thought, as good an education as her master, and as black a heart. It was not that he sensed a trap; it was not illogical that Rider could not be stopped at Valhalla. But, with Rider taken care of, he, James Cutler, became too natural a scapegoat. The fire at the Freedman's Bureau, of which he had not been forewarned, had been in a sense a beacon. Tolliver was commencing to clean things up. Tonight Rider. Tommorrow——?

He walked slowly past the front of the livery stable, pausing to peer in at the door. A black boy lay sleeping on a pile of straw, the smell of manure and fresh hay hung like a sign about the door, while in the dark of the building the horses moved in their stalls, their hoofs thudding heavily from time to time and the sound of their breathing audible even from the street. Cutler went around the block towards the dark church, and Halla remained always by him in the shadows and dark places of the street.

The black people gathered quickly, and Cutler thought it was as well that the meeting had not been the regular one. For the sudden call and the unusual hour had excited them and they were ready for anything. Once he gave them the word, there would be no stopping them.

In a corner, by the door of the church, Halla watched and listened. She had been startled when Cutler lit a torch in the church and she saw that he had put on a black hood. She knew about the Brotherhood, but she had not realized that the Brothers did not know who their leader was. The meeting was short and Halla slipped out before it was over, Cutler's words ringing in her ears. "I've done the work for you," he had shouted. "I've found out your enemy. He's got chains waiting for you, and cabins without windows to lock you up in. He's got white overseers with whips and guns. He'll put you back where you were. You'll be eatin' terrapin again and [illegible]

[illegible]

[illegible] get to Valhalla long before these people could. She waited outside the church until she saw Jim Peter bringing a horse around the corner. Then she slipped out of her retreat and, keeping in the shadow, made her way back to the boarding-house.

Once out of sight, she hurried. There was time, she knew, but she could hear the whole town rustling and she could see people moving in the night. She did not talk to Bourne himself, but sent a message in to him. She waited only long enough to make sure that he had received it before she went, with all the speed she could muster, back to the swamp.

A solitary traveller could cover the distance in a little over four hours, but two or three hundred would take all night, and if they could not get there until day they would lie in the swamps and wait for dark again. There was time.

29

ARCHIBOLD RIDER stood at the gates of Valhalla and faced his son-in-law. He had waited for Kate but she had not come to him, and when at last he knew that she would not come he had started to walk. There was no horse for him, and he could neither beg for one nor steal one. At the gates, Tolliver had overtaken him, bringing him a horse.

"Has Kate changed her mind?" Rider asked.

"Kate will stay with me," Tolliver said. "I am sorry, Rider; I wish things were different. You won't——?"

Rider shook his head.

"I see. Well"—Tolliver tossed the reins of the spare horse to Rider and pointed to a flask on the saddle—"Kate sent you some whiskey. It's a long ride." He looked at the older man as though he were reluctant to leave him. Then, without saying another word, he turned back to the house.

Archibold Rider stared at the flask, and his shoulders sagged. He had known, when Kate did not follow him, that she would not come. And yet he had been possessed of a forlorn hope. She would overtake him. He was only on foot, she could not help but overtake him.

But she had sent him a horse and she had sent him a bottle of whiskey. Kate had changed. A year ago she would have come; she would have run after him, every step of the way. She would never have sent him whiskey. She used to cry when he drank.

He climbed into the saddle and rode slowly away from Valhalla. The flask swung against his knee with each step, but if he felt it he made no gesture to stop it, and only looked down the road at the dust and the sun and the long, dreary distance.

It was a hot, slow ride. Long before he came to McGirth's creek pure physical discomfort overwhelmed his every thought, and he sat his horse with head bowed and eyes unseeing. Twice he looked down at the flask. He was hot and thirsty and aching with fatigue, yet at the sight of it the thoughts came back and he looked away, grimly determined not to touch it. But at McGirth's creek he pulled up his horse and unscrewed the cap. He took a long, burning draught, and sat for a while letting the fire flow through him. Then he took another drink, replaced the cap, and kicked up his horse.

At McGirth's creek the road dipped through a tangle of trees and vines to the ford, a place that was dark even by day. By the time Archibold Rider came to it the sun had long since gone. He let the reins fall loosely, knowing that the horse would find his way better than he himself could. They had crossed the creek and were coming up through the jungle on the far side when he heard a shot and felt something hit him on the back—a hard dull blow, as though a rock had been thrown at him.

The horse shied [illegible] can get him later—we'll have a look at you first——"

Rider closed his eyes, and the voice and the face went away. "Where are you——" he said thickly, but there was no answer.

Bourne leaned over the wounded man and frowned.

Rider was muttering, but his pulse was growing weaker. He opened his eyes again. "Kate!" he said, and he felt as though his voice were ringing—it filled his head and all the earth about him.

Bourne put his ear close to the other's lips; he could scarcely hear him.

"Take care of her. She needs——" But if there was more it was never said. Archibald Rider slumped back on the bank where Bourne had laid him and a small trickle of blood poured from his half-open mouth and dripped lifelessly onto the grass.

KATE slept little that night, but lay with her eyes open, staring at the silver birds that preened so prettily on her blue bed-draperies. She left her lamp going and, when the oil was finished, it smoked blackly for an instant and went out. Still she lay there with her eyes open. Her husband had struck her and locked her up, with a groom to watch over her. When he released her, he had sent her to dress. A hot tub, and Dilsey weeping over her bruises, and dinner in state in the dining-room as though nothing had happened! She had not been able to eat, so he had ordered wine for her and she had swallowed it because of the way he said, "Drink, m'dear. I've no patience with a sulking woman."

Sulking! Kate turned her head and the pain shot up from her neck.

After dinner, he put her in Halla's chair in the music room and played for her, saying briefly, "Halla is busy," and he played the same wild angry music that Halla herself had played on Kate's wedding night, until, unable to endure more, Kate ran weeping from the room. She heard his music half the night, tearing at the very bones of the house. And when he stopped, the silence throbbed like a living thing that had been struck too brutally and too long. But he did not come near her, though she heard him pause by her door and turned her head to watch him enter. She was afraid of him now, and ashamed of herself. When she heard him go down the hall and close his own door, she started to cry. She wondered where her father was and she thought of getting up and going after him. He was right, there was no bond to hold her here. God would not hold her! Her heart, that she had tried to dictate to, would not be dictated to and all the golden apples were rotten. She slept at last, and dreamed. A great black fog was creeping out of the creeks and the swamps and the mud-banks by the river and Kate was fleeing from it, not to Valhalla but up the river to Michael Bourne's place. She never saw him, but she seemed to hear his voice. She awakened, trembling and cold. The dream had been so real that she seemed still to hear his voice. Then she heard a horse on the road, not coming to the house but going away at a gallop. She frowned into the dark. Had her husband gone away? At this hour of night? And why?

Having spent much of the night awake, Kate slept late and came downstairs to find the sun high and the day so warm that every bud in the grove had burst open. The air was heavy with perfume and the drone of young bees at work. Kate rang the small silver bell that stood by her place. Only one place was set. Her husband had had his breakfast and gone out. She sighed with relief. Moses came in, shaking his head.

"Mawnin', Miss Kate," he said. "Mast' Hains done gone to the dock. Hit's some trouble with [illegible]

[illegible]

and eat them cakes right up."

"I'd like to see Alma send a message like that to Mr. Tolliver," Kate said, laughing. And then she stopped laughing, suddenly, and looked down at her hands.

"She used to did," the old man said, "she used to did. But the war done changed that boy a lot."

"Yes, I suppose so." Kate started to eat, not wanting to talk. Later, she went out to the low-walled garden where the sheep used to pasture, and lay down in the sun-warm grass. It was a new day and she had to think. Rightly or wrongly, she had made her decision; still, she had to think. But the thoughts would not come in any coherent pattern. It seemed you couldn't put your mind to a problem and marshal at once the past, the present and the future in a neat array that would spell an answer, that would tell you what to do.

She wished that they had never come South. She wished for the narrow little house in Hartford, from which she was now forever an exile. Her father would go there now. She could see him in the evenings, his face rosy from a brisker air than she would ever feel again. He would sit by the fire in his stocking feet. He would smoke and, every now and then, he would wiggle his toes to express comfort, and Aunt Enid would sew and listen to him. He would not like Mr. Grant and he would not like Mr. Grant's Cabinet. He would tell her what they were doing in

Washington, and what they should be doing, and every so often Aunt Enid would say, "Tut, Tut!" in a distressed voice, but she would never miss one single neat little stitch.

Presently, Papa would go down to the cellar to look at the furnace, and there he would refresh himself with a bottle that he kept among the ash-cans. And then Aunt Enid would leave her sewing and come to the cellar steps and call down, "Archibold! is anything wrong? You are taking so long!" And they would never mention the South, and they would not mention Kate. Kate was dead. Kate had died a worse death than the little mother who was still a part of the family circle. Kate's grave was covered with golden apples, and her mother's was covered with snow. Kate wept into the warm grass. Even if she went after him, she could not go back with him. They had run away together from Hartford and Aunt Enid, but only she had *really* run away, or *really* wanted to, and so only she could not go back.

There were crocuses in the grass and yellow-green buds on the daffodils, with half a handful of trumpets open in the sudden heat. After a while, Kate turned over and looked at her garden: here and there were pale spring colors; later, there would be more color—gay, brilliant color; now the garden was green and growing wildly. There were no weeds, but there was no order either.

"I don't want it all trim and arranged," she had said to her bewildered gardeners; "I want it to grow by itself." Which, considering the amount of work that it required from three boys, was a funny way to put it. In the far corner, where a grassy slope rose up to meet the wall, was the tea-house that her husband had promised her. It was an exquisite little building and not, after all, like the Governor's lady's. It was copied instead from a small temple in Greece, a temple to Athena.

"The Goddess of War, more than suitable for your garden, m'dear, and better to copy, if one must copy, than the Governor's lady's."

He was good to her, though he had struck her. Her memory conjured up the picture of a little boy and girl fighting many years ago and Aunt Enid pulling them apart:

"A gentleman never strikes a female, never!" And to Kate,

with as austere reproach, "And a lady never takes advantage of the fact that she cannot be struck. A lady of any breeding will never strike a man, never!"

Kate started to cry again: she had been wrong, but she [illegible]

[illegible] house that was empty because it was at the end of its life, because it would never have children in it—left her with a husband whom she feared, with shame for herself and with the knowledge of her own wrong in her heart. Michael Bourne would marry some fine, some decent girl, and forget her. Kate sat up. She had no right to think of him, but a bitter envy burned in her at the thought of his marrying someone else. His wife would live in a log cabin and do her own work and be sneered at by the old aristocrats, perhaps be called white trash by the darkies. But she would be all of the heart of her home, and proud of her husband, and the sneers would not outlive a generation.

Kate got up and walked slowly up the path. The bees droned on and a woodcock called. But there was no other sound and she was suddenly aware that there should be. With a hundred darkies coming and going, there was always sound: wood being cut, a big voice singing in the garden or the hen-house, a thin high hymn in the house. There was always a clatter or a pounding, there was always talk, there was always scolding, there was always shouting, at the dogs or the chickens, at one another, at the pickaninnies who came up from the docks to Alma's back door, and there was always singing. It never seemed like noise, but it should be there. She stopped in the path and listened. There was nothing. It was as though no living being but herself were there—the bees and the woodcock and herself. A small chill crept up the back of her neck and she hurried to the house.

There was no one at the back steps, where a gardener and a groom and a batch of pickaninnies could almost always be found, and there was no one in the kitchen. A mixing bowl was on the table, with a batch of batter half whipped in it and there were egg-shells and a fork with cgg-yolk congealing on it. In the dining-room, no place was set for lunch. Kate ran into the hall, calling, though she knew that there would be no one to answer. As though she were calling in a dream, her voice was small, swallowed up in her own tight throat. But there was someone in the house. Coming down the stairs, in the black taffeta dress in which she had first seen her, was Halla. Sun from the high stair window fell upon her like a benediction and she looked proud and, Kate thought again, like someone whom she had seen before and that she would understand something important about if only she could remember where and how she had seen her. As she came closer, Kate saw that she was wearing the heart-shaped amethyst, and she suddenly realized that she had not seen it on Halla since she had come here to live.

"Where is everybody?" Kate cried with a flare of anger, because Halla was too still and because she was frightened.

Halla let her wait, and then she said, "They have gone. There are only you and I—and Mr. Cutler."

"Mr. Cutler?" Kate's hand went to her throat. Fear was making her cold.

"Come." Halla turned and went down the hall to the door of a storeroom that opened opposite the music-room. It was a large room and backed onto the kitchen, where it should properly have opened. But Halla kept the keys to it, and having a door that opened on the front hall further secured its contents from marauders.

She lit the lamp that stood on a table outside the door, and then unlocked the door. There was no window in the room, only shelves going up to the ceiling. James Cutler lay on the floor, bent backwards like a bow, his wrists secured to his ankles, and a rope around his throat also secured to his ankles, so that if he moved he was in danger of strangling. Kate cried out and the fear in her became terror and ran like liquid through her body.

Halla held up the lamp to shine on Kate and said, clearly and cruelly:

"Your father is dead. This man shot him last night. He was waiting at McGirth's creek to shoot him. He waited until he had [illegible]

[illegible] eyes were wide open and his mouth forced open with a gag so tightly drawn that the lips were pulled away from the teeth. Always thin and white, he looked like a skull, live eyes moving helplessly in a dead head. "The Yankee, Bourne, was supposed to catch him red-handed," Halla muttered. "But he was late, he chased him out here. And the master sent Mr. Bourne away."

"I heard his voice last night," Kate whispered. "I thought I was dreaming, and I heard him going away."

"You go now," Halla said. "There is a carriage at the door for you. You will have to drive yourself. Hurry! He is coming soon."

Kate lifted her head with a sudden return of pride. "I will go. But I will send soldiers here. I will tell them what you have told me." She stopped, for Halla was smiling.

"You are his wife. They will not hear you. You cannot testify against him."

Kate's hand flew to her breast. There was the note. That was not a wife's testimony, that was evidence. But Halla still smiled.

"What you have there is nothing but a piece of paper," she said. "I returned the other to the master."

Kate dropped her hand slowly. "There is Mr. Cutler," she said; "they will find him——"

"Mr. Cutler has shaped his own ends," said Halla, looking

fiercely down at the terrified man. "He has stirred up the black people and lied to them. He hoped that they would come out here and kill the master. They will come. They are on the edge of the swamps now. But they will not touch the master. They will be given Mr. Cutler. They will be told how they have been fooled. He will be turned over to them as he is. And they will be satisfied. He has frightened them and stirred them up and they will have to have satisfaction. Tell about him if you want, but he will be dead before you can send help to him."

The prisoner had been moving restlessly as she talked, his feet making little helpless jerks that only brought his head back and made his eyes protrude. Now, suddenly, a sound bubbled in the back of his throat and he relaxed completely. Kate went quickly to his side. "He's fainted," she said, and turned fiercely on Halla. "You can't do such a thing!" she cried. "Let him go."

"Your father's murderer!"

"You are my father's murderer! You and Hains Tolliver," and Kate walked out of the room and out of the house. On all the world outside the sun lay hot and thick, and high in the blue sky one towering cloud sailed before a wind too far up to stir the earth. The perfume of jasmine and orange blossoms mingled and there were red buds on the big camellia bush by the steps. Suddenly the black room and the black-hearted woman and the terrified man were not true. Her husband would come galloping up in a moment and Billy would run to take his horse, and he would come up the steps and say to her coldly:

"You look as though you had been sleeping in your dress! Go and clean up for lunch."

Or, perhaps, for once, he would not wait for night to be warm and gentle with her—he would take her in his arms and say:

"You've been having bad dreams, Little One. But it's all over now. I'm here, you're safe with me."

"Little One!" It was Michael, not Tolliver, who had called her that. Kate leaned on the rail and was sick, with tortured violence. When it was over, she went weakly back to the house. Halla was locking the door of the storeroom. Kate went up the stairs. There was one thing that she had to do, and then she would go quickly, as Halla wanted her to, as she wanted to herself.

She ran, holding her skirts in her two tight fists. There was hardly time, for at any minute Mr. Tolliver might [illegible]

[illegible]

father on the big slow horse that her husband had given him. "He shall have a slow horse—he'll cool off." That is what Mr. Tolliver had said. And when he came to take her out of the locked office and she had begged him to take her to her father, he had said, "Impossible, m'dear, he's headed for home by now." But he had lied. Hains Tolliver had had no intention of risking his life in the hands of an honorable man. And because her father was an honorable man he would have suspected nothing. And because he was tired and heartbroken he would have gone through the dark oak groves with head bent, listening for nothing and caring for nothing. Kate brushed her eyes angrily. There was no time to think. Oh, if only she could remember where her keys were! When she had come to Valhalla she had been given a set of keys. She used to wear them on a loop at her belt, until she discovered that she was only being allowed to play at housekeeping and that they meant nothing. Now that she had to find them, she could not remember where she had put them.

She rummaged through drawer after drawer, looked in her jewelry box, where she knew that they would not be, and in her desk, where they might be but were not. When every hope seemed gone, she thought of Halla. She would get them from Halla. She would say, "give me the keys, let that man go—or I will not go." But Halla certainly would not. And Halla knew already that she *would* go; she had no weapon left. Then suddenly she remembered the hook at the back of the closet. They would be there. She could see them hanging there. And they were. Kate pulled them from the hook, almost weeping. Then she took a pair of shears from her work-basket, snatched up a cloak and went out of the room. In the hall, she hesitated and went back through her room to the piazza. She had to see how much time she had. She went swiftly around the entire piazza. There was no cloud of dust to be seen, no rider coming. On the north side of the house, she stopped suddenly. Someone was in the reception room. There was the sound of something hard striking wood. Kate leaned over as far as she could, but she could see nothing. Again she hesitated. Could Mr. Tolliver be there already, could he have come without her knowing it? She shuddered, and her breath came fast. Oh, why had she taken so long! She could not go past him, she could not face him. She turned toward the house with a little cry and then, as suddenly, her fear left her. He was not there. Halla would have let her know in time. Halla always knew when he was coming. And Halla did not want her to see him. Then what? All at once, Kate understood. Halla was bolting up the shutters. Cutler was to be given to the mob but no chances were going to be taken. That meant the hall would be empty. She had wondered how she would get past Halla to open the storeroom. She leaned down and pulled off her slippers. Providence was helping her and there was not a second to waste.

Halfway down the stairs, Kate paused. The house was silent. And then there was that pounding again in the reception room. She wondered how many shutters were done and where Halla would go next. But she did not hesitate again. The storeroom door took her too long and she started to breathe drily. There were too many keys. But finally the right one slipped in and she stumbled into the room. She thought the noise she made was deafening, but Halla was pounding a bolt to and Kate did not waste time in wondering whether she had heard. If she had, it was already too late to do anything about it. She had not dared light the lamp and the room was dark, without shape or shadow. Kate went down on her hands and knees and crawled along the ground until she felt the legs of the trussed-up man. He must have heard her coming. He jerked a little and called from the back of his throat, and Kate put her hand on his face to warn him.

She worked quickly, digging with the blade of her shears at the rope that held him, and all of the time she whispered [illegible]

[illegible]

[illegible]

[illegible] you hang, do you hear, I hope you hang. But I don't want to see you murdered."

He pulled himself first to his knees, and then to his feet. All at once, his knees buckled under him. Sick with disgust, Kate watched him drag himself to the door. Her face was white and set, but she could not bring herself to touch him again. At the door, Cutler pulled himself up and staggered out. The sound of hammering was in the kitchen now and Kate followed the lurching man across the hall without any fear of being detected.

A light phaeton stood before the house as Halla had promised. Kate went down the steps to it with a surge of relief. Now she could go. Fast and far. There was no one on the road, and no sign of a horseman coming through the groves. She was breathing quickly. At her elbow Cutler spoke, his voice was hoarse, but clear,

"Have you a pistol?"

Kate turned on him. "If I had, I would not give it to you!" They'll catch you and hang you, and I want them to!"

She unfastened the lead on the hitching-post and was in the act of climbing into the carriage when Cutler caught her by the arm and pulled her down. "I guess I need this mor'n you do," he said between his teeth and scrambled up the step, his weakness and pain overwhelmed in fear.

"Oh no!" Kate grabbed at his coat with both fists and might

have pulled him down by the sheer fury of her attack, had he not aimed a kick at her that sent her sprawling. Then he cracked the whip across the horse's back, wheeled the carriage around and set off at a full gallop down the drive.

Kate staggered to her feet, clutching her stomach. She was sick with pain and anger. Behind her, Halla's voice said softly,

"You shouldn't have let him go. You are a fool."

When Kate didn't answer, the black woman said, "It doesn't matter. He'll not get far."

I hope he doesn't! Kate thought, and then she whirled on Halla, outraged at having any thought in common with her. "Go bolt yourself in," she cried. "At least, I'm not a murderer." And she grabbed her skirts and started to run towards the stable.

At the stable she was doomed to disappointment, for every stall was empty, as though some hand had seen to it that no one left on the place should have means of escape. There was nothing to do but to walk. She faced Jacksonville. But she knew that she could not make it. If she tried to go through the swamps, she would be lost. If she went by road, however late he came Hains Tolliver would still overtake her. So she turned eastward and headed through the groves. Someone would be at Michael's place. Perhaps he had gone there last night. He might still be there. Once out of sight of the house, she did not try to go quickly. She had a long walk, a longer walk than any she had ever taken, and she could not fall by the way. The sun had long since passed the top of the sky and, though it was what she would normally have thought of as a pleasant afternoon, it would not last for long. There would be night, and long before that she must be at Michael Bourne's. She did not, strangely enough, think of George Morgan, whose home the small cabin was. It was Michael who made it for her a place of safety.

She stumbled in the deep loam of the grove; her shoes filled with dirt and her skirts grew heavy. She pulled them up and held them in her arms and then her arms grew tired and she dropped them again. She was crying for a part of the way; then the tears dried of their own accord and she went on dully. The trees in this part of the grove were young and of one age and shape. They stretched in every direction with geometric precision. The avenues were diagonal, they were straight, and nowhere was there any mark, any tree that stood out from any other. It made Kate dizzy and she tried closing her eyes. Then she opened them with a [illegible]

Suddenly the grove came to an end and Kate stood on the edge of a young jungle that surrounded the old Valhalla, the house where George Morgan had been born and from which the older Alphonse Morgan had ruled his empire and made an enemy of Stephen Tolliver. Kate sank down to the ground and laughed into her hands. She had never been here before, though she had wanted to come. Nobody had wanted her to come, and she had not had the courage, or the interest, to come of her own accord.

After a while, she looked up and breathed deeply and her eyes were wet. My house will be like this, she thought. Her laughter had been without pleasure. My Valhalla will be like this, like a carrion skeleton, with no memory of how much I loved it. She looked at it dully, but because she had the gift of pictures she saw another young woman there, with her boy and her husband, and the pretty little cousin who came to visit, and all the vines were trimmed and the trees made to keep their distance. Now the trees came close to the house and there was moss on the roof and hanging from the windows. And only here and there was there any glass, wavering, glimmering glass, and where the sun struck it it seemed as though a face peered out from the broken house. Kate thought of her husband, who let this lovely place stand here and rot because of his own hatred or hurt.

Hurt, she decided, and got slowly to her feet. His mind is

crippled and I have come too close to being like him to condemn him. She did not condemn him, and she knew that this sense of justice, or forgiveness, came from a knowledge of his death. The people whom he had exploited and detested were going to kill him that night. All Halla's shutters would not stop them, now that there was no goat to sacrifice. Unless he came early, and has come after me, she thought.

She started, and turned back to stare through the groves. But there was no cloud of dust to warn her. Kate found herself wishing for Halla's special gift, though she had sometimes suspected that it was nothing but scanning the groves from the deck on top of the house. In the finely harrowed orange lands, you could see a man coming from a long distance.

Suddenly she was hurrying. The sun had passed over the groves and Kate had left the old Valhalla behind her. She had not thought to arrive at any decision. Still, she had arrived at it. She could not leave her husband to be murdered, any more than she could leave James Cutler. For an instant, she turned back and then she turned again and went on. She could only help by hurrying on. It was daylight still. Halla had said that nothing would happen until night came.

"They are waiting on the edge of the swamp," she had said. And, even after dark, for a while, there were the shutters. Now that she hurried, she stumbled in the soft earth and twice she fell only to pick herself up and stumble on. She came to the road at last; eight miles back were the gates of Valhalla, and beyond were Mandarin and Jacksonville; ahead, towards the ocean, was Michael Bourne's cabin.

When she came to the edge of the Irishman's groves and looked out on the small cabin, the world was dark. The sun, after a long slow journey across the sky, had dropped like a plummet behind the horizon of pines. For an instant the world was blasphemous with color, and then even that faded, like an echo, behind the trees and night came. If she had been farther away, Kate would gladly have dropped. Hains Tolliver was dying—and so was she! But the yellow light in the cabin gave her new life, and she gathered up her skirts and stumbled on.

Michael Bourne opened the door to her and, for a moment, she stood staring at him dumbly. Though she had hoped to find him she had not, somehow, expected to find him.

"For the love of God!" he cried, drawing her quickly into [illegible]

Bourne frowned. It was hard to see her like this and not take her in his arms. She had lost her cloak somewhere along the way and her dress was limp with dirt. Her face and arms were smudged where she had fallen and then wept and brushed the tears away and wept again.

"I shouldn't have thought he'd send you," he said harshly. "What does he hope to gain?"

"What do you mean?"

"Did you think I'd spare him because he's your husband? Look, Kate—" he came close to her "I told you once what he was. A man like that gets drunk on his own success. Sooner or later he goes too far and we get him."

"You don't understand!" Kate cried, catching at his coat.

"But I do. Did he tell you about the fire? The Freedman's Building? He can't get out of this. We caught one of his men and to save his own skin he's willing to swear where he got his orders. I came out to get Cutler, but I'm going to pick Tolliver up in the morning, and nothing——"

"You don't understand!" Kate cried wildly. "He didn't send me. He doesn't know—— Arrest him, I don't care. Only go help him now, he's going to be murdered if you don't."

Bourne gripped her shoulder, as though to shake some coherence into her. But Kate sagged against him weakly and his arm slipped behind her back.

"Here!" he said, with unexpected gentleness, and he put her

in a chair and poured out a tumbler of wine. "Drink this, and get your breath. You'll have to make more sense."

Kate took the wine gratefully. For a moment he had been gentle, but now again his face was hard and uncompromising. He detested her. And, why should he not! She put the empty glass on the table and told her story as briefly as she could, without color or feeling. While she talked, Bourne paced restlessly up and down. When she had finished, he went to the door and shouted, "George! Sutt! get the horses." Then he came back to stand before her.

For a moment he was silent, giving her a quick close scrutiny, as though to satisfy himself that she was all right. Then he said curtly:

"Mandarin was closer, why did you come here?"

"I knew that you had come out last night—I thought you would still be here."

"And why would you come to me, Mrs. Tolliver?" His voice was cold with repressed anger. "Why should I save the bloody bastard for you?"

"You are the law," Kate said unhappily.

Michael's eyes were contemptuous. "The law is nothing to you. It's your poor conscience is bothering you, and I'm to risk the lives of five decent men to pretty it up for you."

Kate clenched her fists and screamed at him. "Those niggers will tear him to pieces. They're not human beings! They're a mob who've been lied to and cheated and terrified—even the house servants have run away. Do what you want to him afterwards" her voice dropped—"I don't care—I hope you hang him! But save him from them."

"You don't mean that."

Kate sat down suddenly and dropped her face in her hands. At once he spoke kindly, and she commenced to cry.

"I sent a rider back to Jacksonville for help this morning," he said. "They may be at Mandarin even now!"

There was the sound of horses and men before the house, and the door burst open. Kate had an incoherent impression of a crowd of grim faces staring at her. George Morgan was there, and there were two others in ragged gray uniforms. They were thin men and their uniforms were big. Involuntarily the memory of a scarecrow she had once seen dressed in uniform came to her. Her father had scolded her for laughing.

and hating, the rest of her days. For she had come, unreasoningly, to think of Hains Tolliver as omnipotent: no one would ever punish him and he would never let her go. Waves of weakness washed over her. She thought, I am fainting, and, bewildered and unhappy, she dropped into a sound sleep.

31

WHEN the men came into the cabin for their guns Kate lay limply in her chair. Bourne strode across to her with a quick exclamation. In the doorway, the man Sutt, a lanky loose-jointed Cracker, said, "Shor' is purty. Is she daid?"

Behind him, someone laughed. Bourne grinned. "Dead to the world," he said. He lifted Kate and carried her to his bunk and the men tiptoed loudly, collecting their pistol belts and rifles. They had been riding all day in search of Cutler. They were tired, and they had no love for Hains Tolliver. But they went quickly to their horses, and if any one was reluctant he showed no signs of it.

Bourne adjusted his reins. He said, "Sutt, get back to Mandarin. Send any able-bodied man you find on to Tolliver's. If Healy's there, bring him along. Otherwise go on down the road till you meet him. If he's brought help we stand a chance——"

Sutt wheeled his horse and galloped away down the dirt road. Bourne turned to the others. "Keep together," he ordered. "We'll decide what to do when we see how things are. George, you go ahead and show us the quickest way." And with one unhappy scowl towards the unguarded cabin, he dug his heels into his horse.

If it was in his power, he would save Tolliver. Not only because he, Bourne, represented the law, but paradoxically because he would have been glad to see this man killed, above all others. So, to quench the murder in his own heart he would risk his life, and the lives of five others. Not very noble, he told himself grimly; his conscience was no better than Kate's.

He thought of her, bending low in his saddle and keeping his eyes on George Morgan. They had crossed the road and were entering the groves of the old Valhalla; the trees here were unpruned and wild and so low that the riders had to lie almost flat on their saddles to avoid being torn by the thorny branches.

Kate should never have come South, he thought; yet how could he regret her coming? He had known, when he had first seen her, that life in Jacksonville would be hard on her. But he hadn't known how she would fight back. She had gone after the wrong things, and now she would have to pay for them.

They came out of the old grove and the horses stretched their necks and the men settled themselves more comfortably. Bourne dug at his horse with the calves of his legs. There was no moon and the night was dark, and alive with urgency. If they saved Tolliver, he would stand trial. And Bourne knew that he would be found guilty. Jacksonville was a tinder-box. People were afraid of fire. They would not be easy on anyone they found guilty of arson. And what of Kate? He thought suddenly of her father, and wondered if she knew. Poor damn little fool. She's paid already, more than her share, he thought. He could still see her standing in the door in her dirty dress, with the dirt streaks on her face. He realized with a sudden clear understanding that, though Kate had looked physically crushed, some other thing about her had been strong and untouched. She had grown in character. He had been wrong to accuse her. And her father had been wrong to think she needed—help—or him—whatever he had tried to say. Kate had done her own growing, out of her unhappiness and her self-discovery. She would not take help now. She would wait for Tolliver to come out of prison, and stay by [illegible]

"They're chanting," one of them said; "I've heard it before! They burnt my pa's place in Jackson." They were silent, listening.

"Sounds like they're cutting trees?"

"They'd do that. Happen they're gonna cook Tolliver!"

There were fires in the grove and a column of bright smoke was discernible now coming from the house. Down the long avenue of trees the riders could see black silhouettes moving grotesquely in the firelight.

Bourne stood in his stirrups and studied the scene. "If they've got to the liquor, we're beat. There's just a chance——" he sat back for a moment, thinking, "—if Healy and Sutt bring help, so much to the good. But we can't wait. There's one other chance. If we ride in there, yelling and whooping like a regiment, it might work. It's Indian fighting, but those blacks aren't soldiers. If they're not drunk, they'll scare off. If they don't scare," he hesitated, "—nobody'd be wrong not to want to go in—it's likely too late anyway."

He waited. The men moved restlessly in their saddles, but no one spoke.

"Come on, then!" he shouted, and he fired a shot into the air and kicked his heels into his startled horse. "Let's hear that Rebel Yell!" In the night around him there was a bellow of sound and a burst of gunfire and the frenzied pounding of hoofs. The soft earth rose in clouds. Here and there, when a rider got out of line, sharp branches lashed him across the face and the roar of his blasphemy increased in sincerity.

Even before they reached the clearing in front of the house, they saw the line of silhouettes break, startled in the midst of their wild dance. They wavered and a scream went up to join the oncoming thunder. Then the black line thinned and faded, and all about in the night there was a plaintive wailing.

By the time Bourne and his men reined in before the house, there was not a human being in sight. A few trees had been felled and the ground was a bed of blossoms, while the white stumps stood out like tombstones in the night. The roof was on fire in several places and smoke poured out of the house where a bullet-riddled shutter had been torn from its hinges.

As they went up the steps of the piazza, their guns ready and their eyes wary, the door was flung open and Hains Tolliver stood before them. His collar was open halfway to his waist and his chest had been riddled with buck-shot. His shirt was soaked with blood, and his sleeves and collar were grotesquely white. He leaned heavily against the door, but at the sight of Bourne he straightened up and his eyes burned angrily.

"Where is my wife?" he asked, as though the words were wrenched from him.

"She's all right. She's at my place."

Halla appeared suddenly behind Tolliver, and said to him quietly, "Let him have her! She's always been his anyway. Come, let me fix you."

But, at her words, Tolliver's eyes had blazed into Bourne's. "God damn your guts," he said. His voice was soft but his tone was bitter. And he dropped to the ground before any hand could reach him.

Halla bent over him quickly. "He's dead," she said. The men on the porch moved restlessly at the tight sound of her voice. She would not let them touch him, but lifted him herself. And heavy man though he was, she carried him with ease.

In the house, there was the long windy sound of fire and the crackle of wood. The golden draperies were on fire, and fire had fallen in handfuls to the rugs, and lay here and there, like careless largess, on the furniture. The fireplace was perversely dark, but above the mantel the Tagliaferro portrait had begun to burn.

Halla carried her master up the stairs to the smoke-darkened [illegible]

"Danger's from the roof. Reckon I'll get up there."

"Me too."

Morgan came in. "There's a pump in the kitchen," he said, "an' a tool shed directly under the back porch." He had brought an armload of axes and spades and he dumped them on the floor.

Bourne took up an axe and the other men were choosing their tools when Halla came down the stairs. She seemed to carry smoke with her. In the flickering light, she looked down on them and, for an instant, her proud gaunt features were those of the portrait that burned in the reception room.

"Get out," she said to the men. "This is mine." Her dead, and her house, her voice seemed to say.

"I'd be glad to let it burn," Bourne said, "but there's still Mrs. Tolliver."

"Valhalla is mine. He promised it to me. I am his sister," Halla said simply.

Morgan swore under his breath and Bourne turned his back abruptly on Halla. "It's Mrs. Tolliver's, if she wants it," he said. "But I don't think she will. Anyway, we're going to put out the fires."

Smoke was thickening in the hall and the sound of fire was growing. Bourne pulled off his coat. "Bud and I are going up to the roof," he said. "You fellows start breaking it up down here."

They went up the stairs. For an instant Halla stood in their way. But Bourne shifted his axe pointedly. "I'd as soon cut you down, woman," he thundered at her. "Out of my way!" She stood aside then, and she followed them up into the darkness.

When he saw the condition of the roof, Bourne shrugged. It seemed hardly worth while. But he swung his axe and cut into the blazing shingle, and behind him he heard the steady crash of Bud's axe. For a moment the air on the roof had been an agonizing relief to their smoke-filled lungs, but the contrast was short-lived. The heat from the flames was unbearable: they breathed in short quick gasps, the sweat soaked their shirts, and the heat and smoke burned their eyes. But still they cut viciously into the shingle and timbers, and with every blow a fountain of flame leaped into the air and went sliding like burning rain over the side of the house.

While they worked, there was a pounding of hoofs and a company of soldiers came galloping out of the groves and up the road, with Sutt and Healy ahead of them. Bourne lowered his axe and bellowed down at them and then he slid his arm across his forehead and turned to Bud. "We've got it licked," he said. "Fifteen minutes later and we'd have had to get off and let the damn thing burn up."

Even with help, it was another hour before the fire was beaten. When they had finished, there were small streams of smoke in every room. The kitchen pump had broken down, but someone had found the well, and someone the wine-cellar. And all over the house was the pungent smell of wet char. Hains Tolliver lay on his bed covered with a pall of blackened velvet and Halla stood at his door and would not let anyone come near him.

Now that it was over, Bourne remembered Cutler and called the men together. "I'm sorry," he said. "You're tired, but so is he. Tonight he can't get far—tomorrow we'll have lost him."

"Is he a black-haired feller, with a skinny yaller face?" somebody yelled.

"That's him."

"His haid's stuck on a post out back. Sutt found him an' he's still standin' there a-pukin' his guts out."

A roar of laughter followed these words, and then it stopped abruptly and the group of men moved and broke up, not looking at one another.

"Reckon I'm gonna wash up," a big curly-haired man said loudly. But he sat down abruptly on the porch steps and scratched [illegible]

[illegible]

collect a few of these fellows and get over to your Valhalla and look after it!"

The captain looked from one to the other, puzzled at something in their manner.

"It's up to you now," Bourne told Morgan quietly. "There's nothing to keep you from taking over."

Morgan's face was white. "What about Kate?" he said, and his voice was tense.

Bourne said, "Kate's not going to want Valhalla. And Halla can have this house. I'll take care of Kate. I'll give her a Valhalla of her own."

The captain cleared his throat. "If you want some of my men?" he said.

Morgan turned away from his friend. "Thank you, captain," he said, "but there are a few of these other boys are old friends of mine. I reckon they'd like to come with me."

The captain nodded. "If we hear any gunfire," he said, "we'll come have a look."

Bourne watched Morgan go with Sutt and Healy and Bud and the big curly-haired man who had wanted to wash. George had not said a word, but Bourne knew how he felt. There were moments too big for words. He found his horse, and swung into the saddle. His own moment was coming! He headed the horse towards his cabin, and he thought that he too would not know what to say!